THE KOHAT CONNECTION

To Justine

DENISE BEDDOWS

Denise Beddows

SPELLBOUND BOOKS

First edition
Published in 2023 by

A CIP catalogue record for this book is available from the British Library.
Cover design is by ARTEast

CHAPTER ONE

Idrees struggled to breathe as he ran for his life. His head throbbed painfully and he tried to ignore the rising feeling of nausea as he made his way, swiftly but with difficulty, down the densely shrubby hillside. Twice he stumbled and almost fell. The air was thin and dry and he had no real idea where he was headed. He knew that Kohat was a sizeable town. He had passed through it on the way up to Cherat. If he and Waseem could thumb a lift, they could get to Kohat and hide out amongst the locals whilst they worked out how to get home.

He had never been anywhere this high up before and he hoped he never would again. From what their arms instructor, Ruslan, had told them of this place, Idrees understood the Khattak mountains were some four thousand feet higher than his native Ribble Valley. He guessed that accounted for the air being so sparse and his lungs struggling to cope. Growing up in Blackburn, he had spent much of his childhood running around the West Pennine Moors, where he developed his fitness, but nothing had prepared him for this place. He would give anything to be back in his native Lancashire now.

Realising he could no longer hear his brother's footsteps

thudding on the hard earth behind him, he glanced back over his shoulder, but Waseem was nowhere to be seen. Idrees stopped in his tracks. He could still hear gunfire up on the hill but he had to turn back. He had to find Waseem. He was responsible for his younger brother. His mother had always drummed that into him. During their school days, Idrees had spent the long summer holidays playing out around the streets with his mates, but always with Waseem in tow. Whenever Idrees had got himself into trouble, he had managed to get Waseem into trouble, too. Whenever Idrees and his mates had nicked a few chocolate bars from the corner shop and had run away, it had always been Waseem who'd been caught. Poor Waseem. He'd never been able to keep up. Idrees now reasoned that, if he himself was having trouble breathing, then his asthmatic brother certainly would. Backtracking, he soon spotted his brother lying where he had fallen.

'C'mon, our kid ... Gotta go,' he gasped. 'Time enough to ... catch your breath when we ... get off this bloody hill. C'mon.'

He pulled his exhausted sibling up into a sitting position and hooked his forearms under Waseem's armpits in an attempt to raise him to his feet. That was when he felt something sticky running down his brother's back. He thought it must be sweat, for he was perspiring copiously himself, but, when he withdrew his hand, he saw it was blood. He now realised Waseem had caught a bullet in his back. He wasn't just exhausted. He was barely conscious. Idrees would have to carry him down the hill.

Idrees decided to ditch his weapon. The AK103 had jammed on him anyway. He cursed it, and he cursed those who had placed it in his hands. There should have been more training before they were let loose with the new weapons. Whose half-baked idea was it to try and train them under operational conditions, anyway? It should have been done properly back at the training camp. What a farce it had been! And what had it all been for, anyway? This wasn't what they had signed up for. Now, he really had to get off the hill and find help for his brother.

Crouching down, he struggled to pull Waseem onto his own back. He managed to stagger another few hundred yards but the combination of the steep downward slope and difficult terrain, plus his brother's weight, suddenly caused him to topple over. He put out a hand to steady himself but lost his grip on Waseem. The brothers both rolled a few yards further down the hill. Pausing for a few seconds to try and get his breath back, he felt a sharp pain in his left wrist. He hoped it was just a sprain, as he had a long way to go yet before he and Waseem might escape their pursuers. His brother groaned.

'Waseem ... Don't pass out, bro ... C'mon. Try to stand.'

Waseem had clearly lost a lot of blood and was slipping in and out of consciousness. Idrees realised they couldn't go on. He would have to try and hide Waseem somewhere on the hillside and go and fetch help. Yet he knew that, whilst the fighting still raged on the hill, no-one would want to come back with him and help his brother. He was still wondering what to do for the best, when he noticed Waseem had stopped breathing.

'Oh, God! Waseem!'

He rolled his kid brother onto his back and tried to remember the CPR he'd learned in first aid classes at Brookdale Comprehensive a few years back. He placed his lips over Waseem's mouth and pumped two big breaths into his lungs, then started administering chest compressions, to the rhythm of the old Bee Gees hit 'Stayin' Alive'. This proved painful, owing to his weakened wrist. In his head, he could hear his mother's voice urging him to 'take care of your little brother'. She would kill him if he didn't bring Waseem home in one piece. Every few minutes, he paused, to see if Waseem was breathing on his own, but, to his intense frustration, his brother appeared still and lifeless.

Soon, he heard shouts and was aware of movement above him

on the hillside. More of the fighters were retreating down the hill. Perhaps they would help him. He leaned forward and administered two more deep breaths. When he straightened up again, he suddenly became aware of someone standing beside him. He looked up into the angry face of Gul Bahar, his unit leader. Bahar was clutching Idrees's abandoned rifle.

'Help me. Our Waseem's been shot. He's not breathing,' Idrees pleaded.

'Leave him. Take this and re-join your unit. *Vapas jao*!' Bahar commanded.

'No, I'm not leaving my brother,' Idrees gasped as he recommenced administering chest compressions to the motionless body of Waseem.

'We are all brothers in God, and the fight is not finished. Leave him,' Bahar commanded.

'No! It's a stupid fight, anyway. We're ill equipped and undermanned. We haven't a hope in hell of taking the place. It was a fucking stupid idea in the first place!'

Despite the pain in his wrist, Idrees continued his desperate attempt to revive his kid brother. A loud click made him glance up. Bahar had withdrawn the safety catch on his rifle and was pointing it at Waseem. The sudden loud discharge of the weapon took out the side of Waseem's head. A wave of blood and brain matter splashed over Idrees.

'You bastard! You heartless bloody bastard!' a deeply shocked Idrees yelled.

With tears welling up in his eyes and his fists clenched in rage, he rose to his feet and moved towards Bahar, but Bahar raised the rifle again and fired three shots into Idrees, sending him stumbling backwards across his brother's corpse. As his own blood began to seep out onto the foreign soil and mingle with that of his kid brother, Idrees's thoughts were of his parents. What would his father say when he heard he had lost both his sons in a pointless shoot-out? How would their mother cope with the grief? Would she curse him to infinity for his foolishness?

He gazed up at the harsh, sunlit sky and wished himself back under the rainy skies of Lancashire, where the air was more breathable, where he and Waseem had spent their childhood, where they had been happy and safe. As his vision narrowed and his senses began to desert him, he knew now that it had been a mistake coming here. It had been the most God awful, tragic, bloody mistake.

CHAPTER TWO

THE SOFT CHESHIRE RAIN BEAT AGAINST THE WINDOW AS LAURA ROBERTS spread the documents out on the dining table. She thought it wise to go over the paperwork again, just to make sure she had everything with her before she set off. She checked she had each document specified on the funeral director's list. There was the photocopy of the Pakistani death certificate and the notarised official translation from Urdu to English which the British embassy in Islamabad had arranged. Then there was the Pakistani authorities' officially stamped certificate of approval to remove a body. That came with a translation, too.

She had remembered to include the photocopy of his passport details page which Keith had always kept in their bedroom safe. That turned out to have been a wise precaution, since Keith's actual passport had not yet been located. There was the certificate of embalming and freedom from infection, also with attested translation, and the bereavement information pack sent by the embassy. She had included a notarised copy of their marriage certificate, too, to prove she was Keith Roberts' next of kin. Most of the documentation had already been scanned and e-mailed to the various authorities and to the airline. She sighed and shook her head. It all seemed so clinical and so very impersonal.

She replaced all the paperwork in the document wallet and stood for a moment, gazing sadly at the framed photographs on the sideboard. In pride of place, was their wedding photograph with dark-haired Keith in his pin-striped grey suit and herself in the full-skirted wedding dress with leg of mutton sleeves, so fashionable in the 'eighties, but now looking more than a little dated. Her naturally blonde hair had been piled high on her head that day, with soft little tendrils caressing her temples. Her eyes had been of the deepest blue, her complexion creamy, and she'd been so very slim back then.

Her gaze moved along to the next photo, in which Keith stood alongside her, proudly holding their baby daughter, Beth, at her christening. My, hadn't *those* twenty-six years flashed by? Beth's graduation photo occupied the next spot on the sideboard, followed by the photo of Beth in her own wedding dress, sitting in the wedding car alongside the proud father of the bride.

Finally, there was a much more recent photo. The now silver-haired Keith was seated at the golf club dinner. He and their son-in-law, Alan, each held a handle of the silver golfing trophy which Alan had been awarded that evening. The photo had a printed caption set into the mount, proclaiming the event to be the London Golf Club's Annual Dinner. In this case, of course, the London was London, Ontario, where, to Laura's unspoken disappointment, Beth and Alan seemed to be intent on making a life for themselves.

She glanced beyond the photos at her reflection in the large mirror which hung above the sideboard. She wondered how much of her own hair might now be silver, although, thanks to the regular attention by the colourist at her local salon, it was a restrained shade of blonde, and, these days, she kept it short and neat. Her eyes were, she thought, still of the deepest blue, but perhaps a little more tired-looking. She pulled in her diaphragm and drew herself up to her full height of five foot six inches. Sure, she was a few pounds heavier nowadays, and her complexion might have lost its dewy youthfulness, but she didn't think she looked too bad for someone just past their half century. Of course, now that Keith was gone, who would care? Who would even notice how she looked?

The large golf trophy itself, engraved with crossed golf clubs, also stood on the sideboard behind the photo frames. Laura and Keith had agreed to give it house room since Alan and Beth's posting to Canada was only supposed to be for a year, and they couldn't have taken absolutely everything with them. Of course, that was three years ago now, and it was beginning to look as though the move might be permanent. Laura wished Beth wasn't so far away right now. She could use some emotional and practical support from her only child.

She glanced down at the document wallet again. So, that was it, was it? That was the end of the story – her story and Keith's. The three decades she and Keith had spent together, as reflected in the photos on the sideboard, now culminated in a clutch of certificates. A lifetime's partnership was reduced to a handful of official paperwork. She began to feel sorry for herself and she wanted to cry, but she knew she couldn't allow herself to, not yet, at least. She had far too much to do. In any case, it was now time to go. She had to go and make the final arrangements.

The rain had now turned quite heavy as she climbed into the car. Pretty typical of April weather in Cheshire, she thought. When all this was over, she told herself, she would take a holiday. Maybe she would visit Beth in Canada, or perhaps she would go somewhere warm – somewhere with a little less rainfall. She headed out of Bramhall along the A5102 towards Stockport. It was late afternoon and she was relieved to find there were a couple of empty parking spaces right outside the funeral parlour. She explained to the receptionist why she had come and she handed over the paperwork then sat down to wait.

The chairs were silver gilt with black velvet upholstery. It reminded her of the waiting area at the bridal shop where she had sat, excited to see Beth emerge wearing a succession of wedding dresses. That seemed like only yesterday, and yet it was five years ago. She now recalled Keith expressing a theory about why it was that time seemed to go faster, the older one got. He said it was something to do with the proportion of one's life that lay behind one being greater, in relation to the proportion that still lay ahead, though she couldn't remember the exact logic of his reasoning. Keith had held theories and opinions about everything, of course, and he was always right, wasn't he?

There was a display of lilies in a vase on the little table in the funeral parlour's waiting room. Laura grimaced. She hated the scent of lilies. She thought that might be because of their association with death. From time to time, she glanced at the large clock on the wall, and she wondered what could be taking so long. Eventually, the funeral director appeared. He held the documents she had brought. The last time she had met him, when she'd called in to make the initial arrangements to repatriate Keith's body, the undertaker had worn that well-practised expression of solemnity, dignity and sympathy, so typical amongst members of his profession. This time, however, he seemed uncomfortable as he sat down beside her.

'Mrs Roberts,' he began, 'I'm sorry to say that there seems to be a problem with the paperwork.'

Her heart sank. It had taken almost two weeks of telephoning and chasing around to get all the documents he'd said she'd need. The thought that she might have to do it all again was just too much.

'What do you mean, Mr Burgess? What sort of problem?'

He seemed quite ill at ease now.

'Well, if the translation of the death certificate is accurate, it states your husband died from a myocardial infarction – a heart attack.'

'Yes, that's what I was told.'

'Well, the gentleman we collected from the airport today ... I mean, the paperwork that came with the coffin seems in order, but the condition of the ... that is ... it looks as though the cause of death is not as stated on the certificate.'

'I don't understand. What do you mean?'

'I mean, the gentleman whose remains we collected has clearly been the victim of a shooting.'

'A shooting? You're saying my Keith was shot? Good God! Where is he? Can I see him?'

'Yes, of course, Mrs Roberts. If you'll just give us a few minutes more to make him a little more presentable, I'll bring you through.'

If the undertaker was perplexed at this unexpected anomaly, Laura was deeply shocked and confused. Whilst she continued to wait, she wondered how such a thing could have occurred. Keith had been on one of his usual business trips to Pakistan. It was a trip he had made many times over the years in his capacity as purchasing manager for Global Tobacco Products. Several times each year he had visited their suppliers in Nowshera and he had never encountered any trouble whatsoever. He only had a couple more years before his planned retirement. Why on earth would he have been shot? Why him? Why now?

Eventually, Burgess returned and ushered her through the curtained archway into the small room beyond. With some trepidation, she walked across to the casket. The upper part of the lid was open and she gazed in at the occupant of the coffin. She stared for a moment at the dark hair and unfamiliar, youthful features of the dead man before she rounded on the undertaker.

'Mr Burgess,' she said, angrily, 'that's not my husband! I don't know who the hell that is, but it is *not* my husband.'

Later that night, ten miles west of the Roberts' house, in another leafy Cheshire suburb, a car pulled up outside the modern synagogue. It was past midnight and the building was in darkness. A young man, clad in jeans, trainers and a hooded jacket, climbed out of the front passenger seat and looked up and down the quiet road before approaching the entrance of the modern building.

Taking a spray can of paint from his jacket pocket, the young man sprayed a back-to-front swastika in red paint on each of the wooden double doors. His task completed, he bounded back to the car and jumped in, and his accomplice hit the accelerator. In contrast to its quiet arrival, the car now roared off down the street and headed in the direction of the M56. An elderly man, out walking his equally elderly Jack Russell terrier, stepped out of the shadows as the car sped past him. He made a mental note of the car's number plate before taking out his mobile phone to call the police.

An hour and a half later, Rabbi Gerald Solomons stood outside the synagogue. He shook his head sadly. The uniformed constable standing alongside him also looked sad.

'I'm so sorry,' the policeman said.

'Why would *you* be sorry, Officer? You didn't do it, did you?' Solomons asked.

'What I mean, Sir, is that I hate this kind of thing. It's despicable. I'm so sorry it happened to your lovely building. But, judging by the way they got the ... symbol wrong, I suspect it was just kids, just yobs.'

'The *Hakenkreuz*. It's always the *Hakenkreuz,*' the rabbi sighed.

'Sorry?'

'The crooked cross. The swastika. It's probably the most

offensive and fear-provoking thing they could paint. When the Baptist church noticeboard got sprayed it was 'MUFC'. Those amongst the congregation who were Manchester United fans might not have minded so much. But this ... are you sure it was just kids? You don't think it could be the precursor to a more serious attack?'

'I'll have a word back at the station, Sir. We'll try and have the local patrol cars come down here a bit more often. The old gent who called us got the registration number of the car. It was reported stolen in Blackburn earlier today. If we find it and there's any prints in it, we'll get them.'

'I hope you're right. I hope it was just kids. We've never had any trouble like this here before.'

'It's a shame you don't have CCTV,'

'We never thought we needed it. Looks like we were wrong,' the rabbi shook his head again.

CHAPTER THREE

The following day, Laura made herself a strong coffee and went into her dining room. Once again, she sat staring at all the documentation laid out in front of her. It made no sense. She could accept that slip-ups sometimes occurred in funeral parlours, and she knew from past experience that officialdom in far-off countries could sometimes be a bit slipshod, but if the body which had been shipped to England had been murdered or involved in some sort of shoot-out, then what could have happened to Keith? Might he have been buried in a grave intended for the man in the coffin? Had he really died of a heart attack, or had he been involved in the shooting, too? Was he even dead at all? Maybe he was alive somewhere. Maybe he killed the man in the coffin. She dismissed that thought immediately.

She began to imagine all sorts of scenarios, the most likely being that Keith had been the victim of a robbery or some sort of car-jacking incident. She knew such things happened out there, but he should have been safe enough in the city of Nowshera where the company's major supplier was located. After all, he had been there often enough over the years and his business trips had always gone off without incident.

Her call to Global Tobacco Products' London office hadn't reassured her in the slightest, but at least the company had agreed to look into the matter urgently on her behalf. Her confused thoughts were suddenly interrupted by a ring at the front door. She rose to go and answer it, and was pleased to see her next-door neighbour, sixty-year-old Steve Jeffreys, standing there with a casserole dish in his hands.

'I came to see if there's anything I can do,' he said. 'I was sure you wouldn't feel like cooking, what with all the funeral arrangements and everything, so I brought you another sample of my abysmal home cooking.'

'Steve. How kind. Do come in. And you're a wonderful cook. I must give you your other dish back. The lasagne was delicious.'

Steve walked into her kitchen and put the casserole dish down on the worktop. He seemed slightly flushed and there were tiny beads of perspiration on his brow. She suspected he had been standing in his kitchen cooking all morning, oblivious to the pain his bad leg always gave him on rainy days. She felt touched that he should have done so for her. She counted her blessings in having such a good neighbour. Steve ran a hand over his short-cropped, greying hair.

'Did the funeral directors give you an idea when it will be?'

'Oh, Steve, you won't believe what's happened. Come into the lounge. I don't know what to think. I can't make sense of it all.'

Once they were sitting down, Laura told him about viewing the wrong body at the funeral parlour. He was as shocked as she had been.

'They sent the wrong body? That's disgraceful! How could they make such a crass mistake? Have you been in touch with Keith's firm? Have they got an explanation?'

'They said they were stunned, too. They're sending a company representative around to see me this evening – Charles ... someone or other. He's supposed to advise me about Keith's final salary and his pension and insurance entitlements. I'm not sure I'm in the right frame of mind to take it all in, though.'

'Would you like me to be here when he comes?' Steve offered.

'Oh, would you? That would be so kind of you.'

'Not at all. It's been six years since I lost Viv, and you and Keith were so good to me when it happened. I know how the sudden loss of your partner leaves you in shock. It's like a brain fog sets in. There's so much to organise and yet you feel like your head is somewhere else.'

'Yes, that's exactly how it feels. I mean, finding out he'd died was shocking enough, but because it happened overseas, I felt I needed to see his body so I could accept it was true. D'you know what I mean?'

'Yes. I do.'

'Well, you can imagine how awful it was seeing a complete stranger in the coffin – in Keith's coffin, which I'd paid for, by the way. And the fact that the dead stranger had been shot, well, I mean ...'

'What? He'd been *shot*?'

'Yes. That's how Burgess, the undertaker, realised there was something wrong – that and the fact that the dead man was considerably younger than Keith. On the Pakistani death certificate, it says Keith had a heart attack, but the young man in the coffin was a shooting victim. Just imagine, though, if Burgess hadn't spotted that, I might have buried some dead Pakistani stranger in the family plot. Worse still, I might have ended up lying in there beside him, for all eternity.'

'Bloody hell! Look, what time's he coming, this Charles chap?'

'He's travelling up from London, apparently. He should be here about eight this evening.'

'I'll be here when he arrives, Laura. And don't you worry about it. We'll get to the bottom of this, I promise you.'

• • •

Steve was as good as his word and was waiting with Laura when the company man's Mercedes pulled up outside the house.

'We'll see him in the dining room,' she said, as she headed for the front door. 'I've laid out all the paperwork in there.'

'Fine,' Steve said, and he went through and seated himself at the dining table.

Moments later, Laura ushered in a smartly dressed, middle-aged man.

'Steve, this is Charles Markham from Global Tobacco Products. Mr Markham, this is Steve Jeffreys, a close family friend.'

The two men shook hands and Laura bade Markham take a seat. Markham placed a bulky envelope on the table.

'May I offer you a coffee, Mr Markham?' Laura offered. 'You've had a long drive.'

'It's Charles, please, and no thanks. I'm fine. Well, may I begin by expressing my sincere condolences. We were all terribly shocked to hear the news about Keith. The office will be sending a floral tribute, naturally. And I've brought with me all the paperwork regarding the financial side of things.'

He tapped the envelope.

'You won't need to worry about money, and if there's anything you need to query, my contact details are in here, too.'

'Yes, but, right now, I'm more concerned to find out what's happened to Keith's body. I've had to put the funeral arrangements on hold until he's found. And goodness knows what will happen about the other body – the one that's been sent by mistake. Will I have to pay to repatriate him back to Pakistan? I don't even know who he is.'

'Oh, you won't need to worry about that, Mrs Roberts. Our head office is looking into it right now. We've got our contacts in Pakistan liaising with the local authorities. It was most unfortunate what happened, and I can't apologise enough for the terrible mix-up, but I'm sure it'll all be sorted out very soon. And the company will pay any additional expenses that might ensue.'

'Will they?' Laura asked, though she didn't feel greatly reassured.

'Oh yes. In the circumstances, it's the least they can do.'

Laura was far from clear on what the circumstances were, but at least it seemed the money side of it would not be a problem. There was an awkward silence. Laura took in Markham's appearance. The man was in his late forties or maybe early fifties, not exactly tall but rather stocky, with thinning, dark hair. He was well-spoken and his dress suggested accustomed affluence. The high-end car parked beyond her dining room window completed the picture. He said all the right words, and yet, somehow, he didn't sound sincere. There was something glib and condescending about his smile. That and the measured home counties accent didn't exactly endear him to Laura.

Markham glanced around the room. His gaze alighted on the sideboard with its array of family photographs.

'I shall miss Keith, too, you know,' he said. 'He was a good colleague and very good at his work. And, my, didn't he love his golf?'

Markham had obviously spotted the photograph taken at the golf club, and the trophy standing beside it. Surprised, Laura caught Steve's eye.

'Strange, he never mentioned you,' she said.

'Didn't he?' Markham shrugged. 'I don't suppose he talked much shop talk when he was at home. I know he was quite a private man, though he often spoke about you and your lovely daughter. He was so proud of Elizabeth. Spoke of her all the time.'

Again, Laura's glance met Steve's. Steve raised his eyebrows.

'Well, Mrs Roberts, is there anything else I can tell you? Anything else you need to know? Would you like me to talk you through the paperwork?'

'No, I don't think so, thanks. I'll have a good look through the papers tomorrow and I'll await your call when you've tracked down Keith's remains.'

Markham got to his feet and offered his hand.

'Then I'll be off. I'll be staying in Manchester tonight and heading back to London around mid-morning tomorrow. Don't hesitate to ring me on my mobile if you need anything. The number's on my business card. Well, good night to you both.'

'Thank you for coming, Mr Markham,' Laura said, as she showed him to the door.

'Well, what did you make of him?' she asked on her return.

'He's a shifty southern git. And a liar,' Steve declared. 'Keith never played golf. He couldn't see the point of it. He used to say it spoiled a good walk. And when did anyone call your Beth 'Elizabeth'? She'd clock them one if they did.'

'Maybe he was just trying to make me feel better. Funeral directors do that, too. They tell you it's their 'sorrowful duty' to be handling your business, but they don't mean it. I suppose it's a forgivable insincerity, since it's meant to make you feel better.'

'He'd no need to lie, though,' Keith shook his head. 'He could have just said 'I never met Keith, but I hear he was very well thought of at work'. No, I don't know who he is, but clearly, he wasn't a work colleague of Keith's. I doubt he'd even met him.'

'Well, so long as he finds Keith and I can get this funeral sorted, I won't worry about it. But I can't say I'm bothered about meeting Charles Markham ever again.'

CHAPTER FOUR

OPERATIONAL INTELLIGENCE OFFICER HARRY EDWARDS TURNED OFF THE M66 at junction three and followed the signs for the retail park. Sweeping his lank, fair hair back from his eyes, the thirty-six-year-old felt a little more relaxed now they were off the motorway. It had been a long drive from London and it had been raining hard for the last few miles. He opened the car window just enough to allow in some fresh air. At the roundabout, he took a road which was signposted in the opposite direction from the Lancashire market town of Burtby.

'Are we not heading for the town itself, then?' his colleague Kirpal Kohli asked.

'No, Mate. It's in one of those out-of-town retail parks.'

'Does the building have a name?'

'Well, the chap who gave me directions on the phone just referred to it as 'RBP'. I suppose they don't want the whole world to know the exact location of MI5 North.'

'Are we nearly there yet?' a sleepy female voice came from the rear passenger seat.

The incoming fresh air had awoken their colleague, Jo Laska.

She yawned and stretched out her long legs, at least as much as the back seat footwell would allow.

'Yes, Jo. Not far now,' Harry assured her. 'It's a relatively new building, and purpose built. Should be very different from Thames House.'

Driving around the perimeter road of the industrial estate, they came to a large site surrounded by the same sort of galvanised steel palisade which protected other nearby industrial units. Despite the lack of signage – or perhaps because of it – Harry knew they were at the right place.

As they pulled off the road and were admitted beyond the first of two sets of security gates, they saw that the building was indeed very different from MI5's London headquarters. Unlike Thames House, with its ornate, Portland stone exterior and its grand entrance flanked by the patriotic statues of St George and Britannia, this twenty-million-pound, steel-framed, two-storey bloc could have passed for just any large commercial or light industrial unit. It was set beside one of Lancashire's fast-flowing rivers. Harry knew that, once upon a time, rivers like this one would have powered many mills. Those mills had clothed the nation, back in the days when cotton was king. Nowadays, the local industrial scene was more diversified.

Glancing around the industrial park, he could see several double-glazing manufacturers and also a timber mill, where, according to their signage, trees were processed into fibreboard for the construction industry. However, their own latest installation on this site would be more of an information mill. The product processed in this unit was intelligence. Harry knew the Security Service's northern HQ had been constructed with twenty-first century security features and he was pleased to see that, unlike their London office, it benefitted from a multitude of car parking spaces. Once admitted through the second barrier and directed to a designated parking space, Harry could see a garage block which held an array of vans and other commercial type vehicles, which he guessed were used for surveillance.

At reception, they were cleared through security and met by one of the regional office's operational intelligence officers. Sue Shaw was around mid-thirties, Harry guessed, and had short dark hair and what he took to be a local accent. Smiling broadly, she introduced herself and led her three London colleagues upstairs to the section where they would be working on attachment for the next month or so. In contrast to their own counter-espionage section at Thames House, the accommodation occupied by their northern colleagues was open plan. The large windows provided an altogether more extensive and pleasantly rural view than their office windows back in London. Sue took them through to meet the head of the section, Luke Greenwood.

'Boss, these are our attachees from Thames House, Harry Edwards, Jo Laska, and Kirpal Kohli.'

'Welcome,' Luke said. 'Now, Harry and Kirpal I know from my visits to Thames House, but, Jo, we haven't met, have we?'

Smiling, he rose from his desk to shake the hand of the tall, attractive blonde.

'So, you're all from Adrian Curtis's team, I understand. And how is Adrian these days?'

'He's very well, thanks,' Harry replied, 'and he sends you his best regards.'

'Adrian and I joined the firm at around the same time,' Luke explained. 'Of course, Adrian's a soft southerner, but I'm a Lancashire lad, so, when they decided to site a regional office up here, I jumped at the chance to return to my roots. Now, are you all familiar with the area or is this your first time up here?'

'First time for me,' Harry said.

'Furthest north I'd been before today is Leicester,' Kirpal added, 'but the countryside up here looks very beautiful, from what I've seen so far.'

'And how about you, Jo?' Luke asked.

'Oh, I have Polish cousins in Burnley and Manchester. I've spent quite a lot of time up here over the years.'

'Good. Well, I expect Adrian told you that half a dozen of our section's staff are on long-term sick at the moment, and it couldn't have happened at a worse time, as our workload is really picking up. We've some serious targets we're looking at right now and the intel is rolling in, but I'm woefully short of staff to act on it. Kirpal, you speak Punjabi, don't you?'

'Yes, also Hindi and Urdu.'

'That'll be very useful. What about you, Jo? Do you have linguistic skills?

'I'm fluent in Polish and Russian and I have A-level French and German.'

Impressed, Luke nodded, then looked towards Harry, who held up his hands apologetically.

'Schoolboy French and a few Welsh swearwords my granny taught me,' Harry confessed.

'That's okay. Well, Sue here will get you all settled in then we'll have a bit of a briefing. She's booked you in at the Traveller's Inn which is here in the retail park. Their rates are reasonable so you should have enough of your subsistence left for some decent meals out. There's a nice little pub restaurant close by, too. The Pepper Mill. I can recommend it.'

Sue took her three new colleagues back into the main office, showed them where the restrooms and the office kitchen were and offered them tea and coffee. Next, she allocated them each a work station.

'So, was it the Covid virus that decimated your section?' Jo asked, when they were all settled.

'No. We're all double vaccinated and boosted. And most of us had the 'flu jab last autumn, too,' Sue explained. 'No, we've four off with recurring migraines, so we're getting someone in to check that the office lighting isn't to blame. Another one has some kind of vertigo and tinnitus and has been warned not to drive till he's over it, and a sixth is suffering from bouts of nausea. At first, she thought she might be pregnant, but her GP suggested it might be down to the chemicals used on the new carpeting in the building. They still have that horrible chemical odour about them, which is why we try and keep the windows open.'

'I've heard of sick building syndrome,' Jo said, 'but you don't usually hear of that in a new build.'

'Maybe it was the change in climate and altitude,' Harry joked. 'Moving so far up north, I mean. Did anyone get a nosebleed?'

'Not as far as I know,' Sue grinned, 'and, anyway, half of them were recruited locally. Like me, they should be used to the altitude, and the rain. We Mancunians are born with webbed feet, you know.'

Soon, Luke Greenwood re-joined them. Clutching his own mug of coffee, the fifty-year old perched on the edge of a desk and briefed them on his section's main areas of interest.

'Okay, so, our own counter-espionage team has been looking at the exceptionally large numbers of Chinese students studying here in the north. What concerns us in particular is the high ratio of post-doctoral students assigned to collaborate on research and development projects. They seem to seek out projects connected with military weaponry, cyber security and that sort of thing.'

'I thought the government was going to slap a blanket ban on Chinese students getting involved in sensitive research programmes,' Harry said.

'Yes, and they have,' Luke agreed, 'but the Chinese government got around that initially by getting EU passports for some of those post-doc applicants. Maltese and Romanian were the documents of choice. You can get those if you invest heavily enough in those states. Since the UK left the EU, though, the latest scam is mainland Chinese arriving amongst the mass settlers coming in from Hong Kong.'

'It can't be that easy to establish which are genuine Hong Kong citizens and which are actually from China,' Harry observed. 'I imagine the Chinese authorities control the issuing of all identity documents in Hong Kong, so you can't accept at face value what it says in their passports and national ID cards.'

'That's right, Harry,' Luke confirmed. 'And UK universities find it difficult to refuse someone who, on paper, is eminently qualified to join a research team. They can't reject them just on the basis of their suspected loyalties.'

'So, is that what we'll be involved in – academic espionage?' Harry asked.

'No, Harry. That'll be for our own depleted team to take forward. The reason I asked for your assistance here is to run an entirely different operation. Our other major area of concern is that we're seeing some activity involving young men in the local Muslim communities.'

'Radicalisation, you mean?' Kirpal asked.

'Well, maybe, but maybe not. The police and a couple of local MPs have been approached by some Pakistani families who are concerned that their sons have suddenly taken their passports and disappeared. You'd be forgiven for putting that down to radicalisation, but we're not so sure that it is.'

'Why's that?' Kirpal asked.

'A couple of those lads managed to contact their families from overseas, before their mobile phones and passports were taken away from them. They told their folks they'd been offered well-paid jobs overseas, but they'd been told not to say anything about it to their families.'

'Did they say why?' Kirpal asked.

'They'd been told the UK government wouldn't approve of what they'd be doing, because they'd be working for a state which

HMG doesn't recognise. The odd thing is that the youths said they hadn't ended up where they expected to be.'

'Where *did* they expect to be?' Harry asked.

'They'd been told they'd be going to the new Islamic Emirate of Afghanistan,' Luke explained, 'to work as security guards minding sensitive buildings and mining sites, and also to provide security at the country's two main airports in Kabul and Kandahar. But, instead, they found themselves in north west Pakistan in some sort of military training camp.'

'So, do we know what's going on there?' Jo asked.

'Well, one of them said he was receiving basic combat and weapons training. That's all he managed to say before his communication with his family ceased abruptly. They haven't heard from him since.'

'It all sounds a bit sinister,' Jo opined. 'Are the Pakistani authorities recruiting these lads for their army, or something? Are they looking to start a war?'

'Well, that's one possibility,' Luke agreed.

'Aren't the Pakistanis having problems with their own local Taliban?' Harry ventured. 'I suppose they might be expanding their armed forces to deal with that, but why would they need to recruit British lads?'

'Indeed, Harry,' Luke nodded. 'The TTP, or *Tehrik-i-Taliban* of Pakistan is another fundamentalist Islamic group, wholly separate from the Afghan Taliban. The Pakistani authorities have an odd relationship with the TTP, though. On the face of it, the military have been fighting them, but ISI – Pakistan's main intelligence agency – have, on occasion, used their local Taliban fighters for their own purposes. It's a strange situation.'

'Aren't they worried the Pakistani Taliban might join forces with the Afghan Taliban and establish an emirate in Pakistan, like they've done in Afghanistan?' Kirpal asked.

'Not so far,' Luke explained. 'You see, the Pakistani Taliban are distinctly separate from the Afghan Taliban. They're not allied to Islamic State as the Afghan Taliban are. The TTP draw their ideology from Al-Qaeda instead.'

'That would explain how Osama Bin Laden came to be living a protected life in the Pakistani town of Abbottabad,' Kirpal agreed.

'Yes, and, so far at least, the Pakistani TTP don't regard themselves as allies of the Afghan Taliban. What the TTP want is to establish their own independent state all across Pakistan's Federally Administered Territories up in the North West of the country. It's a bugger of a place to administer, so I wouldn't be surprised if some branches of the Pakistani government are happy to let the TTP get on with it.'

'So, who do you think might be recruiting fighters from the UK – the Pakistani government, or the TTP?' Jo asked.

'We're not entirely sure, Jo. Recently, though, according to MI6, there's been a bit of activity in the Khyber region, up in the north west of Pakistan. The Pakistanis say they're simply engaging in military exercises up there, but MI6 think it may be more than just exercises.'

'So, they think there's some sort of actual military conflict going on?' Kirpal asked.

'Yes, but it's difficult to get any meaningful intelligence, especially since western troops pulled out of Afghanistan. We've no intelligence coming from the Afghan side of the border, and Pakistan's ISI aren't sharing intel on what's happening on their side – that's assuming they do actually *know* what's going on. It's impossible for MI6 to get people on the ground to observe and report back. And, of course, recruiting agents locally is tricky, because, in those tribal areas, with their shifting affiliations, you never know who can be trusted.'

'So, what's our role in this?' Harry asked.

'I just need you guys to identify who, at this end of the supply chain, is recruiting the young local men. If we can find out what they're meant to be doing in Pakistan, so much the better, but our main aim is to try and cut off that source of supply. They may be recruiting from other countries as well, but that's not our concern.'

'Do we have any intel?' Harry asked. 'Any potential suspects you'd like us to target?'

'Well, Sue has been liaising with local Special Branch and they passed a few names and addresses her way. We got warrants to check out their communications and our local GCHQ people have been keeping an ear out. So, Sue will take you three into Manchester tomorrow to visit Heron House.'

'Heron House?' Harry queried.

'Our local branch of GCHQ. They'll brief you on the outcome of their COMINT and you can establish some appropriate contacts there. Always better to get out and meet people face to face. In the meantime, you can read some of the reporting we've received thus far. And, by the way, this op has been named *Operation Trebor*. Looks like the current round of operational names Thames House are doling out is based on sweet and toffee manufacturers.'

Kirpal glanced out at the rain, which had been falling steadily since their arrival.

'Maybe *Operation Mackintosh* would have been more appropriate,' he observed, gloomily.

CHAPTER FIVE

Laura Roberts sat at the dining room table at the appointed time of seven o'clock in the evening and switched on her laptop. Soon she was connected, via the internet, to her daughter Beth in Canada. By her reckoning, it was about two o'clock in the afternoon in London, Ontario.

'Hello, Darling. How are you?' She beamed to see her daughter's face on screen.

'Hi, Mummy. I'm fine, but how are you? Your e-mail said there would be an indefinite delay with the funeral. I'd booked a refundable ticket so I'll have no trouble changing my date of travel, but what's happened?'

'Oh, a bit of a mix-up with the repatriation of your father's ... remains. They sent the wrong body back.'

'They did *what*?' Beth was aghast.

'They sent the wrong body. It was most unfortunate, but these things happen sometimes. Anyway, they now tell me they're having a bit of difficulty finding your father. Wasn't that just like him in life? I never knew exactly where he was, or exactly when he'd be back from those interminable business trips. Anyway, I can't re-book the funeral until they locate him.'

'Mummy, that's outrageous! Did they have any explanation? I mean, how do you lose a body? Who's in charge out there?'

'Well, your father's company is liaising with the British Embassy in Islamabad, and they're pressing the local authorities to find out what's happened, but it's been a week now since anyone from the company has been in touch with me. I'm worried that, if they take too long about it, you'll be too far along with your pregnancy to fly. To be honest, I'm thinking of flying out to Pakistan myself to see if I can speed things up.'

'What? Why on earth would you do that? Surely, there's no need for you to go? Let the authorities sort it out.'

'Well, there are some unsatisfactory aspects to this, things I'm not happy with.'

'What sort of things?'

'I tried calling some of your dad's colleagues, you know, Frank Pearson in HR, and your dad's PA, Tilly, to try to find out what they know, but they just clam up. They keep referring me to this chap called Charles Markham from head office in London. I rang head office and all they said was they couldn't connect me to him as he's continually out of office. He doesn't even have an office extension. He can only be contacted on his mobile.'

'Well, that's okay, isn't it, if this man Markham's your point of contact and you have his mobile number?'

'Yes, but most of the time his mobile seems to be either switched off or it goes to a messaging service. And, anyway, I met him and I don't like him. He's too ... smug, too shifty. I don't think he's being very honest with me. And there's another odd thing, darling. The Pakistani death certificate states your father died of a heart attack, but the man in the coffin – you know, the wrong man – he'd been shot.'

'Shot? He'd been *shot*? And you're thinking of going out there? *Really*, Mummy?'

'Well, there's obviously something going on. You'd only have to meet this Markham character to know that. Steve's met him, too, and he doesn't trust him either. Steve sends you his love and best wishes, by the way.'

There was a short silence as Laura's daughter took in what her mother had just told her.

'Mummy, you don't think Dad's been up to his old tricks again, do you?'

'What, other women, you mean? Oh, I shouldn't wonder. He was never faithful to me in all the years of our marriage. But surely, that wouldn't have got him killed? I just feel there's something more to all this. I just know they're not telling me everything. That's why I want to go out there and find out what happened for myself.'

'Mummy, you know I loved Daddy very much, but, as you say, he was never completely loyal to you. Why would you put yourself at risk to find out what happened to him?'

'Oh, I know, Darling, but in the thirty-odd years of our marriage, he was a very good father to you. He always kept a roof over our heads and we never wanted for anything. I feel I at least owe it to him to find out where he is and what happened to him. For all we know, he might not be dead at all. He might still be alive. He could be held captive somewhere. Nobody else seems to be in any hurry to find out what happened. So, if no-one else is going to do anything, then I will.'

'Oh, Mummy, you will be careful, though, won't you?'

'I will, Darling. I promise.'

CHAPTER SIX

It had stopped raining by the following lunchtime, and the Thames House attachees were preparing to visit GCHQ's northern office for the afternoon. Sue Shaw was to accompany them.

'Do you want me to drive?' Harry offered.

'Not necessary, thanks. We'll take the Metrolink,' Sue advised as they donned their coats.

'The Metrolink? What's that?' Kirpal asked.

'It's Manchester's tram system,' Jo said. 'I've used it before and it's good. It's expanded a fair bit since the last time I was up here.'

'That's right,' Sue agreed. 'It goes out to Manchester Airport and it links several of the Lancashire mill towns with the city.'

One of Sue's colleagues dropped them off at the Metrolink station in Burtby where they boarded the modern yellow and grey tram bound for the city. Around half an hour later, they disembarked in St Peter's Square. Kirpal glanced across admiringly at the polished marble façade of the magnificent Midland Hotel.

'Wow, that's a bit posher than our Traveller's Inn,' he exclaimed. 'And what's that big building over there?'

He indicated a huge, white Portland stone rotunda, topped

with a dome to rival St Paul's, and with a magnificent Corinthian portico at the front.

'That's Central Library,' Sue informed him. 'When it was built, back in the nineteen thirties, it was the biggest municipal library in the world. We have some really beautiful buildings here in Manchester, you know – art galleries and museums, and lots of wonderful eateries. You should do some exploring in the city whilst you're up here.'

'That's right,' Jo agreed. 'Manchester's got everything London's got, except it's all in a more accessible space. You can walk between most of its best attractions. And there's great places to eat in the Northern Quarter and in Chinatown.'

'Maybe we should eat out here tonight before we catch the Metrolink back,' Harry suggested. 'We can give the rush hour a miss, that way.'

Leaving St Peter's Square, they walked the short distance into Albert Square, which was dominated by what Sue Shaw described as Alfred Waterhouse's acclaimed town hall, though much of it was hidden behind scaffolding and blue plastic tarpaulin. Sue explained that the Victorian building, which she described as the 'Pride of Manchester' – albeit that the same title was also taken by one of the local beers – was being given a costly overhaul, inside and out. She added that the whole of Albert Square was being pedestrianised, which was one of the reasons GCHQ had agreed to occupy new premises in the square. The tarmacked roads which ran around the square had recently been closed to traffic and paved over.

Directly opposite the Town Hall, Sue pointed out the more modern, red brick edifice of Heron House. Unlike 'The Doughnut' – GCHQ's main nerve centre located out in rural Gloucestershire – this northern regional HQ of Government Communications was right in the heart of the city, and its ground floor level was ringed by retail units and even a pub.

'The town hall, and indeed most of Manchester's fine old buildings were built on cotton,' Sue advised them.

'Built on cotton?' Kirpal queried.

'I mean on the profits from what was known as 'King Cotton',' she explained. 'Of course, the cotton weaving trade is long gone now. Cheap imports from India and Pakistan killed the King.'

'Oh, perhaps I should apologise for that,' Kirpal said. 'My grandfather set up a major textile firm in Gwalior, in India's Madhya Pradesh.'

'You're forgiven,' Sue smiled.

Sue led them into Heron House. Once they had cleared security and been allocated visitor's passes, they headed upstairs in the lift and were met by Yasmeen Mehta, whom Sue introduced as her regular liaison contact within GCHQ. The petite and attractive young woman led them into a small briefing room where she had a large thermos of coffee waiting.

'Please call me Yazz,' she said, as she shook hands with her Thames House visitors. 'I've printed off some of our latest reports for you to see whilst you're here, but I'll send them to you electronically, too. We've been gathering intel which may be pertinent to your *Operation Trebor*. This has come from certain individuals' communications in a few Blackburn locations. In particular, there's an Islamic book shop-cum-café in Blackburn, and a private household also in that town that you may be interested in.'

'Which is the book shop?' Kirpal asked.

'It's called *Sadaqat*,' Yazz told him.

'That means 'truth' or 'fact',' Kirpal explained for Jo and Harry's benefit.

'I'll let you have a little read of these reports whilst we have our coffee. Do ask me if you have any questions,' Yazz said, as she distributed a manilla folder to each of them, then began to pour the coffee.

When they had digested both the coffee and the information in the intel reports, Yazz collected the folders from them and returned them to the safe. She asked if they had any thoughts or queries. Kirpal, in particular, was intrigued.

'I see you've got some useful COMINT between the landline at *Sadaqat* bookshop and a mobile phone being used in Blackburn. Any idea who owns the mobile?'

'No,' Yazz said. 'It's an unregistered pay-as-you-go. But we've got a fix on the user's movements. We think he's living on Trafalgar Street in Blackburn. At least, that's where his mobile signal is static overnight. His phone signal also pings regularly on the tower nearest the *Sadaqat* book shop. We suspect, however, that most of his communications are made via e- mails on the dark web, so we can't access those.'

Sue Shaw had also spotted something of interest.

'One of your HUMINT reports concerning activity in Blackburn has a snippet of intel from a local source. It's an allegation relating to potential radicalisation, I think we'd like to follow that up, as well.'

'Sure,' Yazz said. 'I'll ensure I include that one with the reports I send you electronically.'

Sue turned to Kirpal.

'The local source is a chap with a Muslim name. If he has useful info to impart, maybe you'd like to meet with him, Kirpal? If his info is good, you could become his handler.'

Kirpal confirmed he'd be very keen to do so. Sue thanked Yazz for her time and suggested she would take her charges to have a look around the city before they chose somewhere to have dinner.

'If you guys like Indian food, I can recommend *Firdooz* in the Northern Quarter,' Yazz said, 'and they're open for dinner from about six-thirty, if you don't want to be in town too late.'

'That sounds good,' Harry said. '*Firdooz* it is, then.'

'Will you join us, Yazz?' Kirpal asked.

'Thanks. I will. I'll come straight over after work. Be sure and save me a place.'

As Sue Shaw and her charges left Heron House, they crossed Albert Square, dodging around the roadworks and construction vehicles. As they left the Square, Kirpal glanced up at the massive crane which was lifting building materials up to the roof level of the town hall. The building's main clock tower looked to be, in his estimation, around three hundred feet high, and large chunks of stone and pallets of Welsh slate were being hoisted aloft towards the roof.

'It must be cold and draughty up there,' Kirpal remarked. 'They're taking heaters up there, too.'

Sure enough, two large items being carried into the building resembled old-fashioned industrial fan heaters.

'Doesn't the town hall have central heating?' Jo asked.

'Oh yes,' Sue assured her. 'It's been modernised since it was first built in the late nineteenth century, but I imagine all the electrics and gas will be turned off during the renovations. Most of the staff have been relocated into the more modern town hall extension next door.'

Sue indicated the so-called modern extension which she explained was itself a magnificent building of nineteen thirties' construction, linked to the original, grade one listed, neo-Gothic town hall via two glazed bridges.

Sue next escorted her Thames House colleagues up to Moseley Street to Manchester's Art Gallery and Museum, with its huge Portland stone columns and classical pediment. Since they hadn't had a chance to eat lunch, she took them into the museum's café for tea and cake.

'You know,' Kirpal confided, as he demolished a generous slice of Victoria sponge cake, 'I've spent most of my life in London, and

I like city life, but I'm beginning to see other cities can be just as lively as the capital.'

'Yes, you need to get out more, Mate,' Harry agreed. 'I can understand why Luke was keen to move back. I expect property prices are a lot more reasonable up here, too.'

'Oh, they are,' Jo agreed. 'There's not so much crime around here, either. Of course, they did have the Islamist suicide bomber at the Manchester Arena about five years ago, and that was heart-breaking. Generally, though, it feels much safer up here than in London.'

'Yes, it does,' Sue agreed, 'but we can't afford to be complacent. There are more plots and plotters up here than you'd expect.'

Having spent the afternoon touring the museum and gallery, they next walked up to the once industrial, now fashionable Northern Quarter to look for the restaurant Yazz had recommended. Kirpal suggested the area had a similar vibe to London's Camden Market. They had just reached *Firzdooz* when the drizzle which had followed them around all afternoon suddenly turned into a downpour. They hurried inside and found Yazz already waiting for them. Harry noticed that, whilst he, Sue and Jo took off their damp coats and found the coat rack on which to hang them up, Kirpal strode ahead threw his coat over a chair, and contrived to sit opposite Yazz. When they were all seated and settled, Yazz explained that the owner and chef were *Parsee* and so was the cuisine, and she talked them through the menu options and made some recommendations.

'What's a *Parsee*?' Jo asked.

'They're fire-worshippers,' a grinning Kirpal informed her.

'Zoroastrianism is about rather more than that,' Yazz protested. 'Our ancestors were Persian originally, and when the Muslim Moghul armies invaded, our ancestors fled to India and were welcomed there. The *Parsee* community is a small one, but they are well respected in India. What faith do you follow, Kirpal?'

Kirpal bit his lip and looked as though he could kick himself for his injudicious comment.

'Sorry, Yazz,' he said, sheepishly. 'I wrongly assumed from your name that you'd be Hindu. You'll know from my name that I worship as a Sikh, but, as you can see, I don't embrace the uncut hair or the turban.'

'Why's that?' she asked.

'I'm a Technical Operations Officer now, but I'm trained to do surveillance work, too, and I realised that wearing a turban would make me too conspicuous,' he explained. 'I'm sure God will recognise me, even without my turban. But I do respect other people's religions, too. I hope I didn't offend you. I'm clearly a bit ignorant about Zoroastrianism and I would actually like to know more about it. That's if you'll forgive me for my rudeness.'

Yazz glanced into Kirpal's big, doe eyes and she smiled coyly. Yes, clearly, he was forgiven. Harry nudged Jo. Jo winked back at him, knowingly. They could see there was an instant attraction between their colleague and Yasmeen. The waiter took their order and, before long, there were some wonderful aromas emanating from the kitchen.

'It's still belting down,' Harry sighed, gazing glumly out of the steamed-up windows.

'Is it?' Kirpal replied, not taking his eyes off Yazz.

It seemed to his colleagues that, despite his earlier complaint about the weather, Kirpal no longer minded the rain. In fact, he didn't seem to mind it one little bit.

CHAPTER SEVEN

Silver-haired chairman Sir Stuart Bridgeman called the meeting of the Joint Intelligence Committee to order. He smiled to see a pleasingly full turnout of the Committee at the Cabinet Office on Whitehall that morning. He reserved his broadest smile for Helena Fairbrother, the Director General of MI5 and the committee's sole female member. The Security Service Chief was, as always, well-dressed and her short brown hair was neatly styled. Her fuchsia-pink jacket marked her out from the largely grey-suited men of the committee. Her colourful jackets were something of a personal style statement, and they not only flattered her complexion but made her seem a little more youthful than her fifty-two years.

'Good morning, everyone,' Sir Stuart began. 'Thank you all for attending. Naturally, the main issue on the agenda today is a most urgent one. Clearly, we need to re-visit our national security and defence threat assessment in the light of developments in Afghanistan since the coalition withdrew. As you all know, I was the senior Foreign Office diplomat with responsibility for political issues in the region. Some years before that, I was deputy head of mission in Kabul. As such, it pains me to see how the situation there has deteriorated.'

He turned to Lieutenant Colonel Sir John Hooper, Chief of Britain's defence forces.

'John, will you give us a sitrep?'

Sir John, an impressively tall man with a suitably military bearing, looked grave as he addressed the meeting.

'Thank you, Stuart. I don't think I need to point out that it was against all military advice that, in twenty-twenty-one, the Americans decided to pull their forces out of Afghanistan, and that Downing Street rejected our own Defence Minister's urging that the UK should encourage its fellow NATO members to stay.'

All the committee members nodded in agreement.

'It was just a matter of time before the country fell to the Taliban' Sir John continued. 'Though I don't think anyone could have predicted just how quickly that would happen. Perhaps it was naïve of us to believe the Afghan national army's claim that they had three hundred and fifty thousand soldiers ready to defend their homeland against the Taliban.'

'And hadn't they?' the pin-stripe suited Cabinet Secretary, Sir Henry Mortimer, asked.

'No, Henry,' the Defence Chief explained. 'The Americans were funding those three hundred thousand posts, but it now looks like the entire standing army amounted to, at most, fifty thousand men.'

'Why would they lie about that?' Sir Henry asked.

It was Sir Stuart, the Chairman, who answered his query.

'For the same reason my bearer in Kabul told me he'd hired four sweepers and a cook's assistant for my household. My bearer was pocketing the wages of five 'ghost employees'. The Afghan military seem to have been doing the same, albeit on a vastly grander scale.'

The Defence Chief continued:

'It was inevitable that the Russians would take advantage of the coalition's withdrawal, especially since they've been funding the Afghan Taliban for a number of years now. They learned a painful lesson back in 'seventy-nine when they invaded Afghanistan, and it took ten years of bitter war for them to realise that the best way to control the region and its riches was not by military invasion, but by stealthy manipulation and investment.'

'But how do you think this will impact us, here in the west, John?' Sir Henry asked, idly twiddling the row of pens which poked out of his breast pocket.

Helena smiled as she caught sight of the pens. She sometimes felt that Cabinet Secretary Sir Henry, as Head of the Civil Service, displayed his pens almost as a badge of office. In his appearance, he looked like every other senior official in the vast civilian army of suited administrators. However, despite the beer-glass-bottom spectacles he wore, which gave him both a perpetually myopic expression and a red-veined nose, Sir Henry was, she knew, a highly astute man, a man of integrity, and someone who took his role most seriously. She often thought that, if she had to choose just one of the men seated around the conference table to trust with her life, it would be Sir Henry Mortimer.

'Well,' the Defence Chief appeared thoughtful, 'it may not affect us at all. The various armed insurgent groups around the region may simply continue to fight amongst themselves. Then again, they may decide to bring terrorism back to the west, either separately or in unison. What does Vauxhall Cross make of all this, Bob?'

Sir Robert Vanbrugge, the sartorially elegant MI6 chief, fiddled with his gold cufflinks. Helena noticed he often did so, perhaps as an aid to concentration. She mused that his cufflinks were the equivalent of Sir Henry's pens. He seemed reluctant to appear as the spectre at the feast, and yet he was clearly about to introduce a note of caution.

'Well, Gentlemen – and Lady,' he nodded in deference to Helena, 'it doesn't seem to matter how many intelligence briefings we submit to our present government, nor how earnestly we stress the dangers, they seem always to adopt the strategy of least resistance. Let's be honest, former US President Trump announced the withdrawal of American troops from Afghanistan in order to court popularity with the US electorate, for all the good that did him.'

Again, the committee members nodded.

'We had no choice but to follow suit,' Sir Robert continued. 'We must remember that we're no longer a world super power, but a small and increasingly insignificant cluster of islands. We're still emerging from the crippling economic aftermath of both our withdrawal from the European Union and a major global pandemic. We cannot afford to police the world.'

'Does the world need policing, Bob?' Helena asked.

'I fear it does, Helena. We no longer have an empire to defend, but someone needs to defend democracy.'

'And what are the threats democracy faces currently?' the Cabinet Secretary asked.

'At the moment, Henry, the Taliban regime in Afghanistan presents little threat to us. Sure, some terrible things are befalling the local populace. The bearded and barefoot militiamen in pyjamas are busy wreaking revenge on those locals who supported the coalition, and they're supressing some of the ethnic minorities such as the Hazaras. They're also riding roughshod over the rights of women and girls, as we knew they would. They say their main goal is to establish their new Islamic Emirate of Afghanistan. But I suspect it won't be long before they begin to extend their sphere of influence beyond their own borders.'

'How do you think they'll do that?' Sir Henry asked.

'Our fear is that they'll begin to form alliances with the TTP –

that's the Pakistani Taliban – and with other Islamic insurgents in the region, such as those in Turkmenistan, Uzbekistan, Tajikistan and Kirghizstan. Following the Russian clamp down on protests in Kazakhstan, that state, too, could look to joining a regional insurgency. And Pakistan's TTP is allied with Al-Qaeda, who've carried out some of the worst attacks on the west before now.'

'But, Bob, I thought there was no love lost between the Afghan Taliban and the Pakistani Taliban,' Helena said. 'Is there really any likelihood of them joining forces?'

It was the chairman, Sir Stuart, who answered her question.

'In the world of the Pashtun,' he theorised, 'it's a case of me versus my brother, or my brother and me versus the next village, or my village and the next village versus the tribe over the hill. If the Afghan Taliban ever manage to persuade the other insurgents in the region that their common enemy is the non-believers in the west, then they will all join forces against us.'

'And the Afghan Taliban have already buttered-up Iran by handing all the abandoned US planes, tanks and helicopters over to them,' the Defence Chief added. 'With Iran now having nuclear capabilities, well, it could end up in the biggest *Jihad* imaginable.'

There was a brief but ominous silence. It was the most senior civil servant who broke it.

'Won't China have a role to play in what could be a doomsday scenario for them, too?' Sir Henry asked. 'After all, they constantly risk an insurgency in their own Uighur Muslim region, don't they?'

'Yes,' Sir John nodded, 'and they're chummy with the Russians these days, so, perhaps we should let the Chinese and the Russians sort it all out between them. After all, the threat is on their doorsteps more than on ours, isn't it? And with Putin having lined up so many of his troops on the border with Ukraine, Russia could be weakened by fighting a war on many fronts. Speaking of the Russians, though, are they still pulling the strings next door?'

The Defence Chief indicated the green baize-lined door which led to the passageway linking the cabinet office to the adjacent offices of the prime minister in Downing Street.'

'Well, we'd hoped that source of influence had dried up when the PM was forced to sack his so-called chief advisor, that Russophile Malcolm Donald,' Sir Henry said. 'But Helena tells me they've been seen together again recently.'

'Yes,' Helena agreed. 'Politically speaking, Malcolm Donald's dead, but it seems he won't lie down.'

'Are your people keeping an eye on that relationship, Helena?' the MI6 chief asked.

'We certainly are, Bob,' she assured him.

'We wouldn't want him back in Thompson's fold again, would we?'

'No, Bob. We wouldn't. But if it looks like he might gain re-admittance to Number Ten, then we'll certainly do something about it.'

CHAPTER EIGHT

If Laura Roberts was feeling excited about her forthcoming trip, her neighbour was both incredulous and apprehensive.

'Laura, I can't believe you're really going to do this,' Steve said. 'I've been checking out news reports and looking at the Foreign Office travel advice on that region. It's really not a safe place to travel around, especially for a woman on her own. Maybe you should wait a little longer and see what the authorities can find out. After all, what enquiries could you make that they won't already have done?'

'But that's just it, Steve,' she said, 'they're not *doing* anything. Charles Markham did his best to talk me out of it, too. I told him that, surely, as a private citizen, I can go wherever I please. When he saw I wouldn't be put off, he said he'd make all the travel arrangements. It seems the company has agreed to pay for my flights and accommodation, on condition that Markham comes with me. Can't say I'm wild about that, but, since they're paying ...'

'But don't you need a visa for Pakistan? It says so on the Foreign Office website.'

'Yes, and Markham has got me one. The company asked the

Foreign Office to facilitate my application to the Pakistan Embassy for a thirty-day visit visa on compassionate grounds and it's come through very quickly.'

'So, when do you fly?'

'On Tuesday.'

'So soon?'

'Yes, well, the sooner the better. I mean, if Keith should still be alive but in some kind of trouble out there ...'

'You think he might be?'

'I have no idea. But it's a possibility. I'm booked on Qatar Airways from Manchester to Doha. Markham's travelling out from Heathrow so I'll meet up with him at Doha, and we'll fly on together to Peshawar. Someone from the consular section of our embassy in Islamabad is going to meet us on arrival and he'll take us wherever we need to go. I can't say I'm going to enjoy Markham's company, but, between him and the Consul, at least I should be in safe hands.'

Steve looked worried and Laura was touched by his concern. She regarded Steve Jeffreys as a good neighbour and a true friend, although she sometimes felt that, as a retired civil servant, he was a tad too cautious, too unadventurous. She doubted he'd have found himself in any danger in the London office of the ministry which had hosted his career. She recalled him saying he'd been in the Government Communications Procurement Directorate, or something equally dry. By his own account, his safe career had been cut short a decade earlier, when a tumble down a flight of stone steps had resulted in a serious leg injury. She knew his shattered and pinned thigh bone still caused him pain from time to time. She imagined that was the greatest danger Steve Jeffreys had ever faced.

'Well, since you obviously won't be swayed from your purpose, you'd better take this with you,' he said, as he pressed a mobile phone and charger into her hand.

'Oh, thank you, but I have one,' she said.

'Yes, and I imagine Markham has your number. He won't have the number of this one, though. It's always handy to have a back-up phone anyway, just in case yours should be lost or stolen. The charger is solar-powered, too, in case you find yourself stuck up country somewhere. Oh, and Markham doesn't need to know you have a second phone.'

She smiled. It was typical of Steve to be so ultra-cautious. Still, it was good of him to be concerned about her, and having a second mobile phone certainly wouldn't hurt. Agreeing that she would, if she found herself in the slightest bother, give him a call, any time of day or night, she accepted the phone and promised she would keep it fully charged at all times.

Laura's daughter, too, had expressed her concerns at the trip her mother was about to undertake. Beth phoned twice in the days leading up to Laura's departure. She was reassured, however, to learn that her mother was to have two escorts to keep her out of trouble. Laura promised to text her details of the hotel where she would be staying, just as soon as she got there. She assured Beth the accommodation would be perfectly safe as the embassy would book her into their marker hotel. This, she explained, was one they were satisfied was in a safe location and where diplomatic staff and visiting VIPs would normally stay. Also, all the local officials she would need to see there should be based in the city of Nowshera, so there was absolutely no need for Beth to worry.

The day before she was due to depart, Laura busied herself sorting out some modest clothing and comfortable shoes. When, eventually, all was packed and ready, she began to look forward to the trip. She knew that, if she were being completely honest with herself, part of her motivation in making the trip was the prospect of an adventure. Apart from their one brief visit to Beth in Canada, it had been many years since she had travelled so far afield. She recalled how she had often tried to persuade Keith to take her on one of his many business trips to Pakistan or to Brazil, the countries where he mainly did his purchasing, but the only time he had let her accompany him was on a buying trip to North Carolina. That hadn't been very interesting at all, although they had stopped off in New York on the way home and she'd enjoyed the shopping and a trip to the Museum of the Moving Image.

Keith had declared that the best thing about New York, from his point of view, had been the Starbucks cheesecake Danish pastries he'd insisted on having every morning for breakfast. He had really developed a taste for them. That was typical of Keith, she told herself. He always had that little selfish streak. It hadn't mattered that Laura had wanted to go somewhere that served her favourite eggs Benedict, or that she wanted to try some genuine American pancakes with crispy bacon and maple syrup. New York was famous for its breakfasts, so Keith's insistence on visiting the same coffee house chain every morning had been disappointing, to say the least.

Of course, things had been very different in the early days of their courtship, she reflected. She had some happy and still vivid memories of their travels together as a young couple, but things had seemed to change after Beth was born. Increasingly, Keith had thrown himself into his business travel and she'd been left behind to keep house and raise their daughter, not that she had minded that so much. She had adored motherhood and all the new friends that came with it, from the mother and toddler groups to the clutch of friendly mums she met at the school gates. They had met regularly for coffee back then, and indeed, they still did, albeit that, nowadays, some of them had grandparental responsibilities. She would soon be a grandmother herself, and that prospect thrilled her, but with her daughter and son-in-law seemingly settled in Canada, she feared she wouldn't get to see her grandchild as often as she would wish.

Laura had hoped that, once Beth had left home to go to university, she could accompany Keith on his more exotic travel. But it hadn't happened. Now, however, she told herself that she was a free agent again, and it was entirely up to her where she went. Yes, despite the tragic reason for her trip, she was actually beginning to feel quite excited about it.

The flight from Manchester to Doha took a long seven hours but was comfortable enough, and it gave Laura plenty of time to think. However, now that she was alone, out of her comfort zone and poised to head half way around the world, she began to have second thoughts. It now occurred to her that Steve and Beth, and even Charles Markham might well be right. Perhaps she was completely mad to be undertaking such a trip, especially at her time of life.

'Take the insurance money and start to live a little,' Jason, her hairdresser, had urged, as he had trimmed her fair locks in preparation for her trip. Yet, almost three weeks had now passed since she had learned of Keith's death, and the various authorities were no nearer finding his body or establishing the precise circumstances surrounding his death. As far as she was concerned, that was unacceptable.

She met up with Charles Markham at Doha. His flight from Heathrow had arrived an hour or so before hers and he caught up with her in the airside transfer lounge where they awaited their onward flight to Peshawar. He bought their coffees.

'How was your flight?' he asked, cheerfully.

'It was fine, thank you. And yours?'

'Yes, not too bad. Of course, as a seasoned business traveller, I'm always well-prepared for flying.'

He held open a WH Smith's carrier bag to show her the clutch of newspapers and magazines he had brought with him from Heathrow.

'See, I always bring plenty to read.'

Laura noticed he also had a clutch of chocolate bars in the carrier bag. It reinforced the initial impression she had formed of him as someone who was self-indulgent. She could picture him as a schoolboy, jockeying to get to the head of the queue at his private school's tuck shop. She noted the absence of a wedding ring. Perhaps, as a single man with no responsibilities, he could afford to be self-indulgent. She had brought a couple of paperbacks to read, since the prospect of chatting with Charles Markham all the way to Pakistan held little appeal. However, there were one or two questions she did want to ask him.

'So, which department of GTP are you in?' she asked. 'It didn't say on your business card.'

'Contracts,' he replied, a little too quickly and somewhat bluntly, as he averted his gaze beyond her towards the flight information board.

She guessed that was the sort of answer which rarely attracted further comment or query. After all, who would ever ask someone to expand on his work in negotiating contacts? It sounded deadly dull, as dull, perhaps, as Steve Jeffreys' former employment must have been. She did wonder why the task of liaising with the widow of a deceased employee had fallen to a contracts manager. However, she decided she wouldn't embarrass him by grilling him further on his precise role in the company or on his faulty knowledge of Keith – not yet, at least. She would have to spend the next seven hours or so in his company, so she saw no point in annoying him at this early stage.

Once onboard their flight to Peshawar, as soon as Markham had read a couple of his motoring magazines and had devoured his tuck, he nodded off, and he slept quite soundly. Soon, he began snoring, and Laura began to wish she had asked for them to be seated separately, a few rows apart. She had only just met Markham. He was pretty much a stranger still, and yet here they were, she mused, sleeping together – well, not exactly sleeping together, but sleeping alongside each other, not that she intended to sleep. She found his presence irritating, and his snoring even more so.

She had read the first of her paperback books. It wasn't as good as she'd expected. She started to read the second one, but Markham's snoring kept distracting her. Several times, she found herself glaring at him, willing him to be silent. Then she noticed his passport poking out of the breast pocket of his shirt. It was one of the new dark blue British passports. That told her it would have been issued relatively recently. She kept trying to engage with her book but Markham kept snoring, and her gaze kept returning to his passport. She decided she would love to have a look at it, just to confirm whether he really was who he said he was. Eventually, she could resist the urge no longer. Satisfying herself that no-one was watching, she slowly extended her hand, grasped the edge of the passport between her thumb and forefinger and very gently eased it out of his pocket. So long as he kept snoring, she knew she was safe enough to check the document.

It had indeed been issued to one Charles Markham. It was annoying that, nowadays, passports no longer stated the holder's occupation. She couldn't imagine why the passport people had stopped including that. She wondered if it was because, in these modern times, companies only offered short-term contracts and many people job-hopped. Seemingly, employers preferred to see a prospective employee's extensive and varied resumé rather than evidence of long years of loyalty to one employer. Apparently, long and dedicated service such as Keith's was no longer valued. She wondered whether that was why no-one at GTP was putting himself out to locate Keith's body. Maybe he wasn't so valued an employee as Markham had suggested.

There wasn't a lot of information in the passport. Markham had been born in Chertsey, Surrey in nineteen-seventy. He might indeed have been well travelled, as he had claimed, but it didn't look as though this particular passport had accompanied him anywhere until now. Apart from the Pakistani visa, the travel document bore no other visas or entry stamp endorsements. Then, she noticed the wording of the Pakistani visa. Surprisingly, his was a diplomatic visa and, next to the 'fee paid' section, it was marked 'gratis'. She supposed the Foreign Office must have made his application as if he were one of their own employees, rather than as a tobacco company employee. Yet they hadn't done that for her. Her own visa was a standard visit visa, for which the company had paid a standard visa fee. This struck her as a little odd.

On impulse, she retrieved her mobile phone from her handbag and selected the camera function. Timing things so that the faint click of the shutter would coincide with Markham's inward snorts, she took an image of the passport's biodata page, and then, on his next snort, she photographed the Pakistani visa. She also took a sneaky shot of the sleeping Markham. She didn't think slipping the passport back into his pocket would be as easy as removing it had been, so she didn't take the risk. Instead, she slipped the document into the WH Smith's bag which Markham had stowed in the seat pocket in front of him. Oblivious to this invasion of his privacy, Markham snored on. With her curiosity partly satisfied, Laura returned to her paperback.

CHAPTER NINE

Kirpal Kohli met with Imtiaz Siddiqui at the coffee shop in Burtby's large shopping arcade. Sue Shaw's advice regarding a good meeting place had been spot on. The high glass roof and the big indoor boulevard in which the busy Coffee Craft Café was set ensured their conversation was unlikely to be overheard. Kirpal's first impressions of Imtiaz was that he was around the same age as himself, mid to late twenties, and, judging by his local accent, he, too, was UK-born.

'*Sat, Sri, Akaal,*' Imtiaz gave Kirpal a Sikh greeting as they shook hands.

Since he had eschewed his beard and turban, Kirpal presumed it was from his name that Imtiaz had deduced he was a Sikh. He was gladder than ever now that he had cut his hair and beard, since it would certainly be difficult to conduct any kind of discreet enquiries or covert surveillance wearing a turban in locations like this where, despite there being a significant proportion of ethnic minorities, virtually no Sikhs lived. A turban would have made him stand out like the proverbial sore thumb.

'*Salaam aleikum,*' Kirpal responded, in deference to his new informant's Muslim faith.

Imtiaz had arrived first and had already bought himself a soft drink but Kirpal wasn't in need of a drink himself, so he quickly sat down opposite the young man.

'So, Imtiaz, do you live here in the town?' he asked, by way of kicking off the conversation.

'I do now. I moved here a few months ago from Blackburn when I started my new job. I'm the IT systems manager at a local college. I used to worship at a mosque over in Blackburn. That's where I first met Hamid Gulabzai.'

'He's the man you wanted to speak to me about, right?' Kirpal asked.

'Yeah. Since I moved, I've started attending one of the mosques over here and, blow me, if Gulabzai isn't there as well. Turns out, he hangs out at all the mosques around this part of Lancashire.'

'When you called, you said you felt this Gulabzai character was dangerous. What did you mean by that?'

'He holds fairly radical views, and he seems to be trying to recruit people – young men at the mosques, I mean. I see him hanging around the colleges as well. He tried to get me interested in coming to a meeting of what he calls his young Muslim studies group. My friends and I don't like him, though. He makes us feel uncomfortable.'

'How does he make you feel uncomfortable?'

'He makes derogatory remarks about English people and about black people and Jews. He uses offensive language, you know, like *kuffar* and *hubshi*. He's equally unpleasant about women, too. He thinks females should be confined to the house and not educated. When that girl's school in Afghanistan were attacked by the Taliban, he said at least it would make the girls stay home now.'

'He sounds like a piece of work.'

'Oh, he is. He's always sounding people out, to see if they

agree with his radical views. He's clearly not been in England that long and he doesn't seem to realise that, around here, most young men of our age were born here and went to school here. We have friends of different faiths, and we treat our sisters with respect. My worry, though, is that the elders in the mosque think he's just a joke.'

'But you don't think he is?'

'No. He tells the teenagers fanciful stories about having been a freedom fighter in Afghanistan. Some of them listen to him. I worry that he might be radicalising some of the youngsters.'

'Do you have any proof that's what he's doing?'

'Not really. But I recently tried to arrange a school reunion. I thought it'd be fun to get together some of my former classmates from Brookdale Comprehensive. Turns out some of them have disappeared. No-one seems to know where they've gone, or, if anyone does, they're not saying. They haven't been seen since Gulabzai appeared on the scene. Might be no connection, but who knows?'

'So, what else do you know about this Hamid Gulabzai?'

'Well, he's in his forties, and he says he's Afghan. Says he were born in a region called Paktia near the border between Afghanistan and Pakistan. It's all tribal territories up there and the local Taliban are trying to get control of the area. But my dad's from NWFP – you know, what used to be Pakistan's North West Frontier Province. The region's name was changed to Khyber Pakhtunkhwa, or KPK, some years ago now, but my dad still talks about NWFP. Well, Dad spoke with him a few times at the mosque in Blackburn. He doesn't believe Gulabzai is who he says he is.'

'Really? What did your dad make of him?' Kirpal asked, his curiosity aroused now.

'Dad says Gulabzai speaks the Hindko dialect. From that and his name, and from a few things Gulabzai said, Dad thinks he's probably a Pakistani – a Waziri, in fact. Waziristan is another region that extends from KPK on the Pakistani side across the border into Afghanistan. The Waziris are a tribe that live all over the border areas. They've never recognised political borders. Afghanistan, Pakistan, it's all the same to the Waziris. They come and go across the border as they please.'

'So, do you know where Gulabzai's living now?'

'I don't know the address, but I'm told he's renting a small terraced house somewhere near the old Trafalgar Mill. Seems he's seeking settlement here as an Afghan refugee, but, as me dad says, he's more likely to be Pakistani.'

'And you say your religious elders consider him a joke?'

'Yes. Behind his back, they refer to Gulabzai as *gulab jamun*, you know, like the Indian sweets, the fat dough balls coated in sugary syrup. That certainly seems appropriate, but I think they should take him more seriously, especially as he targets the younger, more impressionable members of our community.'

'So why have you come to us with this? Why not get your Imams to tackle him?'

'The Imams don't see him approaching the young ones outside the mosques. They don't hear how persuasive he is. In many ways, that's typical of the older generation of immigrants. Keep your head down, don't criticise anyone else's beliefs and mind your own business.'

'I know what you mean,' Kirpal nodded.

'I hear my own parents talk about 'in my country they do this' and 'in my country they do that'. They're talking about Pakistan. But they've lived more than half their lives here in Lancashire. Well, I were born here. This is *my* country. In *my* country, they eat bacon baps and black pudding. Those things are traditional but not obligatory. In *my* country, women have careers. That, too, is a matter of choice. Me dad's a Pakistani Muslim, but I've never even been to Pakistan. I'm a British Muslim. I value both those things, and I don't consider them incompatible. I don't feel any conflict between my religion and the culture into which I was born. Do you know what I mean?'

Kirpal nodded again. He knew exactly what Imtiaz meant. That had been quite a speech, and he was impressed with this intelligent young man.

'But, what about you, Kirpal' Imtiaz asked. 'You're not from round here, are you?'

'No. I'm from London. But you and I seem to have a lot in common. I imagine if I'd grown up around here, you and I would've been friends.'

'No reason why we can't be friends,' Imtiaz grinned. 'And I could introduce you to Gulabzai as my British Pakistani friend from London.'

'That would be useful. Thanks.'

'Just one thing, though.'

'What's that?'

'You'd need to ditch the *Kara*.'

Kirpal glanced down at the steel bangle, one of several symbols of his faith, and one which always adorned his right wrist. He smiled to himself. That, too, had told Imtiaz he was a Sikh. The lad had good observational skills. He was a good informant, a good CHIS, or covert human intelligence source. In fact, he might make a good intelligence officer one day.

'So, how soon could I meet this *gulab jamun*?' Kirpal asked.

CHAPTER TEN

On touchdown at Peshawar's Bacha Khan Airport, Laura was advised by her escort, Charles Markham, that the diplomat from the Embassy in Islamabad who would be meeting them was someone he knew, one Martin Hopgood.

'Have you been to Pakistan before, then?' she asked.

'Yes, a few times, but not as often as Keith. This was his patch, of course.'

'Of course. And will we be staying in the hotel where he passed away?'

'No. I thought you might find that a bit upsetting. We're booked into one of the best hotels in Peshawar, though, the Emerald Inter-continental. It's one our embassy uses.'

Laura did wonder why, if the Emerald Inter-continental was the embassy's marker hotel, Keith had not stayed there, but soon they were on their feet and disembarking. They exited the aircraft and walked via the air bridge into the terminal building. They were met at the gate by a slightly-built, fair-haired young Englishman who seemed to recognise Markham on sight.

Martin Hopgood introduced himself to Laura as a Consular

Officer, and from what she could see as she squinted at the ID which hung from a lanyard around his neck, that was indeed his designation. His confident manner and English public-school accent were immediately reassuring as, indeed, Laura imagined they were intended to be. The earnest way in which he expressed his condolences for Laura's bereavement was exactly what one would expect from someone charged with consular responsibilities. Given the reason she was here, however, Laura was not inclined to accept anyone or anything at face value.

Hopgood's airport ID facilitated their seamless passage through the immigration controls. As they waited in the air-conditioned customs baggage hall, Laura gazed at the digital baggage information board which was displayed the message 'Welcome to Peshawar International Airport'. She noted with dismay, however, that the displayed information included the current outside temperature and it stood at thirty-two degrees. She had checked on annual temperatures for the mountain regions and hill stations but she hadn't realised that the city of Peshawar, situated as it was in a valley, was inclined to be much hotter than in the hills, even in late April. She feared the clothes she had brought would be too heavy for this climate. Hopefully, though, things would be a little cooler at Nowshera.

Their passage through customs was as smooth as at the passport control. As Laura had expected, though, as soon as they emerged from the air-conditioned airport building, she felt the hot, dry air immediately assault her eyes and nostrils. It had been a great many years since she had experienced this degree of heat. At least her suspicions regarding their meeter-greeter were further allayed when Hopgood led them across to a car which had diplomatic number plates and, to her great relief, air-conditioning.

Just a short drive along the Khyber Road brought them to the hotel which Hopgood referred to simply as 'The Inter-con'. If she had hoped her accommodation would be in characterful colonial style, she was to be disappointed. But for the row of yellow, scooter-powered taxis parked outside, and the mirror-embroidered waistcoat and baggy *shalwar kameez* worn by the doorman, the Emerald Inter-continental hotel could have been situated anywhere in the world.

Their consular escort's observational skills were evident when Hopgood asked Laura whether she had brought any lighter weight clothes than those in which she had travelled. She said she feared she had nothing which would cope with Peshawar's dry heat. In that case, he suggested, once they had inspected their rooms and freshened up, he would take them all to a local bazaar where they could have lunch and where Laura could, if she wished, purchase some more suitable attire.

Laura's en suite room, with its over-sized lamps and king-sized bed with fake suede padded headboard, was as modern, clean and comfortable as one might expect of an international business standard hotel, but it was also as anonymous and soulless as the rest of the hotel's interior. She consoled herself with the thought that it wasn't costing her anything. After a quick shower and a change of clothes, she re-joined Markham and Hopgood down at reception. Hopgood helped her change some sterling for rupees at the reception desk. Back in the car again, they headed further along the Khyber Road until they spotted signs for *Qissa Khawani Bazaar*.

'This place we're going to is known as 'The Storyteller's Bazaar' and it's Peshawar's oldest market,' Hopgood told them. 'In ancient times, the caravans from Central Asia would stop here and professional storytellers would tell their tall tales for the amusement of the merchants and traders. And this big entrance up ahead is the *Kabuli* Gate. That's *Kabuli* as in Kabul, capital of Afghanistan.'

Laura noticed that Hopgood pronounced the 'K' in Kabul as a

clicking sound from the back of his palate. She was impressed that he should have such a command of the local language that his pronunciation sounded so authentic. As they passed beneath the tall red-brick archway, Laura now felt she was in the beating heart of the city. This was the *real* Pakistan. Crowded, dusty streets and ancient crumbling houses presented a scene which, apart from the presence of so many motor vehicles, was probably unchanged in centuries.

'Look at all these tuk-tuks,' Hopgood complained, indicating the many scooter cabs which buzzed in and out suicidally between the cars, their continuous horns sounding like angry wasps. 'They're the bane of my life.'

It was with difficulty that Hopgood negotiated the dense and seething traffic in the narrow streets and alleys. Laura, however, was enjoying the spectacle of the bazaar. There were spice sellers' stalls resplendent with large bowls and buckets of vividly-coloured powdered spices, all fashioned into impossibly tall mounds, like conical sand-castles. She wondered how the merchants could possibly dispense the spices without dislodging each precarious heap.

There were clusters of fabric shops with brightly-coloured lengths of silk and polyester fluttering like banners from wooden poles overhead. Copper and brass sellers' shops competed with the more workaday aluminium pots and pans on sale from open stalls, and everywhere there were people. There were few pavements to speak of and the Peshawari shoppers dodged in and out of the traffic with reckless abandon.

Although Laura understood Hopgood was based in Islamabad, it was obvious that he also knew his way around the city of Peshawar quite well, and he soon found somewhere to park. Stepping out of the air-conditioned car, Laura breathed in deeply and savoured the scents of the market. There was a distinctive aroma, a combination of fried onions, grilled spiced chicken and jasmine-scented joss sticks, with an undernote of rotting fruit and car exhaust fumes. It was an odd combination but not altogether unpleasant. It was also a combination which was vaguely familiar to her, and it triggered some dim and distant memories. A short walk further on, they came to a clutch of ready-to-wear clothing stalls.

'We'll leave you to browse the ladies' outfits, Mrs Roberts,' Hopgood said, 'and we'll just be having a cup of tea in that café over there. Join us when you're ready. Mind you don't pay the asking price for anything, though. Insist on beating them down. These stallholders have one price for the tourists and another for locals.'

Laura couldn't wait to explore the racks upon racks of *shalwar kameez* suits and matching *dupattas* on display. She worked her way around the stalls, admiring everything they had to offer, but then, beyond the stalls, she came to a shop which had *the* most dazzling outfits in the window. She knew this was a place where she would find something special. She also knew this wasn't the kind of shop in which one haggled over the price. That activity was for the amusement of tourists and the irritation of the stall holders out in the street.

Once inside the air-conditioned shop, she was pleased to see that the *chooridar pyjama* was again in fashion. Many years ago, practically in another lifetime, she had worn and loved these tight-legged pants with the drawstring waist. She now chose several pairs in white and cream. She didn't need to try them on. The classic eastern *chooridar pyjama* was a one-size-fits-all garment. Although fitted snugly to the leg, the waistline of the pants was cut very generously to fit almost any waist, and, if they were a bit on the long side, they could simply be ruched up the leg until they were the right length. She loved this style and she reckoned she still had good legs. In any case, she told herself she wasn't tall enough to wear the baggier style of pants, the *shalwar*. That would make her look dumpy.

Next, she browsed the long tunic-like *Kameez* and chose a selection to go with the pants. There were floaty fine cotton *kurtas* with simple self-coloured embroidery around the neckline, and longer silken *kameez* with ornate Sindhi embroidery down the front. She felt she could have bought up half the shop.

Having selected half a dozen beautiful outfits, she was unable to decide between them and so decided to take them all. She held first one outfit and then another in front of herself and looked at her reflection in the full-length mirror. As much as she was enjoying herself, however, she experienced a sudden pang of guilt. She reminded herself she wasn't here to indulge in retail therapy, she was here to locate the body of her husband. Then again, she told herself, she had to have some lightweight clothing to wear, so she might as well buy something she really liked. She persuaded herself Keith had been sufficiently self-important that he would have wanted his wife to look nice. If it should transpire that he was still alive, he would approve of seeing her smartly and appropriately attired. Soon the saleswoman approached, clearly delighted to see a customer making a bulk purchase.

'Is Madam thinking of buying *all* these things?' the saleswoman asked.

'Madam is,' Laura assured her. 'Madam needs to dress for this heat.'

'Then I can offer you a discount.'

Laura was even more pleased now.

'Is there a changing room? I'd like to wear one of these suits right now.'

'Yes, of course. Please come this way and I'll take the rest of the clothing and pack it for you.'

Ten minutes later, with her purchases packed into brown paper carrier bags along with the sensible outfit she had been wearing when she came in, and her purse a few hundred rupees lighter, Laura left the shop. The gently ruched, white *chooridar* pyjama pants, so named for the fact that the ankles were as narrow as a *choori*, or bangle, flattered her own still slim ankles, and the silky turquoise *kameez* flattered everything else, and fluttered pleasingly as she walked. With the matching white georgette *dupatta* draped over her head and across her shoulders, as she left behind the air-conditioning and headed out into the hot dusty bazaar, she suddenly felt taller and quite elegant. The fifty-five-year-old widow was a girl of twenty-two again – in her head.

'Good heavens!' Charles Markham exclaimed as she entered the café. 'What a transformation.'

'He's right, Mrs Roberts,' Hopgood agreed. 'You look wonderful.'

'Thank you,' she blushed, as she accepted the cardamom tea which Hopgood poured her from the chipped enamel teapot. 'So, did someone suggest lunch?'

The café served up a magnificent *Kabuli pullao*. It came in the form of a huge volcano-shaped mound of fluffy buttered rice, studded with chunks of lamb, carrot, raisins and almonds, and delicately flavoured with cinnamon and cloves. They were each given a bowl and a spoon and Hopgood explained the idea was to shove one's bowl into the mountain of rice and use the spoon to scrape out a generous portion into the bowl. As big as the platter of *pullao* was, it didn't take the three long to demolish it. Laura had thoroughly enjoyed both the shopping and the lunch, but she was impatient to start the search for her late husband's body.

'So, where do we begin?' she asked.

Hopgood glanced at Markham before he answered.

'Well, it's not far from here to the hospital where Mr Roberts was taken. We could go there now, if you're not too tired. Otherwise, we could come back tomorrow.'

'Let's go there now, please,' she said and she took out her purse. 'How much will they want for the food?'

Charles Markham waved his hand to dismiss her offer to pay.

'No, no. GTP will pay. It's the least they can do.'

CHAPTER ELEVEN

At Ten Downing Street, the Joint Intelligence Committee members were seated in the Cabinet Room, awaiting the arrival of the Prime Minister before commencing their meeting.

'He likes to keep us waiting, Helena,' the MI6 chief whispered to his MI5 counterpart. 'That way, he can make a grand entrance. Makes him feel important.'

'Oh, but he *is* important, Bob. He is *El Primo*. The man with his finger on the pulse,' Helena said, sarcastically.

'Yes, well that finger is far too tight, these days,' Sir Robert complained. 'He's cutting off our circulation.'

Heavy footsteps could now be heard approaching along the corridor. Suddenly, however, there was an almighty thud immediately outside the door of the Cabinet Room. It was followed by the familiar loud tones of the Prime Minister.

'Will SOMEONE do SOMETHING about that fucking CAT?' he yelled.

Seconds later, the Cabinet Door burst open and the portly figure of Ivan Thompson barged in, his face red and his suit dishevelled.

'Are you all right, Prime Minister?' Sir Stuart Bridgeman, the Committee chairman asked.

'No,' Thompson spluttered, as he ran his stubby fingers through his thatch of unruly, light-absorbing, black hair. 'I just fell headlong over that bloody cat – again! He has to go. I'm getting rid of him.'

'But Winston has lived here for years. He's a permanent fixture,' Sir Henry Mortimer, the Cabinet Secretary, protested.

'He's right, Prime Minister,' Sir Stuart agreed. 'The Foreign Office have their cat, Palmerston, and the Treasury cat is Gladstone. And Number Ten's Winston serves a useful purpose. He even has an official designation as Mouser-in-Chief. Number Ten was overrun with mice before an official cat was appointed. Indeed, there's been a cat in residence here since seventeen forty-five.'

'And don't forget,' the MI6 chief added, 'he's also known as Agent 009 – he of the nine lives. You surely can't rid Number Ten of its only member of staff who's licensed to kill.'

'He's right,' the Cabinet Secretary added. 'Prime ministers come and prime ministers go, but there's always a cat in residence.'

'Well, *I've* never seen him catch a mouse,' Thompson argued. 'In fact, I've never *seen* a mouse in Number Ten.'

'That's because, like Trident, he's an effective deterrent,' Sir Henry grinned.

'That's right, Henry. He's a WMD,' Sir John Hooper, head of UK's defence forces agreed.

'A WMD?' Thompson spluttered angrily. 'What's a WMD?'

'A Weapon of Mouse Destruction,' the Defence Chief laughed.

The others laughed, too. Thompson, however, was not amused. He banged his black conference folder down on the table and took his seat beneath the portrait of Robert Walpole, the first, and rather more statesmanlike incumbent of the office of Prime Minister.

'So, what's today's crisis, then?' he demanded to know. 'Why are we here?'

'Well, speaking of weapons, it's to do with the latest weapon the Russians are using against us,' Sir John Hooper, the Defence Chief replied.

'And what's that?' Thompson asked.

'Gas,' Sir John replied.

'What, some sort of nerve gas, you mean?'

'No, I mean the gas we use to heat our homes, or at least the ten percent of our gas which we buy from Russia. The Russians have increased the price per therm of their gas by almost forty per cent. They're slowing down the supply and threatening to cut it off altogether if we continue to criticise their occupation of the Crimea, and if we don't support their latest pipeline initiative.'

The Cabinet Secretary also chipped in: 'And it's not just the UK whom they're threatening in this way. They're making the same threats against the EU bloc.'

'But, why?' Thompson asked. 'Don't they want to sell us their gas?'

'What they want,' the MI6 chief, explained, 'is for everyone to put pressure on the Germans to sign up to the Nord Stream 2 gas pipeline. That pipeline will bring Russian gas from Russia to Germany via pipes laid beneath the Baltic Sea.'

'Well, what's wrong with that?' Thompson wrinkled his brow. 'Why won't the Germans sign up to that?'

'Well, for one thing,' Vanbrugge said, 'it would bypass the Ukraine and cut them out of the supply chain. Russia wants to achieve a bloodless *Anschluss* of the entire territory of Ukraine by withholding their gas. If that doesn't work, they may well invade Ukraine. This creates a moral dilemma for the Germans. They've been protesting vehemently against the Russian occupation of the

Crimea, and against the Russian troops now sitting intimidatingly on the Ukraine border, yet Germany's highly dependent on Russian gas. If Germany does accept the pipeline, it will render them, and the rest of Europe, dependent upon Russia. And the revenues from the gas will fund Putin's expansionist efforts. In effect, Vladimir Putin is weaponizing gas.'

'But, if *we* only get a small percentage of our gas from Russia, why is this a crisis for *us*?'

'It's as much a moral dilemma for us as it is for Germany,' Vanbrugge explained. 'We, too, are committed to supporting Ukraine. We've threatened sanctions against Russia if they do actually attempt to occupy a sovereign and independent state.'

'Have we?' Thompson was aghast. 'When did we do that?'

'We did it right after they invaded the Crimea, before you became prime minister, Prime Minister,' Sir Henry Mortimer informed him.

'But can't we manage without the Russians' ten percent?' Thompson asked.

'No, we can't,' Sir Henry explained, 'because, whilst we normally have sizeable stocks of gas held in reserve at this time of year in preparation for winter, this year, because of the poor spring weather, we were consuming last year's gas production much longer into the year. Our stocks are really low. And the pandemic lockdown over the last couple of years meant more people working from home and using gas to heat their houses. Our own gas industries were shut down and production has only just got going again. It's not just domestic consumption which will be affected. Many of our industries rely on gas to fuel their production processes.'

'Well,' Thompson reasoned, 'it sounds to me as though there's nothing else to be done. We have to continue to buy our gas from the Russians, even if that means putting pressure on the Germans to accept that Nord Stream thing.'

'There is another option,' the MI6 chief suggested.

'And what's that?' Thompson asked, hopefully.

'We cut off the pipeline.'

'What do you mean?' Thompson was puzzled.

'We sever the Russian pipeline, just like the Russians severed our electricity cable in the English Channel last month. We've now lost a huge supply of electricity we'd been importing from France. That's caused a sharp increase in electricity prices, too. Putin's waging a major energy war, if you hadn't noticed.'

'Oh, steady on. We don't know for certain that was the Russians. It could have been severed by any ship's anchor,' Thompson protested.

'No ship's captain in his right mind would drop anchor in the world's busiest shipping lane,' Sir Henry argued. 'That cable was severed deliberately. And we know there was at least one Russian submarine in the channel at the time.'

'That's right,' the MI6 Chief agreed. 'So, if we were to reciprocate and cut off their gas pipeline, and tell them we don't want their gas anyway, and if we could persuade the EU bloc to reject their gas as well, it would call their bluff. The Russians would either capitulate, or they'd have to find other customers for their gas. And that would mean building another pipeline.'

'But that would cause us shortages this winter, wouldn't it? Where else would we get that ten percent of gas from?' the prime minister asked.

'Maybe you should be implementing your publicly stated green policies,' Vanbrugge suggested. 'One of your election pledges was to go green and to wean the public off fossil fuels. So, why not lift the taxes and tariff charges on solar panels for domestic homes? Subsidise the cost of solar storage batteries and solar-compatible electric boilers for domestic use. Get the big industries to invest their profits in greener and more sustainable energy sources. It's what was promised in your party's manifesto, after all.'

'Sure, sure, but cutting off their pipeline, I mean, that could spark retaliation from the Russians, couldn't it?' Thompson asked.

'No, Prime Minister,' Sir Henry shook his head, wearily. 'It would *be* retaliation for what the Russians have done to us.'

'But how on earth could we sever their gas pipeline? It's up in the Arctic, isn't it? And wouldn't the Russians see it as an act of war?'

'Only if they know who did it,' Helena added as she smiled across the table at Sir Robert Vanbrugge. 'I think you can leave the details to Bob and me.'

CHAPTER TWELVE

Hopgood drove Laura and Markham down the road towards Peshawar's historic *Bala Hissar* Fort. Driving around behind the fort, they came to the Lady Reading Hospital. Hopgood explained that the hospital was built back in the nineteen twenties by Lord Reading, then Viceroy of India, and it was named for his philanthropic wife. It occurred to Laura that Keith would have appreciated that, as he liked to stay in the best places. At least, he might have appreciated it if he hadn't been dying at the time – apparently.

Inside, following Hopgood's lengthy explanation in Urdu to the reception staff, and after a wait of a good ten minutes, a man appeared and introduced himself as Mr Qasim, the hospital's almoner. Laura thought hospitals back in the UK no longer had such things as almoners to look out for the practical welfare of patients and the interests of the hospital. Her guess was that, nowadays, there were medical social workers for the former role and a raft of administrators for the latter. She knew, though, that a lot of old British-style institutions still existed in this part of the former British empire.

Once they were seated in Qasim's small office, Martin

Hopgood explained to him, in impressively fluent Urdu, that *Memsahib* Roberts, her diplomatic escort and her husband's company representative were there to enquire about Keith Roberts' death. Qasim turned to Laura and spoke directly to her in fluent though heavily accented English.

'Mrs Roberts. I am very sorry for your loss. Your husband was indeed a patient at this hospital. He was brought in by ambulance having suffered a heart attack. We have a tip-top cardiology unit here, with first-class surgeons, and they worked to save him but, tragically, they could not. He passed away later that evening.'

'But, Mr Qasim, what has happened to his remains?'

'His body was prepared in accordance with local health regulations, then he was collected by a local undertaker and sent to England by air for burial.'

'But he never got there. The wrong body was sent,' Laura protested. 'And we need to know where the mix-up occurred and where my husband's body is now.'

'Oh, dear. That is most unfortunate, Mrs Roberts. My sincere apologies. This has never happened here before. We have strict procedures in place in our mortuary. The mix-up must have occurred at the local undertakers. I will give you their business card. It has their address. They are just off the Khyber Road here in Peshawar.'

Laura was puzzled that Qasim should be surprised to hear this. Seemingly, no-one had contacted him before now. She wondered exactly what enquiries GTP had made. Surely, she thought, this hospital would have been the first place they would have contacted. Hopgood took the business card from Qasim and, immediately, he and Markham stood up to leave, but Laura was not yet satisfied.

'Wait a minute, please. I have some more questions. Where was my husband brought in *from*?'

'Where from? I don't know. I don't have any record of that.'

Laura found that very odd, but if they didn't record it, then they didn't record it.

'Well, do you know who arranged for him to come here? Who settled the hospital bill? I assume the treatment wasn't free?'

Qasim shifted his gaze towards Hopgood. So did Laura. She thought she saw Hopgood shake his head. It was a barely perceptible gesture, though, and she wondered if she had imagined it.

'I don't have a record of that, either,' Qasim said, 'only that the bill was paid in full.'

'That would have been the embassy who paid, wouldn't it, Martin?' Markham interjected. 'And Global Tobacco Products would have reimbursed the embassy. There's nothing for you to worry about on that score.'

'And what happened to his personal effects? His passport and his wallet and business papers, where are they?' Laura asked.

'We don't have them here,' Qasim shook his head.

'So, the ambulance which brought him here, how would I get in touch with their office?'

'Well, it depends which ambulance brought him. It would have been a private ambulance company, and there are quite a number of those. As I say, I don't have a record of which ambulance brought him in or where he came from. All we were told was his name and that he was a British citizen, so, naturally, we advised the British Embassy in Islamabad.'

Laura turned to Martin Hopgood.

'Yes,' Hopgood confirmed, 'and, of course, we knew Keith, and we knew which company he worked for. He always let the embassy know of his arrival and departure dates and his movements. That's always a safe precaution for foreigners coming up to KPK, especially in these unsettled times.'

'So, he would have told you where he was staying, then?' Laura reasoned.

Hopgood looked at Markham. Laura sensed all three men

were being guarded in what they said. It was either that, or they were lying.

She turned to Markham.

'Well?'

'Yes,' Markham said. 'Keith usually stayed at the University Guest House here in Peshawar. You see, although his business was in the districts of Nowshera and Kohat, there aren't any upmarket hotels to speak of up there.'

'Yes, that's right,' Hopgood nodded. 'He told us he'd be going to the University Guest House, as usual. We'll take you there tomorrow, after we've spoken to this undertaker chap. Right now, though, we ought to be getting back to the hotel. It's not absolutely safe to be wandering round here when it gets dark.'

Laura glanced at her watch. It wasn't yet three o'clock in the afternoon. She didn't imagine it would be dark for hours yet. She sensed she was being given the bum's rush. However, the long journey and lack of sleep was beginning to catch up with her, and the strain of trying to make sense of what she was being told had added to her weariness. Reluctantly she acquiesced.

Back at the hotel, she took her purchases up to her room and hung her clothes up in the wardrobe. Then she lay down on the bed to think. She suddenly felt alone and just a little bit helpless. In all the years of their marriage, it had been Keith who had taken care of everything official. But Keith wasn't here anymore. She would have to sort this problem out by herself. She couldn't go calling Beth in Canada every time she needed advice or a bit of moral support.

However, she could call Steve Jeffreys. He was a sensible and steady chap. If she could just discuss the situation with him, it might help. Hearing his friendly voice would certainly dispel her feeling of loneliness.

She took out the mobile phone Steve had given her and, as

instructed, she found his number listed in the contacts as 'Steve's mob'. Soon, she was connected.

'Steve? It's Laura.'

'Laura. How are you? And where exactly are you?'

'I'm at the Emerald Inter-continental hotel in Peshawar and I've just got back from the hospital where Keith died. Oh, but, wait a minute. What time is it over there? I'm not calling you in the middle of the night, am I?'

'No. Don't worry. It's almost lunchtime here. The UK is about four hours behind Pakistan. So, what've you found out?'

'Well, not much. The hospital almoner swears the mix-up couldn't have happened in their mortuary, but he can't or won't say where Keith was brought in from, or which ambulance company brought him. Markham and the consular chap who's taking us around, he's called Martin Hopgood, by the way, well, they say he was staying at another hotel here in Peshawar, the University Guest House. We're going there tomorrow, and also to the undertakers who were tasked with despatching Keith to England. But, Steve, I really think I'm being given the run around here.'

'Listen, Laura, I'm going to make some enquiries at this end regarding Messrs Markham and Hopgood, and I'll get back to you as soon as I find out anything.'

'Oh, I managed to take a couple of photos of Markham's passport and visa while he slept on the plane. Got a shot of him, too. I'll text the images to you.'

'Good. In the meantime, though, you'd best not let those two characters know you're suspicious of them. Do call me again tomorrow to let me know how you got on. But, right now, you'd best tell me absolutely everything that happened today. Don't leave out any detail.'

CHAPTER THIRTEEN

THE FOLLOWING DAY, AT MI5'S NORTHERN REGIONAL OFFICE, LUKE Greenwood sought out Harry Edwards.

'Harry, could you spare me half an hour or so, this morning?'

'Sure, Boss.'

'A former colleague of mine is coming in to see us. He used to work at Thames House in our Counter-terrorism section, but he took medical retirement about ten years back. He lives here in the north west nowadays. He contacted Thames House and they referred him to us. He needs our help with an enquiry.'

'Medical retirement? Was he ill?'

'No, he got wounded on duty.'

'Where, in London?'

'No, Northern Ireland. He was under cover. A truly brave chap. We owe him.'

Later that morning, Luke appeared in the main office with his former colleague in tow. Harry left his desk and followed them into Luke's office. Harry observed that Luke's visitor walked with a noticeable limp.

'Harry, this is my former colleague, Steve Jeffreys. Steve, this is

Harry Edwards. He's on attachment from Thames House. He works to Adrian Curtis.'

Steve shook Harry's hand warmly.

'I remember Adrian,' Steve said. 'How is he? Did he ever marry Helena Fairbrother?'

'Er, no. Things got a bit complicated. Helena got promoted to DG, and ...,' Harry shrugged.

'Ah, yes. I can see how that would have complicated things. Anyway, thank you both for seeing me. I really do appreciate it.'

'Well, sit down, Steve. Now, what can we do for you?' Luke asked.

'Well, I hope I'm not wasting your time, but, a very good friend of mine may be in a spot of trouble in Pakistan.'

'Oh, yes?' Luke was interested.

'Laura Roberts. She's my next-door neighbour. She and her husband Keith have been very good to me since I retired and moved back to Cheshire, especially after my wife died. Keith Roberts was a purchasing manager for Global Tobacco Products.'

'Was?' Harry asked. 'Is he retired, too?'

'No. He's dead – allegedly. He visited Pakistan regularly over the years. His company deals with a supplier in the north west of the country. They grow a lot of tobacco out there, you see. Well, he went there a couple of weeks ago for a routine visit to inspect their product and to negotiate a deal, and Laura was told he'd died suddenly in his hotel room.'

'Oh, I'm sorry,' Luke said.

'The company told Laura it was a heart attack and she's run herself ragged sorting out all the paperwork to repatriate his body. Well, they flew the body back and she went to the undertakers in Stockport to view the corpse and say her final goodbye, only it wasn't Keith in the coffin.'

'Good Lord!' Luke exclaimed. 'Who was it?'

'Nobody knows. Some Pakistani bloke. Quite a bit younger

than Keith, according to Laura. Naturally, she was very upset. She contacted Keith's company and they sent some creep to see her. I met him, too. He's clearly a fraud, though. He claimed to have known Keith, and it was obvious he was lying. But the really worrying thing is that the bloke in the coffin had been the victim of a shooting.'

'Good Lord!' Luke exclaimed again. 'So, have they sorted out the mix-up?'

'No. They left Laura kicking her heels for a week or two with no explanation and no dead husband. So, she decided to go out to Pakistan and try and find out for herself what happened to Keith and where his body is.'

'She didn't go alone, did she?' Harry was taken aback.

'No. She wanted to, but the company rep insisted he would go, too, and he's out there with her now. They've hooked up with a guy from the consular section of our embassy in Islamabad, a bloke named Martin Hopgood. Laura called me yesterday. She feels she's being given the run-around by the company rep and the consular officer. She suspects they know what really happened to Keith but they're not saying.'

'What makes her suspicious of them?' Harry asked.

'Well, the company rep, Charles Markham – a smooth git if ever there was one – he's supposed to be based at their head office in London, but Laura could never get hold of him there. She only had a mobile number for him, but his mobile seemed to be switched off for much of the time.'

'Could he just be the kind of company rep who travels around a lot?' Luke asked.

'Well, he told Laura he works in the contracts department at Global Tobacco Products, so I wouldn't have thought so. And there doesn't seem to be a logical reason why he claimed to have known Keith fairly well when it was clear to both of us that he'd never even met him. And why would GTP send someone from contracts? Why not someone from human resources?'

Harry took out his pen and notebook.

'How old is this Charles Markham?'

'Oh, about fifty. Well-spoken. Private school, probably. Maybe five foot seven, a bit on the chubby side, well dressed. Short, greying hair, balding slightly up top. A bit effete, actually. Laura sneaked a snap of his passport photo while he was asleep on the plane, and she took a covert photo of him, too. They're on my mobile phone which is downstairs in your lockers at reception, but when I'm back downstairs I'll e-mail them to you.'

'Good. And did Laura describe the consular chap?' Harry asked.

'Martin Hopgood. He's younger, she said, and quite slightly built. Fair hair. Blue eyes. He speaks fluent Urdu and, although he's based in Islamabad, he seems to know his way around Peshawar pretty well.'

'I'll go and do some checks,' Harry said. 'Meantime, can I get you a coffee, Steve.'

'That'd be grand, Harry. White, no sugar, thanks.'

By the time the coffee was brewed, Harry had completed his checks. He took three mugs of coffee into Luke's office and handed a scribbled note to Luke. Luke perused the note and, apparently surprised at its contents, he glanced up at Harry from beneath raised eyebrows.

'Steve, you're still covered by the Official Secrets Act, right?' Luke asked.

'Yes. Till I die, apparently.'

'Okay, well, you were right. Charles Markham doesn't work for Global Tobacco Products.'

'I knew it. So, who the hell is he working for?'

'You mustn't tell Mrs Roberts this, or anyone else, but Markham is an MI6 officer.'

'Bloody hell!' Steve exploded and turned to look at Harry. 'How did you find that out? Is he on your database as a rogue officer or something?'

'No,' Harry explained. 'Nowadays, we ensure our staff are on each other's systems. It's in case their people get stopped at an immigration check point overseas. If a foreign immigration service got in touch with UK Border Force or Special Branch wanting a Brit checked out, they'd see a marker asking them to check with us before disclosing any info. If the passenger was a Secret Intelligence Service chap, we'd smooth things over. Likewise, if one of our people has to travel overseas and gets held up, an MI6 local team can help out without blowing our officer's cover. It also helps avoid a 'blue on blue' situation occurring. You know what I mean, in case we blunder into each other's ops.'

'I see,' Steve said, clearly disturbed at this disclosure.

'Of course,' Harry continued, 'Charles Markham probably won't be his real name, but it's the one under which he's operating at home and overseas at the moment. It'll be the name in the passport he's using currently, and it's the name in which he's listed on our database.'

'I don't get it,' Steve was baffled. 'Why would MI6 involve themselves in covering up the death of a British businessman? Because that's what they seem to be doing.'

'Dunno,' Harry said. 'And I doubt they'd tell us if we asked. As for Martin Hopgood, I checked the Diplomatic List and he is based at our Islamabad embassy, but he's not in the consular section. He's listed as a third sec in their political section. He'll be MI6, too.'

'So, what's going on?' Steve asked. 'What's Vauxhall Cross's interest in Keith Roberts? Why are they obstructing Laura? And what's happened to Keith? I mean, is he really dead? If these characters do know what's happened to him, why aren't they saying? Maybe *they* killed him. I mean, what the hell's going on?'

'I think you'd better leave this to us for now, Steve,' Luke said.

Once they had finished their coffee, Harry escorted Steve downstairs and reunited him with his mobile phone. He also handed Steve his business card so that Steve could e-mail him the images Laura had taken of Charles Markham and his passport.

As soon as he was back upstairs again, Harry, was summoned into Luke's office, as were Kirpal and Jo. Luke had been considering the phenomenon of the disappearing youths and he had another theory to share with them.

'I've been giving some more thought to the lost boys of Lancashire,' he said, 'and I'm trying to think outside the box a bit.'

'How do you mean, Boss?' Harry asked.

'Well, supposing this recruitment business has nothing to do with the Taliban. Supposing it has nothing to do with Pakistani intelligence either.'

'So, you're thinking someone else might be behind it,' Kirpal surmised. 'But who?'

'Have any of you heard of The Borodin Group?' Luke asked.

Puzzled faces all round told him they hadn't.

'The Borodin Group is a pseudo-private paramilitary company run by a Russian named Potimkin. It supplies fighters, mercenaries, to anywhere in the world where they might be needed. In reality, however, the Russian government uses those mercenaries in places where they might have an interest. For Vladimir Putin, using what appears to be a private company affords him deniability if any atrocities are committed. But we've long known there were traceable links between the Russian state and the Borodin mercenaries.'

'So, where exactly are these mercenaries fighting?' Jo asked.

'They've been spotted in the Central African Republic, in Syria, in Kosovo, and in Libya, and they're believed to be in

Ukraine right now, which is why we believe an invasion there is imminent,' Luke informed them. 'Wherever there's a conflict and the Russians can see some advantage in being involved, that's where you'll find Borodin mercenaries.'

'I thought the Russians were supporting the peace accord in Libya,' Harry said.

'Ah, that's what they'd have us believe. Putin swears he's committed to peace, but, in fact, there's little doubt he's funding and arming these Borodin mercenaries in order to keep the conflict going.'

'Do we know why?' Kirpal asked.

'In a word – oil. Potimkin is not just MD of The Borodin Group, he's a Russian oil and mining magnate. With the help of a rogue Libyan army officer, General Hosseini, he's backing one of the late Colonel Gaddafi's sons to be a future leader of Libya. Borodin mercenaries are supporting Hosseini in suppressing the opposition, and they'll keep the conflict going until they get their man in power. In return, they'll get access to Libyan oil and other mineral deposits. The profits will be split three ways, between Gaddafi junior, Potimkin and the Russian state.'

'I don't get why it's called The Borodin Group,' Jo said. 'Why not The Potimkin Group?'

'Well, rumour has it that it's simply because Potimkin is a big fan of the Russian composer Borodin,' Luke advised. 'The fighters Potimkin recruits aren't just young unemployed Russian men. He recruits many nationalities, Serbs, Kazakhs, Armenians, Moldovans. The pay is generous, but the recruits take the risk of being killed overseas and their bodies will not be brought home for burial. That's all part of the deniability. Maybe they're now finding a new source of recruits here in Lancashire.'

'I can see why Russia would have deployed their mercenaries in Ukraine, but do we know why they might be deploying them in Pakistan?' Kirpal asked.

'Well, in many ways, the tribal areas of Pakistan are pretty much as they were when the British first arrived there in the nineteenth century. It doesn't matter where you draw the borders or who thinks they're in charge, it's a constant war – tribe against tribe, village against village, ideology against ideology. Same as in Afghanistan. There will always be conflict in the region. It's the Pashtun way.'

'But why would Putin want to exploit the conflict in that region?' Jo asked.

It was Harry who suggested an answer to Jo's question.

'It might be because he's worried about his own borders. He's established military bases in Uzbekistan and Tajikistan, which neighbour Pakistan. Those states are Russia's vulnerable under belly. We saw how he reacted to unrest in Kazakhstan, didn't we? He sent his troops in. Same in Georgia. Maybe he's worried about fundamentalists pouring over the borders from Pakistan into the Central Asian states. If he's been funding and controlling the Taliban in Afghanistan so successfully, maybe he also plans to fund and arm the Pakistani Taliban, the TTP. Maybe he's sending his Borodin mercenaries to north west Pakistan to extend his influence there, too.'

'That makes sense,' Luke agreed.

'But why would Lancashire youths rush off so willingly to risk their lives in Pakistan?' Jo asked.

'Well, it looks like they don't know that's where they're headed or what they're expected to do,' Luke suggested. 'From the little bit of intel we have, we know that at least some of those youths thought they were heading for Afghanistan, to take up legitimate and lucrative employment there. Because they expected their destination to be Afghanistan, a state not recognised by us, they accepted the reasons why they shouldn't tell their families they were going. If they are being used as mercenaries, the work would certainly be lucrative – if they survive long enough to collect their pay.'

'Boss,' a thoughtful Kirpal asked, 'how did we even know about this Borodin group?'

'Ah, good question, Kirpal,' Luke smiled. 'We'd heard rumours, of course, but then we had an amazing stroke of luck. One of their Russian fighters was killed in Africa. The authorities found on him a smartphone. The security password was bypassed. I don't have to tell a tech-ops like yourself how that can be done. Astonishingly, the phone gave up all his contacts and their positions.'

'That *was* a stroke of luck,' Harry said.

'Yes. Each of the Borodin mercenaries was listed, not by name, but by code names and service numbers. The phone's journey around Africa, and indeed to other zones where there was conflict, was also established, as was the size of the network. We got an amazing amount of information just from that one phone.'

'So, they weren't using encrypted phones?' Kirpal was surprised.

'Not by that stage, no. Not since that *Phantom Phones* supplier was arrested and put out of business. In fact, there aren't any providers of totally secure encrypted mobile phones around these days.'

'Yes, I'd heard that,' Kirpal said, thoughtfully. 'Of course, *Phantom Phones* going out of business has left a gap in the market. Seems to me there's a big business opportunity there for anyone with the right technical know-how.'

CHAPTER FOURTEEN

Kirpal met up with Imtiaz Siddiqui outside one of the Blackburn mosques after Friday prayers. Together, they stood and watched as all the faithful emerged and headed off in different directions.

'I saw him inside,' Imtiaz confirmed. 'He'll be out shortly.'

Gulabzai did eventually appear. He was, as Imtiaz had suggested, rather more corpulent than might be expected of an alleged freedom fighter. Kirpal imagined it was more than just the similarity of man's name to that of the doughball sweets which had prompted some at the mosque to call him *gulab jamun*. There was something oleaginous about Gulabzai's manner and his smile. Seeing a stranger standing alongside Imtiaz immediately attracted Gulabzai's attention. Imtiaz waved him over.

'*Salaam aleikum*,' Imtiaz greeted him and he held out a book he had been carrying. 'I wanted to return the book you lent my brother. He says to thank you, but it isn't for him. Too radical, I think.'

Gulabzai took the book from him and shrugged. He turned to face Kirpal then held out his hand in greeting.

'*Salaam a leikum*,' Gulabzai said.

'*Wah aleikumu as salaam*,' Kirpal responded, glad he had

remembered to remove his Sikh bangle as he now proffered his hand.

'This is a friend of mine,' Imtiaz indicated Kirpal.

'Muhammed Qureshi,' Kirpal introduced himself.

'Hamid Gulabzai. I don't think I've seen you here at the *masjid* before,' Gulabzai said, maintaining his hold on Kirpal's hand.

'Qureshi is just visiting from London,' Imtiaz explained. 'He's planning to visit Pakistan and I remembered you telling me you knew a good travel agent in Blackburn.'

'Oh, yes? Have you been to Pakistan before?' Gulabzai was clearly interested.

'No,' Kirpal replied. 'The furthest east I've ever been is Leicester. But I thought it was time I went to visit the land of my ancestors.'

'And when do you plan to go?'

'Next month, *Inshallah*,' Kirpal replied, adding the Muslim invocation of God in order to add some authenticity to the impression he was trying to create of being a Muslim himself.

'Do you have relatives to stay with?' Gulabzai asked.

'No. My extended family all left in the 'fifties,' Kirpal dangled the bait.

'Then you must let me arrange somewhere for you to stay,' Gulabzai took the bait. 'I have lots of good connections out there. Look, why don't we all go to a café I know and have a cup of tea.'

'I have to be home soon, but you guys go,' Imtiaz excused himself and, his part in the ruse having been completed, he left.

Over tea and vegetable samosas at the *Sadaqat* book shop and café, Gulabzai began to sound out Kirpal, and Kirpal was more than ready for this.

'So, Qureshi,' the older man began, 'what do you hope to find in Pakistan?'

'Oh, I'd like to get a feel for the place, for the family's village. Maybe see what life was like for my grandparents before they emigrated. I'd like to find my culture, my heritage. I suppose I'm looking to find me.'

'Why now? Are you looking for a wife, perhaps?'

'A wife? Well, I hadn't thought of that. Of course, I've finished my degree, and I've been working on and off with some different companies.'

'And what do you do? What is your job?' Gulabzai asked.

'I'm a software engineer and communications software developer, and I'm quite a good one, actually. I've been training others in my field.'

'Really? Who've you worked for?'

'My last job was as a trainer with an international conglomerate – Lurman Industries,' Kirpal answered, speaking completely off the top of his head and naming a dubious organisation with Russian connections, which he and Harry Edwards had investigated a couple of years earlier.

'I never heard of them. But with computing skills, you could work anywhere in the world, couldn't you? In fact, I happen to know of lots of opportunities opening up for young men out in South Asia. If you needed a new job ...'

'Thanks, but I don't at the moment. What I really need is a long holiday. I think it'd do me good to get away for a while. You see, as well as working for the Lurman Corporation, I've been burning the midnight oil, developing a little communications software project of my own. I hope to go into business myself, you know, be self-employed and all that. For now, though, I just need a break and a change of scene.'

Kirpal glanced out of the window at the dense, cloudy Lancashire skies.

'And maybe somewhere with a bit more sunshine,' he added.

'Well, you must call at Sitara Travel here in Blackburn. Mention my name and they'll get you a good deal. I'll write the address down for you. In the meantime, maybe you'd like to come to my house one evening. I'll introduce you to some other young men from around here. And perhaps you'd like to tell us all about your communications project.'

'Thank you. I'd like that,' Kirpal smiled, genially, pleased that, so far, the plan was working. In fact, it was working very well.

Almost two thousand miles away, in Peshawar, Laura's visit to the undertakers was not going so well. The reception was not as calm and serene as that at the Stockport funeral parlour had been. In fact, it was chaotic. There were a number of families crammed into the small reception area with too few chairs to accommodate them, but at least there were no lilies. A rather flimsy curtain divided the reception from the business area in the rear and the sounds emanating from the back of the premises suggested intense activity. Various dusty vehicles entered and left the yard to the side of the premises whilst they waited.

A flustered employee seemed to be having a disagreement with one set of customers over whether or not they had booked and paid for 'full service', at least that phrase was being uttered frequently in English. After a few minutes of waiting patiently, Hopgood decided to butt in. He introduced himself to the employee as being from the British Embassy and demanded to speak to the 'in-charge'. The flustered man disappeared momentarily but was soon back accompanied by an older man who invited them to go beyond the curtain to his office.

As they passed through to the back, Laura glimpsed a huge, untidy work area which was open at one end to the elements and was stacked from the dusty floor to the rather makeshift corrugated iron roof with fairly basic plywood coffins. In one corner, several large carboys of chemicals took up much of the floor space and, in another, there was a stack of trestles. A radio blared away ceaselessly in the background, as a couple of men busied themselves at various tasks which Laura had no desire to see. It resembled a busy builder's yard rather than a sedate and sombre funeral parlour.

If she was expecting to see any of the substantial, silk-lined viewing caskets such as she had purchased for Keith, she was disappointed. She imagined Keith would have been brought back in one of the more basic plywood boxes and, only after he arrived at the Stockport undertaker's, would he have been placed in the English oak casket she had selected – that is, he would have been if he *had* actually been brought back. She wondered whether, in fact, he had been buried locally in one of those plywood boxes. He would have hated that, she thought.

Like the outer reception area, the manager's small office also lacked sufficient seats so they remained standing. It was also quite untidy. Box files sat gathering dust on rather flimsy shelves, and there were sheaves of papers piled upon the manager's desk. The presence of an electric fan which sat, whirring, on one of the shelves was, she supposed, the reason why there were also various papers strewn around on the floor. The office was a chaotic as the workshop area. At Hopgood's request, the manager opened a large desk diary and began leafing through the pages. His head wobbled from side to side, like a yacht upon an ebb tide, in that classic non-committal gesture Laura knew was typical of local officialdom.

She tried to glimpse what was written on the pages of the diary but, as well as having to view it upside down, she saw it was handwritten in Arabic script. When his gaze alighted on the relevant page, the manager confirmed he had found the record.

'*Ji han*,' he set his head wobbling even more emphatically, 'Mishter Keith Roberts, full embalming and transfer to England.'

'There you are,' Markham said, 'their record shows they sent Keith's remains to England. I suppose the error could have occurred at the UK end.'

'No, it couldn't,' Laura assured him. 'There was only one coffin on board that aircraft and our local undertaker has re-confirmed that with the airline. They say it's actually quite rare to have remains repatriated from Pakistan to the UK. It mostly happens the other way around. Mr Hopgood, please ask him how many other deceased persons they had on the premises when Keith was brought in here.'

Hopgood duly interpreted her question into Urdu and the manager ran his finger down the lines of script on the appropriate diary entry and counted them slowly. Laura counted, too. She couldn't help noticing a supplementary piece of notepaper had been fixed to the bottom of the page with sticky tape.

'*Chubbeese*,' he replied.

'Twenty-six!' Laura exclaimed. 'He did say twenty-six, didn't he? I counted twenty-six entries on his page, too. And looking at his other diary pages, that seems excessive. Look, he's had to extend the page to get them all on. Ask him if we can have the details of the other twenty-five.'

Hopgood looked a little uncomfortable at her suggestion but he put the question to the manager anyway. The man's head wobble increased and he clicked his tongue against the roof of his mouth before replying at some length to Hopgood.

'He says that won't be possible,' Hopgood explained. 'You see, there's the confidentiality aspect. He says he can't give out the names of the other deceased, nor the contact details of their families. He points out that they, too, have been bereaved and it would be most upsetting for them if we were to contact them.'

'But that's ridiculous,' Laura exploded. 'Tell him it's almost certainly the case that one of those families is missing their deceased, and that their loved one is lying unclaimed in a funeral home in England. If we don't find out who he is, he can't be returned to his family. As it is, he hasn't been buried within the short time the

Muslim faith requires. And what about Keith? Ask him about Keith. Surely, he must have had a family come to view the body of their man and seen that it was Keith. Go on, press him further.'

'Well, I'll try, but I get the impression he doesn't want to admit there's been a mistake. I suppose he's worried it might harm business and the firm's reputation if it got out.'

'Sod that! Tell him I'm not leaving here until I know what he's done with my husband!'

A further exchange ensued between Hopgood and the increasingly harassed-looking manager.

'He says he's dreadfully sorry if there's been a mix-up and he asks you to please understand that it was an exceptionally busy day when Keith was brought in, and that it must have been a simple human error. He asks that we leave it with him and he will contact the families personally and see if he can find out what happened to your husband's remains. He adds that he is confident it will all be sorted soon.'

The manager may have been confident, but Laura certainly wasn't. She knew that, in this part of the world, bodies were buried much sooner after death than at home, and, as more than three weeks had now passed since she had learned of his death, she feared it would no longer be possible to retrieve Keith's remains. It was possible he had already been buried. It was all intensely frustrating, but she realised there was little she could do.'

'Please, at least get him to confirm what other details he has recorded, especially what he understands was the cause of my husband's death.'

'Hopgood's fluency now appeared a little more hesitant as he tried to establish what else the undertaker might know about Keith Roberts. Laura concentrated on the manager's reply, expecting to hear him mention the University Guest House, or maybe just the universal word 'hotel', but she didn't hear any of those words mentioned.'

'All he knows is that Keith took ill at the place where he'd been staying and was taken to hospital by some private ambulance or other, but he doesn't have a record of which ambulance company was involved,' Hopgood interpreted, 'so I suggest we waste no further time here and go and check with the hotel.'

Laura had supposed the University Guest House would have been so named for its proximity to Peshawar's fine university and yet it was actually located some distance away, right by the side of the Grand Trunk Road and quite close to the city's bus station. Consequently, the area was quite noisy and very dusty. As Hopgood led her and Charles Markham into the hotel's reception area, Laura could see right away that this was not the sort of hotel Keith would have chosen. It certainly wasn't what Keith would have considered to be of international business standard. It was air-conditioned, but the navy velour sofas and armchairs in the reception area had obviously seen better days. The luminous lemon emulsion paint, which she suspected someone suffering from snow-blindness had chosen, appeared disinclined to adhere to the unevenly plastered walls. Keith had stayed in this part of the world a great many times. Laura had little doubt he would have sussed out the quietest and most comfortable hotels in the area, but she could not believe this would have been one of them.

Once again, Hopgood took the initiative in explaining to the female receptionist why they were here. The receptionist's disinterested expression remained unchanged as she telephoned to summon the hotel manager. Allah Din's name badge confirmed he was the hotel manager and, having shaken hands with Hopgood and Markham, but rudely ignored Laura's outstretched hand, he lifted the large hotel register from the reception desk and led them into his office.

Under different circumstances, Laura might have found it amusing to be asking 'Aladdin' to shed some light on the circumstances of her husband's demise, but she doubted he would have a magic lamp he could rub, or a *genii* of whom he could demand answers. She suspected he would be just as unhelpful as the hospital and undertakers had been. Hopgood asked the manager to confirm that a Mr Roberts had stayed at the hotel during the previous month and what had led to his leaving the hotel. Without consulting the register, the manager launched into an explanation in Urdu, but resorting to English phrases such as 'heart attack' and 'ambulance'.

Laura glanced from Hopgood to Markham and saw that they were smiling politely at the manager. To her frustration, however, they didn't seem to be querying what they were being told. The manager opened the hotel register and offered it to Hopgood for his perusal.

'*Register dekhna chatay hay*?' he offered.

'*Naheen*,' Hopgood declined. '*Yay zuroori naheen*.'

Laura suddenly decided she'd had enough. She was extremely frustrated with her two male escorts being in control and she had reached the end of her tether. Hopgood might not think it necessary to check the register, but she damn well did. She stepped forward, reached across and grabbed the register.

'*Zuroori hay! Meyn register parna chatee hun*,' she insisted, adding, for Markham's benefit, 'actually, I would like to see it.'

She was briefly aware of the shocked glances which passed between Hopgood and Markham, but she ignored them and ran her finger down the page on the relevant date of Keith's arrival. His name did not appear in the hand-written list of guests. She checked the days which followed, and the days before, but the name Keith Roberts was not there. Unsurprisingly, there were no English or European-sounding names at all.

'Mere khavind ka nam ismay naheen hay,' she declared.

Turning to Hopgood, she repeated this in English, again for Charles Markham's benefit.

'My husband's name does *not* appear in the register. This man is lying. I suggest you ask him why he just said my husband stayed here when plainly he did not. And if Keith wasn't here, how did he know he'd had a heart attack? Why would he lie? If he can't explain, then perhaps we'd better inform the police.'

There was a shocked silence, before Hopgood recovered his composure.

'I didn't know you spoke Urdu, Mrs Roberts,' he said.

'I speak Hindi, therefore I understand Urdu,' she explained.

'But, how ...?' Markham asked.

Laura was quite irritated now to think that they were more concerned with how she came to understand the language than with finding out why the man in front of them was being so blatantly obstructive and untruthful. Still, she thought it important that she remain calm.

'I had my own career, albeit a brief one, in diplomatic service,' she explained. 'I was posted to India and was working as PA to the First Sec Commercial in our Delhi High Commission when I met my husband. Keith was on a business trip for GTP and I arranged introductions for him to the relevant local companies. India is the world's third largest producer of tobacco, though I'm sure I don't need to tell *you* that, do I, Mr Markham, you being ... a tobacco company employee?'

She made no attempt to hide her annoyance and her tone was one of stark sarcasm. She continued:

'Well, Keith was quite a charmer back then, and I was only twenty-two. I made all the relevant appointments for him and he was grateful. He asked to buy me lunch. The rest, as they say, is history.'

'I had no idea you'd been to this part of the world before,' Markham said.

'You mean Keith – your esteemed colleague – never mentioned it to you?' Laura said. 'How strange. But that's not the strangest aspect to all this, is it? The strangest thing is why you two are lying to me. Mr Hopgood, I think you may have spent too much time in the storytellers' bazaar. Well, I've heard enough stories. Let's just stop this pretence, shall we, and let's get out of here.'

Laura rose to her feet, handed the register back to the baffled hotel manager and headed for the door. She turned and glared at them both.

'It's time you took me to see where my husband was *really* staying. If you really had known Keith, you'd know he wouldn't have been seen dead in a place like this ...'

The irony of what she had just said suddenly hit Laura and, before she could help herself, her eyes filled with tears. She fled outside to the car and stood by it, stifling her anger and her tears with her handkerchief. She told herself these were tears of frustration rather than grief. She determined that, unless one of those two came clean about Keith, and quickly, she would ditch them and proceed alone.

Some five minutes passed before they followed her, by which time she had regained her composure and they, she imagined, would have got their story straight. At least they both had the good grace to look ashamed.

'I really am terribly sorry, Laura,' Markham squirmed. 'May I call you Laura?'

'Let's stick with Mrs Roberts, shall we, until I decide whether or not I can trust you?' she snapped, 'because, right now, I don't.'

'Fine. I really am sorry, though. Please believe me when I say we fibbed for the best of reasons. We wanted to spare your feelings.'

'What do you mean? Why this ... complicated charade?'

Markham looked to Hopgood for help.

'Mrs Roberts,' Hopgood began, 'please accept my apologies also. You're right. Your late husband wasn't staying here. Whenever he came out here, he didn't stay in hotels. He would stay ... with a friend.'

'A woman friend, I presume. Well, I knew all about Keith's infidelity. I can't say I care about that. I just want to know how and where he died and where his body is. So, are you going to take me to see this woman friend, or not?'

CHAPTER FIFTEEN

BACK AT THE HOTEL, LUNCH WAS TAKEN MOSTLY IN SILENCE. LAURA WAS still angry but Markham and Hopgood looked fairly chastened. She thought they looked like two public schoolboys who'd been caught cheating in an exam. If she hadn't been so grossly deceived, she might almost have felt sorry for them. When they had eaten, Hopgood suggested Laura might like to fetch a jacket before they drove to Kohat, as their destination was a good deal higher and it would be much cooler up there than it was here in Peshawar. Laura collected a fine woollen shawl and joined them in the car park, where Hopgood was just finishing a call on his mobile.

Their drive took them along the N55 and through the Kohat Tunnel which cut through the mountains. Hopgood explained this was known as 'The Friendship Tunnel', since it had been built with Japanese funding. It had not only shortened the journey between the cities of Peshawar and Kohat by half an hour, he said, but it also facilitated the passage by long-bodied trucks which, previously, had found it very difficult to navigate the many hairpin bends of the mountainous Kohat Pass. Laura thought the tour commentary was all very well, but she wasn't the slightest bit interested in the damned tunnel. She wanted to know about their destination.

'So, where is it exactly that we're going, and who are we going to see?' she demanded.

'We're going via the Kohat Wildlife Park up to Tanda Lake,' Hopgood explained. 'It's a local beauty spot and there's a guest-house up there, the Tanda Lodge. The owner of the lodge was Keith's friend.'

'And what's she called, this ... friend?'

'Madame Sophie Benoit,' Hopgood said. 'She's a wealthy French widow. She was married to a French diplomat based at their embassy in Islamabad. On Monsieur Benoit's retirement, they saw a business opportunity here when this area began to open up to tourism and so they stayed on and had some guest bungalows built. It's a lovely location, handy for the wildlife park and the lake, and also for the many hiking trails in the hills.'

Suddenly, Laura was put in mind of a little hotel she and Keith had stayed at in northern France many years ago. The hilariously misspelled brochure had advertised a 'French widow in every room', instead of a 'French window'. Keith had found that deliciously funny. Seemingly, though, he'd had his very own French widow in his room whenever he visited Pakistan. She found herself wondering how far back in her and Keith's relationship his infidelity had actually begun.

'How enterprising,' Laura said, sarcastically. 'So, have you both met this Sophie Benoit?'

'I have,' Hopgood explained, 'but Charles hasn't.'

There didn't seem to be much else to say on the subject, so the drive continued in silence. Laura needed to digest this information and, during their passage via the Kohat tunnel, there was no scenery to distract her thoughts. She had long known that Keith had affairs, and she had no doubt his many forays overseas afforded him opportunities for such liaisons. Somehow, though, she'd thought they would be fleeting affairs, and she hadn't imagined any of those liaisons would happen in Pakistan, this being a strictly Muslim state. She began to wonder what this French widow might look like. Was she Laura's age, or younger? Was she more attractive, or simply available? Most importantly, Laura wondered how the French woman would react when her lover's widow turned up on her doorstep. She steeled herself for the meeting.

Less than an hour after they had set off, they arrived at a series of single-story bungalows set around a lake which was also ringed by mountain peaks. As they climbed out of the car, Laura was struck by the intense pale blue waters of the lake and by the pure, cool air. Yes, this was more Keith's sort of place. The suggestion that he would even have contemplated staying at the University Guest House down by the fume-ridden GT Road seemed even more ludicrous now. She'd have been more inclined to have believed Hopgood and Markham if they'd said Keith had stayed at the Inter-con in Peshawar. Perhaps, though, the staff there couldn't be bribed to lie.

Hopgood had parked in front of the largest and grandest of the bungalows. The front door opened before they even reached it. Laura closely scrutinised the woman who emerged to greet them. She guessed the Benoit woman to be about forty-five, though her skin suggested a life-time's exposure to sunlight, and her olive complexion did not sit well with her long, dyed blonde hair. She was slim and well-dressed and she didn't seem the least bit surprised to see them. Laura now recalled Hopgood being on the phone in the hotel car park back in Peshawar. No doubt he had rung ahead to announce their visit. Laura didn't wait to be introduced but stepped forward and thrust an assertive hand out to the French woman.

'*Madame Benoit? Bonjour. Je m'appelle Laura Roberts. Merçi de nous reçevoir,*' she began, coldly and formally.

'Laura. It's okay. I speak English well. Please, come in.'

Sophie Benoit led them into the well-furnished and cool bungalow. Laura imagined that this particular bungalow was Madame Benoit's private residence. Laura and her escorts followed their host through the to the rear and out onto the large private terrace which was built out over the water and enjoyed one of the best views of the lake and the mountains. She bade them be seated around the large garden table.

'Now, let me offer you a cold drink. It must be hot down in Peshawar now.'

'Nothing for me, thank you,' Laura said.

Hopgood and Markham said they would appreciate something to drink, but water would be fine. Their hostess picked up a small brass bell and rang it. Immediately, a young man appeared.

'Abdul, tanda pani layao,' she commanded and the young man disappeared.

'Well,' Laura began, determined to remain polite but cold. 'I'm sure, when he phoned you, Mr Hopgood told you why we're here.'

'Yes, he did. You want to know what happened to Keith. Firstly, please accept my deepest sympathy. I am desolated for your loss. He was a good man.'

'But not a good husband, it seems,' Laura couldn't resist saying. 'I used to tell him he should have joined the navy, since he liked to have a woman in every port. You probably know there was Sarah, an Anglo-Indian woman in Delhi, and Margarethe in Amsterdam, and quite a number of different girls he saw in London on his trips to head office.'

Laura had simply made up the names but, if she hoped to offend her husband's French mistress by suggesting she was just one of a veritable *harem* of women Keith had, then, disappointingly, her words didn't seem to be having the desired effect.

'I don't doubt it,' Sophie agreed. 'Keith wasn't the sort of man to be content with one woman. But he always returned to his wife at home. He did love you, you know.'

Laura found it quite irritating to have this stranger telling her how Keith had felt about her. It was unacceptably condescending.

'Strange, that of all his ... dalliances, he never mentioned you,' she said. 'Had you known him long?'

'Oh, three or four years, or so. We met at a diplomatic function at the British Embassy. It was the Queen's Birthday Party, wasn't it, Martin?'

Laura glanced at Hopgood, surprised that he should have known about the affair for so long. Perhaps the entire world knew about it, Laura thought, with the exception of herself, of course.

'Goodness, I don't recall,' Martin shifted uncomfortably in his chair, 'but it couldn't have been more than three years ago. I've only been out here three years. All our embassies throw a sort of garden party affair each year in June to celebrate Her Majesty's official birthday,' Hopgood explained for Laura's benefit.

'Yes, the QBP,' Laura nodded. 'I know. I helped arrange one, once.'

Their conversation was interrupted by the arrival of the bearer with a tray of tumblers and a large glass jug of water in which ice and slices of lime floated. He poured out the water but Laura declined. She didn't feel inclined to accept anything from this woman. Even water would stick in her throat.

Sizing up the situation, Laura grasped the message her husband's mistress was intending to impart. Sophie Benoit wasn't just some French floozie Keith had been screwing as a matter of convenience. She'd been to diplomatic functions with him. She'd met Hopgood before and, no doubt, other diplomats and business contacts of Keith's. They'd accepted her into their circle. For all Laura knew, Hopgood might even have introduced them in the first place. This woman had been more to Keith than an occasional lay, she'd been his pseudo-wife. That hurt. Laura realised it was no use continuing the point scoring, as she wasn't going to win. She might as well get straight to the point.

'So, we've established that you know how he lived when he was out here. I'd like to know where and how he died.'

'Of course,' Sophie responded, and she paused briefly as she glanced at Markham and Hopgood.

Laura tried to interpret her expression and wondered if it was one of embarrassment, or was she smirking? She couldn't tell.

'Well,' Sophie explained, 'he took ill here, in my house. He actually had a heart attack in my bedroom, in my bed, in fact.'

'Oh, God!' Laura exclaimed. 'You were having sex when he had a heart attack?'

'Yes, I'm afraid so. He started to make those little gasping noises. Well, you'll know how he always did that, and I just thought it was, you know, *la petite mort*. How do you express it in English, his climax? But it wasn't that. It was his heart. I called the ambulance and I went with him to the cantonment hospital in Kohat. They decided to send him down to the Lady Reading Hospital in Peshawar. They have a better cardio department there. His heart stopped not long after we got there and they tried to revive him, but ... he didn't make it. I'm so sorry, Laura.'

Laura was deeply shocked. She couldn't decide which offended her more, the thought of Keith having a heart attack whilst having sex with this woman, or the fact that this woman thought it okay to call her Laura, as if they'd been friends for years. Well, it seemed Madame Benoit had known all about Laura for years, but Laura had known nothing about her. And it had been some years since Keith had made any little gasping noises with Laura. In fact, she couldn't recall him ever doing exactly that – grunting, maybe, but not gasping. Of course, that could be a translation thing. Or, perhaps he hadn't found sex with his wife as exciting as it had been with his French mistress. My, how that hurt.

'Was that how your husband died, too?' Laura asked, suddenly.

'Well, yes, as a matter of fact, it was,' Sophie replied, almost with a hint of pride.

'Ever thought you might be a bloody jinx?' Laura asked, somewhat savagely.

Sophie laughed. Laura tried to see beyond the red mist as she didn't want her anger to cloud her judgement. There were still some unsatisfactory aspects to all of this. She glanced at Markham and then at Hopgood. Their faces betrayed nothing, no embarrassment, no unease, nothing. Why didn't all of this make them uncomfortable? Laura racked her brains. What was she missing here?

'So, what about Keith's personal effects?' she asked. 'What happened to his luggage, his passport, his wallet? Do you have them?'

Sophie looked baffled for a moment or two. She looked to Hopgood. Laura also looked to Hopgood. His eyes grew bigger but otherwise his expression did not change.

'Ah, now I remember,' she said. 'I took them in the ambulance with us. I remember we had his things with us at the local cantonment hospital. I just can't recall if they came with us to the hospital in Peshawar. I could call both places to enquire, if you'd like.'

'No need. Don't trouble yourself,' Laura assured her. 'I'm sure Mr Hopgood will do that, won't you?'

'Yes, of course, Mrs Roberts. Leave it to me.'

'Well, we won't take up any more of your time, Madame. It was good of you to see us,' Laura said and she picked up her handbag and rose to leave.

Markham and Hopgood stood up also and Sophie walked them all to the door. As they stood on the doorstep, Laura shook hands with her husband's French mistress.

'Oh, just one more thing I'd like to ask you, Madame,' she said.

'Yes?' Sophie Benoit smiled, seeming a little more relaxed now that they were leaving.

'You did tell them at the two hospitals about Keith's pacemaker, didn't you?'

'His ... pacemaker? Yes, of course. That's why I insisted on going with him, to make sure they knew about that.'

'I see. Well, thank you again.'

Laura thought her escorts, too, seemed a little more relaxed now that the ordeal of disclosure was over. As they reached the car, a grinning Markham held the car door open for her.

'Oh,' she exclaimed suddenly. 'My shawl. I've left it behind.'

She quickly walked back to the house and rang the bell. It was the young bearer who answered the door.

'*Afsos*,' she apologised, '*mera pashmina* ...'

The bearer stepped aside to let Laura in, just as Sophie Benoit appeared in the hallway holding the shawl. The bearer stepped away and returned to the kitchen.

'So sorry, Madame,' Laura said, 'I left my shawl.'

With her left hand, Laura took the shawl from her erstwhile host and, with her right hand, she drew back and let fly with a sudden sucker punch to the woman's jaw. Caught wholly off-guard, Sophie Benoit, guest house proprietor and alleged mistress of Laura's late husband, fell backwards onto the floor, dazed, while Laura stepped calmly away and headed triumphantly back to the car.

CHAPTER SIXTEEN

Helena Fairbrother enjoyed her morning stroll along the side of the Thames. The late spring weather was glorious, and she was glad to observe that the capital was almost back to normal following the months of pandemic lockdown. The novelty of working from home had gradually worn off and, as she lived alone, she had missed the camaraderie of the office. Even the rush hour traffic, which she usually considered a nuisance, she now found reassuring. Weaving her way through the waves of on-coming pedestrians, virtually none of whom continued to wear face masks these days, she crossed Vauxhall Bridge. She made her way to Vauxhall Cross, the futuristic headquarters of the Secret Intelligence Service, referred to by some as 'The Ziggurat'. Once admitted through the security air-lock, she signed in at reception and was met by her SIS counterpart, Sir Robert Vanbrugge.

Once they were settled in his office, the MI6 chief angled his desktop screen so Helena could see a series of images.

'So, this is what I wanted to show you. Some of these are satellite images but most were taken by scientists who are studying a most unusual phenomenon occurring on Russia's Yamal Peninsula,' he explained.

'What exactly am I looking at?' Helena asked.

'Sink holes, Helena. Bloody big sink holes. They've been appearing all over the region since the Russians began drilling out the gas up there. See this one, here, with the scientists looking down into it? That gives you an idea of the scale. Some of these sink holes are six hundred meters across, and the depth can be up to seventy metres.'

'Good grief! They look like craters on the moon, except for the fact that they're flooded. So, what's causing them?'

'The boffins say the gas deposits are most unstable. Every now and again, there's a build-up of gas beneath the earth's surface and the earth swells up as the gas begins to expand. Then, the gas ignites somehow and there's a sudden almighty explosion and, bingo, another massive crater appears.'

'I'd have thought it would be rather dangerous for people living and working there.'

'Indeed, it is, Helena. Of course, it's very sparsely populated. The indigenous inhabitants, the Nenets, are semi-nomadic reindeer herders who use the entire peninsula as their grazing lands.'

'So, are there any villages there, or towns?'

'No. They don't build houses there. They erect their *chums* – large tents – wherever they make camp, and then they up sticks and move their camps around with the seasons.'

'I never heard of them – Nenets, you say?'

'They're not Russian but a Samoyedic people. Naturally, they're resentful of the Russian drilling operations up there and of the pipeline, especially since the expansion of the drilling operations and the laying of yet more pipelines. You see, it's forcing them to exist on smaller and smaller parcels of land. They can't roam around the whole peninsula as once they did. It's a similar story to what's been happening on Russia's Tamyr Peninsula where a lot of mining takes place.'

'But what's causing the gas deposits to ignite? Do the scientists know?'

'They're not sure, but they think it might be due to global warming. The permafrost no longer exists up there. Earth that once stayed frozen for much of the year, and which kept the gas underground, is now exposed to sunshine and is heating up. Of course, these sink holes are a relatively new phenomenon. They've only been discovered since the gas drilling operations began. The drilling is causing massive pockets of gas to rise up towards the earth's now warmer surface.'

'I see. So, this phenomenon has come about partly naturally, but partly because of the gas extraction?'

'Yes. It certainly looks that way.'

'And I imagine you're thinking how unfortunate it would be if one of those explosions were to occur beneath a section of the pipeline?'

'Indeed, Helena. That's exactly what I've been thinking,' Vanbrugge smiled mischievously, 'and remember how Putin reacted when there was that dreadful spillage of red diesel up in the Arctic a couple of years back?'

'Yes, twenty thousand gallons of the stuff got into the rivers, didn't it?' Helena recalled.

'It did. The Director of that installation is still in prison. The Russian authorities suspected some foreign saboteur had done it, but eventually, the scientists decided that, too, was due to the permafrost melting and the land becoming unstable. Subsidence had caused a massive storage tank to collapse.'

'Mind you, too big an explosion under the gas pipeline could lead to an uncontrollable fire, and that would create another environmental disaster, wouldn't it?

'Oh, yes, *too* big an explosion would. But I was thinking more of a number of smaller explosions at different points along the pipeline. That would drastically reduce the flow of gas and tie up the engineers for some time in repairing the pipeline. It would reduce Putin's profits, too.'

'I see. And when were you thinking these small, natural explosions might happen?' Helena grinned.

'Well, Vlad the Bad is having his Victory Day celebrations in Moscow on the ninth of May. There's all sorts of celebratory events planned – military parades, an air force fly-past and a big, formal reception. This year will be the biggest ever, since the last few parades had to be cancelled, owing to the pandemic.'

'I suppose he needs something big to distract the Russian public from his failures over the lack of Covid vaccine supply, and also the failed assassination attempts on his political rivals. He probably needs a big show of might to scare the Ukrainians, too, since they've applied to join NATO. What better way to do all that than with a big, patriotic event with all his nuclear missiles on show?'

'Indeed. Various leaders of other nations will be there, too – Hungary, Austria, Belarus and the Stans. And all the foreign ambassadors based in Moscow – our own included. And the forecasts are for an exceptionally warm spring this year. Gas deposits, even in the Arctic, are more likely to combust in warm weather. It would be a shame if a few... accidental ... explosions were to put a dampener on the great parade.'

'Yes, it would, wouldn't it? Dreadful shame.'

Meanwhile, some two hundred and thirty miles away, in the county of Lancashire, another meeting was taking place. MI5's Kirpal Kohli, or as he now introduced himself, Muhammed Qureshi, had joined the circle of young men at Gulabzai's Muslim youth group. He was not surprised to find that most of his fellow recruits were younger than himself. Their ages ranged from mid-teens to early twenties. He was a little surprised, however, to see that two of the newly enlisted were not of Pakistani ethnic origin, but were local English lads. There was nothing about their mode of dress which gave Kirpal the impression they might have embraced the Muslim faith.

As the introductions were made and each young man was encouraged to say what he hoped to get from the group, Kirpal learned that one of the English boys, Darren Wilson, had grown up in care. His path from then on had been a rocky one, strewn with drink, drugs and petty crimes which had led him to a young offenders' institution. Finding himself unemployable, he seemed to be seeking to turn his life around. Or, at least, Gulabzai was offering to do that for him. The lad's thuggish mate, Lee Hardman, didn't seem very bright, however, and looked as though he'd just joined the group to be with his pal.

The rest of the group of fifteen were the sons of Pakistani parents. It seemed to Kirpal they were a pretty mixed bag. As they sat around, cross-legged on the floor in Gulabzai's Trafalgar Street terraced house, each one recounted their personal story. Kirpal thought he detected some similarities in their backgrounds. Some had found themselves in trouble at some point. Most didn't seem to have had great paternal role models in their lives. Several had lost their fathers at a young age, some to illness, some to desertion. Some were seeking a new 'family', and that seemed to be what Gulabzai was offering them – a brotherhood with a shared goal. It just wasn't clear yet what that goal might be. All, it seemed, were seeking a purpose or a direction in life.

'You need to get out of Blackburn,' Gulabzai told the young men. 'You should broaden your horizons and get some experience of life. You should also develop skills which will be useful to you in life.'

He turned to Darren and Lee, the English lads, and addressed them in particular.

'Painting swastikas on synagogues is all very well, but that is no way to prove yourself or, indeed, to improve yourself.'

The lads looked chastened. Kirpal was baffled as he hadn't noticed any synagogues in Blackburn. It seemed, for a moment, however, that Gulabzai's advice might be sound and well meant. Perhaps he was actually doing some good in the community. Kirpal wondered whether, perhaps, Imtiaz had misread the situation. Gulabzai went on to suggest the youths should invest in their own futures by seeking meaningful careers. He said they might redeem past sins and misdemeanours through hard work and self-betterment. He said he could help them achieve this.

The one thing the group did not seem to be about was Islamic scriptures. Kirpal was thankful for this, since he had very little knowledge of the Koran and knew that, if quizzed about it, his ignorance would certainly give him away. That might not be the end of the world here in Gulabzai's house since he would be able to simply walk away. But if, as was just possible, he should find himself in one of their training camps, escape might not be so easy. Thankfully, there was no mention to begin with of training camps or of anyone going overseas. It was suggested, however, that they should all meet up at a local sports field the following Saturday for a game of five-a-side football. Kirpal thought he'd better quickly acquire himself some kit.

That evening, over dinner back at the Pepper Mill restaurant, Kirpal recounted the day's events to Harry and Jo.

'Well, this Gulabzai character does seem to be encouraging the local youths to get fit and to find work, and he's offered to help them with that. He says there are many opportunities overseas. He could well be a *passeur*, though he might not be the only one around here.'

'A *passeur*?' Jo looked puzzled.

'Yes,' Harry said, 'That's a people trafficker. A recruiter, if you like. Someone who passes the trafficked people on through the network. Of course, people trafficking is normally *to* the west, not *from* the west. How does he operate, then, Kirpal?'

'First,' Kirpal said, 'he identifies vulnerable and needy youths, mostly kids who've been in trouble with the police. Next, he invites them to his place, then he fires them with enthusiasm for the *jihad* he claims he had a fighter's role in – the holy war in Afghanistan. Once he's got their attention, though, he only seems to be encouraging them to make something of themselves.'

'So, you've no reason yet to think he's recruiting for this Borodin Group?' Jo asked.

'Not specifically, but my CHIS says that several young men he knew personally, and who had attended Gulabzai's little youth group, had set off overseas weeks ago and they've never been heard of since. Seemingly, this was after Gulabzai had put them in touch with his travel agent. My source fears they might be dead. Perhaps Gulabzai's young students really are fighting a war somewhere in the world. The question is – where?'

'Has he actually told them that's what they're going to do – to fight overseas?' Harry asked.

'No, not at all. He's talked about adventure and about travel broadening the mind. He suggested there are wonderful job opportunities nowadays in Afghanistan for fit lads.'

'Did he say what kind of jobs?' Jo asked.

'He mainly mentioned the airports at Kabul and Kandahar. He said they intend to open up again to international traffic and that they need to employ English-speaking staff, but very few of the Taliban speak English or any other European language, so he suggested the Taliban regime is recruiting overseas for airport security staff and that they'd be paying big wages.'

'You can see how that might appeal to lads who've made themselves unemployable here at home by getting a criminal record,' Jo said.

'Indeed,' Kirpal agreed. 'He also mentioned something about

security jobs in mining out there in the new Islamic Emirate. He said there are big new mining operations underway for coal and copper, and they need security staff to guard them.'

'You're not going to let him recruit *you*, are you?' Jo asked.

'No. I think I'm a bit older than his usual recruits and he wouldn't expect me to be so gullible. No, I've made *him* a proposition – a very different proposition indeed. Oh, and speaking of which, I'll need to use the office car first thing tomorrow morning. I've got to go over to Blackburn really early.'

'How early?' Harry asked.

'About five o'clock.'

CHAPTER SEVENTEEN

THAT EVENING, BACK IN HER ROOM AT THE INTER-CON, LAURA CALLED Steve Jeffreys and related the day's events. She told him about the visit to the undertaker's chaotic premises, and about the attempt by Markham and Hopgood to deceive her into thinking Keith had been staying in a seedy little hotel by the Grand Trunk Road, where the manager had clearly been persuaded to play along with their subterfuge. She also described the exchange she'd had with Sophie Benoit up at the Tanda Lodge resort, though she left out the part about punching her husband's French mistress. Now that she'd had time to reflect on the day's events, she was beginning to regret having done that.

'Oh, Laura, I'm so sorry,' he sympathised. 'That was too bad of Keith. You deserved better than that. And they shouldn't have lied to you. I don't, for one minute, believe they did it to spare your feelings. Still, does this mean you'll be coming home now?

'No. I don't think I'll come home just yet. They still haven't found Keith's body, or his personal effects. And I still don't think they've told me the entire truth.'

'You don't?'

'Well, at first, it sounded believable that Keith and that woman were having an affair. It seemed so like Keith. He didn't have it in him to be faithful. I've always known that. But, well, Markham and Hopgood just looked so ... conspiratorial, that I started to have my doubts about it. I'm beginning to doubt she even knew Keith at all.'

'Why? What makes you think that?'

'Well, when I was leaving, I suddenly got it into my head to ask her whether she'd told the hospital staff about Keith having a pacemaker fitted. You'd normally have to tell them if a patient has a pacemaker, you know, as they're not supposed to use a defibrillator on them. Well, she assured me she *had* told them about his pacemaker.'

'Blimey, Laura. I knew Keith for, what, ten years, and I never knew he'd had a pacemaker fitted.'

'Well, that's just it. He hadn't. I made it up. But she assured me she *had* warned the hospital about his non-existent pacemaker. So, clearly, she's a liar. If she really had slept with Keith, surely, she'd know whether or not he had a pacemaker.'

There was a short silence, as Steve took in what Laura had said. This was weird. It was more than weird. It was a disturbing conspiracy. He debated telling her that Markham didn't work for Keith's company, and that Hopgood wasn't a consular rep, but that both of them worked for the Secret Intelligence Service, and yet he couldn't tell her any of that, not least because that knowledge might put her in danger.

'Laura, I really do think you should come home, now,' he said.

'I can't, Steve. Not until I know what's really happened to Keith. If this story about the affair with the French woman isn't true, if they've lied about that, then it gets even more sinister. They've gone to a hell of a lot of trouble to deceive me. And I'm no nearer finding out where Keith's body is, or even if he really is dead. I really think I'd do better making enquiries on my own, without having ... Laurel and Hardy in tow.'

'Oh, dear. I don't like the sound of that. Laura. That part of the world has its own Taliban, you know. You shouldn't even think of travelling around on your own. But, look, if you won't come home, then I'm coming out to support you.'

'Oh, Steve, I don't want to involve you in all this. There's no need for you to come.'

'I think there is, Laura. I think there's every need. I've got some contacts who might be able to help me out with a fast-tracked visa application and I'll book a flight as soon as I can. Promise me you won't do anything until I get there.'

'You know, Steve, I think the answer to what happened to Keith might just lie up in Kohat, but I'm not sure it's got anything to do with that French woman. I think that's where I need to make further enquiries.'

'But please, Laura, wait until I get there. Don't do *anything* until I get there.'

Laura ended the call and sat for a while, thoughtfully cradling Steve's mobile phone in her hand, whilst she considered what her next move ought to be.

In Blackburn, Hamid Gulabzai, too, was cradling a mobile phone in his hand. Sitting in the travel agency and taking coffee with Tanvir Ahmed, Sitara Travel's forty-five-year-old proprietor, Gulabzai held the phone aloft.

'I got you this,' he said as he handed the phone to Tanvir.

'But I have a phone – several phones, in fact – smart phones and pay-as-you-go burner phones.'

'Yes, but you don't have a smart phone like this one. This one is completely encrypted. I got us six of them. You should use *only* this phone when conducting our business.'

Tanvir shook his head, dismissively.

'My friend, you forget, we've been here before. Those ... what were they called? ... *Phantom Phones* ... were supposed to be completely secure and encrypted. Then one of our drivers got stopped on the motorway and the police found his. It didn't take them long to decrypt it. And they stopped two more of our incoming trucks before they'd even reached Rotterdam. Remember?'

'Yes, that was nearly, how d'you say ... *aafat*?' his associate conceded.

'A disaster,' Tanvir translated. 'It was indeed. We don't want to take any more risks with phones. Maybe giving them cheap, untraceable mobiles which they can smash under their boots if they're stopped, or throw out of the cab window, maybe that's best.'

'But, Tanvir, this is a new kind of smart phone. It's deeply encrypted, with special new features to protect the user's data. I am assured that, with this phone, there's no possibility of what they call digital eavesdropping. This is new on the market. Nobody else has these.'

'What makes you think these will be any better than the *Phantom Phones*?'

'Well, you remember how you used that special gadget to find where our phones were when the police had taken them?'

'The digi-scanner? Yes. It didn't just track down the phones, it was able to send a signal to the phones to wipe all the data. The police were baffled. They couldn't understand how the data had been wiped when they had our phones locked up in their evidence store. That scanner was very expensive, but it worked. It got us off the hook.'

'But the next time, the Rotterdam police put the drivers' phones in those special bags. What did they call them? *Uska nam kya tha*?'

'Faraday bags.'

'Yes. So, they couldn't be tracked or wiped. We were lucky we were not all arrested that time. The British police do the same thing now. If they get hold of your phone and put it in one of those Friday bags ...'

'Faraday bags,' Tanvir corrected him. 'Yes, they now know to put them in Faraday bags which block the signal from a digi-scanner. I know all this. Everyone knows this. That's why *Phantom Phones* went out of business.'

'But the clever young man who's invented these new phones has come up with something most brilliant.'

'So, how do these work any better?' he asked, turning the phone over in his hand.

'First, the servers they use are in Panama. No-one can get into them or get the user's movements tracked. Also, these phones have very special software.'

'Why, what's special about it?'

'These phones will automatically delete all data if the phone is not used for twelve hours. If the user gets arrested, or loses the phone, or if the phone goes into a Faraday bag in a police evidence store, and if it's not switched on within twelve hours, using the owner's personal passcode, all the call history, contacts and data is wiped automatically. The phone wipes itself. No digi-scanner is needed. So, there is no evidence. *Koi evidence naheen.*'

'That sounds like it could work,' Tanvir began to sound more interested.

'Of course, it works. Same happens if the user is killed. Remember how one of our fighters was killed in Somalia and someone found his phone on him? It had all his contacts and their locations on it. It was nearly *aafat* for the whole Borodin network. But, with these phones, if the user is killed, and if his phone isn't activated by him, then, twelve hours, later, *khatam hay* – it's wiped clean.'

'That sounds too good to be true, my friend. Are you sure they work?'

'*Ji han. Zurur.* I was given one to test yesterday. I made a couple of calls, sent some texts and I put some contact details into the phone's address book. Then I left it on my kitchen table overnight. This morning, I awoke at seven o'clock and I checked the phone and it was blank. No contacts listed, no texts, no call history. All gone.'

'So, these phones must be very expensive?'

'The young man who invented these gives you up to four handsets for nothing. You just have to pay two thousand pounds for a six-month contract. That's the same cost as for the *Phantom Phones*, but, back then, we also had to pay for each of the *Phantom* handsets. With this new fellow, Qureshi, if you need more than four of these new handsets, they're five hundred pounds each. This is a much better deal.'

'They're still expensive, though,' Anwar was dubious.

'Not if they save you from prison. And these are completely hacker-proof. One hundred percent guaranteed.'

'So, what are these new phones called?'

'They're called Q-phones. See the logo on the back.'

Tanvir turned over the smartphone and saw the tasteful large letter 'Q' in grey on the back of the black plastic case.

'Hmm,' he mused. 'It sounds too good to be true. I hope you're right.'

Later that afternoon, Gulabzai and Tanvir stood on the side-lines as the youth studies group kicked a football around one of the dozen or so football pitches at Blackburn's Blessington sports ground.

'So, which one is Qureshi?' Tanvir asked.

Gulabzai pointed towards Kirpal.

'That one.'

'He's older than the rest,' Tanvir observed.

'He's smarter than the rest. He could be useful to us.'

'Okay. Bring him along tomorrow night. He may be smart, but we'll see how trustworthy he is.'

CHAPTER EIGHTEEN

THE FOLLOWING MORNING, LAURA ROSE EARLY, SHOWERED AND PUT ON another of her newly acquired local outfits. She packed her toiletries and a couple of changes of clothes in her cabin bag, just in case her enquiries in Kohat might run to a second day. She might have to find somewhere to stay up in Kohat, although, naturally, it wouldn't be at the Tanda Lake Lodge. The only thing she knew for certain about her quest was that she wouldn't be welcomed back there.

She now felt a measure of regret at having walloped her husband's alleged mistress. She was now convinced Sophie Benoit had not been in a long-term relationship with Keith, but why had the French woman told such detailed lies? Clearly, that little scenario up at Tanda Lake had all been staged for Laura's benefit, but why? Why would Keith's company representative go to such lengths to deceive her, and how had he managed to persuade a British diplomat and a French woman to support him in that deception?

Down at reception, she left a note for Martin Hopgood, explaining that she would be taking the day off to go exploring and shopping around Peshawar. She hoped that might keep him and Markham off her back for a while. She asked the hotel receptionist to summon a dependable taxi driver. As she climbed into the cab, she noticed that, instead of the ubiquitous woollen hats which most of the locals seemed to wear, the driver wore a blue turban.

'Where to, Madam?' he asked.

'I'd like you to drive me up to Kohat, to the cantonment hospital, and I'll want you to bring me back again later.'

'Sure thing, Madam.'

'Oh, and *meter lagao*,' she ordered, insisting he switched on his meter.

As they drove along, she was puzzled about his turban.

'Tell me, are you a Sikh?' she asked. 'Only I didn't think there were Sikhs in Pakistan.'

'Oh yes, Madam. I am of the Orakzai people, and many of us are of the Sikh faith. My name is Johar, by the way. Harminder Singh Johar. You can please call me either Mindo or Johar.'

'Johar is a good name,' she smiled. 'I'll call you Johar.'

'Madam, are you happy if we take the tunnel to Kohat? Only it is quicker and cheaper.'

'Yes, but why *wouldn't* we take the tunnel?'

'Well, it is a few years past now, but, one time, the Taliban attacked the tunnel. They took it over. The army had to come and shoot everybody up so they could gain control. There was peoples killed there. Some travellers feel safer going over Kohat pass.'

'Well, Johar, I was driven through the tunnel only yesterday and I made it there and back safely, so I think we'll risk it again today.'

'Very good, Madam.'

'So, where are you from?' Laura asked. 'Where do the Orakzai live?'

'Orakzai district is more north than Kohat. My people had to leave there because of Taliban. We came to live in Peshawar.'

'Is it still dangerous up there?'

'At the moment, it is okay around Kohat city, but it is dangerous to leave the main roads in that area.'

Laura hoped they wouldn't have to leave any main roads, although she didn't yet know where her quest might take her.

Some forty-five minutes later, they reached the hospital and Johar agreed to wait in the car park for her. Once inside the modern building, she was relieved to see there was an enquiries desk, which meant she would not have to queue up with the out-patients. To her further relief, the young man seated at the enquiries desk not only spoke English well, but he was the first person she had met who seemed inclined to be helpful.

'Hello, I'm Mrs Laura Roberts. I'm enquiring about my husband, Keith Roberts, a British citizen. He was out here on business when he took ill and he was admitted here as an emergency case back in early April.'

'Ah, let me check on the computer, Madam,' the young man said, as he punched in the details. 'An emergency admission, you say?'

'Yes, I was told he'd suffered a heart attack.'

'Ah, yes. Here we are. Mr Keith Roberts. He was treated here as an emergency case, but he was transferred the same day to the cardiology department at the Lady Reading Hospital in Peshawar. I hope he has fully recovered.'

'Well, no, in fact, he passed away in the Peshawar hospital, but I'm trying to find out what happened to him and where his personal belongings are. His luggage and his passport are missing, also his wallet and money. In fact, his body is missing, too. I was also wondering who it was who brought him in here.'

The young man tapped at his keyboard again. Eventually, he nodded.

'Yes, I see we had an exceptionally large number of casualties that day, owing to a major shooting incident up near Cherat. The casualties were all brought in by the army.'

'But my husband would have been booked in by some civilian or other.'

The young man again scrutinised his computer screen.

'No, Madam. Mr Roberts, too, was booked in by the army. He was brought here by soldiers.'

'But it *was* a heart attack, wasn't it?' Laura asked, confused now.

'Yes. It says he had suffered a myocardial infarction, exacerbated by his wounds.'

'His wounds? What sort of wounds?' Laura was quite alarmed now.

'It seems that, like all the other casualties we had that day, he'd been shot.'

'Shot? You're saying Keith had been shot? But, how? Where?'

'I'm afraid it doesn't show that on my system. You'd have to enquire with the Ministry of Defense people. All I can tell you is that he arrived in a military ambulance along with other casualties from Cherat. Also, it was a military ambulance which later dispersed him and other casualties who needed specialist treatment.'

'I see. So, where is this place? Where is Cherat?'

'It's a hill station about fifty miles from here, up in the Khattack mountains. It's right at the edge of the Kohat district, but it's not a safe place to visit.'

'Clearly not. Well, thank you. You've been most helpful, not to mention refreshingly truthful.'

'You are most welcome, Madam. And, I'm so sorry about your husband.'

'Yes, me too.'

As Johar drove her back down to Peshawar, Laura pondered over the revelation that Keith had been shot, just like the young man who now occupied his expensive satin-lined coffin. She couldn't imagine how or why Keith would have got himself mixed up in some sort of army shoot-out. It just wasn't like him. He wasn't a young man. He wasn't a fit man. He was just a buyer for the tobacco company – in essence, a travelling salesman. The more she thought about it, the less she understood how he could possibly have ended up being shot.

'Johar, do you know a place called Cherat?' she asked.

'Oh yes, Madam. It is on the border between Kohat District and Nowshera District, up in the Khattak mountains.'

'Do you think it would be safe to go there?'

'Only in daylight, Madam.'

'Then I'd like to book you to take me there first thing tomorrow morning.'

Laura took from her bag the mobile phone Steve had given her. She thought about calling him to relate the surprising news she had received at the hospital. Glancing up at her blue-turbaned driver, however, she decided it probably wasn't a good idea to be discussing this within his earshot.

Steve had warned her to be wary about trusting people out here. Johar seemed a nice enough fellow, but she didn't know him. Steve had said that, out here, one never knew who worked for the government, and who might be connected with the Taliban. No, she decided she would wait until she was in the privacy of her hotel room. She glanced at the mobile phone in her hand and reflected on how very thoughtful it had been for Steve to have given it to her. Everyone she knew had offered her advice of various kinds, but Steve was the only one to offer practical help. Kind, practical, cautious Steve, she thought. Thank heavens for reliable, if dull, civil servant types. She slipped the phone back into her bag.

CHAPTER NINETEEN

Markham and Hopgood had seemed a little suspicious when Laura returned to the hotel after her trip to Kohat carrying her cabin holdall but without any shopping bags. However, she had simply fibbed and tapped her bag, saying she had bought some local jewellery for herself and her daughter. They weren't the only ones who could lie, she told herself. They were clearly concerned that she seemed to have no inclination to leave Peshawar and fly back to the UK, but she told them she absolutely would not be leaving until Keith's body was located. She hadn't told them she had arranged to make an early start the following morning, and nor would she tell her minders where she was going, or, indeed, that she was going anywhere at all. She had asked Johar to pick her up at seven o'clock, before Markham and Hopgood came down to breakfast. She had noted that, unlike herself, they were not habitual early risers.

When morning came, she decided to forego breakfast. In the hotel car park, she found Johar topping up the Suzuki's radiator with water. He had already filled up with petrol ready for the round trip to Cherat, which he explained would be over seventy miles. It was not as far as to Kohat, he informed her, but it was a much trickier road. She had again brought her cabin bag with overnight things and several changes of clothing, just in case her enquiries should take longer than hoped.

'Do you know where in Cherat you wish to go?' he asked as they set off, heading south east towards the mountains.

'No, not really. I suppose I need to speak with local officials. Is it a big place?'

'Not very. It was a hill station in the days of the British Raj. There was a sanatorium, where they sent the soldiers who got sick down on the hot plains. It is too much healthy up there in Cherat.'

'Too much healthy?' Laura smiled at Johar's odd phrasing. 'Does that mean there's still a hospital there?'

'Yes, I believe so.'

'Well, that will be the place to start, perhaps.'

The traffic on the Grand Trunk Road was heavy and Laura was quite shocked at the standard of driving by most of the road users. Overtaking seemed to be the aim of every commercial truck and bus, whether or not there was actually room to pass. She held her breath each time a lorry overtook them. Overtaking on the inside seemed to be as commonplace as was overtaking on the offside. At one point, she really thought they were going to be killed when she saw one of the lorries heading straight for them, on the wrong side of the road, apparently with no room to pass. She couldn't look. When no collision came and she opened her eyes again, she realised that, by a small miracle, the lorry had actually made it through the gap.

It was only after the shock had been replaced by a sense of relief, she realised that, as the lorry had headed straight for them, she had been able to see all four wheels of that truck spread out in a line. That must mean the chassis was so badly deformed that the axles were completely out of alignment. The lorry driver must have had quite a job on his hands to keep his twisted vehicle on a straight path. Her blood ran cold at the thought of what might have happened. She told herself she would be greatly relieved when they actually got to Cherat.

Once they had left the busy Grand Trunk Road, the drive up into the Khattack mountains became much more pleasant. Johar switched off the vehicle's air-conditioning and opened his side window to allow the cool morning air to flow in. Along the quiet country road to Cherat there were trees and shrubs, some of which Laura didn't recognise. There was a honey-scent in the air, mixed with the distinctive smell of burning charcoal. Johar explained that people in the villages would be lighting wood fires to heat their breakfasts, which usually consisted of leftover charcoal-cooked chappatis torn up and soaked in hot milk. It sounded most appealing to Laura, who hadn't yet had any breakfast.

As they approached Cherat, they drove around a gentle bend in the road and saw some high walls and some large and very secure gates. Alongside, was a tall, blue and white road sign which proclaimed in English, 'Welcome to Cherat, Home of the SSG'.

'What's SSG?' Laura asked as they drove past.

'It's the Special Services Group. They're known as the 'maroon berets' – army commandos, you know? I knew they were up in the Khattack hills somewhere but I didn't know they were stationed in Cherat. Madam, I'm beginning to think maybe we need a permit to be here.'

Laura could see Johar's face reflected in the rear-view mirror. His expression was one of mild concern.

As the Suzuki climbed up the final steep incline towards Cherat, Laura was surprised to see a large billboard for a tourist facility which boasted, in English, 'The longest zip wire in Asia'.

There was already a small queue of people awaiting admission to the attraction. Given the obvious lack of maintenance of the lorries they had passed, Laura couldn't see herself trusting her life to a six-hundred-foot zip wire. She could envisage someone having a heart attack as they zipped out on a flimsy harness over the steep-sided valley below them. She wondered briefly whether that might just have been where Keith had come to grief, but then there was the little matter of his wounds. If this was, as it appeared to be, a tourist area, why would there have been shooting here? Why would anyone have shot a tobacco company employee?

Further on, they could see, on top of the hill, a very English-looking church. It seemed somewhat incongruous here amongst the mountains of Pakistan, yet she had seen similar churches in the Indian hill stations of Simla and Mussoorie. Some warm memories now came flooding back. As a young woman, on her first overseas posting, which was also to be her last, she had been bowled over by the sights and the scents of India. Of course, she had also been swept off her feet by Keith. They had explored a few choice corners of India together. It had been so romantic when they had taken the Taj express from Delhi down to Agra and had photographed each other seated on the famous marble bench in front of the magnificent Taj Mahal, that historic monument to eternal love.

Laura recalled how she had suggested they get one of the other tourists to take a photo of both of them together but Keith had said that was a bad idea since most of them seemed to be locals and they might run off with the camera. She had thought that rather unkind of him, but he had laughed at her trusting nature and had assured her he knew this part of the world and its people better than she did. Given the present circumstances, however, she began to doubt that was the case. So, they hadn't had a photo of the two of them together in front of the Taj Mahal, just separate ones. That seemed ironic, somehow, and perhaps a little prophetic. Just as in the tragic story of the world-famous British princess who had been photographed sitting alone on that very same marble bench, Laura's husband had not been true to his wife, either.

On his next business trip to Delhi, Keith had whisked her away to the beaches of Goa. There, they had bathed in the warm waters of the Arabian sea by day, and, in the evenings, they had sat together on the star-lit shore, watching the little night fishing boats heading out to sea at sunset. It had all been so terribly exotic, so romantic. They had sipped *fenny*, the local coconut spirit, before retiring to the little rented beach cabin for nights of passion. Laura had no idea back then that, unlike the timeless romance of the Taj Mahal, although her relationship with Keith would last, their romance would not.

The warmth of those memories was suddenly cooled, however, by the image which now entered her head of Keith making love, not to Laura, but to the bottle-blonde French woman – if, indeed, he really had. Abruptly, the magic of the moment was gone. That woman had intruded into Laura's personal recollections and had burst the bubble of nostalgia. Might Keith's wandering libido have been the death of him, or had he really been shot, as the young man at the hospital had claimed? The truth was frustratingly elusive so far.

She had spent all last night thinking it over. Supposing Sophie Benoit had not been lying. Perhaps Keith's heart really had given out as he had lain in her bed. The overwhelmed hospital staff in Kohat might have simply assumed Keith was one of the casualties of the shooting incident and wrongly entered his condition on their computer. Maybe the wounds shown in the hospital record were not his.

But, then again, the Benoit woman had fallen into Laura's trap. Surely, his lover of three years' standing, if indeed she were his lover, would have known Keith didn't have a pacemaker? And if she did know that, why hadn't she said so? Why had she gone along with Laura's ruse? So, if she *wasn't* Keith's lover, and if he *didn't* have a heart attack in her bed, maybe he really had been shot. But why, and how? Had the French woman shot him? Laura's thoughts just kept going around in circles. She wouldn't even begin to know the truth of it until his body could be found.

Laura now acknowledged that the physical aspects of love no longer played a role in her life. She had accepted that, in the same way she had accepted those tiny, blue spider veins which had begun to appear on the back of her thighs, and the laughter lines around her eyes which didn't disappear when her laughter ceased. The fact that Keith had been three years older than her clearly hadn't killed the romance in *his* life. He had bounced from one affair to another, from one woman's bed to another. It wasn't fair, she thought, suddenly. How bloody dare he! He hadn't been the best of husbands, and yet, here she was, half a world away from home, trying to locate his worthless corpse. For the first time since she had set out on her quest, she began to question the sense of it.

'Are you all right, Madam?' Johar asked.

She hadn't realised how much her thoughts had upset her, but she now found there were tears trickling down her cheeks again. As before, they were tears of anger and frustration, and Johar could see in his rear-view mirror that she was tearful.

'Oh, yes, Johar. I'm fine. I'm just being silly, that's all.'

'We should stop for a cup of tea, I think,' he said, as he turned into the square in front of the church and parked the taxi. 'There's a tea shop over there. Please, come.'

The tea shop was an open-air affair. There was a small, corrugated tin shack, set upon a wooden platform. Within the shack's rusted open doors, a bare-foot *chai walla,* squatted on a large wooden trestle table with a big samovar placed beside him. He dispensed boiling water from the samovar onto tea leaves in the ubiquitous chipped green enamelled tea pots, and a teenaged boy collected the pots and distributed them unceremoniously, along with tea glasses, to the various customers seated at little wooden tables ranged around outside the shack.

Laura noticed there were no women customers. In fact, there were no women out and about at all. In this, she found Pakistan very different from India. In India, women could be seen everywhere in public, wearing brightly coloured saris or gaily patterned *shalwar kameez.* She had even seen some of the poorer, low-caste women labouring on building sites. Many of the better-off young men seen strolling around Delhi wore western jeans and tee shirts with designer logos. By comparison, however, the clothing of the men here in north west Pakistan was drab. Their loose-fitting *shalwar kameez* varied little in colour from brown, through fawn to insipid pale blue. Their flattish, woollen hats, a little like berets but with rolled edges, were of the same dull colours. Many of them also wore drab-coloured shawls that resembled old army blankets.

In order to appear a little more modest, Laura wrapped the chiffon *dupatta* around her head before climbing out of the car, and Johar found them a table positioned away from the other customers, then went to order some tea. The tea, when it came, was hot and milky and already sweetened in the pot. Laura didn't normally take sugar in her tea, but she was glad of the energy it might give her, since she hadn't yet eaten anything.

She watched Johar pour out their tea into the two glasses. She observed him take a deep draft of tea, sucking it in through clenched teeth to strain out the tea leaves which he then swiped from his teeth with his forefinger and flicked into the dust. She had forgotten how country people in this part of the world drank their tea. It had been the same in India. But that was so very long ago. It was the little details like that which one forgot, and it was nice to be reminded of them. She sipped her own tea in the same fashion.

She remembered how surprised she had been to hear Martin Hopgood refer to the little scooter rickshaws as 'tuk-tuks'. They'd never been called that when she had lived and worked in Delhi. She knew they were called 'tuk-tuks' in Thailand, though, as Beth and Alan had holidayed there and had sent photos of themselves sitting in one. She thought perhaps it was the European tourists holidaying in Thailand, and then in India and Pakistan, who had dubbed all the scooter rickshaws 'tuk-tuks' and the Thai name had stuck here, too.

The development of language had always fascinated her. This was something else which saddened her. She reflected that, if it hadn't been for her early marriage to Keith, she might have stayed with the Foreign Office. She might have travelled to even more exotic places and learned more languages. She now regretted what were wasted opportunities. However, she did not regret being a mother to her lovely daughter. She didn't resent the years spent raising Beth, though she did regret the fact that, nowadays, they lived continents apart. As she sipped her tea, she congratulated herself on having remembered some of the Hindi she had learned. Had she forgotten it, she might not have fully understood what Hopgood had been saying to his co-conspirators at the hospital and at that dingy little hotel. She might not have had the confidence to challenge what she was being told.

She also felt glad she had shown them she wasn't the tame little middle-aged housewife they had thought her to be. Asserting herself had given her the courage to continue with her quest. Glancing around her, now, Laura couldn't help noticing the other customers were staring at them. She could understand why. It must be rare to see a European woman frequenting the tea shops, especially a European woman accompanied by a Sikh. She hoped it was just natural curiosity, though, rather than anything more threatening.

'Well, Madam, we are here,' Johar said. 'What do we do next? Was it the hospital you wished to see?'

'Oh, I don't really know where to begin, Johar. You see, the reason I'm here is that I'm trying to find my husband.'

'You have misplaced your husband?'

'Not misplaced, no. He died here in Pakistan, but I'm having some difficulty finding out exactly how and why.'

'Oh, *barri afsos*. I'm very sorry. You think he died here in Cherat?'

Laura noted Johar's expression of genuine concern. Though she hadn't known him long enough to know if she could trust him, she trusted her own judgement. She decided she would entrust him with a little more information.

'Well, he actually died at the hospital in Peshawar, but I found out yesterday that it was here in Cherat that he had taken ill, or perhaps had been shot.'

'Shot?' Johar was surprised. 'Shootings happen here a lot, because of Taliban, but I never heard of *Feringees* getting shot here.'

'*Feringees*?' Laura puzzled for a second. 'Oh, you mean foreigners. Yes, well, not only was he killed, but his body is missing.'

'Oh, that is very bad. Every deceased person should be buried as soon as possible.'

'Well, it's even more complicated than that, Johar. You see, I paid to have his body taken back to England, but there was a mix-up somewhere along the line and they sent the wrong body back.'

'Aiee! So, two families are missing their deceased. That is very bad. You, know, Madam, I think we should not stay too long in this place. These days, not many *feringees* come here. There are too many *dacu* here – too many bandits. If your husband got shot here, maybe it could happen to you, too.'

'Too many bandits, eh? Well, oddly enough, I think I left a couple of bandits back at my hotel.'

Suddenly, a red police jeep appeared and screeched to a halt in the square. A tall, grey-uniformed policeman jumped out. To Laura's dismay, he hurried across towards her and Johar. A rapid conversation broke out between the policeman and the taxi driver, none of which Laura could follow. She guessed they were speaking one of the local Pashto dialects, which was completely unintelligible to her. The policeman seemed quite agitated and kept gesticulating at Laura and then back at the road via which they had arrived. Laura was suddenly fearful that she might be arrested. She stood up suddenly.

'Johar, if he's here to arrest me over that woman, tell him I didn't intend to assault her, but if he knew what she said she did with my husband, well, anybody would have given her a slap.'

Johar stood up, too.

'No Madam, he is not speaking of any woman. He is saying we should have had a permit to come here. It is very dangerous in this district at the moment, especially for foreigners. I am sorry I did not know this. You should please to finish your tea.'

Laura lifted her cup to sip the last of her tea, but the policeman stamped his foot and raised his voice.

'Ubhee! Ubhee! Ek dum!'

Laura knew what that meant. They must go *now*.

'Madam, you should *not* finish your tea,' Johar corrected himself.

She put down her cup and briskly followed Johar back to the taxi. They headed out of the square the same way they had arrived. The policeman stood, hands on hips, and watched them go. With some dismay, the *chai wallah* also watched them leave, since he had not been paid for their tea.

'Did he say why it's so dangerous here now?' she asked as they drove back down the hill again.

'He just said there are insurgents in the neighbourhood. He said that, if we didn't leave, he'd have to take us in.'

'Take us in? You mean, into protective custody?'

'Yes, just so. He wanted to do that anyway, as he was suspicious about why you are here. I told him your husband had recently died and you were going to the hospital to take his body, so he felt bad for you and said we should just go.'

Passing the tourist site with the trip wire again, Laura noticed that the queue of people that had been waiting outside as Johar had driven them up the hill had now dispersed. The leisure facility was deserted. Things suddenly felt different, somehow. Soon, they found themselves approaching the Special Services Group HQ again but, this time, there were barriers across the road and armed soldiers manning them.

Johar slowed down and slid open his window to speak to the soldiers. Once again, Laura couldn't understand the earnest conversation which took place between her driver and the military, but it led to their being directed away from the main road and having to take a detour along an even bumpier, dustier road. As busy and as infested by suicidal truck drivers as the Grand Trunk Road had been, Laura found herself wishing they were back on it, as their progress on this uneven back road was irritatingly slow.

When they came to an unmarked crossroads, it was clear to her that Johar was undecided as to which way led back to Peshawar. The downhill road he did choose, which Laura hoped would take them back down the Peshawar Valley, soon wound around a hill and began to ascend again. The taxi reached the summit of yet another hill then the road ahead of them began to descend again into yet another unfamiliar valley. Johar brought the vehicle to a halt and took his map out of the glove compartment.

'Are we lost?' Laura asked.

'No, Madam. Not lost. Just a little bit off the beating track. I'm just checking the map to see where this road takes us.'

Laura smiled once again at Johar's amusing turn of phrase. It seemed apt, however, as the uneven road surface meant his taxi was taking a bit of a beating.

'I'll stretch my legs for a bit, then,' Laura said as she climbed out and walked to the side of the road.

The valley which fell away beneath her gaze was quite beautiful. There was a sparkling grey river which wound its way along the valley bottom whilst, above, verdant wooded hills gave way to distant, snow-dusted mountain peaks. She couldn't see any major roads ahead, just the dusty track they'd been following, but, in the middle distance, between the road and the river, there was a sizeable fort-like structure. Its tall walls were rendered with sun-baked mud and the only way in appeared to be via two massive corrugated iron gates.

'Is that another army camp over there?' she pointed it out to Johar, thinking it might help him to establish where they were.

'No, Madam. That is a village. Ah, I think I know which one.'

'Really? It doesn't look like any village I've ever seen.'

Johar folded his map up again and joined her by the edge of the road to look at the view.

'It is a *qalat* – a fortified village. Many of the villages in the Khyber Pakhtunkhwa are built like that. The district has a long history of tribes attacking each other, and of invaders coming over the mountains. They still fight tribal feuds around here. This is the territory of the Bangash people. They are Pashtuns. Fierce warrior people. They fought the British and they fought the Russians. Nowadays, they are fighting the local Taliban, and not just the Taliban.'

'So, who else are they fighting besides the Taliban?'

'They are fighting forces within the government itself.'

'What do you mean, Johar? Which forces?'

Laura was intrigued now. There was something scarily magical about the huge fort-like village and the idea that the hills which surrounded it might conceal some kind of dark menace, despite their wild beauty.

'Not all parts of our government are against the Taliban. There are some who work with the Taliban. There are what the foreign press calls unholy alliances, though it is best not to speak openly of them. It would be best if we continue our drive now. We shouldn't spend too much time here on the road. It is not safe. Better to keep moving.'

They returned to the car and resumed their drive down to the valley bottom. There were boulders strewn along the road, which Johar explained would have been washed down from the mountains during the heavy rains earlier in the year. Johar did his best to avoid driving over them. She noticed piles of such boulders and rocks stacked up by the roadside every so often, evidence, she presumed, that the locals had at least made some attempt to clear the road. She wondered why they hadn't finished the job and she wondered whether leaving some rocks in the road was deliberate. Perhaps they'd been left there in order to slow down the traffic, or to dissuade the heavier road users from disturbing the tranquillity of their beautiful valley. It soon became clear, however, that, if the locals' reluctance to clear the boulders from the road was a deliberate measure, then it was an unsuccessful one, as they firstly heard, and then saw one of the local lorries roaring along the road behind them.

The truck seemed massively over-laden, as were most of the trucks Laura had seen speeding recklessly along the Grand Trunk Road, but this dusty track wasn't as wide or as well-surfaced as the GT Road. As she looked over her shoulder, she realised the truck driver was intending to overtake them, and yet there didn't seem to be enough room for him to do so. Alarmingly, he didn't seem to be fully in control of the vehicle either. As the lorry bore down on them, she heard its brakes squealing. Those brakes seemed dangerously ineffective and the truck's tyres seemed to be skidding along, unable to get a grip on the dusty road surface.

'Watch out!' she shouted, 'he's heading straight for us!'

Johar swerved off the road onto what seemed to be the only level bit of verge but which also seemed to have been brought into use as a repository for some of the fallen rocks. There was an almighty crunching sound as the taxi came to a halt up against the heap of boulders, but, thankfully, the lorry swept past without colliding with them. It disappeared in a cloud of dust. Johar got out of the car to inspect the damage. His dismayed expression told Laura it wasn't good. She got out, too.

One of the front wings of the Suzuki Swift was buckled under upon itself, but the worst damage had befallen the front nearside wheel. The tyre was burst but the entire wheel rim was completely bent out of shape. Johar kicked at it with his foot and shook his fist at the direction in which the truck had disappeared.

'*Bay vakoof*!' he shouted, just in case the lorry driver didn't realise what an idiot he was.

'Do you have a spare?' Laura asked, as Johar sank to his knees to look for any damage to the underside of the Suzuki.

'I do, Madam, but I don't think it'll be any use. There's more damage under here.'

Laura didn't imagine there would be any kind of vehicle recovery service so far out in these tribal areas, and they were too far off the main road to flag down someone for help. However, Johar knew what to do. He fetched Laura's cabin bag from the boot of the taxi.

'Madam, if I carry your bag, do you think you could manage to walk with me to that village over there? The people there will help us.'

Laura was disappointed to think she might look as old and incapable as Johar's question suggested. Of course she could walk to the village. It wasn't that far, and, anyway, she was quite intrigued to see what the village looked like from the inside, and to meet some of these Bangash – Johar's fierce warrior people.

CHAPTER TWENTY

It was dark and there was very little traffic in Blackburn at ten o'clock that night, as Tanvir collected Gulabzai and Kirpal from Gulabzai's house. Kirpal had taken the precaution of agreeing to make his own way to the house in Trafalgar Street, as he could hardly have them pick him up from the Travellers' Inn in Burtby, since it was too close to MI5 North. For his own safety's sake, he had no wish to let them know where he was staying or where he was working. He had made the excuse that he was staying with cousins on the other side of Blackburn. In any case, he guessed Gulabzai had no wish to be seen by relatives of the man he knew as Qureshi.

The three sat in the front seat of Tanvir's black transit van. To Kirpal's surprise, Tanvir drove them just a few yards down the street before turning into the yard of the abandoned Trafalgar mill. For a moment, Kirpal's heart began to pound, as he wondered whether they had rumbled him as an impostor and were going to drag him into the old mill and beat him up. To his relief however, Tanvir pulled up in front of the mill's loading bay and, leaving the engine running, he got out of the van and went and hammered on the door. After a few moments, the door was opened and a short exchange passed between Tanvir and a heavily-built man who was waiting inside.

Tanvir and the heavy both glanced towards the street, where all was quiet. Kirpal guessed that, at this time on a Saturday night, most locals would either be out socialising or at home watching television. The heavy now ushered a further four men out of the mill and quickly led them to the back of the transit van where they were hurriedly pushed inside. Kirpal tried to hear what was being said but he could not. Another man now appeared in the doorway of the mill and, stepping outside, locked the mill door behind him and also approached the van. Opening the front passenger door, he clearly expected to sit up front, but was surprised to see Kirpal seated between Gulabzai and Tanvir.

Gulabzai jerked a thumb towards the back of the van and told the man to join the four others who were now in the back of the van with the heavily-built man. Once everyone was aboard, Tanvir reversed the van back around the yard and they headed out through the gates and off towards the centre of Blackburn. Kirpal noticed that Tanvir seemed to be avoiding the main and well-lit roads and was instead taking various detours around residential streets. He guessed this was to avoid police patrols and CCTV cameras.

Soon, they were on their way out of town. Kirpal decided it might appear suspicious if he expressed no curiosity as to their destination.

'So, where are we headed?' he asked at last.

'West Pennine Moors,' Tanvir answered.

'Oh. Shame it's so dark. I'm told the scenery up there is great,' Kirpal said, trying to sound just casually interested and not at all nervous.

'You been there before?' Tanvir asked.

'No. I'm up from London. First time visiting the north.'

Tanvir and Gulabzai seemed disinclined to engage further in

conversation, so Kirpal remained silent, too. As their drive up into the moors progressed, it became darker and darker. Kirpal realised they must be quite high up now, as he could see the bright lights of a town nestling in a valley well below. Indeed, apart from the van's headlights, the glow from down in the valley was the only light around. Eventually, Tanvir brought the van to a halt in what seemed to be a layby.

'We can stretch our legs for a bit,' Tanvir suggested.

Climbing out, Kirpal walked across to the edge of the road and gazed out at the streetlights in the town below. There were no streetlights up here on the moors. In fact, there wasn't much of anything up here. Just a moonless sky above them and an empty road behind and in front of them. The last building they had passed had been a few miles back. The place where they had stopped was quite deserted and eerily silent. Naturally, he wondered why they were here. He had a bad feeling about it.

Looking back over his shoulder, he saw Tanvir standing beside the van, obviously relieving himself. Gulabzai had gone to the back of the van and opened the doors. The heavily-set man now emerged and shouted to one of the passengers to come out, but he indicated that the others should remain inside. The man who had been summoned seemed reluctant to get out. Seemingly, Kirpal wasn't the only one confused about what was happening.

The heavy reached in and pulled the man out, but closed the van doors behind him, leaving the others inside. With a firm grasp on the man's arm, the heavy led him a little further along the roadway until they disappeared into the darkness beyond the beam of light cast by the van's headlamps. Gulabzai now made to follow them. As he, too, walked beyond the beam of the headlights and headed along the darkened road, Kirpal noticed he was carrying a long spade. Just seconds later, he heard a loud noise. It sounded like someone hitting a ball with a cricket bat. The noise came again, and again.

Kirpal stood, frozen with fear, at the sudden realisation that what he was hearing was not someone playing cricket in the dark. Someone had been assaulted with that spade – several times. In fact, it became obvious to him that what he was hearing was the spade hitting someone's head with great force. He heard a grunt each time the spade connected. He knew no-one could survive being hit that hard with that implement. Someone, either Gulabzai or the thuggish man with him, had just killed the man they had escorted out of the back of the van. Kirpal suddenly felt sick to the pit of his stomach.

Tanvir came and stood by Kirpal. Kirpal hoped Tanvir couldn't sense his fear here in the dark. As the sound of earth being struck and shovelled now became apparent, Kirpal tried to steady his hands and his voice.

'Who was that man?' he asked.

'Mushtaq,' Tanvir replied coldly. 'Not someone you should worry about. A *gumrah,* that's all.'

'I don't know what that means,' Kirpal said. 'What's a *gumrah*?'

'You don't have them in London?' Tanvir asked. 'Well, never mind. You'd better wait in the van. We'll be off again in a minute.'

Kirpal climbed back into the front seat of the van and waited. Clasping his shaking hands together, he clamped them between his knees. He knew he had just witnessed, or at least heard, a murder being committed, and he couldn't stop trembling. It wasn't the first time he had heard a man being beaten to death. His mind returned to the time he and Harry and their colleague Dave Lloyd had been concealed in the garage of a Russian killer's house, whilst the Russian's fellow GRU thugs had beaten him to death in his own hallway. That had been sickening. Of course, what had just happened here, along the roadside, was no less stomach turning. However, he knew he had to pull himself together.

After an interminable wait, he saw Gulabzai and the heavy reappearing. Gulabzai handed the spade to his accomplice who walked around to the back of the van. Kirpal heard him climb back in and slam the van door. Gulabzai now climbed into the front beside Kirpal. Tanvir, too, got back into the driver's seat. The third man did not reappear, confirming what Kirpal had feared – that he had just been killed and buried. Kirpal struggled to regain his composure.

'Is that Mushtaq not coming back with us?' asked.

'No, he's gone back to Pakistan,' Tanvir replied, and he and Gulabzai laughed.

'Where to now?' Kirpal asked, trying to control the tremor in his voice.

'Now, we go to Bolton. You been there?' Tanvir asked.

'No,' Kirpal swallowed hard. 'Quite a mystery tour for me.'

They continued the drive in silence. On the outskirts of the town of Bolton, Tanvir pulled off the main road and turned into a yard where several trucks were parked. Feeling slightly more in control of his nerves now, Kirpal glanced at his watch. It was getting on for one o'clock in the morning. Tanvir brought the van to a halt by one of the parked lorries.

'Stay here,' he ordered, and Kirpal was happy to obey.

Tanvir and Gulabzai climbed out and disappeared around towards the back of the van. Glancing in the rear-view mirror, he saw their other passengers emerge. To his relief, it didn't look as though there would be any further killings. The heavy climbed up into the cab of the lorry and started it up, whilst his associate transferred the three remaining men from the back of the van into the rear of the lorry and locked the back, then he, too, climbed up into the lorry cab. Tanvir and Gulabzai exchanged a few words with them then returned to the van. Having watched the lorry start up and swing out of the yard, Tanvir started up the van again and they, too, headed out, taking the A666 north.

As they descended back down into the Ribble Valley towards Blackburn, Kirpal concentrated on fixing the truck's registration number in his mind. He knew this was important. The letters BVM he was easily able to commit to his memory, as he recalled a photograph he had seen on Jo Laska's desk back at Thames House. The photo had shown Jo standing in front of a statue at some religious shrine or other. When he had asked who it was that the statue depicted, Jo had told him it was the Blessed Virgin Mary, so that was how he would now remember the BVM from the number plate. He fixed an image of that statue in his mind.

He usually found it less easy to recall numbers, but he had a method for this, too. He equated each number with an image. For example, the number one represented a bun, two was a shoe, three a bee, and so on. In his mind, he just had to picture an image of the cluster of items which represented each number. Focusing on these images as they headed back into Blackburn helped take his mind off the sickening event he had earlier witnessed up on the moors. Assuring Gulabzai and Tanvir that his cousin would come and pick him up, Kirpal asked to be dropped off in the town centre. As the transit van took off again back to Trafalgar Street, Kirpal took out his mobile phone and called Harry. It took a number of rings before a sleepy Harry answered.

'Morning, Mate. Sorry to wake you at this unearthly hour, but can you come and pick me up, please? I think I've just witnessed a murder.'

CHAPTER TWENTY-ONE

It was two-thirty in the morning and all was quiet in Downing Street. In their private prime ministerial apartments, Ivan Thompson and his live-in mistress, Sally Austin, were asleep, as was their normally sleepless and fractious toddler. The house was entirely in darkness and only their personal security officer and the police on guard outside in the street, were awake and vigilant. However, one regular night-time prowler was making his way stealthily to Number Ten.

Winston, the Mouser-in-chief, entered the rose garden at the rear, by leaping over the garden wall which separated the Cabinet Office on Whitehall from the Prime Minister's historic Downing Street residence. Padding unhurriedly across the lawn, he made his way up the back steps towards the rear entrance. As he approached the cat-flap at his usual languid pace, he was suddenly startled to be overtaken. Instinctively, he reared up and clawed at the humming, disc-shaped drone which hovered above him. He missed. The drone hummed its way through the cat-flap and into the building, followed by the now intensely curious cat.

Down the hallway the drone flew. Again, Winston leapt and tried to paw it out of the air, but again he missed, as it dipped up and down and remained just out of his reach. For a few moments, the flying object hovered and spun slowly around, just above his head. Fired with feline determination, Winston crouched low, flexed his back legs and launched himself up into the air. This time, his determination paid off as he caught the drone and brought it down onto the carpet. Suddenly, however, the drone exploded.

Immediately, loud alarms went off and the police officers on duty outside came running and hammered on the front door, shouting to be let in. The Prime Minister's Personal Protection Officer was first on the scene. Fully clothed with pistol in hand, he leapt out of the upstairs room, where he had been passing the night shift by reading a spy thriller. Switching on lights as he went, he headed swiftly down the grand staircase. Moments later, the Prime Minister appeared on the upper landing, swathed in a dark blue towelling bath robe, and with leather, Turkish style slippers on his feet. Glancing up, the detective noticed the PM was not wearing pyjamas. He had never seen the PM's bare, white legs before, and his attention was briefly drawn to the Premier's knotted varicose veins. Determined to avoid being distracted by the PM's legs, however, he headed along the downstairs hallway.

'What's happened?' Thompson called out. 'What the hell was that noise?'

'Stay there, Sir,' the detective ordered. 'It came from the back of the house.'

The detective ran along the passageway towards the back entrance. He found himself walking through a settling dust cloud and crunching over broken glass. He stepped over chunks of plaster as he felt his way along the wall, trying to locate the light switch to illuminate the rear passage. The building's fire alarm was deafening at this side of the building. The ceiling lights of the rear passage were all smashed but he took out his mobile phone and used its torch function to light his way.

In the gloom, the detective could see exposed eighteenth century wooden laths on the walls where once there had been twentieth century plaster and canary yellow emulsion. He felt the night air on his face as a slight breeze filtered in through the smashed window panes. He stepped over the debris of broken chairs and a splintered Georgian hall table. On the floor of the passageway were smashed pictures which had fallen from the walls. Down, in amongst the detritus, he saw the shattered bits of some electronic gadgetry. He shone his phone torch down upon those bits. To his horror, he saw they were coated in blood and flesh and tabby-coloured fur.

The Prime Minister had his cabinet convene in a conference room at the Cabinet Office in Whitehall later that morning to discuss the incident. Amongst those present were MI5 DG, Helena Fairbrother, Sir Robert Vanbrugge, her MI6 counterpart, and Peter Webb head of SO15, the Metropolitan Police's Counter-Terrorism Command. Sir Henry Mortimer, Permanent Secretary of the Cabinet Office had also been invited along to represent and report back to the Joint Intelligence Committee. They were addressed by the Home Secretary, Rukhsana Chadha.

'Well, the forensic team is still examining the pieces, but it looks as if it was an autonomous drone of some kind,' she announced. 'It was fairly sophisticated – a very small drone, but armed. There wasn't anyone operating it from close proximity to Downing Street. It was navigated remotely via integral cameras.'

'What do you think it was intended to achieve?' Sir Henry asked.

'Had it reached the Prime Minister's private apartments, it would likely have killed him,' the Home Secretary replied.

'But how did it get in?' the Prime Minister wanted to know.

'It could only have entered via the cat-flap, Sir,' Peter Webb replied. 'There were no windows open, and, for obvious security reasons, Number Ten's front door does not have a functioning letter box, only a dummy one. We know they're making small drones such as this now, small enough to fit through a letter box or cat-flap.'

'Oh, for heaven's sake!' The Prime Minister exclaimed. 'The bloody cat-flap? I knew I should have got rid of that cat ages ago.'

There was a momentary surprised silence. Then Joy Cooper, the PM's press secretary spoke.

'But, Prime Minister, it was the cat who stopped the drone getting to you.'

'Yes, but if we didn't have a cat we wouldn't have a cat flap. Then the drone wouldn't have got in at all.

'Maybe so, Prime Minister,' the Home Secretary said, 'but that cat took down the drone before it reached the stairs. Winston saved your life.'

'Oh, well, I suppose we'll have to pin a medal on him or something. Doesn't the Humane Society arrange something like that for animals?'

There was another surprised silence. It was the MI6 chief who broke the sad news.

'You'll have to scrape him off the carpet first.'

It seemed the PM hadn't realised that poor Winston, the feline known as 009 and licensed to kill, had lost all nine of his lives at once in bringing down the drone. The Home secretary's expression was grave.

'I think you should cancel your Moscow trip,' she advised.

'Cancel Moscow?' Thompson asked. 'Why would I want to do that? Absolutely everyone will be there for the celebrations. Putin will take it as a personal affront if I miss the Victory Day Parade. This could be a good opportunity to mend a few bridges. I could persuade him that Ukraine joining NATO wouldn't be a threat to

Russia at all. Of course, we'd have to drop the sanctions we imposed after he took the Crimea.'

'How ironic,' Helena declared. 'The world's biggest Fascist state holding a massive parade to celebrate its historic victory over Fascism.'

'Indeed,' Vanbrugge agreed. 'And all the other right-wing Fascist states will be represented – Belarus, Hungary, Austria. I hear the Chinese Envoy will be there, too.'

'Not just the Fascist states attending, though, is it?' Thompson insisted. 'The Moscow-based ambassadors of most countries will be there.'

'But, Ivan, we don't yet know who tried to kill you last night,' the Home Secretary protested. 'It could well have been the Russians. If they almost succeeded in killing you in Number Ten. Think how much easier it would be to bump you off in Moscow.'

'Why must everything come down to the Russians?' Thompson bristled. 'This attack could have been the Chinese, or the North Koreans, or even the Irish.'

Sir Robert Vanbrugge leaned across and whispered in Helena's ear, 'or his first wife!'

Helena smiled behind her hand, but it was evident the PM had overheard.

'What's that?' Thompson barked.

'Worst time, Prime Minister,' Vanbrugge said, recovering the situation with some aplomb. 'I was saying this could be the worst time to visit Moscow. There are rumours that an attempt might be made on Putin's life during all the parades and fireworks. It's rumoured that some of the Central Asian separatists are out to get him. Alternatively, there are a few thousand dispossessed reindeer herders up in the Arctic who aren't too happy about their traditional grazing lands and the sacred burial places of their ancestors being despoiled by oil and gas drilling and mineral extraction. Any one of a dozen groups could decide to take a pop at him. You could be caught in the crossfire.'

Helena leaned across and whispered in Sir Robert's ear, 'with any luck.'

She saw the PM looking at her quizzically, too.

'With any luck, though, they won't get within a mile of Putin,' she assured him. 'All the same, with Russian troops massing on the border with Ukraine, in a clear threat of invasion, it probably isn't the best time to visit Moscow.'

'There isn't going to be any invasion of Ukraine,' the PM derided, in tones reminiscent of an infant class teacher rebuking small children. 'It's all just threats over the NATO membership issue. Putin's not stupid. He knows he'd never manage to conquer and hold onto such a huge country. Oh, no, he'd have to be stark raving mad to even contemplate invading Ukraine. It simply isn't going to happen, I tell you.'

'I'm sorry to contradict you, Prime Minister,' the MI6 Chief shook his head. 'All the indications are that Putin is hell-bent on expansionism. He's been making overtures to the new regime in Afghanistan, offering them military hardware and other technologies. And we know some of his mercenaries are embedded with the Afghan Taliban. He's also been cosying up to the Pakistani authorities. Word is, he wants Pakistan to side with him when – and that's when, not if – he invades the Ukraine.'

'Nonsense. I am telling you that simply will not happen. Russia will *not* invade Ukraine.'

CHAPTER TWENTY-TWO

JOHAR HAMMERED HARD ON THE MASSIVE CORRUGATED IRON DOORS OF the fortified village. Eventually, one of the gates was opened by a teenaged boy. After a protracted conversation between Johar and the lad, which involved Johar pointing back up the hillside to where they had left his damaged taxi, and swiping the palms of his hands across each other to indicate a collision, the boy nodded but closed the gate on them.

'He is going to ask the *Sardar Sahib*, the village head man, if we can come in,' Johar explained. 'It will be all right, though. They are Pashtuns. They are obliged by their faith and culture to give us assistance.'

Laura didn't see why Johar thought the villagers would be under any obligation to help passing travellers, especially one who was a *ferringhi*, but she hoped he was right.

Soon, the heavy gates were swung open again by the boy. Now, he was accompanied by a man, and from what the boy had said, Laura guessed this was the *Sardar*. Somehow, she had expected the *Sardar* would be an elderly, bearded man. She couldn't have been more wrong. The man who came forward to scrutinise them was in his mid to late forties, she guessed, tall and slim with quite a strong, handsome face and striking hazel eyes. Speaking Pashto, Johar explained their predicament to the *Sardar Sahib*.

'Tourists!' the head man exclaimed, shaking his head and looking Laura up and down.

For one disappointing moment, Laura feared he was going to turn them away. Gripped by a sense of panic at the idea that they might be stranded out on the road in what seemed to be bandit country, she decided to speak up and plead their case.

'*Ham toh tourists naheen*,' she corrected him, politely. '*Meyn idder ai hun kyunkay mere husband yahan mur geya*.'

She wasn't sure whether her clumsy Hindi would adequately explain the situation and persuade him that she wasn't a tourist but had come to find her dead husband. Indeed, she didn't even know whether the man would understand Hindi, but she looked him full in the eye and gave him a most intense look, hoping to stir up a grain of sympathy. The *Sardar* raised his eyebrows in surprise. Clearly, this wasn't a simple case of an improvident tourist coming to gawp at the people of the Khyber and finding herself stranded. There was a much more bizarre and perhaps compassionate reason for this particular *ferringhi* to be presenting herself at the gates of his village. He nodded and offered Laura his hand.

'Suleiman,' he introduced himself. 'And I speak English quite well, actually. I went to Harrow and Cambridge, you know.'

Laura was greatly taken aback. She hadn't expected to find that the head man of the village would be the product of an English public school and university. She put aside her astonishment and grasped his outstretched hand firmly and confidently.

'Laura Roberts. Very pleased to meet you Mr Suleiman. If I may explain, my husband, Keith Roberts, was out here on business and he was killed. His body has gone missing and nobody seems to be doing anything about it, so I came here to look for him.'

It was Suleiman's turn to be taken aback.

'Well, in that case, Mrs Roberts, welcome to *hamara khel*. You must come in and we'll see what is to be done.'

He led Laura and Johal into the compound. Laura gazed around in wonder at the many mud-rendered houses and the narrow, winding passageways which ran between them. Small, well-fed children and scrawny chickens scampered out of their way, whilst women came to their doorways to stare at Laura. Suleiman led them to what seemed to be the only two-storey house within the compound and bade them enter. Laura noticed that her host kicked off his shoes outside the door before entering, so she and Johar followed suit.

'Please, take a seat,' he said, 'and we will have some tea whilst we consider your predicament.'

Laura sat on the well upholstered sofa and gazed around in wonder at the surprisingly sumptuous interior. From outside, the earth-coloured dwelling had given no hint that it might be so well-appointed inside. There were paintings adorning the walls, mainly ancestral portraits and a couple of military battle scenes, and there were stylish ceramic lamps placed on small rosewood tables. There were also rugs and cushions, rather a lot of cushions. A woman, whom Laura took to be in her seventies, now appeared. She had the same aquiline nose and light hazel eyes as Suleiman and Laura guessed she would be his mother. Suleiman asked her to bring their guests some tea. That much, Laura understood.

'Have you had lunch?' Suleiman asked.

Laura hadn't even had any breakfast, and she detected the most wonderful aroma of cooking coming from the back of the house.

'No, we left Peshawar quite early this morning,' she told him. 'We got diverted by an army road block at Cherat.'

'Then you must eat with us,' he insisted, and he spoke again with the woman, who duly returned to the kitchen.

The woman was soon back with a tray on which there was a silver tea pot. To Laura's relief, there was a matching jug of milk, a silver tea strainer and stand, and the sugar was in a silver sugar bowl and not in the teapot. There was also a plate of English-style custard cream biscuits, and the woman offered the plate to Laura. Laura actually hated custard creams, but she was so hungry she took one and consumed it gratefully. She didn't know whether Suleiman's mother would also speak English, but she thanked her in English.

'You're welcome, Dear,' the woman replied, in English.

'I'm Laura,' she smiled at the woman.

'Fatima,' the woman returned her smile before disappearing off once again to the kitchen.

Over tea, Suleiman enquired as to what had befallen their transport, and Johar explained about the *bay vakoof* in the lorry without brakes, and the heap of rocks and his own deformed wheel and twisted axle shaft. Suleiman assured him he would send someone to retrieve the taxi and he would arrange to have it repaired. Johar lamented the fact that parts would have to be obtained from the Suzuki dealers in Islamabad, or maybe even from Japan, and that could take days, or maybe weeks.

'Not necessarily,' his host told him. 'Around here, everyone's a mechanic. We'll send any damaged bits over to the machine shops in Dara Adam Khel. Those Afridis have been manufacturing guns for a couple of hundred years or more. If they can copy a Kalashnikov, they can straighten a wheel. Any parts they can't fix, they'll duplicate. Anyway, Mrs Roberts, tell me what happened to your husband.'

Laura recounted the sorry tale about her husband's unexpected demise, about the wrong body turning up in Stockport, and the conflicting accounts of the cause of Keith's death as given by the undertaker and hotel managers. She didn't mention Markham and Hopgood, or Sophie Benoit. She didn't trust any of them, and she didn't want anyone telling them where she was. In any case, she felt she might evince more sympathy and co-operation from Suleiman if he thought she was a helpless widow and lone traveller. If he learned that, back at her hotel, she had a diplomatic escort and a company executive who was financing her quest, Suleiman might not feel quite so inclined to assist her.

'So, the body that turned up in England had been shot?' he summed up, 'and it now looks as though your husband also had been shot prior to his having a heart attack, and you believe it was because of something that happened in Cherat?'

'Yes,' she agreed, 'and there doesn't seem to have been any reason for him to have been in Cherat. He often visited Pakistan but, as far as I'm aware, he always stayed in Peshawar and visited a tobacco company in the city of Nowshera. At least, that's what he told me.'

'Hmm,' Suleiman was thoughtful. 'We did hear about some incident which took place up at Cherat recently. It wouldn't have been the first such shoot-out up there. Probably the army and some local Taliban. I'll see what I can find out about it. In the meantime, you must accept my hospitality and stay in my house.'

'Oh, that's very kind of you, Mr Suleiman. I would hate to impose ...'

The *Sardar* raised a finger.

'Not at all,' Suleiman insisted. 'To us Pashtuns, it is *nang* – a matter of honour. According to our cultural beliefs, we must offer *nanawatai,* or asylum to those in trouble. I am also obliged, as headman of this village, to offer you *helmestia* – our very best hospitality.'

'Thank you, Mr Suleiman. I am very grateful.'

'Please, Mrs Roberts, just call me Suleiman.'

'And do call me Laura.'

CHAPTER TWENTY-THREE

Luke Greenwood closed his office door and, using his secure line, dialled Adrian Curtis's office in the Counter-espionage section at Thames House. Adrian didn't immediately recognise the caller's number on the digital display.

'Adrian? It's Luke Greenwood.'

'Luke, old chap. How are you?'

'Splendid, thanks. Just calling to thank you once again for lending me your staff. They're doing a wonderful job by the way.'

'Good. It's useful for them to have a change of scenery and to see how you do things up there.'

'Young Mr Kohli, in particular, is doing splendid work. He's cultivated a local CHIS, and that CHIS has identified a major recruiter of young men locally. The recruiter is an Afghan, or at least he claims to be, and Kirpal's been posing as a Muslim when meeting with him. We think the locals are being sent overseas to become mercenaries. You've heard of The Borodin Group, I presume?'

'Indeed, I have. So, you believe there's Russian involvement? Does Kirpal know where the mercenaries are being sent?'

'It looks like they're being sent to Pakistan, to a training camp up in the tribal territories. Kirpal offered to get himself recruited, but I told him I couldn't agree to that. However, he's come up with a much better plan of his own and it seems to be working. He's gained the local target's trust. It's the first major lead we've had on *Trebor* and we'd like to get a handle on others in the network.'

'*Trebor*?'

'Yes, *Operation Trebor*. That's what we've been calling the steady disappearance of young men, mainly Muslims, from this area. We believe they've been enticed with promises of well-paid jobs in the new Islamic Emirate of Afghanistan. Instead, though, they end up fighting somewhere else in the region. We're not sure exactly who it is they're fighting or where, and, so far, none of them has come back. Their families are deeply concerned, as you can imagine.'

Adrian frowned, 'Luke, if this recruiter is connected to The Borodin Group, well, they're a pretty brutal outfit. Nothing's off limits to them. They execute prisoners of war, and they mistreat the locals wherever they're based. They even shoot their own wounded. Kirpal won't be in any danger, will he?'

'No. He should be safe enough here in Lancs. He assures me he's had undercover training and he's certainly put that to good use here. He's also going to take a look at a local travel agent whom we believe is part of the set-up.'

'You won't be sending Kirpal out to Pakistan or anything, will you?'

'Absolutely not, Adrian. But coincidentally, someone you know will be going out there very soon and he'll be keeping his eyes and ears open on our behalf.'

'Who's that?'

'D'you remember Steve Jeffreys? Took medical retirement from Thames House around ten years back.'

'Steve Jeffreys? Yes, I remember him well. Brave fellah. Got badly wounded in Northern Ireland, didn't he? Is he back on the firm's payroll again?'

'No. He's still retired, but he asked for our help. A friend of his recently died in Pakistan in mysterious circumstances. The friend's wife paid to have her husband's body repatriated but the body they sent back wasn't her husband's. And, what's more, the man in the coffin turns out to have been shot dead. Well, the widow insisted on flying out to Pakistan to find out what happened to her husband.'

'Good heavens! That's weird.'

'Oh, it gets even weirder, Adrian. Seems Vauxhall Cross are involved somehow. Anyway, Steve wants to go out there to make sure she doesn't get into any trouble, so we've fast-tracked a Pakistani visa application for him.'

'That's very sporting of you, Old Man.'

'Well, we can do even better than that for a former colleague. We can fix him up with a cut-price local travel agent – the same one Kirpal's looking at.'

'Ah, I see. Killing two birds with one stone, eh? I like it.'

Having updated Adrian, Luke called Kirpal into his office and closed the door again.

'Well, Adrian's as pleased as I am at the progress you've made with Gulabzai. Are you certain you're comfortable to continue with this? Only I'll be held personally responsible if anything happens to you.'

'I'll be fine, boss. As my mum always says, 'you have two good legs, *betaji*, so, if the bad boys come after you, you can always run away'.'

'That's the spirit. Now then, anything turned up on this Sitara Travel?'

'Yes. I'm going to visit them on the pretext of pricing flights to

Pakistan. Jo's been looking into them, too. They're based in Blackburn. The tickets offered to Gulabzai's young men are very cheap indeed. It looks like their travel is being subsidised by someone, or by some organisation. Jo is liaising with Blackburn CID. We'll see whether they know anything about Sitara Travel and its proprietor.'

'Good. Harry is arranging for a retired colleague of ours, Steve Jeffreys, to pay a visit to Sitara Travels, as well. Unlike you, he really is planning to fly to Pakistan. It would be helpful if you could keep in touch with him whilst he's out there. He's a highly experienced man and his experience could be useful to us. But he's also been medically retired a few years now, and, also unlike you, *betaji*, he doesn't have two good legs.'

Back at his desk, Kirpal removed a paper napkin from his jacket pocket and unfolded it. He glanced at the telephone number scrawled on the napkin then picked up the receiver of his desk phone and dialled the number. Moments later, he was connected to an extension at Heron House in Manchester.

'Yazz? It's Kirpal. Kirpal Kohli.'

He smiled to himself and looked around to ensure there was no-one else within earshot.

'I wondered if you fancied meeting up for dinner one night this week? You could tell me more about Zoroastrianism... You do? That's great... Would this Friday be okay?... Great.'

He was suddenly aware that Jo had appeared and was watching him. She had a big grin on her face.

'What?' he said, defensively, as he put the phone down.

'Oh, nothing,' Jo said. 'Just wondering if you'd heard from Yasmeen.'

'I might have done,' he replied cagily. 'Have you heard from Blackburn CID?'

'Yes. Sitara Travel is flagged up with them. It's early days in their investigation, but it looks like Tanvir Ahmed, the man who owns the agency, is associated with some of the principals in a major people smuggling network which Blackburn are investigating. They'd be grateful to know anything you might find out about Sitara Travel and its operation.'

'Sure thing. I'll see what I can dig up. But ... here, are you all right?'

He saw Jo had suddenly closed her eyes tightly and was massaging her temples with her fingertips.

'Yes, just got a thumping headache. It seems to come on each morning as soon as I arrive in the office. You know, it might indeed be the fluorescent lighting in here, or the chemicals on the carpets. You haven't got anything have you, for headaches, I mean?'

'As a matter of fact, I have,' Kirpal reached inside his jacket and pulled out his wallet. From it, he took a bubble pack of aspirin. 'Yes, here you are.'

'Ah, you're a lifesaver, Kirpal. Thanks.'

Jo drained the last of her tea in her cup to help the aspirin go down.

'My dad's GP told him he believes everyone over fifty should carry a pack of aspirin with them, in case of heart attacks or strokes,' Kirpal explained. 'Since then, my mum insists we all carry them, too. I keep telling her I'm too young to have a stroke, but you know what mums are like. Anything to keep her happy.'

'Well, I'm very grateful. You should always listen to your mother, Kirpal.'

It was Suleiman's mother who, with a gentle knock on the bedroom door, awoke Laura from what was the best night's sleep she'd had in weeks. Fatima carried a tea tray which she placed down upon the bedside chest.

'Bed tea, Laura,' she smiled. 'How did you sleep?'

'Wonderfully well, thank you, Fatima. Oh, tea in bed. How very kind you are. I never get tea in bed at home. Never will, now, I suppose.'

Laura pulled herself up into a sitting position, as Fatima poured the tea into a china cup, added some milk and handed her the cup and saucer. This was another local custom she had forgotten about. In this part of the world, the concept of 'bed tea', introduced by the Victorians in the days of the Raj, still persisted. She'd been surprised to be awoken by guest house staff during her travels in India as they, too, had continued this early morning ritual of the British upper classes.

Glancing at her watch, Laura was shocked to see it wasn't actually early morning. It was gone ten-thirty. She never slept this long normally. She now felt deeply embarrassed to have slept in. What would her hosts think of her? She began to apologise, but Fatima silenced her with a wave of her hand.

'It is no matter, Laura. After all, you've had a stressful time. Now, Nasreen showed you where you can shower, didn't she?' Fatima asked.

'Yes, she did, thanks. You've all been so very kind to me. Nasreen is your daughter-in-law, is that right?'

'Yes. And Parvaiz, the younger one is my other daughter-in-law.'

'Oh, so you have two sons?'

'No, only one. Suleiman has two wives, Nasreen and Parvaiz.'

Laura's surprised expression prompted Fatima to explain further.

'We are Shia Muslims, you see. Many Shia men take two wives.'

'Oh, I see. Well, Suleiman is a lucky man. They're beautiful young women.'

'Yes, they are, beautiful and dutiful. And each has her own house here in the village, but Suleiman lives here with me. Oh, by the way, Suleiman and Johar towed Johar's taxi to Dara Adam Khel this morning. The Afridis say they say they can fix it. Hopefully, it will only take a couple of days. Suleiman has now gone up to Cherat to make some enquiries about your husband.'

'Oh, how very kind of him. Will I get to meet *your* husband, Fatima?'

Fatima sighed and sat down on the edge of the bed.

'No, sadly not. He passed away a few years ago. That's why Suleiman had to leave his career in the city of London and come back to take up his duties as *Sardar*.'

'Ah, I'm sorry. So, we're both widows, then.'

'Indeed. So, how many sons do you have Laura?'

'No sons. I have a daughter, Beth. She lives in Canada with her husband. I don't get to see her very often. But, look, I hope Suleiman won't be in danger in Cherat. I understand there's been some trouble up there.'

'He'll be fine. Well, I'll leave you to your tea, Laura. When you are ready, come downstairs and you and I will eat together.'

Fatima departed and Laura stretched out her legs, sank back into the comfortable pillows and drank some of the tea. She had no idea why she'd slept so well or so long. Last evening, Fatima and her daughters-in-law had cooked them all a wonderful meal, comprising a fragrant spiced beef dish, and *alu methi*, which Laura learned was potatoes flavoured with aromatic dried fenugreek leaves. This was accompanied by a cooling yoghurt and cucumber raita and some buttered tandoori breads. Then, exhausted, she had gone to sleep in a room which had scented rattan blinds, through which the cool night breezes permeated. How very different this was from the soulless Inter-con, she thought.

As she sipped at her tea, she reflected that she had achieved very little, so far, in her search for Keith, and the way forward was far from clear. Yet she had felt so very relaxed here, as if she were amongst friends. From Johar's brief description of the fierce Bangash people who lived in their fortified villages, she had expected the *Sardar* and his family to be very traditional, rural types, unsophisticated, perhaps. She now realised that was far from the case. Pakistan was a most surprising place, she thought, a place where appearances were deceptive, a place where visitors should abandon their pre-conceptions. She finished her tea and climbed out of bed. Walking over to the window, she rolled up the rattan blinds to let in the late morning sun.

Taking out the mobile phone which Steve had lent her, she tapped out a quick text message to him.

'Have ditched Laurel & Hardy pro tem. Am staying with a nice family in village Hamara Khel, KPK. Laura'.

Attaching the mobile to its solar charger, she placed it on the sunny window sill to re-charge, then she went to shower and dress.

Nasreen and Parvaiz had already eaten and had gone back to their respective houses in the compound by the time Laura appeared downstairs. She and Fatima sat down together to eat a brunch of Fatima's freshly made chappatis with some of the *alu methi* left over from the night before, and more tea.

'Come,' Fatima said, when they had finished eating. 'Let me show you around *hamara khel*.'

CHAPTER TWENTY-FOUR

Back in Cheshire, it was only eight o'clock in the morning and, still clad in pyjamas and dressing gown, Steve Jeffreys was sitting in his kitchen enjoying his first cup of tea of the day when he received Laura's text. He tried to call her back but there was no reply. He decided he would try again later. This morning, he would need to begin packing some light clothes for his trip to Pakistan. He knew shorts would not be appropriate, and not just for local, cultural reasons.

He glanced down at his thigh, at the purple scar which extended from just above his knee and on up under his pyjama shorts. The scar was a deeply indented one, where a chunk of his flesh had been removed during emergency surgery a decade ago. He could still recall the pain he had experienced that morning in north Belfast, when the violence of the thirty-year conflict had erupted once again, during the mis-named era of peace in the province. When the mortar had exploded and a large shard of red-hot metal had embedded itself in his thigh, the pain had been so intense, and the odour of burning flesh so nauseating, he had passed out cold.

He recalled there had been no official warning beforehand,

though he had been tipped off by one of his own informants and had raised the alarm. He had got there just in time to help the police clear the streets and search the area. They had managed to evacuate the last of the children from the nearby school minutes before the device had exploded. No-one had been killed but a constable was maimed for life in the blast. And, of course, Steve himself had been left with a permanent injury. Yes, it had hurt like the devil, but what had hurt him even more was the pain of giving up a career he had loved. They had offered him a desk job, naturally, but it wouldn't have been the same. He had reluctantly accepted the offer of medical retirement. He greatly missed the job he had lost. However, retiring early had at least given him a few years to spend with his wife, Viv, before he had lost her, too.

His leg still gave him trouble, of course, especially in rainy weather like today's. He thought it might ease up in Peshawar's warmer, drier climate. He hoped it would, since he would be no good to Laura with a stiff and painful leg. He popped a painkiller into his mouth, knocking it back with a sip of his tea, then he picked up his passport from the kitchen table and looked at his photo. The photo had been taken only months earlier when he had renewed his passport, and it was an old man he saw looking back at him. Gone was the energetic idealist; the experienced operational intelligence officer who had feared nothing. He wondered if this sixty-year-old man in the passport photo, this shadow of his former self, would be up to the task of supporting Laura. He told himself his experience had to count for something, and he couldn't leave Laura to pursue her quest alone. For, despite her two escorts, whose motives he deeply mistrusted, he suspected she really was alone.

An hour later, showered and dressed, Steve set off for the funeral parlour in Stockport. Once inside, he explained to the receptionist why he was there and she bade him take a seat whilst she discussed his request with Mr Burgess. While he waited, he grimaced at the cloying scent of the lilies. Why was it always lilies, he wondered? Why not something sweetly scented, like roses, or even dried lavender? Soon, Burgess appeared.

'Good morning. It's Mr ...?' Burgess enquired.

'Roberts. Steve Roberts,' he lied. 'I understand my sister-in-law was quite distressed when she came here to view my brother's remains. She told me she didn't think it was my brother. I find it hard to accept that the wrong body might have been brought back, so, before we start making any fuss, I'd like to see for myself.'

'Oh, I do apologise for the confusion, Mr Roberts. In all my years in this profession, nothing like this has ever occurred. Mrs Roberts was convinced that the ... er ... gentleman we have here isn't her husband, and we've been in contact with the undertakers in Pakistan, but, as yet, we haven't had a response from them. But, if you think she might have been mistaken, since you're his brother, of course you may see him. Would you give us a few minutes to make him presentable?'

'Yes, of course. Thank you.'

Steve took a seat and waited again. Eventually, Burgess returned and escorted him into the viewing area. Steve gazed at the man in the coffin. It certainly wasn't Keith Roberts. Indeed, it wasn't anything like him. This was the corpse of a much younger man. The ashen face was that of a man in his twenties, and the thick black hair and eyebrows were clearly not those of his fifty-eight-year-old friend and next-door-neighbour. He turned to Burgess

'Mr Burgess, I'm quite shocked. Laura was right. This isn't my brother. Unlike you, I'm not used to seeing dead people and ... actually ... I suddenly feel unwell. I don't suppose I could trouble you for a glass of water, could I?' Steve clutched at his chest and headed for a nearby chair.

'Oh goodness! Yes, of course,' the undertaker agreed and he dashed off to the staff kitchen.

As soon as Burgess had withdrawn, Steve took out his camera phone and, stepping back to the coffin, he took several photos of the dead man's face, both full face and in profile. Steeling himself, he quickly pulled aside the satin shroud which enveloped the corpse and made a rapid and cursory visual examination of the body.

Setting aside the revulsion he felt as his fingers briefly brushed against the dead man's ice cold and very dry skin, Steve observed the wounds, at least three of them, with the unmistakable spattering of gunshot residue on the clothing around them. This told him the man had probably been shot at fairly close range. To Steve, that suggested execution. Satisfied that he now knew as much about the dead man as he would ever know, short of learning his identity, he quickly rearranged the shroud and sat down again just as Burgess re-appeared.

'Thank you,' he took the glass and sipped the water. 'I do apologise. I should have had breakfast before I came out.'

'I'm so dreadfully sorry,' the undertaker looked almost as mortified as the man in the coffin. 'I do assure you that we are doing all we can to rectify matters. Hopefully it won't be too long before we retrieve your brother's remains.'

'I hope so, too. Thank you, Mr Burgess,' Steve said, and he handed back the glass and left.

Back in his car, Steve tried several times more to call Laura. He got a ringing tone, but no-one answered. He was a little concerned now. He needed to book his flight to Pakistan, and the sooner the better. Starting up his car, he programmed the co-ordinates he'd been given into his satnav and headed off towards the M60.

It was almost midday when Steve arrived in Burtby. Parking up outside The Pepper Mill, he headed into the restaurant. He spotted Harry seated with Kirpal at a table in a far corner and went over to join him. The delicious aroma of grilled steak emanating from the kitchen reminded him he really hadn't had any breakfast that morning, just a couple of cups of tea and his painkillers.

'Steve, this is my colleague, Kirpal. Kirpal, Steve Jeffreys,' Harry introduced them. 'Can I get you anything, Steve? A coffee, or a proper drink, maybe?'

'Actually, I'm absolutely starving. Are you chaps planning on lunching here? If so, I'll order something too. Have you eaten here? Is there anything you'd recommend?'

They assured him they had indeed eaten there several times since they had arrived in the north west. Harry said he would definitely recommend the steaks.

'Have you heard from your friend, Mrs Roberts?' Harry asked, once they had placed their orders. 'Is she okay?'

'Well, last I heard from her was that she'd ditched Markham and Hopgood. She doesn't know who they really work for, but she knows they were going to great lengths to obstruct her, so she's struck out on her own. She seems to be staying with a family in a village somewhere in the Khyber area. So, just as soon as I book my flight, I'll get out there and see what's really going on. Now then, what's the deal with this travel agent you want me to use?'

'They should get you a good deal on a ticket,' Kirpal assured him, 'but intel suggests they're also involved in people smuggling.'

'What, from Pakistan to UK, you mean?'

'Oddly enough, in both directions, it seems,' Harry explained. 'They're under investigation by local CID and it's known they have contacts with people who provide stolen documentation. This documentation is used by the individuals they're bringing into the UK. The passports and identity cards are genuinely issued but some have been falsified, you know, with substituted photos.

In some cases, though, they simply match up the passports with people who look like the real document holders. They wouldn't pass muster at UK passport controls, but the documents only have to be good enough to get the migrants into Europe via Turkey. Once in eastern Europe they're smuggled to UK by clandestine means.'

'Clandestine means?'

'Hidden in freight lorries or commercial containers,' Harry explained. 'The travel agency owner, Tanvir Ahmed, is associated with a local mill owner. The mill ceased operating years ago and, nowadays, it's used for goods storage. We believe it's also used to store people – a sort of clearing house, until the inbound illegals can be re-distributed around the country.'

'So that's the story with the immigrants,' Steve said, 'but who is it that they're pushing in the opposite direction?'

'Well, CID are concerned with both the in-bound *and* outbound clandestines. They believe that, using the same routes and methods, individuals who are wanted on arrest warrants are being smuggled out of the UK. Instead of taking out empty lorries in order to bring them back full, they carry human cargo on the outbound journey as well.'

'Makes good commercial sense,' Steve nodded.

'However, we believe there's also a third aspect to their activities. We think they're also using the more usual air routes out of the UK to export local youths, young men of fighting age. They provide them with cheap air tickets, on the pretext of getting them lucrative employment overseas, but we believe they end up being used as mercenaries.'

'I guess they don't all make it back, then?' Steve asked.

'No, Steve. None of them has, so far. And their families want answers.'

. . .

Later that afternoon, Luke Greenwood received a call from reception and headed off downstairs. A few moments later, he was back, accompanied by two men wearing visitors' passes.

'CPNI,' he announced to everyone in the section. 'Just the usual routine inspection. Stand by your beds.'

'Who?' Jo asked Harry.

'They're from the Centre for the Protection of National Infrastructures,' Harry informed her.

'The bug hunters,' Kirpal added.

Jo still looked baffled.

'They're the guys who check out the security of our buildings,' Harry explained. 'They regularly sweep for bugs and make sure no-one's using inappropriate devices which might compromise security, that sort of thing.'

'Ah,' Jo laughed. 'When Kirpal said 'bug hunters' I pictured the school nit nurse. Remember? Nitty Norah, the head explorer?'

'God, yes,' Harry laughed. 'I'd forgotten her, and the indignity of those regular examinations for head lice.'

'And remember how they always told us it was no shame if you had them, 'cause the nits preferred the cleanest heads?' Kirpal recalled. 'Back then, wearing a turban was my best defence against the little critters.'

The two CPNI men didn't seem that interested in the staff's individual work stations, and certainly not in their scalps. They immediately took out small yellow meters and began walking around the open plan office, holding the meters aloft and checking their readings. Just moments later, they and Luke Greenwood disappeared into Luke's office. Harry, Kirpal and Jo glanced across and could see, through the glass partition, that Luke and the CPNI men seemed to be in rather earnest discussion. Moments later, Luke emerged and called out to everyone.

'Okay, everyone. I want you all to head down to FC1 immediately. Leave what you're doing and log out of your computers.

Everyone out now. Quick as you can. And take your coats, handbags, wallets, car keys. Don't leave any valuables or personal stuff behind, as you might not be coming back up here again today.'

Despite their bafflement, all the staff reacted immediately. Desktop computers were switched off, drawers locked, and jackets, coats and handbags snatched, as everyone shuffled out of the office towards the lifts and stairs. Everyone, that was, except the two CPNI men and Luke. Harry noticed Luke heading back into his own office, where he closed his door and began to lower the metal blinds at the glass partition which separated his room from the main office.

'What's going on?' Kirpal asked.

'Dunno,' Sue Shaw shrugged. 'Could be a drill of some kind. We've had them before, though usually they want us to muster outside in the car park.'

'Where's FC1?' Harry asked.

'It's in the basement. Follow me and I'll show you,' Sue said, avoiding the queues for the lifts and leading the three attachees down the stairs. 'It's probably a routine precaution, whilst the CPNI chaps make their inspection. I'm sure there's no need to worry.'

When they got there, they saw FC1 wasn't so much a room as a basement of warehouse proportions. They were amongst the first to arrive but, soon, more and more staff began to stream in. Harry was puzzled by the fact that the room number didn't seem to follow the same sequence as that of other rooms in the building.

What does FC1 stand for?' he asked Sue.

It's Faraday Cage, level one,' she explained. There are more levels below this one.'

'Is that like the Faraday Box I keep my car keys in at home?' Kirpal asked.

'Sort of,' Sue said, but she didn't seem inclined to expand on that explanation.

'We're not under attack or anything, are we?' Jo asked.

'Good heavens, no. I expect they just want us out of the way whilst they check everything.'

However, Jo's fears were nearer to the truth than any of them could imagine. Back upstairs, Luke quickly dialled the Thames House extension of his Director General, Helena Fairbrother. Helena had Adrian Curtis in her office to discuss staff appraisal reports, and they were having coffee together as she took the call.

'Luke. Hello. How's thing's up there?' she asked. 'How are the Thames House staff getting on?'

'Helena,' Luke said getting straight to the point. 'We've got a serious problem up here.'

Helena sat forward and put down her coffee cup. She could hear the urgency in Luke's voice.

'What sort of problem?'

'The CPNI chaps are here. They've been conducting tests to see if there's anything in the structure of our building which might be responsible for our staff falling sick.'

'And ... I take it they've found something?'

'Yes. What they've found is something very serious indeed. We're going to have to evacuate immediately.'

'Do you want to call me back from a safe place?'

'It's okay. I'm safe for the moment. I'm in my inner office with the metal blinds down. As soon as I've finished speaking to you, I'll go and get the staff away from the building. Not sure where we'll go, though.'

'Why? What've they found?'

Adrian drained his coffee and placed his cup and saucer back on the desk. He could tell from Helena's expression, as well as from her side of the conversation, that something very serious was occurring. He prayed it wasn't anything to do with Kirpal's part in *Op Trebor*. Soon, Helena ended the call with a request to be kept informed. She looked grave.

'The CPNI are up at our Northern HQ. Luke Greenwood says they've found dangerously high levels of radiation in the building,' she explained.

'Good God! What sort of radiation?'

'They say it's super high frequency microwave energy.'

'What, like you get from smart phones and Wi-Fi routers?'

'Yes, but much stronger than that. It's the kind you get from satellites or phone masts, but at even higher levels than those, and it's not emanating from anything within the building. It's being directed in from some external source.'

'I don't like the sound of that.'

'The way they've explained it to Luke is that the recommended upper limit for exposure to microwave radiation is one microwatt. The readings CPNI are getting are between six hundred and a thousand microwatts. But it could be more than that. The CPNI engineers' meters aren't capable of registering levels beyond that.'

Adrian was horrified.

'So, they suspect this is some sort of hostile activity?'

'Yes. It looks like our northern colleagues are under attack.'

'Bloody hell!'

CHAPTER TWENTY-FIVE

The very next morning saw a number of concerned officials gathered in the Cabinet Office Briefing Room in Whitehall. The meeting of the Civil Contingencies Committee, more generally known as 'COBRA' – shorthand for 'Cabinet Office Briefing', the 'A' being added by a fan of the beer, ostensibly to make it easier to pronounce – was to be chaired by the Prime Minister, who was expected to join them imminently. Since the Cabinet Office backed onto Downing Street, Ivan Thompson had only to leave his PM's office in Number Ten and head through the internal door into the adjoining Cabinet Office building.

'Bad business, this,' Sir Robert Vanbrugge, the MI6 chief, told Helena, while they waited. 'How many of your people have been affected?'

'It's hard to say, Bob, since the symptoms are many and varied. There's almost a dozen signed off sick now, and there's a few more working wounded. It's hard to know who might simply have developed tinnitus or memory problems naturally, and how many have actually been affected by the microwave business.'

The baize-padded door opened suddenly and the PM strode in. Taking his seat, and with an air of authority, slamming his big, black conference folder on the table, he galloped straight to the point.

'So, who has the technical details on this?' he demanded.

'I do,' Helena said. 'A significant number of staff working at our Northern HQ up in Lancashire have been affected by a directed energy source. Around a dozen have now fallen ill, some of them seriously. A couple of them seem to have developed symptoms akin to dementia.'

'So, are we thinking this is down to that ... Havana Syndrome?' Thompson asked.

'Almost certainly,' Helena confirmed.

'We know that the Russians and the Chinese have acquired a new micro-auditory weapon known as Medusa,' Sir Robert Vanbrugge added, 'and this is what we believe may have been responsible.'

'Medusa?' the PM looked doubtful. 'What, like the Gorgon?'

'Well, that's what the Americans have christened it, apparently. You see they invented the technology and the Chinese stole it and developed their own weapon based on the US design. They've sold Medusa on to the Russians and the North Koreans.'

'Why Medusa?' the PM asked.

'The Americans say Medusa stands for 'Mob Excess Deterrent Using Silent Audio',' Vanbrugge answered. 'I know, it's horribly contrived and clunky, but we don't actually know what the Russians and Chinese call it, since they won't admit to having it. The Chinese have used it successfully against mass demonstrations in Hong Kong, and the Americans think it has been directed against their CIA staff, both overseas and in Washington, with devastating effects on their health.'

'So, how does it work?' Thompson asked.

'By directing very high frequency microwaves, either widely into a crowd in order to deter them from gathering, or more narrowly towards an individual. Mostly, the targets hear an intense and painful noise. The effect it has initially is to repel the targets, to make them withdraw from the area. Long term exposure, however, causes brain damage, especially when it's a concentrated beam directed at an individual or a small group of individuals. The damage could be temporary, or it could be permanent, depending on the concentration and duration of exposure.'

'What kind of damage are we talking about?' Thompson asked.

'Many of the Americans believed to have been targeted are suffering effects ranging from confusion, sleeplessness, tinnitus and memory loss, to full-blown dementia. It can cause long-term neurological damage and behavioural issues.'

'But couldn't this have been caused by some internal source,' Thompson asked, 'such as microwave ovens or smart phones?'

'Over time and to a lesser degree, yes,' Vanbrugge said, 'but to have caused such major effects so quickly, the level of the energy has to be massive. The CPNI engineers have found the MI5 building up at Burtby is being bombarded by sound waves over a thousand times in excess of safe levels, and, more significantly, they are being directed from outside the building, not from within. This is a targeted and hostile attack.'

'But who would be behind this? I mean, what would the Chinese have to gain from attacking MI5 staff?' Ivan asked.

It was Sir Henry Mortimer, the bespectacled, pin-striped suited Cabinet Office Permanent Secretary, who answered.

'Well, I don't think you can blame this one on the Chinese or, indeed, on the cat. Surely, it's more likely to have been the Russians.'

'But why would Putin do such a thing?' Thompson was sceptical.

'Because he can,' Sir Henry said. 'Why would he send a military intelligence thug to blackmail a British prime minister? Because he can.'

Thompson blanched. He knew Sir Henry was referring to an incident two or three years earlier when a particularly nasty Russian calling himself WOTAK had tried to blackmail Thompson over his shady business dealings. The Cabinet Office Secretary had offered to have WOTAK dealt with by UK intelligence, in return for a few little considerations in favour of the Civil Service. For this, Thompson would be forever in Sir Henry's debt. He was clearly irritated, however, that Sir Henry had brought this up again now.

Sir Henry glanced across at Helena Fairbrother and winked. He and she were the only people around the table who knew that it hadn't been the Russians who had been behind the blackmail threats. In fact, it had been Helena's head of counter-espionage, Adrian Curtis. Sir Henry pushed his advantage further.

'And we've now learned that the components of the drone which blew up at Number Ten were Russian made. They're clearly perpetrating some very hostile acts against us – against you, Prime Minister.'

'Well, how on earth could the Russians be directing this Medusa beam?' Thompson countered. 'Surely, it couldn't come from Moscow? From outer space, perhaps, or from a satellite? I dunno, it all sounds a bit like a Dan Dare death ray to me. Aren't we venturing into the realms of comic book fiction, here?'

'Not at all,' the MI6 chief insisted. 'We know the technology exists. And it could indeed come from a satellite, but I suspect the source is much nearer to home. The Medusa is a large but portable device, and it doesn't need a big power source. The Americans have evidence that the Russians mount their Medusa weapons in vehicles which can simply be driven to where their targets are located and then parked up nearby.'

'That's right,' Helena agreed. 'Moscow citizens protesting

against the invasion of the Crimea weren't surprised to see police vans parked up near their demonstrations, but they wouldn't have known whether there was a Medusa on board. Our northern HQ is situated on an industrial estate. There could be any number of factory units or vehicles close by which could house a Medusa weapon. CPNI are checking out the area as fast as they can.'

'Won't that alarm the locals?' Thompson asked. 'It'll draw attention to the location of your northern HQ, won't it?'

'No, Prime Minister,' Helena assured him. 'The CPNI chaps know what they're doing. They carry a variety of IDs. In this case, they're gas inspectors, checking the site for gas leaks, except they're using microwave sensors rather than gas detectors. We've evacuated all the staff from our building already. Ellis Graham has also sent up some of his people from the National Cyber Security Centre, and local CID are involved. Between them, they should be able to track down the source.'

'And, when they do, what can they do to disrupt it?' Thompson asked.

'Well, they can take it out, and arrest whoever's behind it,' Helena said, 'but they're also doing whatever's necessary to make the building impervious to any further such attacks. That's going to be a costly and time-consuming process. In the meantime, I have to find somewhere for a hundred staff members to work.'

Sir Arnold Mayhew, the Director General of GCHQ, readily offered a solution.

'If you can get them all into Manchester, Helena, I'm sure we can make space for them in Heron House, our local HQ. Parking might be the only issue, though.'

'Thank you, Arnold,' Helena nodded. 'That would be ideal. We'll send them into town on the tram system, in relays. It'll attract less attention that way. I'll call Luke Greenwood as soon as we're done here and let him know.'

Sir John Hooper, head of UK Defences, also chipped in.

'We'll get a Gorgoneion up there, too. It'll deflect the microwaves back at the source and help pinpoint it.'

'A Gorgoneion?' Thompson spluttered. 'I know what that is. It's an ancient amulet, isn't it? As in the legend of the Gorgons?'

Helena smiled at the PM's regurgitation of his Oxford classics degree. He'd probably hoped his knowledge of Greek mythology might one day come in useful in his political role. However, today was not that day.

'Gorgoneion is also a device we have in our armoury, Prime Minister,' the Chief of Defence informed him. 'The Americans alerted us about the theft of the Medusa technology, and our own weapons scientists developed a device to counter the worst effects of Medusa attacks. It's a device which deflects the microwave radiation back towards the source. And, since the Americans called their device Medusa, we named our device Gorgoneion, after, as you say, the magic protective amulet worn by the Greek deities.'

'Ah,' Thompson nodded. 'But, wait a minute, why haven't *we* got one of those Medusa things?'

'Because they're very dangerous, and highly unethical,' the Defence Chief explained. 'It's not the sort of weapon we in UK would be comfortable using.'

'Well, that's a typically British response,' the Prime Minister spluttered. 'When I was Mayor of London and I bought German water cannons for tackling London demonstrations, I wasn't even allowed to use them. They had to be scrapped and we lost over three hundred thousand quid on that deal. This Medusa is pretty much the same thing, isn't it? A sort of sonic water cannon.'

'But it's much more dangerous than a water cannon, Prime Minister,' the MI6 chief said. 'Medusa can kill people.'

'That's what they said about my water cannons,' Thompson sulked.

'You'll be pleased to know, though, that CPNI are rolling out monitoring equipment to other Security Service properties and to all the other intelligence agencies' premises,' the MI6 chief assured him. 'RBP is unlikely to be the only building that's being targeted. Others may be under attack right now, or may be targeted in future.'

'Well, so long as they're doing something about it,' the PM said, 'presumably we can all get back to business, now. Today, we've got to discuss arrangements for my visit to Moscow and ...'

'Hardly, Prime Minister,' the Cabinet Office Secretary interrupted. 'I mean, what are *you* going to do about it?'

'What do you mean, Henry?' Thompson looked irritated.

Sir Henry pushed his heavy spectacles further up his red-veined nose and looked directly at the Prime Minister.

'Well, surely, this a deeply serious matter. Number Ten has been bombed, and now the UK's domestic intelligence agency has been subjected to a hostile attack – and not for the first time in recent years. A significant number of Helena's staff have been seriously affected, possibly with life-changing injuries. This is no different from when that bomb was sent to Thames House a couple of years back. Surely, every effort must now be made to identify the hostile state behind this attack and to bring them to book.'

'Yes, of course,' Thompson snapped, 'but we can't start mud-slinging until we know who to sling it at, can we?'

'But you will be issuing a statement to the press, won't you?' Helena asked. 'I mean, we don't have to specify the exact location of the attack, but the public needs to be warned. The Russians aren't just attacking intelligence personnel. They targeted you, and they could target anyone in government next.'

Irritated, Thompson ran his stubby fingers through his unruly, black hair, as he often did whenever he felt he wasn't getting his own way.

'No, I won't be speaking to the press. There's absolutely no need to start spreading fear and gloom. We don't yet know who did this. Anyone could have used a Russian-made drone on Number Ten. We can't even be sure that was an attack on your regional HQ. It could be due to some faulty equipment near the site, or even to some natural phenomenon locally, like the radiation they have in Cornwall's granite. They say that makes people sick, doesn't it? No, it's far too soon to be alarmist about this. Let's wait until we know more about it. Helena, let me have your report on this first thing in the morning.'

Snatching up his big, black folder, which the other COBRA attendees might be forgiven for thinking had been brought along simply for effect, since the Prime Minister hadn't actually opened it, he rose, kicked back his chair and disappeared back through the baize-lined door.

There was a disappointed silence following the PM's departure. Eventually, it was Sir Henry Mortimer who spoke.

'Well, everyone. As I said at our last meeting, prime ministers come and prime ministers go, but some prime ministers stay too long. Damn that cat!'

CHAPTER TWENTY-SIX

It was later that evening when Suleiman arrived back at his village. He had a little news for Laura, which he imparted as they all sat down together for the family's evening meal.

'I went to see my cousin Liaqat,' he explained. 'He has a friend in SOCU.'

'SOCU?' Laura asked.

'The Special Operations and Communications Unit of Zarrar Company. Zarrar is the elite counter-terrorism section of the SSG.'

'Ah, now I know about the SSG,' Laura said. 'That's the Special Service Group of commandoes, isn't it? Johar told me they're known as the maroon berets. We passed their headquarters up at Cherat. In fact, the reason Johar's vehicle got damaged, and the reason we're here is because we got re-directed away from the main road by the SSG's road block.'

'Did you, now? Well, that's interesting, because, a few weeks ago, in early April in fact, there was a major engagement up there. Liaqat told me – in confidence – that some armed dissident group attacked the SSG base at Cherat. It's thought the attackers were TTP.'

'What's TTP?'

'*Tehrik-i-Taliban Pakistan*. They're a particularly nasty Pakistani Taliban group. They're not the same outfit as the Afghan Taliban. In fact, in some respects, they make the Afghan Taliban look like boy scouts. The Pakistani group is backed by Al-Qaeda and is dedicated to setting up its own fundamentalist homeland here in Pakistan's tribal areas. They want to establish their own Islamic emirate right across the Khyber Pakhtunkhwa.'

'God spare us!' Fatima exclaimed.

'He will, Mother. Liaqat heard there was also a unit of foreign nationals fighting alongside the TTP,' Suleiman continued. 'It seems there were many casualties, including some of this foreign brigade, whoever they were. Many of the dead and wounded were abandoned on the hillsides around Cherat.'

'Allah!' Fatima exclaimed.

'Liaqat also says some of the locals looted the site the following day for guns and wristwatches. A few of the foreigners' passports ended up being sold to the document forgers in the smugglers' bazaar at Landi Kotal. He believes some of the passports were British.'

Laura took all this in for a moment. It occurred to her that Keith had died in early April.

'Oh, my God! You don't think my Keith would have been one of the British casualties, do you? I mean ... no, that's ridiculous ... he was fifty-eight years old. He couldn't have been involved in fighting anyone. He wouldn't have been caught up in that ... unless it was by accident.'

'I'm sure you're right, Laura,' Suleiman agreed. 'Liaqat is going to see what else he can find out. We'll know more tomorrow. Anyway, put it out of your mind until we do know. Let us eat, now.'

The meal was most appealing, yet Laura didn't have a great appetite. She couldn't dispel the image of bodies lying on that steep hillside which led down from Cherat. She kept picturing one of those bodies being Keith's. It wouldn't have been such a vivid image, perhaps, if she hadn't already been there and seen those hills for herself. She could picture the scene all too clearly in her mind's eye.

However, she told herself, the idea that Keith might have been running round those shrubby hills, waving a gun and getting himself killed, was just too fantastical. It was so very unlikely. His arthritis wouldn't let him wield a golf club, not that he'd ever felt the slightest inclination to do so. So, it was most unlikely he'd have been brandishing an assault weapon. Then again, if he had died in some sort of guerrilla-style combat, that might explain the fact that his body was missing. Might he still be up on that hillside, being picked apart by crows and vultures? Try as she might, she couldn't stop thinking about it.

After the meal was finished, Fatima declined her houseguest's offer to help with the dishes. Nasreen and Parvaiz saw to the clearing up, then took themselves off to their respective quarters in the compound. As Fatima had explained it to Laura, Suleiman lived with her in the main house, where he had a peaceful bedroom and study, but he paid his wives conjugal visits in their separate quarters whenever he wished. Neither wife would know when or how often he called upon the other, so they would not feel rejected.

Laura had thought this a most curious arrangement, but she recalled a long ago visit to Fatehpur Sikri, the abandoned Indian palace. The palace had a raised marble terrace – the highest in the palace – to which, according to the account given by the tour guide, the Sultan would summon one of his wives to attend his pleasure. The reason he had this canopied platform, set so high up, was so as not to offend the wives who had not been summoned. That, too, had seemed curious to Laura, but at least it seemed a more honest arrangement than her own husband had apparently enjoyed with various women to whom he was not married.

Soon, Fatima too disappeared to attend to her domestic tasks. Suleiman could see Laura was disturbed by the news he had brought.

'Would you like some tea, Laura?' he asked. 'I could make us some. Or some cold milk. Milk is good for making you sleep, and our local milk is very good.'

'No, thank you. A stiff drink would be more use, but this being Pakistan ...'

'Alcohol never solved any problems, Laura.'

'Nor did milk, for that matter. Oh, Suleiman, you and your mother have been so very kind to me, so hospitable. And it's so good of you to make these enquiries on my behalf. I promise you I won't outstay my welcome.'

'You are welcome to stay as long as you need to, Laura.'

'Thank you. But whether I find out what happened to Keith or not, as soon as Johar's taxi is fixed I think I should head back to Peshawar with him. I'm beginning to think it was very foolish of me to come out here and think I could find Keith when the hospital authorities couldn't, and nor could the British Consul in Islamabad. Maybe I should just give up and go home.'

'I'm very impressed that you have already gone to so much trouble to find him. You must have loved him very deeply.'

'Oh, well, I did ... once.'

'Not anymore?' he seemed surprised.

'Well, you see, I think he fell out of love with me a long time ago. He wasn't faithful to me. He had many affairs over the years. It's hard to love someone who doesn't love you.'

'That's true. Yet you came out here, to a place that's virtually a war zone, to try and find him. You must love him just a little bit, Laura?'

Laura shook her head.

'Not love. I don't think so. I think it's more about duty, responsibility. He's the father of my child. He's ...he *was* my husband for the past thirty-odd years. I suppose I owe it to him to find his body and to bring him home. It's the least I can do.'

She saw Suleiman looking at her with admiration in his eyes. However, she didn't feel she deserved his admiration.

'You are ... a very spirited woman, Laura. I admire that. I'm sorry your husband had fallen out of love with you.'

'Well, I'm middle-aged, Suleiman. Men don't love women when they're past their prime.'

'Why, what age are you?'

Laura was taken aback by his rather forthright question. She was torn between being honest in order to evince a little sympathy and wanting to lie for vanity's sake. She laughed.

'My age? Well, let's just say, there's a five in it, and leave it at that, shall we?'

Suleiman laughed, too. He reached out and placed a hand on her cheek, tilting her face up to the lamplight.

'You are still very beautiful, though, Laura. A beautiful *and* spirited woman, whatever her age, is like a bright star in a cloudy night sky. I'm going to kiss you, Laura.'

And he did. It was an unexpected announcement and an even more unexpected gesture, and it didn't leave her much time to react. She knew she could have pushed him away gently without offending him, but there was something rather nice in the warmth of his hand on her cheek, and the light reflected in those hazel eyes, as his handsome face drew near hers. It touched something within her. She felt a fluttering sensation she hadn't felt in years. She suddenly had a random thought, that the Hindi word for 'butterflies' was *kittlien.* The word fluttered into her mind, for that was exactly what she felt – the fluttering of butterflies somewhere deep within her.

She had expected a peck on the cheek, but the light pressure of his lips upon hers increased with pleasing intensity, as his hand slid from her cheek to her neck and caressed it. This was folly! She had no idea why this attractive man, this attractive younger man, with his two beautiful young wives just across the courtyard, waiting to fulfil his every wish, should be kissing a middle-aged English widow. She couldn't fathom why he wanted to kiss her, but, actually, she really didn't care. She only knew she liked it. She liked it very much.

CHAPTER TWENTY-SEVEN

In Blackburn, Kirpal met up once again with his source, Imtiaz Siddiqui, in the same busy café.

'How's it going? Or am I not allowed to ask?' Imtiaz greeted him.

'All I can say is that I'm well in with *Gulab Jamun* and his cronies, thanks to you,' Kirpal told him. 'But have you heard of any other young men going missing, or, indeed, have any come back?'

'Not since we last spoke. But I'm keeping my eyes and ears open. If I do hear anything, I'll give you a call.'

'Thanks. Obviously, we're interested in young men disappearing, but if you hear of any other odd incidents – other people suddenly disappearing, or maybe small groups of people arriving in the community – I'd be interested to hear.'

'Well ...' Imtiaz began, then he shook his head. 'No, I don't think you'd be interested in that.'

'In what?'

'It's just that there's a local bloke who's been missing for a week or so. He's not a youth, though. He's a teacher at the local primary school where me mam teaches, and he didn't turn up for school all last week. Mam said it were odd. No-one's heard from him and the headmistress went around to his house, you know, to see if he were ill or owt, but she got no reply. She knocked on his neighbours' door and they said he'd gone home to Pakistan and he wouldn't be coming back. Thing is, he didn't tell anyone at school. Didn't hand in his notice, neither.'

'That was odd. Did your mum say what his name is?'

'Yeah, Mohammed Mushtaq.'

'Mushtaq, eh? And what about his family? Did they go with him?'

'Oh, he's not married. A bachelor in his forties, according to Mam.'

'So, maybe he went to Pakistan to get married?' Kirpal suggested, pointedly.

'Oh, I don't think so. Mam said he were a confirmed bachelor. I can ask her to let me know if he re-appears,' Imtiaz offered. 'Is there anything else I can help you with?'

'Well, just one thing. Your Urdu will be much better than mine. Would you know what the word *gumrah* means?'

'*Gumrah*? Well, yes. It's not something you'd say to someone's face. It means ... a pervert, like, maybe a paedophile. Why do you ask? Nobody called you that, did they?'

'No, not me,' Kirpal said.

'Oh, you don't mean this Mushtaq fellah, do you? Is that what you're suggesting?'

'Oh, no. I wouldn't suggest anything of the sort, Imtiaz. After all, I don't know the guy.'

Kirpal didn't have to suggest anything. Imtiaz had clearly made the connection for himself.

'Well, if I do hear anything about any *gumrah* in the community, I'll certainly let you know. If somebody were accused of that, they probably would disappear off to Pakistan pretty damned quick, if they knew what was good for them. That's if local folks didn't take matters into their own hands first.'

'How do you mean?'

'Well, he wouldn't be the first child molester to have left for Pakistan in a hurry – allegedly, that is.'

'Allegedly? Why allegedly? Where would they have gone, then?'

'Probably no further than the moors. But that's just conjecture on my part – just the kind of talk one hears around the neighbourhood. '*Gone back to Pakistan*' is sometimes used as a euphemism for someone being taken up ont' moors and not brought down again, if you get my drift.'

Kirpal had little doubt about where Mohammed Mushtaq had gone. He now understood who it was who had been murdered up on the moors, and why. Unpleasant and criminal as it was, it had little to do with *Operation Trebor*. He speculated that Gulabzai and his cohorts might have lured Mushtaq out of town on a promise of sneaking him out of the country, perhaps because there had been some complaints about his behaviour, but Kirpal wouldn't waste any time or sympathy on Mushtaq's fate.

He took his leave of Imtiaz and made his way to Sitara Travel. His excuse for going there was to enquire about the cost of air tickets to Pakistan, not that he had the slightest intention of travelling anywhere away from his home shores, but he wanted to have a look around for himself. As he approached the agency, he was surprised to find Darren and Lee, the two English youths from Gulabzai's study group, coming out.

'Hi,' he greeted them. 'Fancy bumping into you guys here.'

'Hi, Qureshi. We've just booked our flight tickets,' Darren replied.

'Where are you off to, then?'

'We're going to Peshawar in Pakistan, to a training school, then, two weeks later, we're off to Afghanistan – to Kandahar. Do you know it?'

'No, Mate. Never been further east than Leicester. Have either of you been to Kandahar before?' Kirpal asked.

'No, we've never been further than Manchester. But it sounds good, dunnit? Romantic, like. Kandahar. Like *The Arabian Nights* and all that.'

'Yes, I suppose it does. So, did Gulabzai fix you up with work out there?'

'Yeah, we're going to be working as security officers at Kandahar Airport and the pay's great. We'd never have got a job at Manchester Airport, not with our records, and not without qualifications. It's worked out brilliant.'

'Yeah,' his mate Lee echoed. 'It's worked out brilliant.'

'What about you?' Darren asked. 'Is he gonna fix you up with a job?'

'No, Mate,' Kirpal shook his head. 'I've decided to join the ranks of the self-employed. Got a business plan which seems to be working well. But I'm thinking of booking myself a holiday, first. So, when do you guys travel?'

'Thirty-first of May,' Darren waved his Emirates tickets. 'Seven-twenty int' morning. We change in Dubai and again in Peshawar. The tickets were well cheap, an' all. And the travel agent knows someone at the Pakistani embassy. He's gonna get us visas.'

'Well, I wish you both the very best of luck. I hope you enjoy your new careers.'

'Cheers, Mate,' Darren grinned.

'Yeah, cheers,' Lee grinned, and the two lads headed off.

Kirpal made a mental note of the date and time of the youths' travel. He would have to make sure they didn't board that

Emirates plane to Dubai. It would be a big disappointment to them, he knew, but he also knew their optimism was misplaced. They weren't going to be working at Kandahar Airport. They would most likely be travelling out to their deaths. Well, he would have to ensure that didn't happen. His impression of Darren and Lee was that they were a pair of tearaways, and they weren't the sharpest tools in the box, but they didn't deserve to be used as cannon fodder in someone else's war.

Kirpal was welcomed into the travel agency by Tanvir.

'Hello again, Qureshi. What can I do for you?' Tanvir asked as he bade Kirpal take a seat.

'Hamid Gulabzai said you might be able to fix me up with a competitively priced flight to Pakistan next month. I'm thinking of having a little holiday. It'll be my first trip out there, to the place my folks were born.'

'Right, well, nothing's too much trouble for a friend of Gulabzai's. Now, if you let me know which city in Pakistan you want to travel to, and your dates of travel, I'll see if I can get you the best deal.'

Kirpal mentioned Karachi and quoted some dates on which he had no intention of travelling anywhere, and Tanvir tapped all the information into his computer then handed him a printout. Kirpal perused the list of potential flights. The prices quoted were a little less than he would have expected to pay had he booked directly with the airlines concerned, but they were not *that* cheap. He reasoned that was probably because his trip was not part of the same deal the unwitting mercenaries would be getting. This, in itself, was useful intel.

'Okay, well, many thanks for these quotes. I'll need to mull it over and get back to you, all right?'

Tanvir looked a little disappointed that he wasn't going to make a sale right away, but he nodded, yanked open his desk drawer and took out a business card which he handed to Kirpal.

'Here's my card. You can give me a call any time.'

As Kirpal arose and took the business card, he noticed a smartphone sitting in the open desk drawer. It was black and it bore a distinctive large letter 'Q' in grey on the back of the plastic case. He smiled to himself, as he left. As Darren and Lee would have said, so far, everything was working out 'brilliant'.

CHAPTER TWENTY-EIGHT

IT WAS SEVEN-THIRTY IN THE MORNING WHEN PAKISTAN AIRLINES FLIGHT PK 286 from Doha touched down at Peshawar's Bacha Khan airport. Steve Jeffreys experienced no delay clearing immigration. He had supposed that there might be some scrutiny of young foreign males coming to this region during the present unsettled times, but a sixty-year-old, retired British civil servant with a gammy leg attracted no particular attention. For today, at least, his age was in his favour. Emerging from the airport arrivals building, he hailed a taxi and asked to be taken to the Emerald Inter-continental Hotel.

At the hotel reception desk, he was advised it was too early to check in, but the receptionist agreed to store his holdall until his room was ready, and she suggested he could take coffee at the breakfast buffet if he wished. In the hotel's dining room, he helped himself to a coffee and found a quiet table. Taking a seat, he tried to call Laura once again. Her own mobile phone was switched off, as he had suggested it should be, and the phone he had given her continued to ring but still went unanswered. However, he persuaded himself it was too soon to be worried, especially as the last text message he had received from her had sounded upbeat.

Hotel guests began to appear for the breakfast buffet and, eventually, Steve saw the familiar, stocky form of Charles Markham entering the dining room. He was accompanied by a younger, more slightly-built, fair-haired man. This, Steve guessed, would be Martin Hopgood. They hadn't noticed him and so he watched as they helped themselves to food from the buffet. He noted that Markham in particular, had loaded his tray with a substantial amount of food. This persuaded him that Markham, at least, wasn't particularly worried about Laura's absence. He decided to give the pair time to get settled at their table and to get stuck into their breakfast before he joined them. That way, they were unlikely to abandon their food and make excuses to leave when he approached them, or at least, if they did so, their discomfort at his appearance would appear very obvious. As soon as they began eating, he picked up his coffee and wandered across to their table.

'Good morning, Charles,' he said as, without asking, he sat down.

For a moment, Markham looked at him blankly, trying, Steve supposed, to remember where he had seen him before.

'Oh, it's ... Mr ..., er,' Markham stuttered, his mouth full of *Fauji Flakes*, the local brand of breakfast cereal.

'Jeffreys,' Steve reminded him.

'Yes, of course. Mr. Jeffreys. Martin, this is Mr Jeffreys, a friend of Mrs Roberts.'

'Martin Hopgood,' Markham's companion introduced himself.

Hopgood offered his hand. Steve shook it firmly.

'Steve,' he responded.

'I wasn't expecting to see you here,' Markham said.

'I'll bet you weren't,' Steve thought to himself.

'No, well, I hadn't heard from Laura in a few days, so I thought I'd come and check she was all right. Is she joining you for breakfast?' Steve asked, though he knew very well she would not be.

Markham looked at Hopgood and Hopgood returned his glance. They both looked a little uncomfortable.

'Well, er, Steve, we're not sure,' Markham floundered. 'Truth is, we haven't seen a great deal of her in the past three days or so. She's been coming and going, doing a bit of sightseeing and shopping, while we were waiting to hear about, you know, the mix up. It's still not been sorted out, you see.'

'Sightseeing and shopping? Where, in Peshawar? On her own? Is that safe?' Steve asked.

Markham was quick to reassure him.

'Oh, well, we took her to quite a few places in the city, showed her where the dress shops were and all that, and we were perfectly happy to continue accompanying her wherever she wished to go, but to be honest, I think she got a bit fed up having two hairy-arsed chaps in tow. She said she wanted to go off on her own. Reception here assured us she's been with the same reliable taxi driver – someone they recommended to her.'

'I see. And you say there's still no sign of Keith's remains?'

'No, unfortunately not,' Hopgood said. 'But we're hopeful the undertakers will find him soon. They're contacting all the families whose deceased relatives came into their establishment the same day as Keith.'

'What happens if they don't find him?'

'Oh, I don't think we need to be pessimistic just yet,' Markham assured him. 'We should receive some news in the next day or two.'

'I see,' Steve smiled affably. 'So, when do you have to be back at Vauxhall Cross?'

'Oh, not until next w ...' Markham broke off suddenly. 'I'm sorry?'

'When do you have to be back at work – at Vauxhall Cross?'

'At GTP, you mean?' Markham squirmed.

'Come off it, Charles. Let's stop this pretence, shall we? I know you don't work for Global Tobacco Products. I know who pays your salary. And yours, too, Martin. Now, where is Laura *really*?'

There was an embarrassed silence, as the two Secret Intelligence Service officers looked at each other. Eventually, Charles spoke.

'To be honest ..., we don't know exactly. She went off on her own, probably to make her own enquiries. I'm afraid she hasn't been back to the hotel in a few days, and she hasn't been in touch. But she is with a reputable taxi driver, as I said. We don't think she's come to any harm.'

'You don't *think*?' Steve said. 'But you don't know for sure?'

'No. But it's not her first time in this part of the world. I mean, she's lived and worked in India, hasn't she? And she speaks Hindi, doesn't she? Quite took us by surprise with that one, she did,' Markham laughed nervously.

'There's a lot you don't know about Laura Roberts,' Steve told them. 'She's a resourceful woman. And there's a lot you *do* know about Keith Roberts, but you're not saying.'

Once again, Markham and Hopgood exchanged uncomfortable glances. Clearly, they didn't know how much Steve actually knew.

'I'm pretty certain Keith didn't work for SIS,' Steve continued, 'so I'm assuming SIS were running him as an asset. Am I right?'

Steve could see the two men were struggling, weighing up the safest response, trying to decide whether to confirm or deny Steve's suggestion. After a few minutes' silence, it was Hopgood who spoke. He leaned forward and lowered his voice, conspiratorially.

'Keith Roberts knew this part of the world like the back of his hand. He had many useful contacts, in business and local government, and he had legitimate business reasons for being here so often. There aren't many Brits still doing business in this part of Pakistan. He was simply keeping his eyes and ears open and reporting back to us. Keith passed his observations through me, and Charles was his handler back in London.'

'You make him sound like a modern day Greville Wynne,' Steve said. 'And we all know what happened to him. So, what's happened to Keith? Is he dead, or have you just lost him, like you've lost Laura?'

'Do you think we could continue this conversation outside?' Charles interrupted. 'Only, some walls have ears, you know.'

'Okay. Well, I'll let you gents finish your breakfast first.'

'No, it's all right. I've not got as much of an appetite as I'd thought,' Charles said.

Outside, in the hotel car park, the sun was up now and it was clearly much too hot to stand around talking, so Hopgood suggested they go to his car. He switched on the engine so the air-conditioning would kick in.

'I've signed the Official Secrets Act, by the way,' Steve assured them. 'I'm ex-Security Service, so you can speak freely, and I would appreciate it if you did.'

He waited for Hopgood to continue his explanation. Hopgood cleared his throat.

'Ah, I see. Well, Keith knew his way around the districts of Nowshera and Kohat. He was often up that way, meeting with suppliers. He was indeed a useful asset. We'd heard there was something unusual going on in Kohat. Many foreigners had been seen in the area – young men, mercenaries, probably. Intelligence suggested the Russians might be involved. I don't know whether you're familiar with The Borodin Group?'

Steve shook his head. Hopgood continued:

'They're private mercenaries used by the Russians in areas of the world where they'd like to establish influence. Well, Keith was tasked ... well, not tasked actually, he volunteered to go and have a look. But he never came back and we lost contact with him.'

'When?' Steve asked.

'Back in early April, not long after he went up there,' Markham said.

'We heard there'd been some sort of assault on the military at a place called Cherat,' Hopgood continued. 'It's up in the Khattack mountains which divide the districts of Kohat and Nowshera. It's a great look-out spot across the region, quite a strategic location. For that reason, Pakistan has a big military unit based up there, the SSG.'

'SSG?' Steve queried.

'A commando unit,' Hopgood explained. 'They engage in border reconnaissance, counter-terrorism, hostage crises. A bit like our SAS.'

'So, what happened?' Steve asked.

'Locals reported hearing one helluva fire fight, and seeing bodies strewn around the hillside. We don't know for certain, but we suspect Keith might have got a bit too close and ... well ... he might have got caught in the cross fire.'

'Jesus Christ!' Steve exploded. 'You people! He was a fifty-eight-year-old businessman. He was overweight and over the hill. He was about to retire and he was about to become a grandfather. And you sent him into a blood bath.'

'We didn't know this was going to happen,' Markham grovelled. 'And he wasn't ordered in. We only requested that he should keep his ear to the ground. He volunteered to go up there and see what was going down.'

Steve shook his head.

'Have you told Laura any of this?'

'No,' Markham said. 'We didn't want to upset her any more than she already was on hearing of his death. It seemed kindest to suggest it was natural causes. And there was also the issue of his life insurance. Keith's insurance company would almost certainly refuse to pay out if they knew how he'd died.'

'So, you must have got a lot of local officials onboard to assist you in this ... conspiracy,' Steve reasoned, 'the doctor who signed off the post-mortem certificate, the local health official, the undertaker ... none of them mentioned he'd been shot.'

'This is Pakistan,' Hopgood explained. 'Not everyone's wealthy. People can be bought.'

'And the French woman?' Steve asked. 'Was she in on it, too?'

'Oh, you heard about her?' Hopgood said. 'Yes, she's one of our assets, too. I suppose Mrs Roberts told you she chinned her? Laid her out flat, she did.'

Steve was surprised. Laura hadn't mentioned that bit of the story. His anger suddenly gave way to mirth and he burst out laughing.

'Did she, by God? Well, that's our Laura for you. She's a formidable woman. And a shrewd one. She didn't fall for any of your lies.'

'Obviously not,' Markham conceded.

'So, she's been in touch with you since we took her up to Tanda Lake,' Hopgood observed. 'Did she tell you where she is? Is she all right?'

Steve got the impression that, unlike Markham, Hopgood was genuinely concerned.

'Yes, she did. She's not answering her phone at the moment, but, last time I spoke with her, she told me she's staying in a village not too far from Cherat.'

'Which village,' Hopgood asked, hopefully.

'She said it's called *Hamara Khel*.'

Hopgood's face fell.

'What?' Steve asked. 'Is that a dangerous place?'

'It's not a place at all.'

'What do you mean, 'it's not a place'?'

'I mean it's not a specific place. *Hamara Khel* just means 'our village'.'

'Oh, shit!' Steve exploded again. 'If anything has happened to Laura ...'

Laura, meanwhile, had awoken early. Feeling well rested, she stretched out languorously in the bed and felt the scented morning breeze on her face. She now remembered what had occurred the night before. Suleiman had kissed her. It wasn't a chaste kiss. It was passionate. Then he had said nothing more but had left her and had retired to his room and she had retired to hers. She had lain awake for some time, thinking about that kiss. She had been puzzled by it. She had wondered whether he intended to follow her to her room. He was the head of the household, indeed head of the village, and she was a guest in his home; a vulnerable lone female traveller. Perhaps he intended to exercise some sort of *droit de seigneur* over her. Perhaps he might come to her room and pursue that intimacy further. And she had wondered how she would react if he did. She hadn't known what to think. She was confused. In the event, he hadn't re-appeared, and for that, she was relieved. She wasn't confident enough in herself to feel comfortable about further intimacy. It had been a very long time since Keith had made love to her. She had almost forgotten how that felt.

Now, she closed her eyes, and her toes curled up in pleasure at the thought of that kiss. Yes, it had been most pleasant and intense, but she knew there would be no further physical contact between them. Even if he did seek to do so, she wouldn't allow it. It was true that she hadn't felt like that in ... well, in years. In fact, she couldn't recall *ever* having felt like that with Keith. She cast her mind back to those nights spent in the beach hut in Goa all those years ago. Had it been as exciting as she remembered it?

Honestly, despite the romance of the location, she didn't think it had been. Last night, she had come very close to casting off the inhibitions of middle-age; of overlooking the hang-ups she had about being fifty-five; the awareness of the spider veins and the increasing crêpiness of her neck and knees. No, nothing more would occur between them. If anything like that *had* happened, she knew she would now be feeling mortified.

Once again, she felt a twinge of guilt. She had come here to find Keith, not to find romance. If it turned out that Keith was still alive, what would he have thought if he knew she had been intimate with another, younger man? He had never been faithful to her, it was true, but, in all the years of their marriage, she had never been unfaithful to him. She had never even thought of doing so. And now, now that he was missing and might even be alive and needing her help, well, now didn't seem the time to start.

She climbed out of bed and headed for the bathroom. Once she was showered and dressed, she went downstairs. She could hear Fatima and the girls in the kitchen. Soon, Fatima appeared with tea and chappatis and they both sat down to breakfast. Fatima advised her that Suleiman had risen early to call on his cousin Liaqat once more.

'*Inshallah*, he will have news of your husband, Laura,' Fatima said.

'I hope so,' Laura agreed. 'It's so very kind of Suleiman.'

'He will also go to Dara Adam Khel, to check on the progress of Johar's taxi. He said he will phone to let us know if there is any news'

'Oh,' Laura remembered. 'I left my phone on charge upstairs, I'd better fetch it.'

Heading upstairs to her room, she found the phone where she had left it, on the windowsill. She checked it and saw there were a number of missed calls from Steve's mobile.

She sat on the bed and called Steve's number. She was pleased to hear his voice.

'Steve, it's Laura.'

'Oh, thank God, Laura! I'm relieved to hear from you at last. Are you all right? Where are you?'

'Oh, Steve, I'm fine. I'm staying with the loveliest family. They've looked after me so well.'

'Yes, but *where* are you?'

'It's one of those fortified villages. You won't believe how nice they are inside, more like a compound.'

'But which village? What's the name of it?'

'They told me it's *Hamara Khel.*'

'Laura, that just means 'our village'. It must have a proper name.'

'*Hamara* ...? Oh, of course it does. How stupid of me. I should have realised that. It seems many of the villages around here are called something *Khel*. Wait a minute and I'll ask.'

Rushing down the stairs again, phone in hand, Laura found Fatima in the kitchen.

'Fatima, what's the name of this village, please?'

'This village? It's Kotli Qalat.'

'Thank you,' she said and she hurried back up the stairs.

'Steve, I don't know if you heard that, but it's Kotli Qalat. But where are *you*?'

'I arrived in Peshawar this morning, I'm at the Emerald Intercontinental. Just been speaking with Laurel and Hardy. What a pair of shysters! I managed to get a bit more information out of them about Keith's movements. But I need to know you're safe.'

'Yes, I'm very safe. I was travelling up here in a taxi, and a lorry caused us to have a bit of a crash. Neither Johar nor I were hurt, but the taxi's badly damaged. It'll be another day or two before it's fixed and he can drive me back to Peshawar.'

'Who's Johar?'

'My taxi driver. A thoroughly decent chap. He arranged for me to stay with a lovely family here. But I've been up to a place called Cherat. I think that's where Keith was seen last. I'm hoping to get up there again to have another look around. The area's under martial law and you're supposed to have a permit to be there, but I might have a look anyway. Meanwhile, Suleiman's speaking to his cousin Liaqat who seems to know what's going on.'

'Who's this Suleiman? And Liaqat? No, never mind. Look, don't go anywhere near Cherat. It's too dangerous at the moment. Wait until I get to you. Do you hear me, Laura? Please, don't do *anything* until I get there.'

CHAPTER TWENTY-NINE

Back in London, at Thames House, Adrian Curtis's desk phone rang. He was pleased to see the display register the office number of his golfing chum, *The Times* editor, Ronan Rogers. Usually, when Ronan rang, it was to extend a lunch invitation. Not only did Ronan know all the best places to eat, but he also had a very generous expense account.

'Ronan. How are you, Old Man?' he chirped.

'Fine, thanks, Adrian. But, listen, I'll get straight to the point. I just received a call from the Prime Minister in person. He dropped a bit of a bomb shell, and I thought I'd better check with you whether what he told me is true and whether I can put it in our lunchtime edition.'

'Why, what did he say?'

'He told me there's been some sort of attack on your Northern HQ. He said it was like that Havana syndrome thing the Americans have been reporting. This is worrying after that drone bombing at Number Ten. He says you've had to evacuate all your staff and that all current operations up there have been disrupted. Is this true?'

Adrian was shocked.

'Good God! Um, well, that's news to me, Ronan. Let me check it out and I'll get right back to you, okay?'

'Okay. Don't take too long, will you, Adrian? I don't know who else he's called. Don't want the tabloids to steal a march on us.'

Adrian headed upstairs to Helena's office. He decided speaking to her in person would be better than phoning, and the stairs would be quicker than waiting for the lift. Taking the stairs two at a time he gave Helena's PA, Eileen, the thumbs up sign to ask if it was okay to barge straight in. Eileen nodded. Closing the door behind him, he didn't wait for Helena to ask him to sit, he threw himself into the chair.

'Adrian, you're out of breath. What's up?'

'I thought you said the PM didn't want details of the Medusa attack released to the press?'

'That's right. He's dead set against it.'

'But it seems he just rang the editor of *The Times* and told him all about the attack on our Northern HQ. He even told him where it's located.'

'What? The cretin! I wanted him to make a general statement about a sonic attack on a government building but not to mention it was on one of *our* buildings. Most of the public don't even know we *have* a northern HQ, let alone where it's located, but he was adamant that no-one should say anything about it at all. As usual, he didn't want to accuse the Russians. So, why's he changed his mind? What the hell's come over him?'

Helena's questions were clearly rhetorical. She snatched up her phone receiver and spun the cards on her Rolodex. She found the number she wanted and jabbed angrily at the phone's keypad.

'We'll see what his Press Secretary has to say about it.'

Seconds later, she was connected.

'Joy Cooper, please ... yes, Joy, it's Helena Fairbrother over at Thames House. I'm rather taken aback by the PM's change of heart over releasing details of an incident at one of our regional offices. Do you know why he's been in touch with *The Times* about it? ... Yes, this morning.'

Helena covered the mouthpiece with her hand and whispered to Adrian.

'She says she knows nothing about it.'

'Well, Joy, I'd be extremely grateful if you'd ask him about it,' she continued with measured politeness, 'only he told the JIC they weren't to speak of it, on pain of death. However, it seems he rang *The Times* himself. We weren't expecting him to do that. Would you ask him and get back to me PDQ? Only, they may run with the story this lunchtime and we'll need to have our own response ready. Thanks.'

'You look like you could use a coffee, Adrian,' she said as she put the phone down. I'll get Eileen to get us both a strong one. Eileen!'

Eileen had obviously anticipated their need for coffee, owing to the urgency of Adrian's arrival.

'Coffee's coming,' Eileen called back.

'I hope you get a quick response, Helena,' Adrian said. 'I've asked Ronan to hold off on this until we clarify things with Number Ten, but we don't know if Ivan has rung any other newspapers. It's odd that he hasn't told his press sec what he intended to do. D'you think he's had some kind of brain storm?'

The call back from Number Ten arrived even before the coffee did. To Helena's surprise, it was the Prime Minister himself who called. Frustratingly for Adrian, he could only hear Helena's side of the conversation.

'No, not I, Prime Minister. *The Times*' editor says you called him personally and gave him details of the attack. I must say I was dismayed to hear that ... what? ... well, then who? ... Well maybe your Press Sec could call him back and explain that? ... Yes, we'll deny it, too.'

Helena looked baffled as she ended the call.

'He says he didn't call *The Times*. He says he hasn't discussed the incident with anyone outside of the JIC. He says it must have been an impostor who called. Do you think that's possible?'

'Well, Ronan seemed pretty certain it was the PM he was speaking with. I'll get back to him and find out more about the call and what was said, but I take it we're going for deniability?'

'Oh, yes. And Thompson's furious. He insists we mustn't say a word about the attack, but we should also do our best to find out who it was who called *The Times*. Isn't that just like him? He's more outraged about the call to the press than he is about the attack on our staff.'

As he left Helena's office, Adrian saw her PA was pouring out the coffee.

'I'll take mine to go, please, Eileen,' he said and, grabbing one of the elegant china cups and saucers, he headed for the lifts.

That lunchtime, Adrian and Ronan chatted over the matter as they tucked into their dessert and coffee at a quiet corner table in Ronan's favourite bistro in St Thomas's Street.

'This is lovely. What's it called again?' Adrian asked.

'*Choux façon Paris-Brest*,' Ronan said. 'Choux pastry, crème Anglaise, chocolate and raspberries and, I think, some sort of pistachio paste. Raspberries aren't in season, though, are they? Must be imported. So, you think the Russians may have their very own John Culshaw, then, do you?'

'Well, I can't think of any other explanation for it. Thompson swears blind it wasn't him. And the Russians have carried out some phone pranks before. But you wouldn't think they'd be capable of imitating the PM. I mean, his voice is quite distinctive, isn't it? The occasional stammer, and the way he pronounces 'to' as 'tuh'. You didn't get any hint of a Russian accent, or any grammar slip-ups, did you?'

'No, not at all. I mean, I've spoken to him in person before, and, of course, he's on television all the time. His voice is really unmistakable – that English public-school piffle-waffle. You don't think he's had some kind of mental blip, do you? Could he have called and then forgotten about it?'

'No, I very much doubt it. I mean, he looks like a buffoon, all right, and he often behaves like one, though I sometimes think that's partly an act – you know, a bit of bluff and bluster to dodge certain issues. I've not seen any evidence that he's lost his mental acuity, though. He's sharp enough, and he's also a slippery sod. I'm beginning to wonder if he did do it. But I can't see what his motive would be, other than to embarrass the service, but why would he do that?'

'Hmm. But he's continuing to deny it was him?'

'Yes. Insists he's incensed about it.'

'So, um, the story's true then, is it?' Ronan looked quizzically at his friend.

'Can't say, Ronan. But if it *were* true, I mean, if something like that *should* happen sometime, you know you'd be the first one I'd tell.'

'Good. Well, I'm sure you'll tell me when the time is right. Now, then, how about another coffee and perhaps a small cognac to go with it?'

'Splendid. Thanks, Old Man.'

CHAPTER THIRTY

SULEIMAN HAD MORE NEWS FOR LAURA WHEN HE FINALLY APPEARED LATER that morning. His demeanour was perfectly normal and he made no mention of what had occurred the previous evening. She wondered whether he had sensed a need in her, a need she herself hadn't realised was there. Well, if he wasn't going to mention it, she resolved she wouldn't refer to it either.

'Liaqat tells me there are a number of bodies in the mortuary at the old military hospital up in Cherat,' he told her. 'It seems they aren't local. They're foreigners.'

'But, if they had died during that shoot-out in early April, wouldn't they have buried them before now?' Laura asked.

'They'll definitely have buried any local Muslim casualties. But they probably don't know what to do with the foreigners. They may be waiting for their bodies to be identified and claimed. If you have a photograph of your husband, I could take it up there and see if he is amongst them.'

Laura had to think for a moment. She couldn't recall whether she did have any photos of Keith with her. Taking her personal mobile from her bag, she flipped through the images she had saved on it. There were numerous photos of Beth and some of her son-in-law Alan, but none of Keith. He never seemed to be at home long enough to have family snaps taken. His passport was still missing, and she'd left the photocopy of his passport bio page with the undertaker back in Stockport.

'No, I don't seem to have any on my phone.'

'Well, what about his social media accounts?' Suleiman asked. 'Is he on Facebook?'

'No, he wasn't really into social media. But I suppose there might be some photos of him on my daughter's Facebook page.

Suleman quickly produced a laptop and he sat down at the table and logged on to Facebook. Laura was surprised. Somehow, she hadn't expected there to be access to the internet and social media in Pakistan, especially not in a remote Khyber village. When she'd lived and worked in India, over three decades ago, the internet had only just been created. The Foreign Office was still a decade away from being computerised back then. Her letters from Keith had taken a full two weeks to reach her via the diplomatic mail. Sometimes, Keith had arrived in Delhi even before his letter advising her that he was coming. Of course, the world had moved on since then, though she really hadn't expected there to be anything as sophisticated as an internet signal in this mud-walled village. Her host sensed her surprise.

'What? You didn't think we'd have internet access here? You must have missed the satellite dish on the roof. It's next to the solar panels. We no longer use buffalo dung for cooking and heating our water. Not very observant of you, Laura,' he chided gently.

She *was* embarrassed now. She sat down next to him at the table and he turned the laptop over to her. She logged herself into her Facebook page. She didn't have any photos saved on there either. She only ever used it to communicate with Beth and her coffee morning friends. She found Beth's page, however, and saw there were hundreds of photos saved. They were sorted into albums according to date. There was the Vancouver trip, and a trip over the border into the USA. There was also Beth and Alan's wedding album. There were bound to be photos of Alan there. He'd given Beth away. To her annoyance, however, though she could see the various posts on Beth's page, she couldn't access her albums. Apparently, her security-conscious daughter had password protected them.

'She's locked her images,' Laura explained. 'But I could send her a message asking her to send us one of her photos of Alan.'

'She's in the UK?'

'No, she lives in Canada.'

'Canada's nine hours behind Pakistan. It's the middle of the night over there. She wouldn't see it for hours yet. That would take too long. Maybe you could give me a general description of your husband and, if I see anyone up there that vaguely fits that description, I could take a photo with my phone and send it to your phone.'

'You might still bring back the wrong body, though. I mean, he might be unrecognisable. I have a much better idea. I'll come with you?'

'No, Laura. I can't take you with me to Cherat. Not right now. It's far too dangerous. There are some cut-throat characters roaming about those hills, Taliban militia and all sorts. And there are more police and army road blocks along the way. I might have problems enough persuading them to let me through, but I'm sure I'd have even more problems trying to explain your presence. Supposing they think your husband was one of those foreign fighters? They'd probably arrest you. You have no idea what conditions are like in a police lock-up out here.'

'But, Suleiman, if you do find Keith's body, they're unlikely to take instruction from you to have it repatriated. I'm his next of kin, though. They'd have to act on my instruction.'

'Yes, I suppose you've got a point.'

'Yes, and if they needed to confirm my entitlement, they could call the British Embassy in Islamabad. They know I'm here, and they know why I'm here. They have copies of his death certificate and all the paperwork there, because they got it all translated for me. There's a chap called Martin Hopgood who works in the Consular Section there. They could call him and get him to vouch for me.'

Laura chose her words carefully. She had no intention of telling Suleiman that it was Hopgood who had brought her to Peshawar, or that he was probably still sitting, twiddling his thumbs back at the Inter-con, awaiting her return. Suleiman thought it over for a moment or two.

'I have to admit you're right. They probably wouldn't let me take charge of an Englishman's body. Especially if they thought he was mixed up in the attack on the SSG barracks. They'd probably arrest me. It would sound more credible if I had his grieving widow with me. You could get them to call his company in the UK to confirm what he was doing out here. I'm not entirely happy with this, but, yes, you'd better come too.'

Laura packed her clothes into her cabin bag once more and Suleiman explained to Fatima and Johar where they were going. Johar wanted to accompany them, but Suleiman said he should remain behind and await news of the repairs to his vehicle. Besides, an Englishwoman and a Pakistani man seeking Laura's deceased husband might take some explaining if they encountered any police or army road blocks. The inclusion of a Sikh in their party, however, would take even more explaining.

Soon, they were heading along those same honey-scented roads once more and ascending higher and higher into the Khattack hills. Once again, Laura entertained doubts as to whether she was doing the right thing. It didn't seem fair to be exposing Suleiman to potential danger all for the sake of her faithless husband. Several times during the journey, she thought of asking

Suleiman to stop the car and turn around. She felt she had imposed upon his goodwill too much already. Dragging him into an area where, quite recently, the Taliban had apparently been fighting with local commandoes, now seemed like a really bad idea. Yet, still, she felt this inexplicable duty to find Keith's body and to bring him home. She felt she owed it to Beth to uncover the truth about her father's death. When she looked at it that way, she was able to justify her search. Yes, she told herself, she wasn't doing this for Keith or for herself. She was doing this mainly for Beth.

CHAPTER THIRTY-ONE

Yazz Mehta booked in the first twenty-five Security Service personnel as they arrived from Burtby. The harassed custodian at reception complained that he wouldn't have enough visitors' passes for the next wave. They weren't used to receiving so many visitors in one go. Yasmeen promised to clear it with GCHQ central security that the evacuees could use their Security Service staff passes to access Heron House. She left the custodian grappling with the logistics of getting the automated door swipe machinery to recognise around a hundred MI5 IDs. Yasmeen was pleased to see that the Thames House attachees had been included in the first wave. As she escorted the group towards the stairwell, Kirpal stepped forward to open the door for her.

'Are you sure you can accommodate us all?' he asked.

'Well, there'll have to be a degree of hot-desking and desk-sharing,' she explained, 'but I'm sure we'll manage to absorb you all, somehow.'

'So, who will I be desk-sharing with?' he asked.

'Well, since liaison with MI5 is part of my job description, and as you're the first one through the door, I suppose you'd better share with me,' she smiled, coyly.

Kirpal turned and looked at Harry and Jo, who were following close behind him as they climbed the stairs. He grinned broadly at them. They grinned back.

'Did you return our digital scanner, by the way?' Yazz asked. 'It's an expensive bit of kit, that one.'

'No, I've still got it. Is it okay if I hang onto it for a while yet?'

'I should think so. Did it do what you wanted it to do?'

'Oh, yes. I parked outside a house in Blackburn very early one morning and I used the scanner to wipe clean the occupant's mobile phone data. When I called at his friend's travel agency yesterday, it was clear to me that it had worked just as I'd hoped it would. Now, they'll be using the phones I supplied to them, so I'm keen to hear what they've been saying and who they've been calling using my special Q-phones.'

Yazz showed Kirpal to her desk and assigned Harry and Jo two nearby desks.

'Make yourselves at home. I'll try and find some more chairs. I fear we're going to run out of office chairs. It's lucky that you guys got here first. I think some of the Burtby crowd may end up sitting on green plastic garden chairs. The custodians have been doling them out. We've asked to borrow some chairs from the town hall, too. They have lots of those gilded ones with velvet cushions, you know, the kind used for civic occasions.'

'Are we still on for dinner tonight?' Kirpal asked when, eventually, Yazz took a few moments out from her allocation of office furniture.

'We are, but I thought I'd cook us dinner back at my place and then we could watch a film together, if you like.'

The expression on Kirpal's face told her that yes, he would like that very much. He now remembered he had promised to call Adrian and let him know where they would be and what their new telephone extension numbers would be. He used Yazz's desk phone to call Thames House.

'Adrian, it's Kirpal, just calling to let you know we're all settled in here at Heron House. It's going to be ridiculously cramped, but it'll be cosy ... yes, Harry and Jo are with me. Did I ... what? ... Sorry? ... tell anyone about the attack? No, of course not. You told us not to. Why? ... What?... The Prime Minister did? But why would he do that? He says he didn't? ... No, don't worry, boss. All the GCHQ staff here have been asked not to say anything.'

Kirpal put the phone down and sat thinking. It seemed most puzzling that the PM should have revealed to the press details of the sonic attack at Burtby. Even more puzzling was the fact that he'd denied having done so. As Kirpal sat considering this, he gazed out of the window. Opposite, he could see glimpses of the stately, Victorian town hall of which Sue Shaw was clearly so proud. However much of the building was still clad in scaffolding and swathed in blue, plastic tarpaulin.

'Yazz, remind me what Sue Shaw said they're doing over at the town hall,' he said.

'A major refurb,' she replied. 'The first they've had since it was built, or at least since the gas lights were replaced with electric ones. All the electrics have to be re-wired. And a lot of the exterior stonework needs re-pointing or something. Why do you ask?'

'Well,' Kirpal stood and walked over to the window, 'it looks as though the contractors are expecting to still be working there when winter comes. They're taking more of those industrial heaters into the building.'

Yazz joined him at the window and saw for herself.

'Like I said, it's a major refurbishment. Shame you can't see the whole place under that tarp. It's magnificent.'

At six o'clock that evening, Yazz ushered Kirpal into her modern apartment in the popular Canal Basin area.

'Fancy a glass of wine whilst I'm cooking?' she asked.

'Yes, please.'

Kirpal looked around the apartment. It wasn't huge but it was tastefully decorated and it had a small balcony with a pleasant outlook over the Ashton Canal. Glancing down, he saw a couple of swans floating lazily along on the water. They seemed emblematic of the area's metamorphosis from heavy industry to modern residences and commerce. He next checked out Yazz's bookcase and browsed her selection of books. He noticed a whole array of DVDs on the bottom shelf of the book case, so he knelt down to have a better look at them.

'Hey, I see you've got all the Terminator films. Don't tell me you're a Terminator fan, too?'

Yazz reappeared with a large glass of wine for him.

'Yes, I've always been a fan. Wasn't too impressed with the last one, though. Do you think there'll be any more?'

'Maybe not. Not after 'Dark Fear' bombed at the box office. Shame, though. Which one's your favourite?'

'Well, I liked the first few. I think Terminator Two is one of the best. We could watch that later, if you'd like?'

'Fantastic. I'd love that. Can I give you a hand with dinner?'

'No, you're all right. I'm a messy cook. You sit and drink your wine. Dinner won't be long.'

After they had eaten, Yazz and Kirpal made themselves comfortable on her large leather sofa and began to watch the film. Kirpal remarked that he'd been just a toddler when Terminator Two had been released, and Yazz told him she wasn't even born then. Kirpal reflected on the fact that it had been his dad who had got him interested in the Terminator films when Kirpal was in his teens. The clothes and hairstyles the actors wore in this early nineteen-nineties' film now seemed very dated. But the action was still good and he loved the concept of the battle between the human race and synthetic intelligence. The science appealed to his technical mind.

Soon, they were watching Edward Furlong as John Connor, time travelling back to his own childhood trying to save his younger self. One of the more intriguing scenes from the film saw one of the characters phoning the young John Connor's mother and fooling her into thinking she was speaking to her son, as he electronically mimicked the boy's voice. When the film was ended, Yazz got up to make them some coffee.

'That series was quite prophetic, in its way,' Kirpal remarked. 'A lot of the AI stuff you see in these films actually did come to pass.'

'Yeah,' Yazz called from the kitchen. 'Especially that VCT.'

'VCT?' he queried.

Yazz reappeared and placed two mugs of coffee down on the coffee table.

'Yeah, voice cloning technology. It's a thing now, you know. That artificial voice the late Stephen Hawking used wasn't very human sounding. It must have annoyed him being saddled with that monotone voice, not to mention the American accent that was nothing like his own. But VCT has come on in leaps and bounds now.'

'Has it? What do they use it for, then?'

'Well, mostly for people who have lost their voices, say from throat cancer. What they do now, is they make a recording of the patient's voice before they are operated on, or before they lose the power of speech entirely. With modern analytic machine-learning techniques, the person's voice can then be replicated by artificial intelligence and spoken via a small gadget. The VCT doesn't just copy the nuances and emotions of the human voice, it actually mimics the specific characteristics of the individual person's speech.'

'That's amazing. But how do you even know all this?'

'Well, it's something GCHQ is keeping an eye on. You see, there's also the potential for VCT to be abused. If you think about it, it could be used to get around voice activated computers or building entry systems. We heard of a case where an employee got a call he believed was from his boss, asking him to deposit a hundred grand from the firm's account into an overseas account. Of course, it wasn't his boss, it was a fraudster.'

'But wouldn't you need the owner of the voice to co-operate, you know, to give you a recording of their speech for it to be imitated?'

'Not necessarily. A fraudster could just ring someone and secretly record them. It doesn't even require a lengthy exchange of conversation. When you think about it, someone could phone the US military pretending to be the President of the United States and could order someone to push the button to detonate a nuclear device. Though you'd hope there'd be some stringent safeguards in place.'

'Yes. I suppose the possibilities are endless,' Kirpal mused. 'I imagine someone could impersonate the Prime Minister using that VCT technology, couldn't they?'

'No reason why not. They could capture his speech patterns by recording one of his television interviews.'

Kirpal considered this for a few moments. All of a sudden, he grabbed his mobile phone from his pocket.

'I wonder what time my boss goes to bed. I think I need to give him a call.'

The following morning found Adrian in Helena's office eagerly awaiting her arrival.

'I think Kirpal Kohli might have solved the mystery of the PM's call to *The Times*,' he declared, before Helena had even removed her coat.

'I've been thinking about that overnight, myself,' she said. 'Do you think it could have been those two Russian pranksters that tricked him before? What were they called, Lexus and someone?'

'Lexus and Vovan, you mean? No, I don't think it was them. At least, Ronan assures me the caller didn't have a Russian accent, and those guys do. But it could be that the Russians were behind it. Kirpal's been telling me about voice cloning technology.'

'How does that work?' Helena asked, as she hung up her coat and sat at her desk.

'Through artificial intelligence. Using a recording of the PM's voice, the new technology can analyse it and convert a caller's speech into the same voice and speech patterns as that of the person they've recorded. I haven't seen this gadgetry myself, but GCHQ are aware of it. It has great potential for fraud, apparently.'

'So, we need to consider why the caller might have done this, and that might tell us who he was. Can we assume it was a 'he'?'

'No, the technology conceals the caller's own voice and gender. I suspect that, just like the Russian pranksters' japes, it was intended to embarrass.'

'Embarrass who, though? The PM or us?'

'Maybe all of us. But it still begs the question how did they find out about the Havana type attack? I mean, a lot of people knew about it – all the staff of our northern HQ, probably some at GCHQ's Manchester office, the CPNI, the Corsham people, CID. But all were warned to keep quiet about it.'

'Well, I suppose it only takes one of those employees to tell their wife or husband, or even to discuss possible symptoms with their GP, and word gets out. But there's also Downing Street, don't forget. Someone there could have let it slip. Who on the Downing Street staff might want to embarrass the PM?'

Adrian couldn't help laughing. Helena smiled.

'Yes, you're right,' she agreed. 'That would be *everyone* in Downing Street.'

'Actually, Helena, I think it more likely that the call was made by, or on behalf of whoever's responsible for the attack. My money would be on the Russians.'

'Well, Adrian, I'd be very grateful if you were able to find out who did leak it. You, see, the Prime Minister is convinced it was me.'

Later that morning, Helena made her way to the Cabinet Office for another meeting of the COBRA committee. The Prime Minister was uncharacteristically prompt this time. He rolled into the meeting room even before everyone had taken their seats.

'Prime minister, did you *really* call the press and tell them about the attack on MI5's northern offices?' Sir Henry Mortimer, the Cabinet Secretary asked.

'No, of course I didn't,' Thompson spluttered. 'At least, I don't think I did.'

'You don't *think* you did?' Sir Robert Vanbrugge asked. 'You mean, you might have?'

'No, I'm sure I didn't.'

'You don't *sound* very sure,' Sir Henry said.

'Well, I honestly don't remember doing it. No, I'm pretty sure I didn't.'

'Well,' Helena chipped in, 'I know none of my staff did it. The call was made just after nine o'clock in the morning and we've checked all outgoing calls from Thames House at around the relevant time, and from RBP. Every single staff member's mobile phone has been checked, too. And similar checks have been made at Heron House, so it wasn't any of my staff nor GCHQ staff who made the call. If you didn't make the call, then it must have been someone using the most sophisticated voice cloning technology.'

'Is there such a thing?' Thompson asked, hopefully.

'There is, but, as far as we know, only the Russians have developed anything that advanced.'

'But why would they do it?' the Prime Minister asked.

'To make you look foolish and inept, perhaps?' Sir Robert suggested.

'Oh, but ... well, I ..., I mean *The Times* didn't carry the story, did they?'

'No, but *The Daily Mirror* did,' Helena advised him. 'We didn't get through to them in time to warn them off.'

'Ah, yes, well, hopefully there's no harm done, eh?' Thompson said. 'I mean, it'll soon blow over, won't it?'

'I don't think so,' Sir Henry shook his head. 'The British public are demanding to know who carried out the attack. They're outraged at the idea of an attack of this nature on civil servants, especially those civil servants charged with safeguarding the nation's security. They want to know who did it and what you're going to do about it.'

'Well, I'll probably do what I usually do when the British public gets outraged about something I've said or done,' Johnson resolved.

'What's that?' Sir Robert asked, fearfully.

'I'll throw in a dead cat.'

'What? You'd dig up poor Winston's remains?' Sir Henry looked horrified.

'No, Henry. Not *that* dead cat. I was speaking metaphorically. I mean I'll give them something else that'll get their collective knickers in a twist. I'll announce something else that'll distract them.'

'Such as ... what?' Helena asked.

'Your resignation, perhaps, Prime Minister?' the MI6 Chief suggested.

'Absolutely not. No, I know. I'll get the Chancellor to announce he's to abolish the triple lock on state pensions. That threat always causes fear and indignation, especially in times of severe inflation like we're seeing at the moment.'

'But that's unthinkable,' Helena said. 'You wouldn't attack pensioners' incomes just to cover up your own embarrassment, would you?'

'No, of course not. I'm not a *complete* monster. No, we'll get him to announce that it's likely to happen and then, when all the furore is at its height, he'll say it was just a possibility and one of many he'd been considering, but that he's now found other ways of saving on public expenditure. By then, they'll have forgotten all about my gaffe – not that it was a gaffe, of course.'

Sir Henry Mortimer looked from Helena to Sir Robert Vanbrugge, and shook his head despairingly. The MI6 Chief acknowledged his look, but Helena looked thoughtful.

'Prime Minister,' she said. 'The Times editor says this is the phone number you called him from. It's not an extension at Number Ten. Do you recognise this number?'

Thompson gazed at the piece of paper Helena now showed him. He looked surprised.

'You're right, this isn't a Downing Street number. It's a mobile number. But it's not my official issue mobile. Actually, it's my own personal mobile number. Very few people have this number. I mean, I don't give it to journalists. I don't even give it out to my fellow cabinet ministers. This is just for personal friends and family.'

'But, surely, none of your friends or family members would reveal your personal number to the Russians, would they?' Helena asked, pointedly.

The Prime Minister looked baffled for a few moments.

'Does Malcolm Donald know this number?' she asked, even more pointedly

'Yes, he does. But ... I ... ah, that is, I shouldn't think he ... ah ... I mean, how would my phone have been used to make the call? I keep it in my pocket at all times.'

'It's unlikely to have been used,' Helena suggested. 'But there are ways it could have been made to *look* as if the call came from your personal mobile. Of course, the number would have to be disclosed to the fraudsters by someone who *knew* that was your personal mobile number. Someone with an axe to grind. Someone who wanted to cause you extreme and very public embarrassment. Someone you'd sacked, perhaps.'

Thompson ceased looking surprised. He now looked angry – very angry indeed.

Meanwhile, up in Burtby, the comings and goings of the white-overall clad men with ladders, paint pots and sheets of aluminium wall cladding drew no particular attention from the occupants of the various industrial units around the business park. It was not unusual for newish buildings to develop faults or to require what builders termed 'snagging' to be put right. Although if anyone was observing them closely, they might have been surprised to see the painters and decorators working at an impressive speed. What observers might take to be rolls of wallpaper was actually special radiation-resistant film to be applied to window glass, and anodised aluminium sheets were intended to give interior walls similar protection from microwaves.

As well as the interior refurbishment which was taking place at RBP, however, a casual observer might also have spotted what seemed to be electronic equipment being taken into the building. The technicians from the Centre for the Protection of National Infrastructures, assisted by their counterparts from the Wiltshire-based National Cyber Security Centre, soon had the Gorgoneion up and running. Their meters still showed dangerously high levels of microwave radiation being directed at the building but, more importantly, with the Gorgoneion fired up, they could now tell from which direction that radiation was emanating. The gadget was quickly employed in the task of redirecting that wave of energy right back at the source.

Two of the CPNI technicians, looking wholly credible in their gas company inspector's uniforms and armed with their meters, walked out through the RBP security gates and along the pavement towards the next industrial unit further down the block. According to the signs at the gate, this unit was home to El Nova Business Solutions. The two technicians made a show of standing outside the building's entrance, tapping on their hand-held meters and nodding their heads. The building's security guard soon appeared.

'North West Gas,' one of the technicians explained to the guard. 'There's a significant gas leak on the site and we believe it's in your building.'

The security guard seemed suspicious as he squinted at the identity cards the CPNI men wore on lanyards around their necks.

'Can't be here,' he shook his head. 'There in't no gas supply in this unit.'

'No, but there's gas pipes running under the whole site,' one of the CPNI men assured him. 'There must be, as the building next door has gas appliances in their canteen. And there's no leak over there, but there's definitely gas coming up from the ground over here. Could be dangerous if there's been a slow build-up of gas under the foundations. You could be sitting on a time bomb. Your whole building could go up at any minute.'

'Bloody Norah! You sure?' the guard asked.

'Quickest way to evacuate the staff would be to set off your fire alarm. Have everyone assemble in the car park while we check all the offices to see if it's getting into the building and where exactly it's coming from.'

The guard headed back into the reception area, followed by the two 'gas men'.

'Look, I'm getting a strong reading even here in reception,' one of them urged. 'Best move quick, Mate.'

Shocked, the security man pressed the button on his microphone and put out an urgent Tannoy call for all staff to evacuate immediately. He added, assertively, that this was not a drill. Moments later, staff began to appear from all directions. The Security guard stood by the front door and directed all the building's occupants towards the car park, leaving the two technicians to begin their inspection.

It was up on the first floor that the source of the radiation was soon located. The CPNI men had no idea what a Medusa would look like, but their meters led them to a machine resembling an old-fashioned fan heater. Though unfamiliar with the way the machine operated, it was fairly obvious which of its control buttons would be the 'off' switch, so one of the technicians donned his gloves, switched off the machine and quickly disconnected it from the power socket beneath the desk. His colleague, meanwhile, made a quick call on his mobile phone to confirm the source had been located and disabled. Moments later, a North West Gas van pulled onto the site and four more 'gas men' emerged and entered the building. Making their way quickly to the first-floor office, they produced their police warrants and identified themselves to the technicians.

'Right,' one of them barked at his colleagues, 'start with taking any prints off the gadget, then check out this desk. Whose is it? Then check the rest of this room. We'll take this place apart.'

Outside, the staff of El Nova stood around in small surprised groups, all chatting and some smoking – until their security guard approached and advised them against this. Most of them were not at all put out at having been evacuated. In fact, they were pleased to have an unscheduled break. They were, however, blissfully unaware they were being subjected to covert photographic surveillance from within the van bearing the North West Gas logo.

CHAPTER THIRTY-TWO

THE ROUTE SULEIMAN HAD TAKEN UP TO CHERAT WASN'T THE SAME route Laura had taken with Johar, and she guessed Suleiman knew his way around the area better than her Peshawar-resident taxi driver. This time, they didn't have to pass the headquarters of the Special Services Group. She guessed that must be located on the other side of the mountain, and they saw no road blocks on their way to the former hill station. Although they didn't hold a permit, this time, no angry policeman came to chase them away.

Suleiman pulled up outside Cherat's Combined Military Hospital. It didn't look at all as Laura had expected. Since there had once been a British military hospital here, she somehow expected the same British Raj-era buildings to be in use still. However, there were no single-storey wooden huts or barracks in sight. Instead, the hospital comprised several buildings of more modern construction. First, Suleiman had to convince the armed soldiers guarding the car park entrance that they were there on legitimate business. After a protracted explanation involving much hand gesturing, they were allowed in and he found a parking space.

He explained that security here was understandably tight

because the local Taliban often targeted the Pakistani army and their families wherever they encountered them. It seemed the Taliban had no compunction about attacking injured patients in military hospitals, or shooting their wives and children in army quarters. He said they had even shot at the soldiers who guarded medical staff engaged in vaccinating village children against polio. Laura was shocked to hear this but she was even more horrified to hear that, a few years back, the Taliban had attacked a school in Peshawar where the children of the military were at their lessons, and they had killed over a hundred and thirty children. If she hadn't really taken this in before, Suleiman's recounting of the violence now brought it home to her just how dangerous a place this really was. She hoped she wasn't leading Suleiman into danger, but she felt she had come this far and couldn't give up now.

After presenting themselves to the uniformed man at reception, they were directed to another building which Suleiman explained was the mortuary. Once inside the solid, brick-built block, Laura found the atmosphere morbidly if necessarily chilly. She wrapped her pashmina more firmly about her head and shoulders, but still she shivered. There was an odd smell about the place and it seemed to hit the innermost reaches of her nose. It wasn't quite the antiseptic smell of a hospital ward but was more redolent of the strong disinfectant which school janitors used to pour down drains in the school playground of her childhood. She thought she would rather experience the cloying smell of undertakers' lilies than the sharp floral bleach fumes which hung around the mortuary corridors.

They were met by an army officer who wore a white coat over his uniform and who had clearly been advised of their presence by the soldier on reception. Suleiman shook the officer's hand and explained the situation once more in Pashto. The officer turned to look at Laura and, to her relief, he spoke English well.

'Mrs Roberts. How do you do? I'm Captain Nawaz, one of the medical officers. I understand you think we may have your husband's body here. Do you know when he died?'

'Well, according to the death certificate, it was on the fifth of April,' she confirmed, 'though I'm not sure how accurate the death certificate is.'

'And I take it he would be a European gentleman?'

'Yes. He was fifty-eight, silver-haired, with blue eyes, well-built and about five feet ten inches tall.'

'Did he have any special distinguishing marks? Any tattoos or scars?'

'Um, no, nothing major. Oh, he had a mole on the third finger of his left hand, though you might not notice it if he still has his wedding ring.'

Laura had been wondering whether, in fact, Keith would still be in possession of his ring, given what Suleiman had said about bodies being looted following the shootout in the hills nearby.

'Let me just check my paperwork,' the captain said, as he walked over to his desk and opened a manilla folder.

After a few minutes leafing through the paperwork, he approached them again.

'We have three sets of remains which might fit that description. Will you be all right to view them? It could be upsetting.'

'I'll be fine,' she assured him. 'I've come half way around the world to find my husband. I mustn't chicken out now.'

Clutching the open folder in his left hand, the captain led them through into another room. If Laura had found the outer room chilly, the inner room was positively Arctic. As the officer led them to one of a large bank of metal drawers, Laura began to shiver uncontrollably. She wasn't sure how much this was due to the icy temperature or to her horror at what she might see. She suddenly felt Suleiman's hand encircle her upper arm. It was the first physical contact he had instigated since the night they had kissed, but she knew it was intended purely to be reassuring, and reassuring it was. The captain slid open the deep drawer and revealed a body shrouded in white cotton. Laura steeled herself as he unwrapped the part of the shroud which covered the deceased's face. She leaned over and peered down. The dead man before her did look European, but his hair was fair, rather than silver. It certainly wasn't Keith. She shook her head.

Closing the drawer again, the captain led them to a second drawer which he slid open, producing another corpse for their inspection. This turned out to be another fair-haired man with hooded eyelids. Laura thought there was a distinct eastern European look about his face, and it wasn't Keith either. When the Captain pulled out the third drawer and drew back the shroud for her inspection, Laura recoiled in horror. The dead man's eye appeared to have been shot out. His mouth was twisted in a painful grimace and his whole head seemed badly contorted. Again, she shook her head.

'No, I'm afraid none of these men is my husband,' she told him. 'Are there any more who might be the right age?'

'No, I'm afraid not. All the rest are much younger men.'

'Are these *all* the non-Pakistani victims there were from the recent shooting incident up here?' Suleiman asked him.

'Not all of them, no. There are more of them down at our other Combined Military Hospital in Kohat. Even after we'd buried the ones we knew to be of the Muslim faith, we didn't have enough room here in our mortuary for all the deceased. The mortuary down in Kohat has a greater capacity than ours.'

'So, Mrs Roberts' husband could be there?'

'Quite a lot of the men who died in that incident were foreigners, and none could be identified, so I can't confirm whether Mr Roberts was one of those transferred, but, if you wish to go there and enquire, I can ring them and tell them to expect you.'

Suleiman looked enquiringly at Laura. She nodded.

'Yes, please,' she said. 'If you wouldn't mind. And thank you for your time, Captain.'

Once outside the building, even though she had left the stench of disinfectant behind her and was back in the sunshine again, she began to feel light-headed. She saw a bench by the entrance.

'Suleiman, would you mind if we sat down, for a bit? I'm feeling a bit giddy.'

He took her arm again and led her over to the seat.

'We can go to Kohat next if you'd like, but are you sure you're okay to do this?' he asked.

She noticed that he didn't let go of her arm. His touch was gentle. She glanced into his light hazel eyes. The other night, she had seen passion in those eyes. Now what she saw was more akin to compassion.

'This is very kind of you, Suleiman. I think I'm being a burden to you.'

'Not at all, Laura. As I told you before, for me it is *nang* – a matter of honour. But, from here, it'll take us the best part of three hours to get to Kohat, and we don't want to be driving through Dara Adam Khel after dark. That's real bandit country. We should make a start right now.'

CHAPTER THIRTY-THREE

HARRY EDWARDS DROVE THE OFFICE CAR SLOWLY ALONG TRAFALGAR Street and parked up outside Blackburn's Trafalgar Mill.

'Are you getting the signal?' he asked.

'Yes, but we'll have to wait until he makes a call.'

'Supposing he doesn't?'

'Oh, he will, just as soon as he checks his Q phone and realises how well it works.'

Kirpal manoeuvred the digital scanner around on his lap and adjusted the tuner. When he was happy he was receiving the intermittent signal emanating from the Q phone, the two colleagues settled down to wait. As the minutes ticked by, Harry began humming to himself.

'Harry, you're humming,' Kirpal said.

'Yeah. Can't get this tune out of my head.'

'What tune?'

'It's from Borodin's opera, 'Prince Igor'. We sixth formers at St Gregory's used to have a lunchtime music club. This was one of the pieces we used to play.'

'Ah, the benefits of private education,' Kirpal sighed.

'So, what did you do in your school lunch hours?'

'Detention, mostly.'

'It was also adapted to a nineteen fifty-three stage musical – *Kismet*,' Harry informed him. 'They put lyrics to it. It was called *Stranger in Paradise*.'

'I wouldn't know, Mate. I wasn't born then.'

'Nor was I,' Harry protested. 'It was one of my parents' favourites. They had it on an LP.'

'What's an LP?'

'Give over. Anyway, it's Luke Greenwood's fault. Ever since he mentioned Borodin, I can't stop humming that tune.'

Suddenly, a voice could be heard coming over the scanner. Kirpal sat upright and listened.

'Yes. That's Gulabzai now. His voice is distinctive. He's an oily git. That's his house just over there.'

'And Yazz has stuck an intercept on his landline, too, has she?'

'Yes, and on the landline at the *Sadaqat* book shop, and at the travel agents. We can listen to the recordings tomorrow. But I wanted to be sure Gulabzai's using his Q-phone. He's given one to Tanvir at the travel agency, and we should soon find out who else in the network has them. Then we can track their movements and scan their calls whenever we want.'

'Good stuff. We won't have to sit here in the car outside his house for hours on end listening to his calls, though, will we?'

'No. GCHQ will pick it all up for us.'

'So, he fell for it? He really thinks he's using encrypted mobiles?'

'Yes. Well, he bought them straight from the inventor, you know – a highly gifted young man, I'll have you know.'

'Highly plausible, too. Maybe you should have pursued a career in sales, Mate. What's he saying, then?'

Kirpal listened attentively for a few moments, before he shook his head.

'No idea. I think he's probably speaking Hindko. I can't understand much of that. It's very different from Urdu and Punjabi. It's more like Farsi – you know, Persian.'

'Well, now we know we've got full access to his comms, we should head back to the Travel Inn. I've booked a table for this evening at the Pepper Mill for you, me and Jo.'

'Ah, no, would you just drop me off at the Metro station in Burtby. I've promised to return GCHQ's scanner,' Kirpal asked as he fastened the scanner back into its carrying case.

'But Heron House will be closed by the time you get into Manchester.'

'No, I'm dropping it off at Yazz's flat. And ... she's cooking me dinner again.'

'Oh, I see. And how will you get back tonight? What time's the last tram?'

'Don't worry about that, Harry. Since we're working out of Heron House now, it'll be more convenient if I stay over at Yazz's. No point coming back to Burtby. Not until the work's finished on the building.'

'You jammy bugger!' Harry grinned, and he turned the key in the ignition.

Reaching into his pocket, Harry took out his mobile phone, logged onto his e mails, then handed his phone to Kirpal.

'Here, scroll through my e-mails, would you,' he said, as he put the car into gear and headed off out of Blackburn.

'What am I looking for?'

'There's a couple from Steve Jeffreys. One of them's got images of passport pages attached. He got them from Laura Roberts, his neighbour who went to Pakistan to find her husband's body.'

'The UK passport bio page? Is that the one?'

'Yeah. That's the SIS chap I told you about. He's out there with Mrs Roberts. He's posing as a rep from the tobacco company her late husband worked for. And he isn't doing a very good job of it, because she sussed him as a fake as soon as she met him. He's hooked up with another SIS chap who's based at the Embassy in Islamabad. His legend is that he's Vice Consul there or something.'

'MI6 amateurs!' Kirpal sniffed. 'You've got another e-mail on here from Jeffreys with photos of someone else attached. Is that the other MI6 bloke?

'I hope not. Cause, if you look closely, you'll see he's dead. No, that's the body that got sent from Pakistan in error. Before he flew out there himself, Jeffreys went along to the Stockport undertakers and took some covert snaps of the dead man.'

'It's hard to see how they messed up. This bloke looks to be, what, mid-twenties? And he doesn't look European either.'

Kirpal studied the image of the young man in the coffin for a few moments.

'Harry, would you mind if I forwarded this e-mail to my phone? Only, it may be a long shot, but ...'

'But?'

'Well, there's always a chance this young man could be one of the lads who went missing from Blackburn.'

'I never considered that. How would we find that out, though?'

'I can think of someone who might know.'

On the Saturday afternoon, Kirpal alighted from the Metro tram and made his way again to Burtby's main shopping arcade. The Coffee Craft Café was buzzing with weary shoppers taking the weight off their feet and indulging in freshly brewed coffee and freshly baked Eccles cakes. Kirpal bought himself a strawberry milkshake and was already seated and sipping it when Imtiaz arrived and joined him.

'D'you want a drink, Mate?' Kirpal asked.

'No, ta. I'm good,' Imtiaz said. 'Are things still going well with Gulabzai?'

'Yeah. Good. Thanks for the heads up on him. You'll appreciate why I can't tell you whether or not any investigation is ongoing, though.'

'No problem. I've done my bit. Don't need to know about your bit. Just happy if I've been of help.'

'You have indeed, my friend. But there's something else you might be able to help me with.'

'Sure.'

'You told me a number of young men had gone missing from around here. If I showed you a photo, would you have a look and see if this might be someone you recognise?'

'Of course.'

'But I should say that the photo won't be pleasant to see. Unfortunately, the young man in the photo is dead.'

'Okay. Let's have a look.'

Kirpal took out his mobile phone and scrolled through the recently uploaded images until he found one of the photos Steve Jeffreys had sent. He handed the phone to Imtiaz, who scrutinised the image carefully. After just a few seconds, he nodded.

'Oh, yes. I know him. That's Idrees Khan. He went to my school. He and his younger brother Waseem haven't been seen in a long time. They're his parents' only children. His mam and dad will be devastated. What happened to him, do you know?'

'We don't know exactly, but we're still looking into it.'

'So where is he now? Where was this photo taken?'

'He's being taken care of in a very nice funeral parlour in Stockport. I'll find out the exact address and text it to you. Maybe you could let his folks know and they could go and make a positive identification. I have to notify the coroner's office first, though.'

'Yes, of course. So, he was killed in Stockport, was he? What was it? Traffic accident.'

'No. It's a bit more complicated than that. It seems he died in Pakistan. That's why I need to inform the local coroner, as no post mortem has been carried out on him. Have you any idea why he might have gone to Pakistan?'

'No, only that it probably had something to do with Gulabzai. Any word on Waseem?'

'No, I'm afraid not. Are you okay about breaking the news to his family?'

Imtiaz nodded. Absent-mindedly, he swiped the screen and brought up the next image on Kirpal's phone.

'Oh, my. Now, this is a much nicer photo. Who's the babe?'

Kirpal snatched the phone from him. The image was a selfie Yazz had taken of herself standing next to Kirpal on the balcony of her flat.

'Oh, that ... that's my girlfriend,' Kirpal said proudly.

CHAPTER THIRTY-FOUR

Suleiman and Laura were a couple of hours into their drive south along the N55 and the light was beginning to fade, but they still had some twenty-odd miles to go before they reached the city of Kohat. Suleiman said he wanted to get past Dara Adam Khel before the sun set. He explained that he rarely visited the town these days, as it had become very dangerous. He had taken Johar's taxi to a body repair shop on the outskirts of the town, but that had been in daylight.

His description of the place put Laura in mind of one of those Wild West towns in the cowboy movies, with a single main street running through and lots of back streets where the town's main industry flourished, the main industry in Dara being the many small gunsmiths' shops where stolen guns were traded and copied. Much of the heroin and cannabis cultivated across the border in Afghanistan made its way through here, too, he told her. He warned her that it was not unusual to see and hear customers stepping out of a gunsmith's and testing a potential purchase by firing off a few rounds into the air. If she heard gunshots, he advised, she should not immediately conclude there was a war on. It was quite normal – well, normal for Dara.

The village had once been a popular stopping off spot for curious tourists coming up the Khyber Pass, he explained. This, and the smugglers' market at Landi Kotal, had been firm fixtures on the tourist trail. During the past couple of decades, however, tourists had stopped coming here. The main outsiders who came nowadays were Taliban selling drugs and buying weapons. He told her he'd heard of a series of car bombs and suicide bombings which had occurred locally. There had even been an attack on the local mosque in which a suicide bomber had slaughtered over sixty people gathered for their Friday prayers. Suleiman warned her that, nowadays, this was the most dangerous and lawless town in the Khyber district.

As they reached the start of Dara's main street, he slowed down so as not to draw undue attention from the mainly Afridi locals. Tensions ran high here these days, and it was far from clear what sort of reaction a man from the Bangash tribe, especially one accompanied by an English woman, might attract. Half way along the main street, however, the traffic slowed down to a halt. Pulling up behind the sizeable queue of cars, he put on the hand-brake, opened the driver's door and, setting one foot out of the vehicle, he stood up to see what was ahead.

'What is it?' Laura asked.

'It's a roadblock.'

'Police?'

'No. Armed men. Not in uniform, but local dress. This can only mean one thing – Taliban.'

He glanced behind to see if it might be possible to turn around and head back the way they had come, but, by now, several more cars and lorries had joined the queue behind them. This was a busy route and most of the southbound traffic passed through the town. He climbed back into the driver's seat and waited.

'You'd best cover your head, Laura,' he warned. 'I'm not sure how they'll react to us.'

Laura didn't need telling twice. She pulled her *dupatta* up over her head, throwing one end over her shoulder to cover her blonde hair whilst also concealing the lower part of her face. Very slowly, the queue of traffic inched forward, as the assortment of cars and trucks was cleared at a snail's pace through the road block. As they neared the road block, she could feel Suleiman's tension increasing. Village head man or not, she knew he would have absolutely no control over what might happen in this town. He was out of his own territory.

After what seemed an age, they reached the head of the queue. Laura kept a tight hold on her *dupatta* and slipped on her sunglasses to hide her blue eyes. The mob of heavily bearded, heavily armed characters glared in through the car windows at both of them. Suleiman began his explanation as to their presence, only a few words of which were intelligible to Laura – 'Kohat', then 'Combined Military *Aspital*'. The rough looking man whose rifle was now intruding into the car, just inches from Suleiman's face, nodded and repeated '*hahn, hahn,*' – 'yes, yes'. He seemed to be accepting what Suleiman was saying as a valid reason for their intrusion into what he considered to be his territory.

However, another red-faced man wearing an oversized black turban now strutted forward and began berating the man with the rifle. It seemed that black turban was in charge and *he* wanted to decide who would be allowed to pass and who wouldn't. To their dismay, he indicated they should pull off the main road into a side alley. As they did so, they could see it was a dead end and, even if they thought of accelerating and taking off, there was no egress that way. Laura glanced fearfully at Suleiman.

'Don't worry,' he said, 'they're just asserting their authority. They can't see us as a threat, surely. They'll let us go when I explain the situation more fully.'

Black Turban ordered Suleiman to get out of the car, and he

obeyed without question. Laura stayed put. She could hardly do otherwise, since the other man with the rifle now had it pointed through the passenger window into her face. Glancing slowly over her right shoulder, she could see Suleiman arguing with the self-appointed bandit chief. Keeping one eye on the man holding the rifle just inches from her face, and noting that his attention, too, was turned to the conversation Suleiman and Black Turban were having, she slowly slipped a hand into the handbag in her lap and felt around until she found the mobile phone Steve had given her. Slowly and surreptitiously, she withdrew it. Slipping it under her *kameez*, she slid it down under the waistband of her *shalwar* and tucked it into her underwear.

Moments later, Suleiman returned to the vehicle. For a moment, it looked as though they would be allowed to proceed, but it was not to be.

'You'd better climb out,' Suleiman told her. 'They want to question us further.'

As she got out of the car, the man with the rifle grabbed her bag from her and walked around to the front of the car. Slamming the bag down onto the bonnet, he began to search through her belongings. He found her own mobile phone and her passport and thrust them into his pocket. He also found her purse and he removed all the cash and pocketed that, too. She saw that Suleiman was being frisked and had his wallet and car keys taken from him. For a moment, she feared she would be body-searched also, but, luckily, this didn't happen. Seemingly, this lawless bunch at least had some rules.

Laura and Suleiman were escorted at gunpoint down the alleyway and into a back room in one of the mud-walled gun shops. There was a further exchange of rapid conversation between Suleiman and their captors, none of which sounded exactly amicable. Black Turban thumped on the table a few times and, disconcertingly, kept gesturing towards Laura. She had no idea what they were saying, and, slowly, her trepidation began to turn to terror. Suddenly, however, black turban and the rifle-toting man turned and left. Laura's heart sank even more as she heard them lock the door from the outside. She could see from Suleiman's expression that he was as worried as she.

'You'd best sit down, Laura,' he said. 'I think we may be here for some time.'

'Why, what do they want from us?'

Suleiman made no reply but walked over to the window and checked the strength of the bars which protected the gun shop from thieves. Laura looked around at the sparsely furnished room. It seemed to be some sort of kitchen, with a basic sink and single cold tap. There was a battered wooden table and two wooden chairs. There was also a curtained recess. She walked over to it and drew back the curtain. Behind it, flush with the floor, was a *pishani*, one of the basic village toilets, alongside which was a cold water tap and a plastic jug. There was no window in the alcove. She turned back to Suleiman again.

'Suleiman, did they tell you what they want?'

'Ransom, Laura,' he sighed, as he lowered himself onto one of the chairs. 'A bloody big ransom.'

Turning away from him, Laura fished inside her clothing and removed the mobile phone Steve had given her.

'I'm going to switch this on. If it makes a noise when I do, could you start shouting or something. Only, if they think we have a phone, they'll take it off us.'

Suleiman nodded and went to listen at the door.

'I don't think there's anyone immediately outside. It's worth the risk,' he nodded.

Laura switched on the phone and was relieved that it made no sound. She quickly found Steve's mobile number listed and she tapped in a quick text. Fearing that, if he did reply, whether by calling or texting, the phone certainly would make a noise, she immediately switched it off again.

'Who did you text?' Suleiman asked.

'My next-door neighbour.'

'Your neighbour? What, your neighbour back in England?'

'Yes.'

Baffled, Suleiman shook his head.

CHAPTER THIRTY-FIVE

AT HERON HOUSE IN MANCHESTER'S ALBERT SQUARE, HARRY EDWARDS had just finished speaking on the phone with his wife, Detective Inspector Kit McGlone of New Scotland Yard's Counter-Terrorism Command.

'Kirpal, I've got some good news for you,' he said.

Kirpal turned away from the window, from where he had been watching the progress the builders were making on the town hall renovations.

'Oh, yes?'

'Kit tells me she's been liaising with Kent Constabulary over your tip off about that lorry. It seems the lorry's progress was followed all the way down to Kent and the channel ports were put on alert. It was searched at Dover and the men you saw being packed into the back of the lorry were nicked. Counter-terrorism South East just confirmed all of them were wanted on police warrant.'

'I thought they would be. Did they say what they're wanted for?'

'It seems one of them was the husband of a Blackburn woman, Anita Begum, who was found dead in her home ten days ago. She'd been subjected to a beating then strangled, but no sign of sexual assault or robbery. Her Pakistani husband had gone missing so the local police suspected he'd killed her and they put out a warrant. They're pleased he was stopped in time.'

'And the others?' Kirpal asked.

'All suspects wanted for planning terrorist offences. They'd been lying low for some time and no-one knew where they were. Kent Police were very grateful for the info. They send their thanks and they say if you get any more intel on the network they'd be delighted to know.'

'Any news on the driver?'

'Yes, he's been arrested, too. He isn't talking and he didn't seem too worried that the police confiscated his mobile phone. He's a cocky sod, apparently.'

'That's probably because he doesn't think his mobile will hold its data for very long,' Kirpal grinned. 'But, of course, it will. Once the police analyst gets the phone data charted up, the links with Gulabzai and Tanvir should be a good starting point to investigate the rest of the network.'

'They might need a bit more evidence for a murder charge over that victim up on the moors, though,' Harry surmised. 'Have you any idea why they even invited you along on that jaunt?'

'I've been asking myself that. I'm wondering if it's because they think I'm like them, so they assume I'd be sympathetic and supportive to what they're doing. Or, maybe they involved me in moving the wanted men and let me witness a murder because they thought that might compromise me. Maybe they're hoping to coerce me into doing more for them. I suspect I'll find out if I stick around with them a bit more.'

'I think you should pull out,' Harry warned. 'Now that we know they're cold-blooded killers, if you should slip up, they might decide to take *you* on a one-way excursion up to the moors.'

'You might be right, Mate,' Kirpal conceded.

'I contacted local CID about that Mushtaq chap,' Jo said. 'No-one's reported him missing as yet, but I called the school and asked to speak to him and they say he still hasn't returned. He didn't have a CRO so, if he was behaving inappropriately around children, nobody seems to have reported it to the police.'

'From what my informant says,' Kirpal added, 'some in the local Pakistani community believe that, for certain types of crimes, local justice is swifter and surer than involving the police. I guess we'll never know if it was him that went up to the moors but didn't come down again.'

'I don't suppose you could find the spot again?' Harry asked.

'Not a chance, Mate. It was pitch black up there. And anyway, it's not like London. No street signs. It's just miles and miles of open country. Just hills and valleys and big, big country.'

Meanwhile, Steve Jeffreys, found himself speeding by taxi through another big, big country. The sandy plains and shrubby hills of the Khyber Pakhtunkhwa seemed quite alien to him. There were no fields or fences, just vast expanses of land separating the fortified villages; no hedges or boundaries. He wondered how the locals established which bits of land belonged to whom. Maybe they didn't. Maybe land ownership was one of the factors which led to the regular feuds which he'd been warned about. Eventually, the taxi came to a halt outside one of the fortress villages. He climbed out of the taxi and glanced around him. He gazed up at the high mud-lined walls and two enormous corrugated metal gates.

'Are you sure this is the place?' he asked.

'Yes. Kotli Qalat,' the taxi driver assured him.

'Okay. Please wait for me.'

'No. You pay me first.'

Steve looked again at the tall, forbidding gates. He could

understand why the driver wouldn't want his passenger disappearing through those gates, possibly never to reappear to pay his fare, or perhaps just never to reappear. He checked the amount displayed on the meter, put his holdall down on the ground and, taking out his wallet, he paid the driver.

'Will you wait here for me anyw ...' he began to ask, but the driver took off in a cloud of dust. Steve watched him head back along the boulder-strewn road and disappear off into the distance. It had better be the right place, he thought, or he would be stranded in a place where he didn't speak the language.

Picking up his holdall again, he walked up to the big gates and hammered upon them. When there was no immediate response, he hammered again. He had no idea what he would do if nobody came. Even assuming this was the right place, and he hadn't been dropped off in the middle of nowhere by the taxi driver, they'd come a long way from the nearest town and it would be too far and too hot for him to walk back. Eventually, to his relief, he heard someone unbolting the gate and it creaked open. It was a teenaged boy who stood before him.

'Hello. Do you speak English?' he asked.

The boy looked blankly at him.

'English lady. Mrs Laura Roberts. I'm looking for her. Is she here?' he pointed beyond the gates.

'Memsahib Roberts?' the boy said, then he raised a finger to signal Steve should wait, and he retreated back inside and closed the gate again. This was promising, Steve felt, as he waited. Soon the boy was back accompanied by a veiled woman.

'Yes? What do you want here?' she asked him, to his surprise, in English.

'Hello, Madam. I'm sorry to disturb you, but I'm looking for Mrs Laura Roberts. I'm her friend. My name is Steve Jeffreys. I live next door to her in England. Have you seen her? Is she here?'

'I'm Fatima,' she said, and, though she didn't lower her veil, he could tell from her voice that she was smiling. 'Yes, Laura has been our house guest. She spoke of you. She said you might come. Please, come in.'

Steve followed her into the compound and gazed around in wonder as she led him, via the maze of narrow mud-walled passageways, to her home. Fatima spoke to the youth and it seemed she wanted him to accompany her and Steve into the house. Steve guessed the boy must be a relative and that Fatima wouldn't wish to receive a strange man in her home without a chaperone. He noticed that the woman and the boy removed their shoes at the door, so Steve did likewise.

Inside, he took in the pleasant interior. He could see why Laura had said she'd been comfortable and well looked after here. He declined the offer of tea but accepted Fatima's invitation to sit on the well-stuffed sofa. His bad leg was a little stiff, owing to his having sat so long in the taxi so he sat down gingerly.

'Thank you. So, is Laura here now?'

'This morning, she and my son drove up to Cherat to the military hospital there. They'd been advised there were some deceased foreigners in the mortuary and Laura hoped one of them would be her husband.'

Steve glanced at his watch. He'd set it to local time on arrival at the airport. It was gone four-thirty now.

'Your son is Suleiman, I understand? So, have you heard from them since they left?'

'No. I thought I would have heard something by now. I didn't call my son in case he was on the road. Perhaps I will give him a call now, though. I can let Laura know you are here.'

Fatima, went to a carved rosewood chest of drawers. Opening one of the drawers, she took out a mobile phone. Tapping in a quick-dial number, she waited. After a few moments, she shook her head.

'Suleiman's mobile is switched off. He must be driving back

now. I'm sure they'll be here soon. Do let me make you some tea whilst we wait.'

Steve decided it would be ill-mannered not to accept a cup of tea, so he agreed and thanked her. Fatima disappeared into the kitchen, leaving him under the watchful eye of the teenaged boy. Steve decided to call Laura. Taking out his mobile phone, which had been switched off during his flight, he turned it on. He was about to call the number of the mobile phone he'd given Laura, when a text message from that phone suddenly appeared. As he read Laura's brief text, the hairs on the back of his neck stood up.

'S and I being held hostage in gun shop, back street, Dara Adam Khel. Get help. L.'

When Fatima returned with the tea, she saw the alarm on his face.

'What is it?'

'Fatima, where's Dara Adam Khel?'

'It's a couple of hours' drive from here, in Taliban territory. Why? You wouldn't want to go there, surely?'

'I'm afraid it looks as though Laura and your son are being held captive there.'

Fatima sat down suddenly.

'Oh, God!' she exclaimed.

'I must go there. Is there a police post around here, Fatima?'

'The police won't go to Dara,' she shook her head. 'Too many of them have lost their lives there. Even the army are afraid to go there.'

Steve quickly dialled the mobile number but it now looked as though Laura had switched off the phone. Various thoughts occurred to him. Why would Laura send a message asking for help and then immediately switch off the phone? Perhaps one of their captors had suddenly appeared and she'd had to hide the phone. Or maybe they'd taken the phone off her. Or perhaps the message wasn't from Laura. It was possible that her captors had sent the message, hoping to lure others into a trap.

He recalled the Foreign Office website warnings that kidnapping was a real risk in this area. Of course, there were other possibilities. She might simply have lost the phone, and whoever had found it had sent the message. But, no, that was unlikely. How would they know to message him specifically? And how would they know the user of the phone was 'L'? No, it seemed likely that Laura was indeed being held hostage and that the text was from her.

'How would I get to this Dara Adam Khel?' he asked. 'Is there any public transport around here?'

'I will arrange transport for you,' Fatima said. 'You cannot go alone. Not to Dara.'

She turned to the youth and barked some instructions at him. He leapt to his feet and left the house.

'My nephews and some of our villagers will want to go with you. But first, you should take some tea. It will give you time to think.'

Fatima was right. He realised he did need to think this through. He didn't think rushing over there mob-handed would be the best thing to do. Before he had finished his tea, the youth was back and he ushered Steve outside. Out in the courtyard he was confronted by around a dozen village men of varying ages, all of them armed, and there were two Land Rovers, revving up and ready to go. Another man in a blue turban stepped forward and offered Steve his hand.

'Mister Steve, I am Johar. I brought Mrs Roberts here from Peshawar and my taxi was too much bashed up on the way. It is fixed now and I was to go to Dara Adam Khel tomorrow to collect it. Then I was to take Mrs Roberts back to Peshawar. But the boy tells me Suleiman and Mrs Roberts have been captured by Taliban. These men say they will go and get them back.'

Steve looked at the assembled villagers and he shook his head. He could see this developing into a blood bath.

'Johar, I think just two of us should go. Will you explain that, and ask them if we can hold the cavalry here in reserve? I want to find where Laura is and try and get her out by stealth. If this lot charge in, all guns blazing, she and Fatima's son will most likely be killed. Will you explain that?'

There followed a great deal of argument, and Steve could see that the villagers, having got themselves all excited about heading off for a gunfight, were not going to back down without much argument. He could tell, though, that Johar was doing his best to dissuade them. Eventually, their collective adrenalin subsided and reason won out. One of the villagers handed Johar the keys to one of the Land Rovers and the youth was sent to open the gates of the compound.

'I will go with you,' Johar said. 'I brought Mrs Roberts here. I should be the one to get her safely back to Peshawar.'

Steve thanked Johar and asked him to enter Fatima's mobile number into his and Johar's mobile phones so they could keep in contact with the village. Having given Johar her mobile number, Fatima asked them to wait for a moment and she disappeared into her house. Moments later, she reappeared, carrying some clothing which she handed to Steve. He was baffled.

'Please, these are Suleiman's. You should not go to Dara dressed like a westerner. Take this *shalwar Kameez* with you. You can change on the way. And there is a *pugree* for around your head.'

With Fatima's exhortations for them to be careful, and with some of the villagers still expressing their doubts as to the likely success of the rescue operation, Johar started up the Land Rover and Steve hopped into the passenger seat.

CHAPTER THIRTY-SIX

In Dara Adam Khel, Laura was beginning to feel sick. She and Suleiman had not eaten all day, so she thought her nausea was probably due to a mixture of hunger and anxiety. She hoped Steve would have received her message, but she wondered what, if anything, he might be able to do to help. She had no idea how helpful the local police might be, if he should decide to enlist their help. This wasn't England, after all. They might not be as effective as the police back home, and nor might they feel inclined to risk their lives to rescue a *ferringhi.* And it wasn't as though Steve would be able to come to their aid himself, not with his gammy leg. He might have been a whizz with communication devices in his civil service days, but it seemed to her most unlikely that his particular skillset could help her now. She told herself that, having stepped well and truly outside of her comfort zone, she might have to find a way of helping herself and Suleiman out of this mess.

Her thoughts were interrupted by the sound of a key unlocking the door to the room where they were incarcerated. Laura backed away apprehensively. Suleman stood up from the chair he'd been sitting at and stepped in front of Laura in a protective stance. The door was flung open and the men who had brought them here entered. Another armed individual, an older man in a woollen hat, strode into the room after them. Their captors stepped aside, seemingly deferring to the older man. Glancing only briefly at Suleiman, he stepped around him and approached Laura, looking her up and down. Suleiman attempted to step between him and Laura again, but the man lashed out viciously and punched him on the jaw. Suleiman reeled back.

'Stop!' Laura reacted. 'Leave him alone!'

The man seemed surprised to hear Laura order him to desist. His expression was one of curiosity.

'Who are you?' he asked, in English.

'I'm Mrs Laura Roberts.'

'British?'

'Yes.'

'What are you doing here, travelling with a man who is not your husband?' he demanded.

'My husband is dead. He came here for his company, Global Tobacco Products. They've been trading with Pakistan for many years. He had a heart attack and died, but the Pakistani authorities have mislaid his body. Global Tobacco paid for me to come here to find him. I want to bring him home. My friend, Mr Suleiman here, is helping me to look for him.'

Laura scrutinised the man's face, trying to assess whether her words were having any effect on him. She couldn't tell. She decided to lay it on a bit thicker.

'Mr Suleiman and his mother have been extremely kind to me. They have offered me ... the *nanawatai* of the Pashtun people. They are honourable people who have shown me kindness and honour – *Izzat*.'

If she had hoped her words would shame the man into behaving with equal kindness and honour, she was to be disappointed.

'This company, they will pay to bring you home also,' he said.

Turning to the others, he barked an order at them. Lifting their weapons, the men gestured at Laura and Suleiman to leave the room. They had no choice but to obey.

It was almost nine o'clock that night when Steve and Johar saw the lights of Dara Adam Khel appearing in the distance.

'We'd better find somewhere on this side of the town to leave the Land Rover,' Steve advised. 'It would be better to stroll into town than to arrive with a big fanfare.'

'Yes, Mister Steve. But we'll need to park near enough that we can make a fast getaway if we have to.

They came to what appeared to be a bus station with many cars parked around it.

'This is ideal,' Steve declared.

He had always felt the best place to hide a car was in plain sight in a car park. He had changed into Suleiman's *shalwar kameez* on the way. They alighted and Johar helped him to wind the bulk of the *pugree* around his head, tucking the long end around his jaw then back up into the head section just above his ear.

'You don't want to stand out as the only man in Dara without a beard,' Johar explained.

The town was bigger than Steve had expected. Despite the late hour, all the shops were lit up and the shopkeepers were still hard at it, shouting out to attract custom and engaging in protracted and very loud bargaining. To Steve, every commercial transaction sounded like a full-scale argument.

'How will we know where to find them?' Johar asked.

'That won't be a problem,' Steve assured him, 'but, first, I understand this town is a good place to buy a gun.'

'Yes, but back at Kotli Qalat, we could have borrowed many

guns – AK 47s, Kalashnikovs, even genuine American M-16s, taken from Americans in Afghanistan who ... no longer needed them.'

'I know, my friend. But we're not here to start a war, just to effect a hostage rescue. How much do you think a handgun and silencer would set me back?'

Meanwhile, just a few blocks away, Laura and Suleiman found themselves in a different building. It seemed to be a house, rather than business premises. They were frogmarched into an inner, windowless storeroom and, once again, they were locked in. Laura glanced around and saw there were shelves laden with tinned food, and sacks of rice and pulses, but no furniture. Suleiman tried the stout wooden door, but it held firm, so he sat himself down on a sack of rice.

'I can see why they've moved us here,' he observed. 'This is even more secure than the last place. I can't see us getting out of here in a hurry.'

Laura sat herself down on a sack of lentils. She couldn't believe she had ended up in the hands of the ruthless Taliban. She wondered how she could have been so stupid, so reckless. Worse still, she had plunged Suleiman into mortal danger, too. And his poor mother – a widow with no other children – she'd be devastated if anything happened to her only son. Laura would be entirely to blame, and it would all be for the sake of finding Keith's wretched corpse.

It seemed to Laura that, the longer the search for his remains went on, the less success her efforts seemed to be yielding and the more pointless her quest began to seem. It suddenly occurred to her, however, that, if she and Suleiman had been kidnapped with such ease, despite Suleiman being a local village head man, then maybe that was what had happened to Keith, too. Maybe he'd been held for ransom. In that case, maybe he was still alive somewhere. He might even be here in Dara Adam Khel.

Then again, he'd been missing for the best part of a month now, and no-one had contacted her to demand money for his return. Of course, they probably wouldn't have had her contact details, unless they could persuade Keith to disclose them. Or maybe, in the case of kidnapped foreigners, they'd contact the British Embassy, or even Keith's employers, thinking they would have more funds at their disposal than his wife would. She now regretted having told the man in the woollen hat that Keith worked for GTP. That was stupid. She'd said it because she wanted to sound credible, to persuade them her presence there was legitimate. Now, though, their captors knew who to contact to demand a ransom. If Keith had been abducted, had Markham and Hopgood known this? But, why would they go to all that trouble, obtaining a fake death certificate and bribing people to lie? Why not just pay the ransom?

'You're right,' she said. 'We won't get out of here. Not without help, at least.'

Turning away from Suleiman, she reached a hand up under her *kameez* and located the mobile phone she had secreted in her underwear. At Suleiman's suggestion, she'd kept it switched off in case Steve, having received her text, had decided to text or call her back. If their captors were standing guard just outside the door and heard the ring tone, they would take the phone away, but it was their one life line. Now, she decided to risk switching the phone back on. It occurred to her that, if it did ring, and if the men heard and came rushing back in, maybe she and Suleiman could jump them from behind the door and steal their guns – or did that only succeed in movies? The phone did, indeed, bleep to indicate an incoming text.

The text, from Steve, simply said: *'On my way to you. Be strong.'* Emerging from the alcove, she showed the phone to Suleiman.

'I know you said to keep it turned off until we needed it, but, look, Steve Jeffreys is on his way.'

'Your next-door neighbour? The retired guy you told me about?'

'Yes, he's arrived in Pakistan. He's on his way here.'

'Well, I hope he's bringing the army. I think only the maroon berets could get us out of here – maybe.'

Suddenly, they heard footsteps approaching and the door being unlocked. Laura looked around for somewhere to hide the phone. She didn't want to be parted from it, but she feared angering their captors if it should be found on her person. Suleiman stood up and, on impulse, Laura stuffed the phone into the open sack of rice. She quickly stepped away from the sack just as the door flew open and two of their captors burst in. They spat words she didn't understand at Suleiman and she guessed they had heard the phone. She couldn't understand the heated exchange but she also guessed, from the way Suleiman raised his hands, palms towards them, that he was denying culpability.

One of the Taliban, rifle in hand, stepped forward and began frisking Suleiman again. The other approached Laura and began to do likewise. Suleiman immediately objected, and was slammed up against the wall, as a tirade of verbal abuse followed. Laura cringed as she was pushed against the small wooden table and her captor's hands roamed freely and savagely all over her body. Suleiman continued to object, but to no avail. She heard him spit one phrase she recognised at the man searching her, '*haram zadeh!*' – 'bastard!'

When nothing was found on either of them, the men began to search the room. They swept tins from the shelves and one of them stood on the sack of rice so he could reach the level of the highest shelves. Laura's heart was in her mouth as he stood, perusing the shelves and glancing all around him. Eventually, he stepped down. Mercifully, he didn't think to look inside the rice sack. Eventually, after what seemed to be more threats from the men and objections from Suleiman, the men left, locking the door once more. Suleiman was apologetic for their gross manhandling of her, but Laura felt relieved that they had got off lightly.

Meanwhile, just blocks away, Steve stood outside a gunsmith's shop. He remained hidden in the shadows under the trees, whilst Johar bargained for an appropriate hand gun. Eventually, Johar appeared and showed him a potential purchase. It was an American-made Maxim, nine-millimetre hand gun with an integral silencer. Johal fired it into the air. It made a restrained popping sound.

'How much?' Steve asked.

'With a single magazine, it will cost six hundred and fifty thousand rupees.'

'Six ...? Bloody hell, that's three thousand quid! Tell him I'll pay two hundred thousand and no more.'

After several trips back and too, between the trees and the shop, the Maxim was purchased, along with its ammunition, in exchange for almost all the cash Steve had on him. Steve examined the semi-automatic pistol. It was quite bulky, being around ten inches long, and he guessed it weighed more than two pounds, but he'd handled bigger guns, and he was confident it would do the job. He tucked it up under his *kameez* and into the waistband of his *shalwar*.

'Okay, Mister Steve. What do we do now?' Johar asked.

'Let's go down there, to that alley that runs behind the shops, while I take some bearings.'

Johar had no idea what Steve intended to do but he followed, looking around continually to ensure they had not attracted any unwanted attention. Every now and again, without warning, someone would step out of one of the lighted shops into the darkness of the alley and let off a few rounds to test fire a gun, causing both Steve and Johar to jump out of their skins.

'I couldn't live in this neighbourhood,' Steve remarked.

Pausing in a darkened corner, Steve took out his mobile and began pressing various keys and scrolling. Soon, a small red light began flashing on the phone's screen. Steve slowly turned around, firstly to his left then to his right and stopped when he was at a forty-five-degree angle to Johar.

'What's that? What are you doing?' Johar whispered.

'It's a signal.'

'What sort of signal?'

'One that will lead us to Laura,' he said, cryptically, and he set off walking down the alley, with Johar following.

About five blocks further on, Steve stopped outside a house. The red light on his mobile had now stopped flashing. Looking around, he placed a finger to his lips to warn Johar to be silent, then he circled around the property until he came to a narrow alleyway to the rear. Glancing surreptitiously around the corner, he saw two armed men in the alley, one leaning against a wall smoking, and the other squatting down on his haunches, his back resting against a wooden gate with peeling paint. Clearly, the men were there to guard that gate.

'I think she's in there,' he whispered to Johar. 'We don't want to panic them. Tell me, around here, do men drink alcohol?'

'No. It is *haram* – forbidden.'

'What about drugs, cannabis and so on?'

'Yes. Too much cannabis is grown around here. There is heroin here, too. Taliban say they don't approve of it, but they're happy to deal in it.'

'Okay, well I want you to make like you're under the influence of drugs, and I'll crack on I'm trying to get you home. Okay? When the shooting starts, though, you just jump back out of the way.'

Johar looked highly alarmed, but he did as bid. He walked, all limp and loose-limbed, ahead of Steve, who supported him. As they got nearer the two guards, Johar let his head flop in all directions and giggled. The guard who was squatting stood up slowly and slipped his rifle from his shoulder. The standing guard also tensed but, on hearing Johar laughing maniacally, they relaxed and simply tutted disgustedly in his direction. As soon as they were within a few feet of the guards, Steve quickly pushed Johar aside, raised the pistol and fired two almost inaudible shots into the chest of first one guard, then the other. As the second man went down, he began to raise his weapon, but Steve let off another shot into his face. Both men lay still and lifeless.

'Get their guns off them,' he ordered, and a shocked Johar complied without question.

Looking both ways up and down the alley to ensure there was no-one around, Steve rushed to the door and tried the handle. It was locked. He quickly searched the clothing of each guard in turn, but could find no keys. Stepping back to the door, he tapped on it and called out, in a loud whisper:

'Laura.'

There was no response and, for a moment, he wondered if he had just killed two innocent watchmen by mistake. Signalling Johar to stand back, he fired a shot into the lock on the gate and, thankfully, it swung open. Peering inside, he satisfied himself that the silenced shots had not been heard and that the courtyard beyond the gate was clear. He crept in and made his way towards the house. Johar followed close behind, clutching onto the two seized weapons. Steve could hear music coming from within. Dimly flashing lights told him it came from a television someone was watching in one of the back rooms of the house.

Kicking open the door to the room where the noise and lights came from, he leapt inside and saw just one occupant. The man, seated before the television and eating, suddenly threw his plate of food to the floor, reached down beside his chair and began to raise a rifle. Before he could even point it at them, Steve shot him dead.

Racing from the room and down the hallway, still with a shocked, gun-carrying Johar in tow, he paused to listen. No-one else came, so he assumed he had eliminated the present danger. He followed the cooking smells down to the kitchen. There was no-one there either. A rear reception room, too, was empty. He tried another door, but it was locked. He called out Laura's name. Suddenly there was a response from within.

'Steve? Is that you?'

'Yes, keep well away from the door,' he ordered. 'We're coming in.'

Placing the pistol against the lock mechanism of the door, and angling it downwards, he pumped out another shot. The lock disintegrated instantly and Steve kicked the door open. He was relieved to see Laura appear unharmed.

'Come on,' he urged. 'We should get out of here fast.'

He led an equally relieved Laura and Suleiman out of the house and towards the gate leading to the darkened back alley. He checked carefully in both directions to ensure there was no-one in the alley, before he led them out into it. Neither he nor Johar thought to look upwards, however. On one of the flat rooftops of a neighbouring house, the *chaukidar*, a night watchman, had been sleeping on his *charpoi*. The watchman had managed to doze despite the occasional bursts of gunfire from the town's gun shops, and yet, seemingly, he had been awoken by the sound of the gate being kicked open in the alleyway beneath where he slept. He arose from the stringed wooden bedframe and came to the edge of the roof to see what was going on. As Steve emerged with Laura and Suleiman, the watchman continued to observe them from his roof top position. He took out a mobile phone and quickly tapped at the keys.

'Steve, thank God you found us. This is Suleiman,' Laura

began to introduce her host, then she spotted the two dead Taliban lying on the ground. She also noticed the pistol in Steve's hand. She was appalled at the sight of the destroyed face of the man who had so recently laid his hands upon her, but she was also baffled.

'Did you ...?' she asked, her face registering astonishment at the possibility that Steve was responsible.

'Yes. I'm afraid it was necessary. Come on. We need to get away from here.'

They crept out into the alley, stepping over the two dead guards as they did so. Laura glanced down at them, horrified. She had lived most of her fifty-five years so far without ever having seen a dead person and now, in the space of just a couple of weeks, she had seen half a dozen – one in the Stockport undertakers, three in the hospital morgue and, now, two fresh corpses lying in an alleyway. Johar led the way back down the alleyways and backstreets, heading across town towards the bus station. As they fled, they caught sight of a four-wheel drive vehicle heading slowly in the same direction as themselves, but a block further down from them. The vehicle seemed to be keeping pace with them. Whenever they paused, the vehicle slowed down and stopped. When they set off again along the alleys which ran parallel to the main street, the vehicle coasted off along the main street. It was fairly obvious they were being followed.

Steve signalled to them to follow him into a darkened doorway and wait.

'Looks like we've been seen. Someone's definitely following us. It probably isn't safe to head back to the Land Rover.'

Johar produced a set of keys from his pocket and waved them triumphantly.

'Let's get my taxi?' he suggested, and he led them back a couple of blocks in the direction from which they had come.

When they arrived at what looked like a cross between a car

lot and a scrap yard, the place was in darkness. Steve used the barrel of the Maxim to prise off the padlock which secured the gates of the repair shop and they quickly located the taxi. Johar started up the engine and they all climbed in. Johar headed off, back towards the bus station car park.

'I think we're still being followed,' Johar announced, as he glimpsed headlights reflected in his rear mirror.

'Listen,' Suleiman said. 'Why don't you drop me near the spot where you've parked. You can head back to my village in the taxi and I'll take the vehicle you brought. I'll get between you and whoever is following and I'll lead them on a bit of a chase around town. Once I've lost them, I'll join you back at Kotli Qalat.'

'Oh, you will be careful, though, won't you?' Laura said. 'If they're Taliban ...'

'Don't worry, Laura. I'll be fine.'

Even in the dim light, Steve could see the concern etched on Laura's face. He was glad Johar was driving them, since he doubted that he would have found his way back along the unlit roads. Laura was exhausted after her nerve-wracking experience but was too wired to sleep. Once they had dropped Suleiman off near the bus station and had quickly taken off again in the taxi, she rested her head on Steve's shoulder. She knew she wouldn't feel completely relieved until they arrived back at Suleiman's village. When, eventually, they pulled into Kotli Qalat, the armed village men were still awake and awaiting their arrival. The man whose Land Rover they had borrowed looked a little concerned that they had not returned it, but Johar explained that Suleiman would be back very soon with his vehicle. Steve handed the Maxim pistol and the two confiscated rifles to the Land Rover's worried owner and told him he could keep them as payment for the use of his vehicle. The man seemed pleased enough.

'Where did you get that gun?' Laura asked.

'I bought it in that town where you were held,' Steve explained. 'Or, at least, Johar negotiated to buy it for me.'

'But when did *you* learn how to use a gun?' she asked.

'Oh, a few years ago now.'

'And how did you find us? I mean, how did you know which house, which alleyway ...?'

'The phone I gave you. I'd put a tracker in it.'

'A tracker? How did *you* get hold of a tracker?'

'I told you I used to work for the Government Communications Procurement Directorate, remember?'

'Yes.'

'Well, they source and procure that sort of thing. When I retired, I ... kept a few bits of kit for myself. You know, stuff that was surplus to requirements. Thought it might come in handy one day. And it did, didn't it?'

Laura didn't seem entirely convinced by his explanation, but she was too tired to give it any more thought, and now Fatima had come out to usher them all into her house. Laura reassured her that Suleiman would be back very soon. At least, she hoped and prayed that he would.

CHAPTER
THIRTY-SEVEN

AT HERON HOUSE IN MANCHESTER, KIRPAL WAS NURSING A CUP OF coffee which Yazz had made him and he was trawling through GCHQ's translated texts of the calls intercepted from the Q-phones he had supplied to Gulabzai and his network. From their conversations, it seemed that communications between Gulabzai, his travel agent friend Tanvir and a third man, Rahul, who owned the former cotton mill on Trafalgar Street, had suddenly become more frequent. There were numerous calls between them on a daily basis, and, although they still spoke in guarded tones, it was clear something else was about to happen.

'How's it going?' Yazz asked, as she put her phone down.

'Well, according to these transcripts, they've been talking in terms of goods deliveries and freight ferry bookings. No specific mention of dates, so I'm not sure when it's going to happen, but my feeling is that it'll be soon.'

'Your boss, Adrian Curtis, just called. He says to call him back when convenient. It's not urgent, he says.'

'Thanks, Yazz. I'll give him a call now, before I start on this last transcript.'

Kirpal dialled Adrian's desk number. Whilst he waited for

Adrian to pick up, he stood up to stretch his legs. Gazing out of the window at what was a fine, spring morning in the city, he saw the freshly unfurled foliage on the trees in the square, and, beyond them, the temporary hoardings erected around the town hall. Suddenly, he was connected to his boss, who wanted to know how Jo Laska was.

'She's feeling better, now, Boss. She's on duty today here at Heron House if you'd like to speak to her. But, did you unravel the mystery of the PM's phone call to *The Times*? ... Ah, so the voice cloning is being considered then? Oh, and another question, the gadgetry which was seized from that business solutions place at Burtby, did Luke say what it looked like? I mean, would it look sort of like one of those old-fashioned room fan heaters, you know, slightly tilted back, and with a domed top? ... Why? Well, because I've just seen a couple of similar-looking devices around here. They were being taken into the building just opposite Heron House. ... Yeah. They could be. I'll see if I can have a discreet look. I'll pass your call on to Jo, now. Bye, Boss.'

Kirpal pressed a few keys on his phone to transfer Adrian across to the extension where Jo was sitting, then he walked over to the office window and stared out.

'Yazz,' he said, 'what did you say was being done over at the town hall?'

'Renovations,' Yazz replied. 'And they're also digging up some of the old paving slabs immediately in front of the entrance, hence the big hoardings. It's part of a grand plan to pedestrianise the whole square. Why?'

'Given that the town hall towers over us here, I think I should have a little walk over there and make sure everything's above board. Fancy coming with me?'

Amid clouds of cement dust, Kirpal and Yasmeen slipped in behind the temporary hoardings and, dodging around the scaffolding poles, they crept up the steps and into the town hall's main building. There was quite a lot of noise, mainly from drilling by the men who were lifting paving stones outside, and there was a great deal of hammering from within, together with loud music from the workmen's radio. The site was a hive of industry and, initially, nothing seemed to be amiss. They headed for the building's main staircase.

'Do you know your way around?' Kirpal asked.

'No,' Yazz shook her head. 'This is the first time I've ever been inside.'

They walked up the big oak staircase which led to the upper floors. Halfway up, they were challenged by a man in a yellow hard hat.

'Security Service,' Kirpal said as he produced his warrant.

The man shrugged and headed past them back down the stairs. Several flights of stairs further up, they came to a corridor with green linoleum on the floor and a series of doors of various heights leading off it. The high, vaulted ceiling, told them they had reached the top floor. Several open oak doors led to what seemed to be empty offices or meeting rooms. A low, narrow door, on the other hand, seemed to be exactly the sort of door he would expect to be used by anyone conducting an inspection of the clock tower.

The door was not locked and so they decided to take a look up inside the tower. Immediately beyond the door was a flight of ascending spiral, stone steps. There were a great many steps, far more than they had expected. They began to climb. The further they climbed, the colder it got and the more breathless they became.

'What are we looking for?' Yazz asked.

'Something that looks like old-fashioned fan heaters,' Kirpal told her.

'Good idea. I'm freezing.'

Eventually, after pausing several times to catch their breath, they reached another small door. A modern grey sign affixed to the door announced this to be the mechanism room. Entering the room, they saw bell ropes which stretched from holes in the floor up to the ceiling and disappeared on up into the bell tower. To one side, there was a polished wooden cabinet with glazed doors. Within the cabinet the clock's main Victorian mechanism was housed. Kirpal walked around the room, looking for any piece of machinery or gadgetry which looked as though it didn't belong there, but he could see nothing untoward.

They continued up the next set of spiral steps and checked out a couple more rooms, including one where the largest of the tower's twenty-odd bells hung. Still, nothing seemed to be amiss, so they climbed further on up the stairs. The stairwell grew ever narrower, so they guessed they must be fairly near the top of the tower.

Eventually, they could feel a draught of cold air coming down the stairs and, soon, they found themselves exiting via the final wooden door and emerging out onto a balcony. The view below them was dizzying. Before them, lay the city with its many tall, modern office blocks, each vying for supremacy with the white Portland stone banks and older commercial buildings. They followed the walkway around the tower, getting their bearings from the massive roof of the nearby town hall extension, until, at last they found themselves looking down onto Albert square.

'This is what we came to find,' Kirpal declared, as he spotted one of the machines strapped to the stonework of the balustrade and angled downwards, facing in the direction of Heron House far below them.

'I'm guessing that's not a heater,' Yazz surmised.

'No. I'm guessing it's a Medusa. We'd better get back across the road and give the 'bug hunters' a call.

'Good,' Yazz said, as she shivered in her short-sleeved blouse. 'I'm *really* cold now.'

Kirpal guided her back to the exit and they began to descend the spiral stone steps once again. When they came to the first wooden door, however, it would not open. Kirpal rattled the handle and pushed at the door with his shoulder.

'It's locked,' he said. 'Someone must have followed us and locked the door behind us.'

'What do we do now? We'll die of hyperthermia if we stay up here much longer.'

'Give me your phone. We'll call Harry.'

Kirpal stretched out his hand. Then he noticed Yazz had neither bag nor coat with her. She wore only a thin cotton shirt and a knee-length skirt.

'I didn't bring my phone. Where's yours?' she shivered.

'In my jacket pocket – back in the office.'

'Did you tell Harry we were coming over here?'

'No. I didn't tell anyone. Yeah, I know, stupid, wasn't it?'

The cold was beginning to get to Kirpal now, too. He threw his arms around Yazz and pulled her to him.

'Sorry, Love,' he said. 'I seem to have got us into a bit of a fix. I don't suppose you've got a pen and paper on you, so's we could write a message on a paper aeroplane?'

'I don't even have a pocket. All I've got is my ID and lanyard. I've got a few hairpins in my hair, but they won't be up to picking that lock,' she nodded towards the stout oak door with its strong iron work. 'What have you got in your pockets?'

Kirpal stuffed a hand into each pocket and pulled out his warrant card and a handful of coins.

'I suppose we could catch someone's attention by dropping coins,' he suggested.

'You'd have to be bloody careful to time it right. You could kill someone if a coin hit them from up here. We must be three hundred feet up.'

'Yes, you're right. It could be dangerous. I'll be careful.'

Just at that moment, they heard a whirring noise coming from within the tower. Kirpal glanced at his watch. It was midday.

'Cover your ears,' he warned. 'The bells are about to go off.'

Seconds later, bells did indeed begin to ring, chiming all four quarters of the hour. The sound was truly deafening. Next, 'Big Abel', the clock-tower's eight-ton main bell, began to strike twelve times. Kirpal noticed that the vibrations seemed to activate the Medusa machine. A red light came on and the gadget began to emit a high-pitched and piercing sound. It was only audible between the dozen strikes of the great bell, but it was audible. Kirpal checked the casing of the Medusa until he found what appeared to be an off-switch. At least, when he depressed the switch, the red light went out and the high-pitched humming ceased.

Leaning over the balustrade, Kirpal saw that office workers were beginning to emerge onto the square and head off in search of lunch. Taking a coin from his pocket, he tried to work out how long it might take the coin to reach the ground and how far from the next passing pedestrian he should aim it. He decided to err on the side of caution. The first pound coin he dropped took several seconds to reach the pavement, from where it rolled into the gutter unnoticed. His timing on lobbing over the second one was more successful. A construction worker saw the coin land. Looking up, he spotted Kirpal and Yazz waving frantically. He waved back, picked up the one-pound coin and gave them a thumbs-up sign before pocketing the coin and continuing on his way.

'This is hopeless,' Yazz declared. 'There must be something else we can do to let someone know we're in trouble.'

Kirpal walked again around the full circuit of the balcony to see what he could find. He came back with a roof slate.

'It was lucky that had come loose,' Yazz remarked.

'It didn't. I had to yank it off. They won't miss it until the next rainy day,' he said.

'That'll be tomorrow, probably,' Yazz suggested.

Kneeling down, he began to rub the sharp edge of the slate against one of the two plastic cable-ties which held the Medusa machine in place against the balustrade. It took quite a while for the slate to make any impression on the plastic, but, eventually, the first cable-tie was severed. While Yazz shivered and rubbed her upper arms in an attempt to warm herself up, Kirpal sawed away at the remaining plastic tie.

'You're not thinking of chucking that over, surely?' Yazz asked. 'That really would kill someone.'

'Can't see any other option. I'll be careful, though.'

Kirpal pulled on a wire which led from the gadget in under the door, and which was clearly its link to a power source indoors. Once it was disconnected, it took both of them to lift the heavy gadget up onto the edge of the parapet and hold it steady, whilst Kirpal checked the square below.

'*This* won't go unnoticed or get pocketed,' he promised. 'Here, help me steady it.'

Having worked out that the machine would make its descent much more quickly than the coins had done, he and Yazz held the machine balanced on the edge of the balustrade and watched intently until they spotted a break in the clusters of passers-by down below.

'Now!' Kirpal urged, and they tipped the Medusa over the edge.

The machine bounced off the edge of the roof below, which slowed its descent slightly, and Kirpal feared he might have miscalculated. However, the heavy machine did indeed achieve a much quicker descent than the coins had done. Seconds later, they heard it hit the pavement with an almighty crash, missing the passers-by and splintering in the process. Suddenly, numerous faces were turned skywards to see where the gadget had fallen from. Kirpal and Yazz began waving wildly, and, to their relief, they saw several pedestrians take out their mobile phones.

Within a quarter of an hour, several police patrol cars had pulled up in the square and, soon, they heard footsteps and voices from within the oak door. It was clear that someone had found a keyholder as the door was unlocked and several angry-looking constables firmly escorted Kirpal and Yazz back inside the building. Despite Kirpal's attempts to explain, they were arrested and were marched along to the police station which was all too conveniently located within the nearby town hall extension.

Once booked in, Kirpal was allowed to exercise his right to make a phone call.

'Harry? It's Kirpal. I need you to come and rescue me again, Mate.'

CHAPTER THIRTY-EIGHT

THE BEGINNING OF MAY BROUGHT MILD AND SUNNY WEATHER TO Moscow. The annual Victory Day parade commenced as it usually did, with the arrival of the Russian President and his Prime Minister who took their seats in the specially erected grandstand in front of Lenin's mausoleum. Vladimir Putin, was flanked by his defence minister and his military chiefs. Seated behind them were the serried ranks of the leaders of other nations within the Russian Federation, with the coveted central position immediately behind the president being granted to the Belorussian leader. The principal grandstand was flanked by two other smaller grandstands, one for a select band of war veterans and their families, and the other for officers of the Presidential Guard.

At ten o'clock on the dot, as the chimes of the clock on the Kremlin's Spasskaya Tower began to chime, the Red Army band struck up the opening bars of Alexandrov's patriotic song 'The Sacred War', and the massed regiments of troops, tanks and armoured vehicles, massive missiles and other chilling symbols of war, began to process into the square. Overhead, a flypast of the Russian Air Force briefly captured the attention of the assembled crowds. Television cameras set at various locations and levels broadcast views from different angles of the impressive display, and also of the dignitaries in the grandstand. Many world leaders had been invited but few had chosen to attend, demonstrating instead their disapproval of Russia's increasing military presence in the occupied areas of Ukraine.

In Downing Street, Ivan Thompson was still unhappy that he had allowed himself to be dissuaded from going to Moscow. Seated in his study, alongside his Press Secretary, Joy Cooper, he sulked as they watched the highlights of the parade on television.

'I should have been there,' he pouted. 'I could have used the occasion to negotiate a deal for Russian gas.'

'We don't need Russian gas,' his Press Secretary reassured him. 'And, in any case, you'd have been the only western leader there. Everyone else has snubbed Putin and declined their invitations in protest at his invasion of the Crimea. You can hardly impose sanctions on Putin then attend his party.'

'I like a good parade, though, and they don't come much better than this one. It's been three years since they've been able to hold the parade 'cause of the Covid pandemic. You can't have thousands of troops marching along socially distanced, can you?'

'No, indeed. It must have been disappointing for Putin having to cancel the twenty-twenty parade, as that was the seventy-fifth anniversary of Russia's victory over the Nazis. Still, I think this year's parade is the most important yet, for Putin.'

'Why's that?'

'Well,' Joy explained, 'he's got to show the Russian people that, contrary to all appearances, Russia isn't on the brink of economic collapse owing to the western sanctions imposed over the Crimea invasion. He's got to divert their attention away from domestic difficulties and persuade them that the real threat to Russia is the nuclear threat posed by NATO and by western liberal democracies. If he can persuade the public of that, he might be able to justify invading the Ukraine.'

'Oh, don't you start, Joy. Putin isn't going to invade Ukraine. It's just sabre-rattling.'

'Two hundred thousand troops lined up on Ukraine's borders is a bloody big sabre.'

'Well, it looks as though he can spare them. I mean, look how many are marching in the parade.'

The interminable lines of troops goose-stepped past the presidential stand, most of them khaki-uniformed men with excessively broad caps. There were also regiments of female troops, oddly dressed in impractical white mini-skirts, fashion boots and military-style jackets, and looking more like American cheerleaders than a fighting force.

'Some of those men are women,' Joy protested. 'And did you see that incredibly tall man, the one with the prominent cheekbones and a look of Abraham Lincoln?'

'No. What about him?'

'Well, he's very distinctive. He stands head and shoulders above his fellow troops, and, unless he's one of triplets whose brothers are in two other regiments, I think I've seen him pass three times. I wonder if the troops are changing their caps around the back and marching round again.'

Ivan Thompson drew his chair nearer to the television to see if he could spot the tall man. Just then, however, the cameras switched back to the presidential stand where one of Putin's generals, seated alongside Putin, could be seen taking out his mobile phone and placing it to his left ear. Cupping his other hand over his right ear, and ignoring a disapproving look from Putin, the General seemed to be taking a call. Whilst the Russian President beamed proudly at the massive display which he doubtless hoped would rival NATO's armies, by contrast, the General's expression slowly grew grave. The General handed the mobile phone to his president, just as the camera panned away and focused back on the parading soldiers.

Moments later, however, the camera returned to the dignitaries in the grandstand and it could be seen that Putin was speaking into the General's mobile phone.

'Hello, he looks angry,' Joy commented. 'I wonder who had the temerity to call him during his Victory Day parade.'

'You're right,' Thompson agreed. 'In fact, he looks furious.'

The Russian Premier's face was like thunder as he turned to his General and spoke at length into his ear. White-faced, the General arose and pushed past the other front rankers as he made his way out of the stand. Another General slid along the row and occupied the seat vacated by his comrade. He, in turn, had Putin speaking confidentially and apparently angrily into his ear. This General, too, looked shocked. Once again, however, the camera pulled away to focus on the military hardware which was now processing past the stand.

'Well, I wonder what's going on there?' Thompson said.

Two miles away, across the river at Vauxhall Cross, Sir Robert Vanbrugge, DG of MI6, was also watching the parade on television whilst having coffee with his MI5 counterpart.

'Looks like they've just told him,' Sir Robert surmised.

'Mmh. Doesn't look too happy, does he?' Helena commented. 'Do you have any idea yet how extensive the damage was?'

'They're not saying. Probably won't admit what's happened. It wouldn't be good for public trust to admit the State's pipeline is vulnerable to natural calamities. What we do know, though, is there's been a huge drop in gas pressure throughout the system. By tomorrow, we should have some satellite images to look at. I understand there were at least three major breaches in the pipeline at some very strategic locations. At least three. Could be more.'

'How did you manage it, Bob?' Helena asked.

'With a little help from our reindeer herding friends. Once we'd convinced them the pipeline could be fractured safely, without igniting the gas and polluting the environment, they were happy to help. Of course, some of our European friends won't be too happy. They're highly dependent upon Russian gas. But maybe the erratic nature of the supply, which the Russians will be reluctant to explain, might make them look elsewhere for their gas.'

'That would be quite a blow for Putin.'

'Yes, it would, wouldn't it,' the MI6 chief grinned.

'Bob, you don't think Putin *really* intends to invade the Ukraine, do you?'

'It's hard to say, Helena. Our intel suggests the troops he's got massed on the border are mainly cadets and conscripts. I'd be surprised if he intended to take on the Ukrainian national forces with raw Russian recruits. Though, of course, that may be what he wants us to think. On the other hand, he is just insane enough to invade.'

The early May weather was much hotter in the Khyber Pakhtunkhwa than it was in either Moscow or London. The nights were almost as hot as the days, and yet Steve Jeffreys had no trouble sleeping after the tension of the previous evening. It was very early morning but still dark when he awoke. For a moment, he didn't know where he was. It was Suleiman shaking his arm which roused him from his deep sleep, and he now remembered the night's events and that he was in a small bedroom in Suleiman's house in the compound of Kotli Qalat.

'Suleiman, you got back okay. What time is it?' he yawned.

'It's a quarter to five. Listen, I know it's early, but I think you and I should head over to Kohat now. That way, we could get through Dara Adam Khel before the town is awake.'

'But why do we need to go there?'

'Because Laura and I never got there. We still need to check if her husband is in the mortuary in the military hospital over there. You would be able to identify him, wouldn't you?'

'Yes, but what about you? Did you get any sleep? Are you okay to drive?'

'I can sleep later. Put on the *shalwar kameez* again. I think we'll draw less attention without Laura. Hopefully, we'll get there and back without any problems.'

Suleiman started up a four-wheel drive Toyota which he explained was one of several vehicles he owned. Encountering no traffic along the way, they reached Kohat's Combined Military Hospital before seven o'clock that morning. Suleiman explained the purpose of their visit to the guard at the gates of the hospital compound, who phoned through to his 'in-charge' for permission to admit them.

The medical officer who met them in reception didn't seem too annoyed to have been disturbed so early. Speaking a language Steve could not identify, let alone understand, Suleiman gave a prolonged explanation as to why they had come. Steve imagined he was emphasising the problems they might have encountered in transiting through Dara Adam Khel had they journeyed any later, since he heard the name of that town mentioned several times during the conversation.

'I understand,' the medic confirmed in English, for Steve's benefit. 'Follow me to the mortuary.'

'Are you a relative of the deceased?' the MO asked Steve, as he led them into the ice-cold interior of the mortuary.

Steve guessed this would be important if any decisions needed to be made regarding what would happen next to Keith's remains – if, by any small miracle, his remains were amongst the many casualties in the mortuary.

'Yes, I'm his brother,' he said, throwing a warning glance in Suleiman's direction.

'Then please wait here and I will summon a *chaprassi*,' the medic said and he left them.

'A *chaprassi*?' Steve queried.

'The *chaprassis* are peons. Unskilled workers,' Suleiman explained. 'The doctors don't actually touch the bodies themselves. That is repugnant to Muslims. They have mortuary assistants who are *chaprassis* and who do that instead.'

Steve thought this was somewhat odd.

'Well, how do they conduct post mortem examinations if they don't touch the bodies?'

'The *chaprassi* will carry out the actual incisions as directed by the doctor, and remove any organs. The medic will simply observe. It will be a *chaprassi* who will get out some of the bodies for you to inspect. The medical officer will not touch them himself. That is *haram* – forbidden for Muslims.'

'But aren't the morgue assistants Muslims, too? Isn't touching the dead just as repugnant to them?'

'No, they're mostly Christians. They don't have any medical training and, indeed, not much education. However, working under the direction of a qualified medic, they get the autopsies done.'

Moments later, the medic was back with a sleepy and slightly-built man in tow. Steve noticed that the *chaprassi* wore surgical gloves. Steve and Suleiman followed the MO and his assistant into a long inner room lined with large metal drawers. The MO indicated the drawers along one side.

'The foreigners are all on this side. The assistant here will open the drawers for you.'

'Are these deceased persons from that incident up at Cherat?' Steve asked.

'Yes,' the medic said. 'The army took the casualties they

thought could be saved to the main hospitals in Peshawar first. Not all survived, however, so the deceased ones were brought here, for us to store pending possible identification.'

'Why here?' Steve asked.

'Well, for one thing, we have a bigger mortuary. These days, there are so many incidents, so much conflict in the area, that we have extended our mortuary block. The army are bringing in victims all the time. Another difficulty is that the deceased are usually from two different sides in the conflict. We wouldn't want hostiles trying to reclaim the body of one of their fighters. Alternatively, they might want to interfere with forensic evidence that's been gathered. This place is more secure than the average hospital mortuary. You saw the armed guards on the gates.'

'Yes, I see,' Steve nodded.

'Anyway, it's good that you came, because we don't know who any of these foreigners are. Nobody has come to claim them. We thought we had identified one as Mr Roberts. He had a UK airline booking receipt in the name Keith Roberts in his jacket pocket. That told us he had come here recently from London, so we notified the British Embassy in Islamabad. They asked for him to be prepared for repatriation to the UK, so we had the undertaker come and collect him.'

Steve glanced at Suleiman. It occurred to him that perhaps this was how the mix-up had occurred. If it had been left to an unskilled and possibly illiterate mortuary assistant to select Keith's body from the many currently in there, and to hand it over to an undertaker to begin its journey to England, maybe it wasn't so surprising the wrong body had been sent.

The *chaprassi* now slid open each drawer in turn and pulled back the shrouds so Steve could view the corpses. Each time, as his gaze fell upon an unfamiliar face, Steve shook his head. They were almost at the last row of drawers when the occupant who emerged did actually look a little like Keith Roberts. Raising his hand as a signal to the man not to shut the drawer just yet, Steve inclined his head to get a closer look. The silver-haired man in the drawer was very pale and his eyes had sunk back into his head, but his features were unmistakable. Yes, this was indeed the elusive body of Steve's neighbour.

'Yes, that's him,' Steve confirmed.

'You're absolutely sure?' the medic asked.

'Absolutely. That's ... my brother, Keith Roberts.'

Ignoring protocol, Steve reached forward and pulled back the two halves of the shroud which enveloped his neighbour. Immediately, he saw a large darkened area on the chest of the cadaver. In the centre of what he took to be a patch of darkened, suffused and subcutaneous blood, was a neat round hole. Steve had little doubt this was a bullet wound, and, given its position, his experience told him it would have proved fatal, if not instantly, then certainly not long after it had been inflicted.

'So, what do we do now?' he asked.

'Now we have release papers to complete,' the officer said. 'Please come with me.'

CHAPTER THIRTY-NINE

The staff of MI5's northern HQ were all very glad to be installed back in their building at Burtby. The Medusa machine had been removed and the police had taken away several managers of El Nova and a significant quantity of their paperwork and computers. Harry Edwards had some interesting facts about the company to report. He took his notes into Luke's office.

'I've completed background checks on El Nova Business Solutions.'

'Oh yes, and what are they? A Spanish outfit, or something?'

'Not Spanish, no. They're one of a number of front companies run by a much bigger organisation with Russian connections. It's one we at Thames House have encountered several times and we've reported on it extensively before.'

'Would I have heard of it?'

'Maybe. Lurman Industries is a huge corporation, and a very slippery one. It was founded by Evgeny Lurmaninov, an oligarch who made his fortune in the Russian energy industry. Lurmaninov had close connections with Putin and Russian intelligence.'

'Had?' Luke asked.

'Yes, apparently, he died last year whilst being held in a German prison. He'd been awaiting extradition to the US to face corruption charges in connection with the twenty-sixteen US Presidential elections.'

'And was his death due to natural causes?'

'Unlikely. He suffered a heart attack, yet the medical examination he'd had on admission to the prison suggested his heart was as sound as a bell. Seems he'd ingested some chemical substance, most likely unwittingly, and no doubt provided by the Russians who'd want to shut him up.'

'So, if Lurmaninov is dead, do we know who's running Lurman Industries now?'

'Yes, all the companies under Lurman Industries' control have been re-registered in the name of his widow, Elena Lurmaninova. I'm guessing the name of this particular company is a contraction of her own name. From Elena Lurmaninova to El Nova. I'll give Adrian a ring and let him know. He takes a personal interest in Lurman Industries, because one of their non-executive directors is someone he's crossed swords with before, and I see that man's name is on the board of El Nova, too.'

'Whose name would that be?' Luke asked.

'Do you remember the PM's sacked chief advisor, Malcolm Donald? Arrogant sod. Ginger hair and beady eyes? He was arrested for theft of government property but charges were dropped on condition he resigned his post at Number Ten and stopped talking to the press. We're looking into his communications right now. If further, more recent links with the Russians can be proved, then we might be able to arrest him for something which will stick this time.'

'Malcolm Donald?' Luke exploded. 'The same Malcolm Donald who, for five minutes, was our own Director General? *That* Malcolm Donald? So, he's still in bed with the Russians, is he?'

'Yes. Has been for years, now. But at least there are only two parties in that particular bed, these days. Intelligence suggests he's fallen out big time with the Prime Minister. What once was a *ménage à trois* is now just a *folie à deux*.'

'Your schoolboy French is better than you thought, Harry,' Luke grinned.

'Thanks. Oh, and I had a call from Steve Jeffries in Pakistan.'

'Did he find his friend, Mrs Roberts? Is she safe?'

'Yes, he did. She's fine, but her husband really is dead. It wasn't a heart attack, though. He was caught up in a shoot-out between the army and the local Taliban up in the Khattak Mountains.'

'What the devil was he doing in a shoot-out?' Luke was astonished. 'I thought he was some kind of travelling salesman?'

'Yes, he was. He was out there on legitimate business for his company, but Steve's found out that SIS had been using him as an asset. He'd been reporting back to them on the conflict that was going on up at the SSG HQ. That's Pakistan's equivalent of our SAS. Unfortunately, Roberts got a bit too close to the action and he copped a bullet.'

'Poor sod. I wonder if Vauxhall Cross were paying him, or whether he just did it out of patriotism.'

'We don't know, and they're not saying. But Steve Jeffries has come up with something else of relevance to our *Op Trebor*. Seems there's quite a lot of foreigners got killed in that action and Steve saw a bunch of them in a local military hospital mortuary.'

'Did he? And do we know who they were?'

'Well, the bodies had been looted where they fell, so few of them had passports or money on them, or any jewellery which might help identify them. But some of them had other bits of paper on them, such as airline booking receipts or ticket stubs, showing they'd travelled there from the UK and other countries. Steve saw some of those documents at the mortuary.'

'So, what'll happen to them?'

'Unfortunately, he was only able to make a mental note of some of the names to scribble down later, but some of those names match names of young men on our list of missing Lancashire youths.'

'I don't suppose he managed to find any links between that action and The Borodin Group, or links to the Kremlin.'

'No. But I've found something which might suggest there's a link. I've been interrogating APIS.'

'APIS?'

'The advanced passenger information database. I checked out the names he'd provided of the missing Lancashire lads against historic travel bookings by air to Peshawar over the past few months. I found them all on the database. I searched to see if there'd been any return bookings in those names, but there weren't. But I saw something else that was interesting.'

'Go on.'

Harry referred to some notes he had made.

'I found an unusual booking for a man whose name was familiar to me. He's come to our attention previously as a suspected Borodin member. The booking was for a couple of weeks ago and it was a strange routing. This suspect, a Chechen former soldier named Ruslan Dudaev, was booked to travel from Peshawar to Islamabad International Airport, then from there to Baku in Azerbaijan and on to Minsk in Belarus. If there was one known member of Borodin present in north west Pakistan, it's very likely there were more. And my thinking is that, from Belarus, he may have been intending to travel overland to neighbouring Ukraine. Ukraine could be the next location in which Russia will deploy the Borodin mercenaries.'

'You said he *was* booked. Did he not travel?'

'No. According to APIS, he was denied boarding in Islamabad.'

'Do we know why?'

'Well, that information isn't noted on APIS, but our original information on him came from the Americans, so I called my contact at the US embassy. Corey Hart is with the National Security Agency, and he tells me they had a report from ISI – Pakistani intelligence – confirming they arrested Dudaev at Islamabad airport in connection with the attack on their SSG HQ in April.'

'So,' Luke reasoned, 'if this Ruslan Dudaev is a Borodin mercenary, and if he was in the Peshawar area and was involved in that attack on the SSG, where some of the Lancashire lads were killed, then it adds weight to our theory that those lads were recruited to fight as Borodin mercenaries.'

'Yes, and it looks like the Russian-backed mercenaries are now moving on to Ukraine.'

Luke sat back in his chair and considered the import of what Harry had just told him.

'That's a great piece of work, Harry. Well, done. You've turned up some good stuff there. And well done, Steve Jeffreys. However, it sounds like it's bad news for Ukraine. Get that turned into an intel report, will you. We need to send that up the line, and fast.'

Meanwhile, in Manchester, Kirpal Kohli, had arranged for the CPNI to retrieve the remains of the Medusa for examination. Several more Medusa machines had been found concealed within Manchester's town hall. Kirpal suspected these machines had been stored there whilst awaiting removal to sites near other potential targets. No Medusa gadgets had been found in any other locations, however, despite thorough searches of the areas surrounding some of the intelligence agencies' more sensitive sites. Kirpal suspected whoever had planted them had been testing their effect upon the Security Service staff at Burtby before bringing more Medusas into play against other UK targets.

Despite his brief arrest, Kirpal was happy to remain in the city for the time being, and he had Luke Greenwood's blessing to do so. Luke was happy for him to stay on at Heron House to continue evaluating the signals intelligence gleaned from the Q-phones and the landlines at Sitara Travel as well as those at the homes of Gulabzai and Tanvir. That suited Kirpal who felt that the scenery out around Burtby was all very lovely, but, as a Londoner, he preferred city life. Of course, the buzz of Manchester's many shops and restaurants wasn't the main attraction for Kirpal. He and Yasmeen were still sharing a desk, but they were also still sharing her city flat.

'Why did you call them Q-phones?' Yazz asked.

'Well, the targets know me as Qureshi. As much as it would have appealed to my ego to call them K-phones, Q-phones fits better with my legend.'

'And are you finding much of interest in the SIGINT?'

'I certainly am. For one thing, from what they've been discussing, it's clear they're planning another run. I checked with the ferry companies and I see that one of their phone associates' lorries is booked on the overnight ferry from Rotterdam.'

'When?'

'Tonight. It's due to arrive in Hull early tomorrow morning. Border Force will give it a tug for us.'

'A tug?' Yazz was puzzled. 'That's a boat, isn't it?'

'Apparently, it's also Border Force speak for pulling the driver over. Normally, it's a roll-on roll-off service, unless there's any intel on any specific driver or freight company. The ferry company have sent me details of who booked and paid for the crossing. It's Tanvir's associate, a bloke named Rahul. Someone Tanvir contacts regularly.'

'Will you head up to Hull, then, to be there for the ... tug?'

'No need. There'll be a reception committee awaiting the lorry as it disembarks. Both Border Force and Humberside Police are on to it. Harry's missus will be there with, too, her team.'

'Harry's missus?'

'Yes, Kit McGlone. She's a DI with the Metropolitan Police's Counter-terrorism Command.'

'So, what's CTC's interest?' Yazz's own interest was piqued.

'Kit and her team will be up there in case any of the incoming migrants might be known or suspected terrorists. See, the network's been smuggling some wanted terrorists *out* of the UK and it's wholly possible they'll be bringing some replacements *in*. Kit's also liaising with the *Marechaussee*, the Dutch border police. I've given her details we've got from the network's comms of some of our targets' contacts in the Netherlands.'

'So, what'll happen to the lorry driver if he is caught smuggling people?'

'He'll be arrested, though I suspect he'll be pretty calm about it. He probably thinks all the evidence on his Q-phone will be wiped automatically whilst the phone's in police hands. He's going to be pretty upset when he finds it won't be.'

'Assuming he's convicted, what sort of sentence d'you think he'll get?'

'Could be fourteen years for facilitation of illegal entry. Of course, his lorry will be seized and then his finances will be looked at under the Proceeds of Crime Act. After all that, depending on what passport he holds, he might even be recommended for deportation.'

'What about the other principles – the men you've been looking at in Blackburn?'

'Well, Blackburn CID will be happy. We'll give them all the intel we've got on Tanvir Ahmed, the travel agent, and also Hamid Gulabzai. No doubt they'll get warrants to search their homes and business premises. They'll liaise with Humberside police and, hopefully, there'll be sufficient evidence to prosecute them as well.'

'How exciting. Are you sure you don't want to be over in Hull to witness the fun and games? After all, you've done most of the work on this.'

'No need. Kit has promised to give me a call as soon as the driver's been arrested. Then, Yazz, I thought I might treat you to a little celebratory dinner. That's all the excitement I need.'

The next morning, Mohammed Lateef sat in the cab of his truck, his arms folded, listening to the radio. He was parked on the freight deck of the *Pride of Hull*, awaiting disembarkation. His was only the fourth vehicle back from the gangway, so he was confident of a prompt getaway. The twelve-hour crossing had actually been quite a pleasant one. The sea had been fairly calm during the night and he had treated himself to a cabin which had guaranteed him a good sleep before he had to hit the M62. The food on board was always hot and plentiful and there was good company to be had in the drivers' lounge.

He had completed so many of these runs now that the nerves from which he used to suffer no longer troubled him. At least they wouldn't have the sniffer dogs waiting at the Border control. He knew that for a fact because Tanvir had someone on the inside, someone who was in a position to reveal which port the dog team would be sent to on any given day. It seemed Border Force didn't have a lot of dogs, and the dog team worked to a fixed shift rota. The typed rotas were pinned to the Border Force office wall, and Tanvir made regular payments to one of the office cleaners to take a crafty photo on her phone of each new rota and e-mail it to him. Knowing exactly where the dog team would be, and when, made it easy for Tanvir to book the ferry trips a couple of weeks in advance. This morning, the dogs were at Immingham, not Hull. Tanvir had it all sorted, so Lateef sat back, relaxed in the knowledge that he had absolutely nothing to worry about.

Daylight now began to flood the into the gloomy freight deck as the big sea doors were opened. Lateef blinked at the light. The ferry crew began marshalling the lorries off the ship and up the ramp onto the quayside, starting with Lateef's Lane. He switched on his engine and gradually rolled forward then accelerated up the ramp and out into a pleasant Humberside morning. The weather was still good, so he was anticipating a pleasant drive home. He would be back in Blackburn within two and a half hours. They would be waiting for him at the old mill. He just had to unload his human cargo, collect his payment, and then he'd be home in time for lunch.

Three freight lorries ahead of him passed through the controls and headed towards the exit from the dock area. Lateef was ready to follow them but, to his disappointment, a couple of uniformed officers stepped out in front of him and signalled him to stop. His offside door was suddenly flung opened and another officer climbed up and jumped into the passenger seat beside him.

'Pull in over there, Mate,' the officer ordered.

'What for?' Lateef asked, with some trepidation.

'Routine medical checks. Covid. Got your proof of vaccination, have you?'

'Oh, yeah. I got all that,' Lateef breathed a sigh of relief.

Once he had pulled over into the examination bay, Lateef climbed down from the cab and pulled out his wallet to retrieve his medical papers. To his consternation, however, the officer suddenly snatched the keys from his hand. From the corner of his eye, he saw several more uniformed officers heading for the back of the truck.

'Just need to take a look in the back, Mate,' the officer said. 'Routine examination.'

Lateef's heart sank. It sank all the way down to his smart new Caterpillar boots. His eyes darted swiftly all around him, looking for the best direction in which to run. Of course, they had all his papers. They knew who he was, yet still, if he could escape ... but the officer who had taken his keys now took hold of his arm and led him towards the back of the lorry. He started to shake. He felt sick. He told himself that, maybe, this would just result in a fine. It might not mean prison. But he knew they could, and almost certainly would, impound his truck.

The Border Force officers checked the seal on the lorry. It was intact. One of the officers had a steel mirror on a long pole and was running it over the top of the rig, checking for any signs that the truck might have been broken into from above. Lateef realised he wouldn't get away with feigning ignorance. He could hardly claim the clandestine migrants had sneaked into the truck without his knowledge, not with the seal unbroken.

The seal was now broken by one of the officers and the heavy doors of the truck were swung open. One of the officers climbed up inside and clambered over the tightly stacked bales of paper. Lateef really felt sick, now. There was no way the truck's illicit human cargo, crouching in the void behind the bales, would go undiscovered. Even Lateef was now aware of the smell, the unmistakable evidence of multiple human occupation; the hot sweat and breath and urine odours which now emanated from the back of the compartment and dissipated into the cold morning air. The officer stopped short as he reached the innermost bales and shone his torch down into the space behind them. He turned back to look at his colleagues, a wide grin on his face.

'Bingo! There's at least a dozen back here,' he called out, then, turning to the migrants, he grinned at them, too. 'Mornin' all. Welcome to Yorkshire.'

Once all the clandestines had been escorted into the holding area, they were searched for weapons and for any identity documents. All of them held travel documents of one sort or another. One of the men even had a British passport. The officer conducting the body searches drew this to the attention of his superior, the regional search team's Higher Officer.

The HO perused the British passport, which he noted was in poor condition. Some of the visa pages had reddish-brown stains on them, but, equally noticeably, was a fairly obvious photo substitution. The passport had been issued almost eight years earlier, yet what was evidently a recent photo of the migrant now in possession of it had been pasted in on top of the laser-printed image of the document's real holder, and a clear plastic laminate had been crudely applied over the page. The HO glanced up at the Pakistani male whose image now appeared in the passport.

'So, you're Keith Roberts, are you?' he asked with not a little sarcasm.

'Yes, please,' the stowaway replied.

'And where did you obtain your passport?'

'Uh, Landi Kotal.'

'Never heard of the place, but I'm pretty sure we don't have a passport office there,' the HO replied.

'If he's Keith Roberts,' the officer told his HO, 'then I'm King Constantine of Spain.'

'Constantine was King of Greece, you daft bugger!' his boss laughed.

Lateef sat to one side, his head in his hands, observing the searching process. When his turn came to be searched, the officer found his Q-phone and tucked it into an evidence bag. Lateef smirked. He told himself, they wouldn't get any evidence out of that. He consoled himself that all his contacts and his communications with Gulabzai and Tanvir would automatically be wiped from the phone in twelve hours' time. Yes, he told himself, things might not go too badly for him after all.

Half an hour later, in the Border Force's back office, DI Kit McGlone slipped a scrunchie from her coat pocket and used it to tie up her voluminous auburn hair, the better to examine the travel documents which had been taken from the migrants. Her sergeant, Paul Graham, checked the documents and the names of the rightful holders against the police intelligence database. There was quite a mixed bag of documents, mainly issued by countries which were not required to have visas to enter European states. Most had been reported lost and all had been falsified in one way or another.

Kit glanced out of the HO's office to where the arrested driver sat. She smiled to herself. He would have no idea that the outbound human cargo he'd dropped off in Rotterdam the previous day had already been intercepted by the Dutch authorities. He wouldn't have known this because Kit had agreed with the *Marechausee* that Mohammed Lateef would be allowed to drive off before they swooped and rounded up his passengers. Co-operation between UK and Dutch immigration and police was legendary, and so the Dutch had been content to have the UK authorities arrest the driver on his return trip. Kit's gaze now alighted on one document in particular. It was the sole British passport in the cache of impounded documents.

'Now, where did I hear the name Keith Roberts, and very recently?' she asked herself. She took out her own mobile and dialled her home number.

'Hi Love,' she said as her husband answered. 'Yes, Harry, a good haul, but let me run a name past you ...'

CHAPTER FORTY

AFTER BREAKFAST, LAURA HUGGED FATIMA.

'Fatima, I can't thank you enough for all you have done. Thank you for your kindness and your hospitality. Steve and I are very grateful.'

'We will miss you Laura,' Fatima smiled. 'We rarely get visitors, especially lady visitors.'

Laura offered her hand to Suleiman. He raised her hand and pressed it to his lips. She felt that pleasant fluttering sensation once again as he raised those hazel eyes to meet hers.

'I shall miss you, too, Laura,' he said, as he held on to her hand for just a moment longer than necessary.

'Yes, thank you both,' Steve said. 'You've been enormously kind to Laura and me.'

Laura thought he made it sound as if she and Steve were a couple. She wondered if he might be just the tiniest bit jealous.

'If ever you're coming to the north of England, you will come to my house and let me repay your hospitality, won't you,' Laura said.

'Thank you, Dear Lady,' Suleiman smiled. 'But it's about as likely as your coming back here to the Khyber. I have many responsibilities here, and, as you know, these are difficult times for my people. But it's been very nice knowing you, and quite exciting to join in your quest.'

Johar was waiting for them outside, his engine running. Steve loaded their bags into the boot of the newly repaired taxi and climbed into the back beside Laura. As the big gates were opened for them and the taxi pulled out, Laura glanced back over her shoulder to steal a last view of Kotli Qalat and to wave goodbye. Sighing, she looked back at Steve. She expected him to be relieved to be leaving, but she thought his expression was a mixture of puzzlement and hurt.

'Good looking bloke, that Suleiman,' he remarked.

'Yes, very good looking,' she agreed.

'You weren't tempted ...?'

'Temptation's not a bad thing,' she answered, cryptically. 'Of course, he has two beautiful young wives, you know.'

'Two? Really? Well, that's just plain greedy,' Steve smiled.

Now he looked just a little relieved, she thought.

Back at the Emerald Inter-con in Peshawar, Steve checked with reception that their rooms had been kept for them. He was assured they had. The receptionist summoned a porter to take their bags up to their rooms. Steve also enquired as to whether Messrs Markham and Hopgood were still in residence and this, too, was confirmed. Their keys had not been returned to reception, he was informed, so they were probably still somewhere within the hotel.

'Shall we go and look for Laurel and Hardy?' he asked.

'Yes, let's,' Laura grinned.

They found the two MI6 officers sitting outside at a poolside table. The two leapt to their feet on seeing Laura arrive.

'Mrs Roberts, we were very worried about you,' the younger man said.

'Yes, it looks like it,' she said, glancing at the large club sandwich and French fries Charles Markham was about to consume.

'Did you succeed in tracing Keith?' Markham asked, sitting back down to his lunch.

'Yes, we did,' Steve replied, handing Martin Hopgood a slip of paper. 'His remains are in the mortuary at the Combined Military Hospital in Kohat. Perhaps you ... consular chaps would be able to arrange the necessary documentation for his repatriation as soon as possible. That's the mortuary's reference number. They're aware of what happened so, hopefully, there won't be any mix up, this time.'

'We'll get it sorted,' Hopgood assured them. 'Leave everything to me.'

'Oh, and you won't need to make any arrangements regarding the body at the Stockport undertakers,' Steve informed them.

'Oh, why's that?' Hopgood asked.

'My contacts back in the UK have identified him as a UK resident, and the undertaker in Stockport now has contact details for the deceased man's family.'

'Oh, Steve, that's wonderful,' Laura said, as relieved as she was surprised.

'Yes, well done, Mr Jeffreys,' Markham effused, with no sincerity whatsoever.

'Will you both join us for a spot of lunch?' Hopgood asked.

'No thanks,' Laura declined. 'I'm going to take Steve sightseeing in town.'

'Shall I drive you?' Hopgood offered.

'Not necessary, thanks. We'll take a scooter rickshaw – that's a *tuk-tuk*, to you, I think. But, before we go, there are a few other things to be sorted.'

'I need to buy some more rupees, so I'll see you at reception,'

Steve said, waving his credit card, and he headed off to the hotel lobby.

'Now that you're back safe and sound and the little mix-up has been sorted,' Markham said, 'I expect you'll be eager to go home. I'll be heading back to London tomorrow. Shall I book you on tomorrow's flight to Doha as well?'

'No. We've had a pretty fraught few days up in KPK, actually,' Laura told him. 'I was taken prisoner by the Taliban and they stole my passport and money. Mr Hopgood, if I write down my details, would your Consular colleagues in Islamabad be able to arrange a replacement passport for me?'

'Yes, of course. It should only take a day or two to get it to you. Is there anything else I can do for you?'

Laura turned to Charles Markham.

'Well, since I can't travel until I have my new passport, perhaps Global Tobacco Products would be willing to pay for my hotel room for a couple more days, so I can recover and await my new document. What do you think?'

Charles Markham seemed unable to think of a reason to refuse.

'Yes, of course,' he grinned uncomfortably.

'And, since it was Steve who located my husband's body, at significant risk to himself, and as he has been left considerably out of pocket financially, perhaps GTP would be willing to pay his hotel bill, too. What do you think?' she asked.

'Er, yes. I'm sure they will,' Markham assured her, and he began to look a little less apprehensive. 'I should think it's the very least they could do.'

'Now, I'd like to ask you gentleman a question,' Laura said, as she sat down, 'and, this time, just for once, I really would like you to be truthful.'

Markham's discomfort seemed to return as he wondered what was coming. Laura continued:

'I don't expect you to tell me who it is you really work for, but I would like you to tell me something else.'

'What's that?' Hopgood asked.

'The Government Communications Procurement Directorate, what do they do?'

'Those amateurs!' Markham snorted.

'They're MI5, aren't they?' she asked.

'Er, yes,' Hopgood answered. 'That's a sort of pseudonym they use, you know, when they need to publicly account for government funding and that sort of thing. But why do you ask?'

'No reason,' Laura smiled.

Moments later, Steve returned, tucking some crisp new rupee notes into his wallet. Laura took his arm.

'Steve, Mr Hopgood here showed me the nicest place to have lunch down in the old storyteller's bazaar. Do you fancy a *Kabuli Pullao* for lunch?'

'I don't know what that is, Laura, but it sounds wonderful. Lead on.'

CHAPTER FORTY-ONE

By the time she and Steve were comfortably settled in their business class seats on the Doha-Manchester leg of their journey and were actually in the air, heading west, Laura at last felt she could relax. Her unexpected journey to exotic places would be her last ever such trip, she promised herself, for she knew she would never head east again. She told herself that, the next time she felt like conversing in Hindi, she could chat with Dilip Kumar, her local newsagent, or with Doctor Durrani down at the health centre. She decided the last couple of weeks had provided her with enough adventure to last the rest of her life.

'Glad to be going home?' Steve asked, as he unscrewed the cap from one of the individual bottles of Sauvignon Blanc and poured it into her glass.

'Oh, very much,' she smiled at him as she took a sip of the perfectly chilled wine. 'And I'm so glad of your company. I'd much rather sleep with you than with Charles Markham.'

Steve gave her a quizzical look.

'Pardon?'

'Oh, I mean sleep *alongside* you. On the plane. Markham snored terribly.'

Steve laughed.

'Still, it was nice of him to pay for our upgrade,' he said, as he raised his glass in a silent toast.

'It was the very least he could do. But you never did tell me who he really works for,' she said.

'It's probably best you don't know.'

'And I still don't know exactly what it was that Keith was doing up there in Kohat, or wherever it was that he actually died. Did they tell you?'

'Well, Keith was checking out the Cherat area ... with a view to identifying ... new product. It was just unfortunate that he managed to be in the wrong place at the wrong time, and he got caught up in the crossfire of a local shootout.'

'Well, I suppose I'll never know the full story. He never really told me anything he was up to. He was a very good liar, you know. He lied to me about so many things over the years.'

'Yes, I imagine he did.'

'Steve, you wouldn't ever lie to me, would you?'

'If I did, it would only ever be a white lie, so as not to worry you or hurt you. You know you can trust me, don't you?'

'Yes, I do.'

Laura was thoughtful as she sipped her wine. Eventually, she decided there was a nettle to be grasped.

'That Government Communications Procurement outfit you worked for, do they really exist?' she asked.

'Oh, yes. That was one of several ... names my firm went by.'

'Was that how you injured your leg, working in communications?'

Steve recalled that day, ten years ago, when he and uniformed police officers had run from house to house, knocking on doors and shouting for everyone to get out, and had quickly evacuated the school, just before that fateful moment when the explosion came and he had blacked out.

'In a manner of speaking, yes, it was all due to urgent communications.'

Steve sipped at his own wine and was equally thoughtful. He, too needed to grasp a nettle that was causing him some discomfort.

'I suppose ... if I asked you whether anything happened between you and Suleiman ... you'd tell me to mind my own business?' he ventured.

'No. I'd tell you a white lie, so as not to hurt you,' she said.

'Well, as you said, Laura, temptation isn't a bad thing, and nor is an occasional white lie.'

Steve slipped his hand over hers and held it gently. She gazed into his eyes. They weren't hazel or intense like Suleiman's. They were grey like the seas around Britain, and they were such kind eyes. Kind, dependable, Steve, who had been so cautious on her behalf, wasn't at all the unadventurous ministry man she had long supposed him to be. He had indeed been a civil servant, but, clearly, he'd been much more than that. Now, he was her rescuer, her champion. He had succeeded in finding her late husband's remains when Markham and Hopgood had been disinclined to help her, and he had also succeeded in finding her, too. Steve had even killed for her. She breathed out slowly and placed her other hand onto her stomach.

'Indigestion?' he asked.

'*Naheen*,' she shook her head, '*apnay bhet mey kittlien hoteyn hayn.*'

'What does that mean?' he asked.

'Well, it probably isn't very accurate Hindi, but it means ... I have butterflies in my stomach.'

Acting on a sudden impulse, she leaned across and kissed him.

. . .

The following evening, having opened all her post and dealt with any urgent matters, Laura showered and changed. This evening, for a change, she would be cooking dinner for Steve. He was due to come over at seven and she wanted to look presentable, or, perhaps, rather better than presentable. She'd had a brief conversation with Beth to tell her that her father's remains were now on the way home. She'd promised Beth they would speak for longer tomorrow, when Mr Burgess had made revised arrangements for the funeral. She promised she would tell her daughter all about her trip then. She headed into the kitchen and began preparing the vegetables whilst listening to the news on the radio.

Suddenly, however, the doorbell rang. She glanced at her wristwatch. If it was Steve, then he was half an hour early. She switched off the radio, removed her apron and quickly checked her appearance in the hall mirror as she went to answer the door. A middle-aged couple, whom she didn't recognise, stood on the doorstep.

'Mrs Roberts? So sorry to bother you,' the man said. 'We're Mr and Mrs Khan from Blackburn. Mr Burgess at the funeral parlour said you would be happy to meet with us.'

'Yes, of course. Please, come into the lounge. Can I get you something? Some tea, perhaps?'

'No, nothing,' Mrs Khan said. 'We won't intrude. We just came to thank you.'

'Please, sit down. And may I offer you my sincere condolences. I was so sorry to hear about your son.'

'Sons, actually,' Mr Khan said. 'We lost both our boys. Thank you for bringing Idrees back to us, at least.'

'Not at all. Did Mr Burgess tell you about the mix-up? They brought your son back in my husband's coffin by mistake.'

'Well, that must have been quite a shock for you, but it was lucky for us,' Mr Khan said, dolefully. 'You see we didn't even know our boys had gone to Pakistan. If it hadn't been for that mix-up, we might never have known. We still don't know what happened to our other son, Waseem. I don't suppose you know, do you?'

'All I know is that there was some sort of conflict, a gun battle, up in the hills above Kohat. A lot of men were killed. That's where my husband died, too. I visited one of the local mortuaries where the bodies were taken. They assured me that all the Muslims who were killed were buried with all the proper rites and proprieties, and within twenty-four hours of the battle. All except your boy Idrees, since he'd been despatched to England by mistake.'

'So, Waseem would likely have been buried there, in Pakistan, in accordance with our religion. That's some small consolation, I suppose. And at least we will get to see Idrees before we bury him,' Mrs Khan said.

Laura could see what a strain the Khans had been under and that Mrs Khan was struggling to hold back her tears. She reached out and placed her hand over Mrs Khan's.

'But we must pay you for the costs you have incurred in bringing his body back,' Mr Khan, said, 'for the coffin, and the airfare and everything.'

'Oh, no,' Laura insisted, 'that won't be necessary. Everything has been paid for by, um, by my husband's firm.'

'But Mr Burgess said you had to fly out there yourself to look for your husband's body, and you had to pay to bring him back, too? So much money you must have spent,' Mr Khan said. 'We must give you something towards the cost.'

'No, Mr. Khan. It's fine, really it is. The firm paid for everything, including my trip.'

'They did?'

'Yes, they did. You see, my husband was out there on ... the firm's business when he was killed. So, of course, it was the very *least* they could do, wasn't it?'

ALSO BY THIS AUTHOR:

More books in *The Thames House Files,* a series of espionage novels:

The Hunt for WOTAK

By Denise Beddows

The Cold War has never been colder than in 2020's Brexit-era Britain. In the midst of the mounting chaos of cyber-attacks and a global pandemic, a sinister entity calling himself WOTAK claims responsibility for much of this 'hybrid warfare' and seeks to hold the nation to ransom. A series of brutal murders, including that of the Foreign Secretary, raises the pressure on the Joint Intelligence Committee to establish who or what is WOTAK. With a little help from his friends, the Security Service's Harry Edwards seeks to track down and neutralise WOTAK. However, he has no idea of the enormous personal cost this complicated operation will involve.

Amazon #3 best seller in Espionage thrillers

'Full of intrigue, beautifully written and meticulously researched ... a really impressive read' – Robert Howe, author of 'A Short Life on the Ocean Wave'

'Fast-paced with a good story line and feels as if it has been meticulously researched' – Geoffrey Gudgion, Author of 'Saxon's Bane' and 'Draca'.

'An original and tense spy thriller, set in a wholly believable, locked-down, apocalyptical Brexit-era Britain. A salutary warning of what might be and, at

the same time, a gripping read.' – Joe Silmon-Monerri, author of 'A Secret Son'.

WHEN THE GREY WOLF SINGS

BY DENISE BEDDOWS

When an elderly Russian is burned to death in his car in north London, his 72-year-old friend, former KGB man Nikolai Volkov, determines to avenge his death. Meanwhile, the 'cyber-war' waged on the west by Russia, and a global viral pandemic, both threaten the health, the economy and the security of the nation. When former policeman turned MI5 agent-handler, Dave Lloyd and his colleagues are tasked with identifying the mysterious 'Ringmaster', help comes from an unexpected source.

Amazon #5 best seller in Espionage thrillers

'I thoroughly enjoyed the concept of the tale. In fact, it is all too believable... Shades of John Le Carré are all through the book, but, I think, with a lot more humour.' – ***** Librarything Reviewer.

'A resourceful and likeable central character with an exciting plot.' – ***** Amazon reviewer

'Superb spy novel! Have friends retired from US intelligence agencies

and this rings true. Most spy literature puts me to sleep, but this book is a refreshing exception to the norm' ***** Amazon reviewer, retired US homicide sergeant

A LONG ROAD TO REVENGE

BY DENISE BEDDOWS

A decades-old Russian bio-terror weapon is being deployed on the streets of London. People with no apparent connection are dying, horribly, and there is no clear motive. MI5's Harry Edwards and Counter Terrorism Command's Detective Inspector Kit McGlone identify potential suspects – only to see them assassinated too. What deadly secret did the murder victims share, and who is killing the killers?

Rated amongst Amazon reader's Top Ten spy/political thrillers

'A complex but intriguing web that spans cultures, political machinations and devious trade craft. This has a 'Line of Duty' feel about it and would make a cracking TV drama.' – ***** Amazon reviewer

'A well-written tale of intrigue with a glimpse of intelligence operations in the modern world ... shows us the human side of this shadowy struggle between nations. There are twists and turns enough to keep the reader fully engaged.' –

**** Goodreads reviewer

'I love the topicality of the story which is set in our present COVID ridden, Brexit ridden, political 'circus' of 2020 and 2021. Moves at a fast pace and is difficult to put down.' –
***** Amazon reviewer

SHEARWATER POINT

BY DENISE BEDDOWS

Boston lawyer Dom Caffrey arrives in Northern Ireland to seek his biological parents, but soon finds himself arrested on suspicion of murder.

MI5 intelligence analyst Carole Murray also comes to the province to bury her murdered uncle. Events lead them to Shearwater Point, a stunning spot on the County Down coast.

However, the breath-taking beauty of the location hides a dark history of cruelty, human exploitation and murder. Meanwhile, nearby, a sinister, ultra-right group is plotting a major terror attack.

Amazon's #1 best seller in Northern Irish Crime and Spy Thrillers
Awarded 'Chill With A Book' Reader's Premium Book Award and also their Book of the Month Award.

"Possibly the next John Le Carré, (she) has produced yet another winner. Gripping, enthralling and bang up to date." – Robert Howe, author of 'Men of Letters'.

"Secrets, assassins and betrayals, with a lost boy who finds himself at

the centre of a deadly storm, Shearwater Point is a fast-paced thriller set on the beautiful Northern Ireland coast by an author who clearly loves the place." – Paul Waters, author of 'Blackwatertown'.

"With sinister themes including identity theft, historic institutional abuse, an assassination plot hatched by a murderous neo-Nazi group, and a detective with a heart-breaking cross to bear, the intense beauty of the story's location conceals the dark cruelty of its past, and yet, there are spotlights of humour to lighten the darkness." – Murder Monthly Blog.

"Beddows has concocted a fascinating mix of old influences and new challenges in her modern Ulster Noir. Gripping, and with a terrific sense of place, a worthy addition to this burgeoning genre." – J.A. Marley, author of 'Standstill'

TRUE CRIME:

ODD MAN OUT – A MOTIVELESS MURDER?

BY DENISE BEDDOWS

This is the true and tragic story of transgendered bus conductress Margaret 'Bill' Allen who, despite desperate campaigning by loving friend Annie, was hanged for the 1948 murder in Rawtenstall, Lancashire, of Nancy Chadwick, an eccentric old woman whom Bill barely knew. Did she do it? If so, why did she do it? If not, who did it? The author uncovers evidence which was suppressed at the time, questions the death sentence and asks whether society's treatment of Bill would be very much different today.

Winner of the Julia Hartley-Woore Award for non-fiction

'... a vivid picture of post-war Rawtenstall and of the difficult lives of three women – a murder victim, her killer and the killer's lover ... an exceptionally well researched account of a true crime and a sensitive exploration of the difficult life and brutal death of this transgendered woman whom history has forgotten.' – Murder Monthly

The Cheetham Hill Murder – A Convenient Killing?
By Denise Beddows

One hot July afternoon in 1933 saw Frances Levin brutally and fatally attacked in her own home in one of Manchester's affluent districts. A recent BBC TV programme revealed that the man hanged for the killing could not have done it. The Author uncovers police corruption, malpractice and suppression of crucial evidence, and reveals a more likely motive and an obvious suspect who was never investigated.

'An old murder case is re-visited in this highly readable book ... a shameful miscarriage of justice is explored and fresh research brings up fresh motives and fresh suspects. The author's conclusions are indeed persuasive' – Bloggs on True Crime

All are available from Amazon or from all good book shops

Printed in Great Britain
by Amazon

37479857R00182